Thank

MW00613258

THE SCRIBE

❦

Elizabeth R. Andersen

Elizabeth R. Andersen

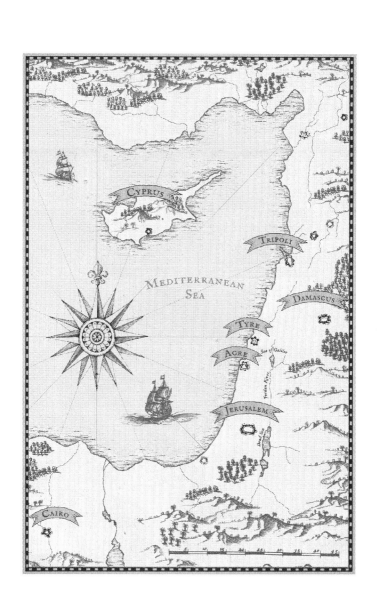

CYPRUS

TRIPOLI

MEDITERRANEAN
SEA

DAMASCUS

TYRE

Sea of Galilee

AGRE

Jordan River

JERUSALEM

Dead Sea

CAIRO

5   10   15   20   25   30   35   40   45

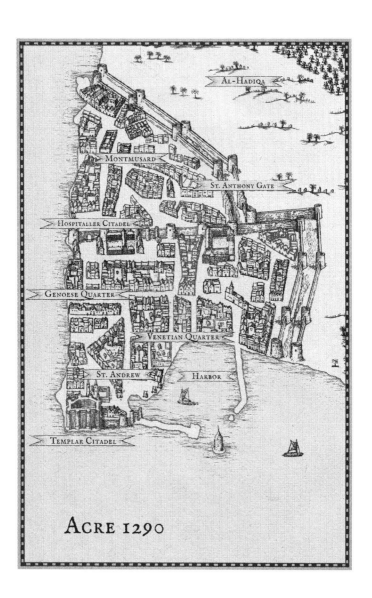

AL-HADIQA

MONTMUSARD

ST. ANTHONY GATE

HOSPITALLER CITADEL

GENOESE QUARTER

VENETIAN QUARTER

ST. ANDREW

HARBOR

TEMPLAR CITADEL

ACRE 1290

PART 1

July 1277 – March 1290

And lower to them the wing of humility out of mercy and say, "My Lord, have mercy upon them as they brought me up [when I was] small."

~ Al-Israa' 17:24 – The Book of the Qur'an

1

DAMASCUS. JULY 1277

Tamrat flung his arms out and marveled at the feeling of weightlessness as he flew, the warm air rushing beneath his body, his robes snapping like flags before a battle. He zipped over the Nile, watching the rippling water blink and flash in the mellow summer sunlight. Beyond the river to the west, he saw the peaks of the great tombs, pointing like fingers toward the heavens. Now he turned toward Cairo, with its towers and minarets shadowed in the gray dawn, swooped around the three domes of the al-Azhar mosque, rose back into the air and paused, looking down on the city. There was his house, the little square semi-detached building at the end of the Street of Quills. He looked left and saw the Ibn-Tu-lun mosque, with gracefully arched arcades surrounding the smooth white limestone sahn where worshippers would gather soon for morning prayers. Beyond that, the citadel of Cairo hulked on the horizon; a manmade mountain of stone and crenelated walls that crouched predatorily between the city and the desert.

An albatross swooped near him with a harsh cry, and he swatted it away. It was time to fly again. He would glide down to his street, scoop Dejen up in his arms, and together he and his son would circle the city like ravens in search of shiny objects. They would alight on the fine-edged peak of the great pharaoh's tomb and watch as the desert slowly woke up.

The albatross screamed again, and Tamrat looked around at the ground, the sky. All appeared as it should. His beard fluttered in the light breeze, its coarse blackness only now beginning to show flashes of gray. And why shouldn't it? He had just reached the age of forty-four and relished every wiry silver strand.

Gathering his deep blue robe about his legs, he flipped to his back on a cushion of air and gazed at the sky, which was cloudless but cool, despite it being early summer. He had not felt this alive, this young and fit, in years. He reveled in it.

More screaming from that infernal bird. Tamrat clawed at the air, but new voices joined in what was no longer the cry of an albatross but a prolonged howl of angst.

He opened his eyes and blinked blearily into the darkness of his house. He was in his bed. It had been months since he had relocated his family from Cairo to Damascus to seek out better commissions and clients, but he still dreamed of the Nile and the great tombs as if he had never left the magnificent capital city of the Mamluk sultanate.

Outside, the wailing grew louder as more voices joined, and soon the cries echoed from every hill in the city. Tamrat sat up and his wife, Sara, stirred next to him. She had her arm slung protectively around Dejen, and the boy nuzzled closer to her for warmth. Extricating himself gently from the tangle of arms and legs on their narrow, straw-stuffed mattress, he pulled on a robe and eased out the door into the street. His neighbors, yawning and blinking in the early gray light, also waited, listening and speculating quietly to each other about the cause of the cries. He felt a touch on his back. Sara had woken and joined him, pulling a scarf over her hair.

"I will find out what is happening. Rouse Dejen, make sure he is dressed, and keep the door barred until I return." Tamrat placed his hands on Sara's shoulders and kissed her, gently pushing her back into the house. Then he set out, briskly walking past the shops and tea houses of his street until he reached the main road.

Hundreds of men had gathered in the small square near the grand public baths, merging into nervous clusters to talk, then breaking apart to relay the news to friends and wives. Was it an attack? Surely not, for Baybars and his Bahri warriors were currently in Damascus and his fearsome reputation was enough to protect the city while he visited. A coup, perhaps? A murder?

A muezzin stumbled up to his post in the square pinnacle of the Minaret of the Bride and began to wail. In between his anguished cries could be heard, first in Turkish and then in broken Arabic, "Our great sultan is dead! Baybars, the master, the victorious king, the pillar of our faith, entered Paradise only just last night!"

Next to Tamrat, a man snatched at his ankle-length thawb, tore the loose garment to his waist, then covered his face and sobbed into his hands. All around, the crowd gasped and shouted with disbelief. Hands raised to the sky in supplication, and some men dropped to the ground, weeping until their beards were wet with tears.

Tamrat looked around nervously and then shouted, waving his hands toward the heavens. He had no great attachment to Baybars, who had caused the death or capture of thousands of innocents, but neither did he want to seem like an easy target for a mob of impassioned mourners. He hurried back to his house and tapped on the door.

"Sara, it is me. Let me in!"

The bar slid back and Tamrat hurried inside, slamming the door behind him. "Gather your bandages and poultices, my love. There may be injuries."

Sara climbed on a chair to a shelf loaded with supplies and pulled her basket of linen bandages down onto a strong shoulder. Tamrat would tell her more when he was ready, but he was wrenching the ring to the little plank-lined hole underneath the floor and transferring chests of books below ground in case a mob should loot the house. Dejen, nine years old, shrank back into the shadows so that Tamrat could only see the whites of his wide, frightened eyes.

"The sultan is dead," Tamrat said quickly. "I am sure all will be well, but the crowd is anguished and uneasy. We will stay inside the house until it is safe to go out, then assess how we may help."

"Father?" Dejen emerged from the shadows. "Will they riot?"

Tamrat smiled and rubbed the boy's head affectionately.

"No, my son, I do not think they will riot. They are just grieving, but we will take caution. Come now. You and I have work to do! This event must be documented. Fetch the ink and quills, and Sara, please light all the lamps. Dejen and I will need plenty of light."

He closed the wooden shutter over the window and unlocked a large iron-banded trunk that sat in the corner, withdrawing several smooth sheets of hemp paper. These he placed on the wooden table in the center of the room, which Sara had illuminated with two oil lamps. A third lamp swung over their heads on an iron chain. Dejen set two small dishes of black ink on the table along with a bundle of quills in various sizes, then sat on his stool.

Tamrat smiled again and squeezed the boy's shoulder.

"We are witnessing history, son, and when this happens, a scribe's first thought should always be to capture the details. We will write these words not for a patron but for your grandchildren."

Dejen nodded, eyes still wide, and smoothed the piece of paper in front of him.

"Do we write in Arabic or in Latin, Father?"

"Let us do both, side by side. It is good practice."

"And what shall we say?"

"I shall say what I saw, and you shall say what you experienced. Two perspectives will give a well-rounded account."

"Father, may I first go outside and look? I have experienced very little here in the house."

"No!" Tamrat stopped inspecting the featureless piece of paper and looked at Dejen seriously. "My son, I know that you survived crowds in Cairo, but I feel it would not be safe for you out there. Our neighbors know that we are Jews, and I have no wish to provide them a reminder when their blood is up."

"They rarely assume I am a Jew, Father," Dejen smiled.

Tamrat looked at him sternly. "You will stay inside. It is unsafe to be out in that crowd."

"Yes, Father, but the next time I am a witness to history, I would like to see it with my own eyes."

"You will, my boy. You will live to see much history as it unfolds! And I hope that you will always document what you see so that others may know the truth of it later."

"Father..." Dejen said slowly, "might I also learn how to protect myself from the crowds?"

Tamrat looked up, and Dejen continued quickly. "Abid ibn-Nabawy invited me to come with him while he teaches Salih to shoot. If he teaches me, may I also go hunting?"

Tamrat grinned. "You may, in time. You can hunt the rats that live behind the night kitchens."

"May I have a bow as well?"

"Here, now! You press your luck very far, young man!" Tamrat laughed. "Now, let us set to our work, and when things calm down, I will speak to ibn-Nabawy about his proposition."

Dejen beamed and bent over his paper, dipping his quill into the black ink. Tamrat cast an uneasy glance at the shuttered window. The transition from one sultan to another was often a bloody business, but Baybars had declared his intention to name his son as his successor. This was certainly not the usual way that the sultanate moved from one sultan to another under the Mamluks, although this new regime had only managed to maintain their power for less than forty years after they wrenched it from the long-reigning Ayyubids.

To think that he could have stayed asleep, dreaming of flight! Tamrat rubbed his eyes and smiled appreciatively at Sara as she placed a steaming clay dish of steeping mint tea in front of him. A dreadful premonition settled over him, and he sensed change approaching, softly, as on the feet of a little child. He looked at his wife and son, both busy at their work. Change could come roaring through their lives, but they would weather it together.

2

— . —

AMANOS MOUNTAINS. MARCH 1279

"Stop crying!" the soldier shouted. "Stop, or I will silence you myself, pagan!"

He leaned over the boy, a tower of angry flesh and creaking leather, with spittle flying from his mouth onto the child's soot-smudged face. He spoke in a thick Kipchak accent, which the boy, who had lived his entire life in the mountains of southern Cilicia, had trouble understanding, but the man's meaning was clear. The boy had watched the soldier club another child with the pommel of his curved sword for trying to escape the tent. He could do it again.

The boy, whose parents called him Emre, shuddered, gulped his tears back, and held his breath. The air inside the wool-felt tent was hot and damp, and the little light that crept through the cracks around the stitched seams was inadequate. The tent had belonged to the tribe's elder, but now the old man lay just outside, a headless corpse, collecting flies in the late afternoon while the invaders used his beautiful, prized tent as a prison.

A frigid gust of mountain air pummeled the side of the tent, and dozens of bells, pots, hooks, and other metal pieces jingled. The sound of it used to bring Emre comfort – the sounds of home for a nomad boy in the hills, along with the bleating of goats and the wind soughing along the tree-stripped hillsides. Now the noise just sounded ominous. Emre knew that the rest of his tribe's tents still burned outside.

He took a deep drag of air to steady himself, but it felt like breathing through a wet blanket.

The soldier grabbed the front of his tunic and shook him.

"There is worse coming for you. Save your tears for when they are really needed... when you reach Cairo."

"Wahid!"

Emre jerked at the sound of another man's voice. He looked up and felt himself go cold and still with fear. The amir stood just inside the tent, his arms crossed. Clad in a blood-spattered blue tunic and surcoat with his scale-like armor covering his chest, he leveled Wahid with a disapproving stare. It was this amir who had pulled Emre from between the warm corpses of his parents and tossed him into Wahid's tent full of frightened children hours earlier.

"I asked you to prepare them for inspection and load them into the wagons, not to terrorize them."

"Many pardons, Amir. It was not possible to inspect them while they were all crying like babes."

"Then I suggest that you find a way to calm them down. After all, it was not so long ago that you were just another frightened child like them, was it not?" The amir raked his eyes along the line of terrified boys, all between the ages of eight and nineteen years old. His gaze stopped at Emre, and he pointed with his deeply curved bow. "That one. He goes with my household."

"But my lord, Amir Qalāwūn says—"

"I know what Qalāwūn says!" the amir snapped. "This one is mine. After he is inspected, place him in my wagon."

Wahid bowed shallowly. "Yes, Amir."

"And Wahid." The amir paused before he exited the tent. "I do not wish to find any more bruises on him... no more than the ones I can already see."

Wahid nodded. The boys stared, wide-eyed, at the retreating back of the amir until Wahid clapped his hands loudly for attention. "You will all take off your clothes now," he commanded. "Place them in front of you where you stand. The physician will be here shortly."

The boys looked at him in stunned silence.

"Now!" Wahid roared, and the boys slowly began to peel away their scorched and muddy clothes, dropping them in piles at their feet.

Emre gingerly pulled his arm from the wide sleeve of his gray and red embroidered tunic, which was flecked with black holes where ash and sparks had singed the fabric. The blood on his arm was clotted and dried where he had gashed it against a rock, but the skin around the wound stung as he pulled the rough sheepswool cloth over it. As he loosened his sash, something soft tumbled onto the ground from his tunic. Wahid strode over and snatched it up.

"So, you still play with dolls, do you? I doubt you will last long in the meydan once you arrive."

"It was my sister's doll."

Wahid's face softened for a moment. "Tell me her name. I will take it to her in the women's wagon."

"She is dead," Emre answered, his voice dull.

Wahid inspected the doll. It was stitched from brown sacking and stuffed with wool, with a red embroidered mouth, braided yarn hair, and two black stone beads for eyes. The doll's dress was elaborately embroidered in the Seljuk style, with bright colors and vivid patterns. Wahid squeezed it, feeling for weapons and hidden objects, then tossed it on top of Emre's discarded clothes. The boy stared straight ahead, stark naked and shivering, with the remnant survivors of his tribe. Each of them quietly considered the last few hours; where they had been when they first heard the drums pounding on the hill, the sight of a hundred Mamluk warriors on horses swarming their settlement, the last look they gave their fathers.

When the attack started, Emre had barely had enough time to escape the camp with Ela before the Mamluk force struck. They were unable to make it to the high forests before he heard screams coming from behind them, so he changed course, bodily snatching up his little sister and sliding down a sandy bluff to the river.

Ela whimpered, and Emre shushed her harshly, forcing her onto her knees in the freezing mud at the base of a large boulder. "You stay here until I can come back," he whispered, and Ela's hazel eyes grew large with tears. "Do not cry, or they will hear!" Emre clamped a muddy hand over her mouth.

"Here is your doll, Ela. Can you comfort your doll until I return?"

Ela nodded and clutched the doll close to her chest. Emre kissed her plump pink cheek and peeked around the dusty rock, taking in the plume of black smoke that gathered in a stagnant haze in the plain below. Smoke and ash were all that remained of his tribe. One regiment of Mamluks raged through the village, slaughtering the survivors, while another smaller group on horseback rounded up the grazing livestock and herded them to the east.

"Emre!" he heard Ela whisper behind him. She was holding the doll out in a trembling hand. "Take Ece with you. She will keep you safe. She knows how to use a bow."

Emre supposed that it must have worked. He was alive now, and Ela wasn't.

The tent flap flicked open, and another Mamluk ducked inside. Instead of the scale armor and colorful robes of the soldiers, this one wore a black knee-length robe underneath light leather armor and loose blue sirwal pants tucked into his black felt boots. After a brief conversation with Wahid, he stalked along the line of boys, checking their limbs and inspecting their teeth. Some of them he pulled out of the line as he muttered, "Weak wrist. It must have broken at some point," or "Cross-eyed. This one will not be able to sight an arrow properly."

Wahid rifled through the piles of clothes, pulling out the occasional coin or concealed slingshot. Then the boys were instructed to dress and were led into the harsh winter sunlight of the Amanos mountains toward a waiting cart.

Women and girls sat close to another nearby wagon with their hands bound, some crying, others staring silently, in shock. Emre scanned the group for his sister's green and red dress and telltale mop of curls, but the women and girls were all so filthy with soot and dirt from their ordeal that everyone seemed to be clad in a gray of mourning.

Ela was not with them.

Wahid prodded the boys into their two-wheeled cart, or tossed them if they refused to move. Four Mamluk soldiers hopped in with them, and Wahid swatted the camel with a grunted order. The beast groaned as it folded its legs and sat, and he climbed onto the blanket saddle, shouting the animal forward.

As the cart ponderously turned and made its way toward the plain, Emre looked back at the blackened bones of his tribe's burned tents and felt his fear come rushing in. He was eleven years old. Everyone he loved and trusted was dead.

He was alone.

3

T he thin light of the moon painted the charred remains of the tents and their burned timbers silvery-blue, and they rattled and swayed in the chill wind gliding off the mountains. Sarangerel crept through the wreckage, which had finally ceased to smolder, walking delicately on the balls of her feet, careful not to make any noise.

It was still winter, and the bitter cold breeze stained her broad cheekbones a rosy red and chapped her lips. She pulled the flaps of her pointed fur-lined hat under her chin and tightened the leather straps that tied it closed, pausing to look longingly back at her *ger*, the tent of thick felt and horsehide, which was warm and snug against the biting wind. In the darkness, the ger was barely visible.

She and her tribe had seen the smoke of the burning tents days before and had hidden in a deep, narrow valley. It was easy to do since they mounted their ger on large wheeled platforms, which could roll ponderously with their herds to fresh pastures. Once they had settled in the valley, it was just a matter of waiting. As soon as the danger of Mamluks had passed, they descended upon the ruins to scavenge whatever loot the army had managed to miss. They were lucky to be the first on the scene after the massacre of the nomads, although it meant that they had to deal with the bodies.

Sarangerel flicked a stray strand of hair that had escaped her braid and snorted with annoyance, sending a puff of white mist above her head into the clear air. Batabayar, their tribe leader, insisted on searching everyone after they pillaged a camp, and the plunder was piled onto a horsehide in his tent where he doled it out in pittances, saving the best for himself and his two wives. During her scavenge earlier that day, Sarangerel had found a hammered silver box, which she buried in the blackened dirt underneath a charred wagon wheel to mark the spot. She was tired of Batabayar's iron-fisted management of the tribe's wealth, and she intended to keep something of value for herself.

Sarangerel hoped that the full moon would be enough for her to find her way back to the wagon wheel, although the settlement was pathetically small already, even for nomads. Crouching low, she swept her eyes over the ruins and spotted the telltale curve of a wheel leaning against a large stone.

Nine years earlier, the mighty sultan Baybars al-Bunduqdari and his Bahri warriors had besieged the city of Antioch to the east, slaughtering every last Christian male and carrying the women and children off as household slaves or new warrior recruits for the Mamluk war machine. The city had burned like a torch for days. The ensuing years saw the city begin to rebuild, now under Sunni rule, but the danger was still present for the nomadic people of the plains. An uneasy peace settled over the land, but with the death of Baybars and the ascension of his son, al-Said Barakah, conflicts had begun to flare, and again, the nomadic tribes became targets.

The fearsome Mamluk amir, Qalāwūn aṣ-Ṣāliḥī, roared through the plains with his troops, and the nomads had packed their tents, fleeing toward the Amanos mountains in Cilicia and beyond. But Qalāwūn's reach was far, and nomad tribes known to be on friendly terms with the Mongols were frequently attacked. The Mamluk message was clear: Join our ranks or be annihilated and enslaved.

They are hypocrites and tricksters, those Mamluks, Sarangerel thought as she picked her way through the wreckage toward the wagon wheel. *They let our Mongol lords sell them slaves, and then they train those slaves to kill Mongols.* The whole thing stank of betrayal to her, but her husband disagreed. Güyük thought the arrangement made practical sense. It was simply their misfortune to be the target of a bad-tempered sultan, he told her.

Stepping around the bloated and rotting carcass of a horse, she clucked her tongue with disapproval. These Mamluks wasted horses like they were throwing pieces of gold into a river. The carcass could have been used for meat, the hair for clothing, the leather for armor, and the urine – what was left in the bladder – could have been harvested to cure the leather. The bones would have made fine weapons, and the hooves could have been boiled to create a thickener for stews. Now it rotted uselessly into a stinking pool of scum.

She reached the wagon wheel and grasped the crumbling, blackened rim to lift it away. Two wide-set eyes belonging to a frightened little face stared up at her from behind the wheel.

"Blue mighty eternal heaven!" Sarangerel shouted, throwing the wheel down and looking over her shoulder to see if there was any movement from the darkened gers.

She pulled a dagger from her belt. The child moved back into the darkness with a whimper, and Sarangerel saw that she was only clad in a dress and sodden wool socks, with no other wraps to protect her from the sharp cold.

"Little girl," she whispered, "are you from the tribe that the Mamluk beasts slaughtered?"

The girl stared back, uncomprehending. Sarangerel lowered her dagger and regarded the child.

Children were valuable as slaves, and a girl could be worth as much as ten alham of silk cloth if she was pretty or talented. She could sell this girl with the silver box and be richer than Batabayar, if only she could hide them from him.

Sarangerel's wind-chapped face broke into a smile. Slowly, she untied the strings of her thick felt deel and wrapped the robe-like jacket around the shivering child. Reaching into her bag, she withdrew a piece of horse-milk cheese and offered it. The little girl backed away again, so Sarangerel unwrapped the cheese and took a bite, and as the tangy flavor danced along her tongue, she smiled and held out the rest to the child. The girl took the cheese, sniffed it, and wrinkled her nose at its sour, musky scent.

"Come now. These tents burned days ago. You must be hungry," Sarangerel murmured, pulling out her leather flask and offering it to the child instead.

Kumis, the fermented horse-milk drink favored by her people, was just as tart but slightly less pungent than the cheese. The little girl took the flask and drank tentatively, choking as the liquid poured into her mouth, but continuing to drink the salty beverage greedily.

"There it is, baby. Drink it all," Sarangerel cooed to her.

When the flask was empty, the little girl's eyes drooped as the alcohol in the kumis soothed her, and she was soon sleeping with her head propped against the wagon wheel.

Great Sky, she must be exhausted after what she has seen. Sarangerel scrabbled in the dirt with a charred stick until she had unearthed her silver box, then scooped the semi-conscious child into her arms and made her way back to her tent. The mighty eternal heaven had been good to her today. Güyük would be concerned, but no worry, she was savvier than him. All they needed to do was conceal the child until they found a slave trader, and then they would be rich.

4

AL-HADIQA, ACRE. APRIL 1279

Henri held his breath, his little hands clasped around the smooth lateral branch of the lemon tree. Below him, Nasir walked slowly, sweeping his head from left to right as he searched the walled citronnier for his prey. This was the third time Nasir had passed directly underneath the tree without looking up, and Henri glowed with the delight of his secret, barely stifling a giggle. Spotting movement, Nasir parted the tangle of grass near him, revealing a head of tousled brown hair. Abdülhamit had attempted to hide in a particularly tall clump of twitch grass but only succeeded in feathering his thawb with seed husks. He sneezed loudly.

"Found you!" Nasir yelled.

Abdülhamit squealed, jumping to his feet to run. In his haste, the edge of his sandal caught on a stone, and he tripped, rolling over in the grass as Nasir pounced on him.

"You are dead, infidel!" Nasir cried, ducking as his prey swiped at him with a closed fist.

Lying on his back in the grass, Abdülhamit swore, then looked up. Henri put a finger over his mouth for silence, but Abdülhamit's eyes narrowed with malice.

"Henri is there! I see him! Henri is there in the tree!"

Henri dropped heavily from the tree and took off running, but Nasir was too quick, snatching the loose fabric of Henri's thawb so they both fell and tumbled over each other, arms and legs sprawling and twisting together.

"This is not fair!" Henri stood and yelled as Nasir crowed in triumph. "Abdülhamit gave away my position. This was an unfair game!"

"Next time, find a better place to hide," Abdülhamit smirked. At seven, he was a year older than Henri, although no taller.

"We are on the same team! You betrayed me!" Henri charged, wrapping his arms around Abdülhamit's waist, dragging him to the ground.

Abdülhamit grabbed a fistful of Henri's dark, curling hair, pulling viciously, and soon the two boys were rolling in the dirt, punching and biting.

"Abdülhamit, stop it!" Nasir screamed, but the boys continued to kick and claw at each other until Henri's nose dribbled crimson dots on his pale blue thawb. "Stop it now! Lord Rogier is coming!"

Abdülhamit pushed Henri away and turned in alarm.

Two men waited at the gate of the citronnier: Hugh de Lusignan - the king of Cyprus and ruler of the Kingdom of Jerusalem - splendidly dressed in a brocade robe and silk hose, and Lord Rogier of Maron, Henri's father. Rogier, fair-haired and heavily freckled, wore a deep scowl as he looked at his son's torn, bloody clothing and dusty hair. The king's two younger sons, Prince Henry de Lusignan and his younger brother Prince Amalric, stood nearby, staring. Both boys wore brocade to match their father.

Picking up his filthy taqiya and wiping his nose on his sleeve, Abdülhamit bowed deeply.

Behind him, Henri stood up, defiant. "Father, they cheated!"

Rogier raised an eyebrow but said nothing. Henri knew that look. It was best to keep his mouth shut.

Rogier turned to his companion.

"My lord, would you prefer to make an inspection of the groves now or take refreshment inside, where it is less... violent?"

The king removed a velvet cap from his head and mopped his sweat-beaded brow with a cloth. Beyond him, Henri saw a servant in the king's livery hurry to take the cloth and hand the king a fresh one.

"Inside, I think. I prefer to keep out of the sun during the heat of the day. Let us leave our little savages to work out their differences on their own."

Rogier bowed shallowly, gesturing toward the towering wooden doors of the house and shooting a warning look at his son.

Knowing what was expected of him, Henri approached the two princes and solemnly shook their hands.

"Do you wish to join us? We are playing 'catch the infidels.' Nasir was the knight, but you can be the knight next if you want." Henri addressed Prince Henry, the older of the two boys, who scanned the grove with a lazy-eyed gaze, and obvious boredom.

The prince's lip curled. "Looks like I have already found three infidels right here."

Nasir and Abdülhamit lowered their eyes submissively, but Henri balled his fists. "My father is a lord of Francia, and Nasir and Abdülhamit converted. Take it back!"

"Why should I? Infidels have dark skin, like you. And your father is stupid. He let people kill your brother and then kidnap you. He is not able to protect you, and he cannot fight, so how is he of any use to the Kingdom of Jerusalem?"

Henri shouted, but before he could rush toward the prince, Amalric stepped between them. "Stop! Henri, you know what will happen to you if you hit him."

Amalric de Lusignan, third in line to the throne, had mousy brown hair that brushed his shoulders. His eyelashes and eyebrows were blond, giving his tanned face a somewhat featureless look from a distance. Despite the two-year difference in their age, the boys had always been friends, with Amalric's level-headed pragmatism balancing Henri's rash impulsivity.

"Just because he is a prince does not mean he can call my father stupid," Henri glared.

"I can call your father whatever I want. Some day, he will be my brother's subject, and maybe even mine!" Prince Henry taunted.

Amalric turned to him. "Henry, stop being a prig, or I will tell Father that you lied about having one of your twitchy fits in order to escape your astrology lessons yesterday so that you could kiss with that ugly kitchen maid instead."

Prince Henry reddened. "I do not want to play with babies anyway," he declared, stalking out of the citronnier toward the house.

Amalric waited until his brother had left, then turned a critical gaze on Nasir and Abdülhamit. "If they cheat, have them beaten," he said simply. "They are just slaves."

Nasir looked up sharply. "I am not a slave. My mother and father are servants at this house."

"Yeah, Lord Rogier does not keep slaves!" Abdülhamit said defiantly.

Amalric slapped Abdülhamit hard across the face. The boy put a hand to his cheek, and his eyes burned with tears.

"Slaves and servants are not allowed to talk freely around me, and they must not cheat. Why do you even play with them, Henri?"

"Because they are my friends," Henri said, glancing at the two boys, feeling self-conscious. Suddenly he noticed their too-short thawbs – cast-off clothing – and Nasir's dirty face and hands.

"You should not be friends with servants. You are even dressed like one."

Henri shrugged, looking at his feet. He could feel the eyes of Nasir and Abdülhamit on him, waiting for him to come to their defense. Amalric watched, arms crossed.

"I think you two have chores to do right now, do you not?" Henri mumbled, still looking at the ground. He didn't watch them as they turned and slowly walked toward the house.

Amalric snorted. "My father says it is a scandal that your father allows you to play with the servants. He is here to tell your father to send you to Sir Geoffroi to train with me. You and I will live there, and we will be brothers together. Will you come, Henri?"

Henri felt a stake of fear drive through his chest. He had overheard his father talking about sending him away for his knightly training, but his mother, still mourning the death of her oldest son, always ended the conversation quickly.

"What about your brothers? Are they not also coming?"

"Henry cannot come because of his fits. He has to stay at home with his physicians. More the better because he is a liar and he is mean. And John has to be king someday, so Father's personal guards are training him."

"I cannot go to Sir Geoffroi's," Henri said, "my mother will not hear of it. She needs me here."

Amalric laughed. "Your mother? Who cares what your mother says? It is your father's decision, not hers, and my father says Lord Rogier would be a fool to leave you here after the kidnapping. Come, let us go into the house. I want something cool to drink."

Henri followed Amalric reluctantly out of the citronnier into the passage that led to the house. The April air was humid from the brackish standing water that rapidly evaporated near the city of Acre, but it was cool among the lemon trees, and he wanted nothing more than to linger in the sweet-smelling grove to hide his shame over how he had treated Nasir and Abdülhamit. They would likely be in the kitchens now, turning the roasting spits and running up and down from the cellars with pitchers of ale and supplies for the preparation of the evening meal.

When Nasir and Abdülhamit had chores, Rogier let Henri work with them in the kitchens, where they would tell jokes and giggle while pumping the bellows or turning the spits. Sometimes Rogier even let Henri take Nasir with him when they rode east to inspect the Maron villages, or allowed Abdülhamit to join them as a companion on trips into the city of Acre. Although they were of different castes, Nasir and Abdülhamit had been born at the estate, just as Henri had. Inside the walls of his house, none of that mattered.

***

Rogier of Maron gripped the smooth limestone lip of his terrace balustrade and stared toward Acre as he often did in the evenings. His eyes rested briefly on the city. It was a collision of pale minarets, church towers, citadels, and laundry lines set against the brilliant pink backdrop of a Mediterranean sunset. As his gaze wandered toward the sea, he could see the smooth curve of the Bay of Acre, with its flat salty plains leading to the blue slopes of the mountains to the south. Due west was the sea and across it – weeks away by ship – lay Francia, the green jewel of his homeland. Although Rogier had lived in Palestine since the age of sixteen, he still recalled the steep forested mountains and clear stony rivers of his home in the Rouergue as if he had wandered there only the day before. In his dreams, he saw leaves that turned russet in the fall and velvety hillsides of grass for grazing. He sometimes woke with the scent of damp, rich earth in his nostrils.

He tried to cultivate green things in Palestine, building his house outside Acre's towering walls near the Yasaf creek and diverting its slow, muddy water to flood his sugarcane fields and lemon groves. Even the name of his estate, al-Hadiqa, meant "the garden." He filled the courtyard of his Eden with almond and pomegranate trees, beds of sweet herbs, and flowers that were entirely useless except for their vibrant colors and pleasing shapes and scents. And then there were the bright eyes of his children, as green as the luminous shallows of the sea.

But it was not the same. Would that he could show his family the land of his birth, where the leaves changed from emeralds to rubies in the autumn, and the hoar frost coated every branch and spider web in the winter so that the meanest field and croft looked like the silvered halls of a faerie kingdom.

His chamber door squeaked as his wife slipped quietly into the room, which glowed from the last light of the setting sun. He smiled, and his gaze lingered on her for a moment. She had released her hair from her dark blue wimple, and it cascaded around her face in shining black waves. Her large brown eyes squinted against the sun, and in the room's dying light, her skin gleamed like polished olive wood.

"Close the drapes, my love. The sun is heating your chambers until it will be insufferably hot in here," she chided. She slipped her feet out of her pointed slippers and walked softly across the richly carpeted floor.

"Come join me out here and close them behind you."

Nasira stepped out onto the terrace and surveyed the city. "Did you refuse the king, or has he convinced you to send my son away at last?"

"He made a strong case. I feel that I cannot adequately protect or prepare him here."

"You have an entire militia. Twenty-five fighting men residing in our walls," Nasira replied, staring out over the sea.

"And yet that bastard and his mercenaries still managed to take my son from under our protection. They still managed to...." He took a steadying breath.

He still could not say the name of his dead son aloud. *Little Rogier. They still managed to kill my heir and namesake.*

"Henri should not be allowed to wander alone. That is the reason why—"

"No," Rogier interrupted her. "He must be trained. He must learn how to protect himself."

"And why can his father not train him? Henri is not some Turkish second son that we can sell to the Mamluks to raise!"

Her temper was rising. Rogier heard the warning in her tone of voice.

"Wife, you know that I can barely lift a sword."

"Durant can train him. Why else would we even employ a master at arms if not for this reason?"

Rogier sighed. Nasira, his beautiful, forbidden wife, protected her children like a lioness. If she knew the full extent of the threats that remained against the lives of her family, she would learn to swing a sword herself. He did not regret marrying her, but it had certainly pushed his life in a direction he had not anticipated. For a French nobleman to marry a penniless serving girl was a scandal in itself, but she was also a Saracen, the derogatory name that his countrymen used to classify all Arabs, Bedouins, Mamluks, or otherwise Muslim people in the Holy Land. Saracens were raiders and murderers. Saracens were dark-skinned and dishonest. While it wasn't uncommon for a lonely knight or pilgrim from the West to take a local woman as a wife and have children by her, it was unheard of for a noble of Rogier's patronage to marry outside of his social rank. A wife of passion, not of fortune. He was unwise, his peers told him, not to marry a rich woman and simply take Nasira on as a mistress.

Nasira fidgeted with her hands, and unconsciously they clutched at her stomach, as if the loss of her first child pulled at her womb. He could not allow this evil to continue.

"This is my decision, Nasira, and I will make it before mass this week."

The discussion was closed. Setting her mouth in a hard line, Nasira turned and stalked from his chamber, leaving her slippers behind. He knew he would be sleeping alone tonight, and probably every night for the rest of the month. He turned back into his room, closed the drapes, and wearily pulled his sweat-soaked black and yellow surcoat over his head. Palestine was his home, but today the heat sapped his energy. Stripping down to his undergarments, he lay across his bed, staring dully at the rich blue velvet canopy above him.

The greatest threat to his family was now gone from Palestine, and for that he was thankful, but he could never rest easy again, knowing that a man had sought out his children to kill them. Rogier tallied the number of people who would benefit from his and his family's deaths. Two. Two more living threats remained. He would be ready for whoever came next.

5

— . —

LA COUVERTOIRADE, FRANCE. OCTOBER 1279

Philip hunched over his small fire and blew on it gently to coax the anemic flames back to life. This unseasonably wet weather was just one more in a series of misfortunes to befall him of late, but at the moment, the soggy kindling and smoking fire felt the most injurious. Nothing had gone to plan, absolutely nothing. Well, he had caught a small pheasant in his snare, but it was hardly consoling. He hated the taste of pheasant.

He was a lean man of about thirty-one, tall and sinewy, with a full head of brown hair that hung in greasy lengths around his jaw. On the rare occasions that he smiled, it did little to convey a feeling of joy or pleasure. His mouth was usually pressed in a hard line, and a wrinkle of concentration tattooed the space between his eyebrows. Notable about Philip were his pale green eyes, which stood out on his freckled face. He was not a beautiful man, but he was striking in the severity of his countenance, even when unremarkably attired.

Angrily, he ripped the feathers from the pheasant and threw them aside until the bird was naked enough to skewer on a stick. As he sat, miserably rotating his dinner over the fire, a gentle rain began to fall, hissing and steaming on the smoldering logs as the shadows grew around him. At least, back in Palestine, he rarely had to deal with wet tinder.

"Damn it all to hell!" he shouted, jumping to his feet and throwing the stick aside and then immediately doubling over in pain, clutching his chest. The wound that he had received months ago, a dagger to the breast that narrowly missed his heart, still throbbed, although it had finally stopped oozing. The old woman in the Genoese quarter of Acre who had treated him advised caution, but Philip made his living by fighting and taking the lives of other men. Too much caution was just as likely to kill him.

Philip froze, listening intently. Was that a voice he heard? He had caught the pheasant illegally in a forest belonging to a local lord, and if a gamekeeper were to find him, he would surely be dragged into prison. Since his luck had already failed him all year, he was not going to take chances. He picked up the stick with the muddy pheasant on it and hid it in the branches of a tree. There was no way to hide the fire. It would have been seen by now, smoky as it was. He snatched his leather scrip and turned to run deeper into the tangled forest when he heard the sound again.

A cry for help. Slowly, Philip put his scrip down.

"Please help me!" came the cry again from the direction of the road.

Philip cautiously walked toward it, taking care not to make any noise in the scraggly yew thickets that bordered the main thoroughfare between La Couvertoirade and Fons Bleaudi. When he reached the road, he saw a man walking unevenly toward him, hunched forward and holding his stomach. Philip eased his dagger from his tunic and approached the man cautiously.

"Friend," the man panted, "I saw the smoke from your fire. Please— " He stopped and clutched his middle for a moment, then tried again. "My retinue was set upon and my men were all killed. Please may I take refuge at your fire? If you assist me, I promise to reward you handsomely when I reach my estate." At these words, the man fell to his knees, retching.

Estate? This is a wealthy man, Philip thought, looking around. His hand tightened on the grip of the dagger, which he kept concealed at his side.

"Let me help you to your feet," Philip mumbled and grasped the man around the waist, probing him for a scrip or a money purse as he heaved the man to his feet. The man was dressed in velvet, but he wore no money bag on his belt. He must have been robbed already. Philip considered dropping him and letting him die of his injuries right there in the road, but the man gasped.

"Thank you," he grimaced. "Please, I am afraid to be on this road. Can we move away? I walked for half a day, but my attackers may still follow."

Philip led the injured man off the wagon track and through the yew thicket until the shrubs melted into the full-grown oaks of the forest. It was slightly lighter here, and Philip could get a better look at his companion. The man was in his late thirties, with a severely receding hairline and bright blue eyes. His clothes, although rich, were covered in bloodstains and mud, and he only wore one shoe.

Philip helped him sit by the fire, which was now little more than a twist of smoke and steam, and he attempted to coax the flame back to life. The man sighed heavily and rolled to his side, pulling his knees to his chest like a small child.

"Thank you for your kindness, friend," he whispered, still clutching his middle.

Philip poked at the fire pensively, trying to decide what to do. There was not much worth taking from this lord, although the velvet cotehardie could be worth something, ripped though it was.

"What is your name?" Philip grunted, not looking up from his fire.

"Georges de Fons Bleaudi. Look here; I have dry tinder in my purse." He dug painfully in his cotehardie and withdrew a small leather sack.

So that is where he keeps his money, Philip thought grimly.

Georges pulled out a handful of small dried oat straws, handed them to Philip, and then collapsed back onto his side. Philip could hear the man's stomach growling loudly.

"I have food," Philip said gruffly, "I hunted it in the forest of Fons Bleaudi...."

"I will not press charges," Georges said weakly. "Please, if I can only shelter here for a day, and if you return me to my father, you will be rewarded."

Philip stood and retrieved his pheasant from the branches of the tree. Georges did not seem to notice how muddy the bird was. He ate ravenously, then vomited most of it up afterward.

"I apologize," Georges said, wiping his mouth. "It is a waste to keep food in your gullet for only a short time."

Philip shrugged and poked the fire with a stick.

"In my terror, I did not ask your name, friend. What are you called?"

"Philip. Philip de Rouergue."

Georges' eyes watered, and he squeezed them shut for a moment. "My brother's name was Philip," he whispered, "but he is dead now. Dead on the side of the road, along with my guards. He is probably still rotting there." His teeth clenched together as pain stabbed through him.

Philip shifted uncomfortably, and Georges continued. "I had traveled at my father's request to collect my brother at his preceptory in Baudelu. My father is very ill, you see – his mind is no longer sound – and he wanted to see my brother before he lost his faculties altogether. I collected Philip, and we were traveling home when we were set upon by some kind of gypsies or Jews who robbed us and killed everyone. I only survived because I fainted from my pain underneath the wagon."

Philip was watching Georges more attentively now. "This is a misfortune indeed. Your brother, was he older or younger than you?"

"Younger. He has lived with the Templars since his tender years, and my father has not seen him as a grown man." Georges sighed, a smile on his face. "How handsome he looked! The last time I saw him, he was just a boy. My father would have been so blessed to set eyes on a man such as Philip and to know that he was his son."

The details of this story rattled around in Philip's head, and he tried to keep his face neutral, but at the mention of the Templars, his expression grew stony. He had seen enough Templars to satisfy him for the rest of his life. *Holy, arrogant sons of bitches, all of them. Just because they wear those white robes, they think they can do anything and go anywhere.*

Philip sat up straight. The solution to his troubles was so obvious that it took his breath away. He looked sideways at Georges and pulled out his wine skin, handing it to the injured man.

"You have had a trying time, my friend. Drink of this, and we shall talk of happier things, eh?"

Georges took the skin gratefully. "This will help dull the pain, for sure. I appreciate your generosity."

Philip smiled. It was a genuine smile. For the first time since he returned to Francia, he felt optimistic.

***

The next morning, Philip wiped the blade of his ornately jeweled dagger on Georges' velvet sleeve and checked to ensure that the man did not breathe. Blood still seeped from the wide slash across the throat, and one of his blue eyes was half-open, staring dully at the sky. Philip slid the dagger back into its sheath with a snap and stood, looking down.

"You should be more careful who you talk to, *friend*," he sneered, then shouldered his bag and set out toward the road.

***

Five days later, Philip knelt, head bowed, on the stone floor of the modest estate belonging to Lord Georges de Fons

Bleaudi. Before him, seated in an oversized wooden chair and cocooned by a thick wool blanket, Lord Georges moaned and howled, wiping his tears on the hem of his moth-chewed robe. Servants rushed in and attempted to offer the old man a cup of wine, but he swatted it away and continued to cry. Philip rose to his feet. It bothered him that the white robe he wore was slightly too short in the hem and sleeves, but in their grief, no one at the Fons Bleaudi fief seemed to take notice. He walked to the old man and put a hand on his shoulder.

"First your three sisters, then your mother, and now this!" Lord Fons Bleaudi wailed. "How much grief can one man take? My heir is dead!"

"I am also aggrieved, Father, although I had weeks to shed my tears on the road. I have prayed for the soul of my brother Georges on every one of those days that I drew nearer to you. When I travel to the Holy Land, I shall say a prayer for the souls of my mother, sisters, and brother in Acre, where God will hear them more clearly."

Lord Fons Bleaudi looked up at Philip from red, swollen eyes. "Acre? Where is that, my son?"

"It is the seat of the Kingdom of Jerusalem. A mighty city of Christian men in Outremer. It is the greatest honor of a knight of the Temple to serve in that city to protect God's land from the infidels." Philip had spent enough time around Templars and Hospitallers to know how they spoke. The old man held out a liver-spotted hand, and Philip took it, masking his disgust. He only had to keep this charade up for a few more days.

"Philip, my son... how it must have torn at your heart to see your brother Georges slaughtered in such a way. Please, do you have the rosary that your mother gave to him? Did you save it? I would like to have it. It will give me comfort."

"We were robbed, Father. Nothing of value remained."

"Ah," the old man sighed. "I am sorry that this is to be your welcome home, my child. Please pray with me so that we may find solace together."

Although he wanted to roll his eyes, Philip kept a straight face. *Only a few more days. I just need to wait until he acknowledges me as his heir, and then I can leave.*

After a quick prayer, he rose to his feet, kissed the old man's hand, and retreated, fingering the silver and amber rosary that he had found on Georges de Fons Bleaudi.

God is good, he thought. *Finally.*

6

— · —

MEYDAN OF THE CITADEL, CAIRO. AUGUST 1281

"Zahed!"

Emre trudged toward the shady gateway of the tebaq, his thoughts focused on a clean change of clothes and a meal. After a long day of lance training in the sun, his forearms and shoulders ached, and greasy sweat made his leather helmet stick uncomfortably to his head. The meydan, a bare, circular training yard near the grand citadel in Cairo, emptied as the other boys scattered to their next lesson, but Emre diverted toward the palm-shaded benches lining the yard for a drink from the fountain. The boys had adjusted to the climate after being taken from the mild Cilician mountains, but Emre had never grown accustomed to drinking fetid warm water from a flask, try as he might.

"ZAHED!"

Emre stopped. That was his name being screamed across the meydan by the tawash – the instructor in charge of lance training. Mamluk boys were expected to be responsive, loyal, and unquestioning. Ignoring the tawash would earn him a beating.

He turned and bowed. "Apologies, tawash Izem, I did not hear you calling my name."

Izem, a thick-armed eunuch of middle height with a pale pink scar that incurred deeply into his left temple, leaned over Emre.

"No," Izem said, "you heard me. You just do not know your own name. Well, I think I have devised a way for you to remember – a way that will stick inside your empty head!"

Emre's shoulders slumped. His exhaustion wore on him. Whatever punishment the tawash had in mind would most certainly be severe.

"Hold, Izem!"

An authoritative voice spoke from across the training ground, and Emre stiffened as he saw Badahir, the amir who had killed his parents and kidnapped him two years ago, striding purposely toward them. This man had committed unspeakable crimes against Emre's people, and yet he treated Emre preferentially, giving him better armor than the other boys and a larger allocation of food in the tebaq. Despite Badahir's efforts, Emre's hatred for the man burned hotter as each day passed. He knew there would come a day when he would sink his dagger into Badahir's stomach, but today was not that day. Years of being a slave soldier had taught Emre patience.

After being taken from their tribe, Emre and the boys had spent days jolting and bouncing in a wagon to Aleppo, where they were transferred to a more comfortable wagon and transported to Damascus, and then came the tortuous journey to Cairo via Jerusalem and the great rocky desert. After that, it had been nothing but constant drilling; stringing and restringing their sharply curved composite bows and pulling the string back for days at a time to strengthen their arms, although it mostly just seemed to make the muscles in Emre's neck and shoulders feel like they were breaking.

On some days, Emre and the other boys had to run next to a horse as it slowly trotted in a circle. On other days, they had to run alongside the horse with their hand on its withers or the pommel of the saddle. There were endless marshal drills with long, slender sticks. *Step-slash-step-lunge-thrust-re-peat.* Each evening, Emre walked stiffly back to the tebaq, where he would eat a meal with the other recruits and be sent straight to bed.

Now that he had lived and trained in Cairo for two years, he found he had the strength to pull himself onto the horse while it ran, with or without a saddle. The interminable days of stringing and restringing a bow melted into thrilling games where he and other boys thundered on their horses in figure-eight patterns around targets set atop posts of varying heights, attempting to fire three arrows into the target within a count of three. Tawash Izem placed a pointed lance in his hands and taught him graceful movements with it, thrusting, tossing, and sweeping in a deadly dance until no one could defeat him.

On other days, the boys spent hours sitting cross-legged on rugs inside a madrasa, learning to speak Arabic, to write their names, and memorizing the verses of the Qur'an. Like the other people of the mountains, Emre knew of Islam, Allah, and the Prophet Mohammed, but as nomads who lived a life without walls, they were more comfortable worshipping Tengri and the pantheon of gods who ruled the earth, water, and mountains. A deity of nature helped explain the harshness of life in the elements with wild animals and storms that swelled the rivers and swept tribes away in a single night, or cold that could kill an entire herd. Some of the boys simply added Allah and Jesu Christi to the list of gods that could help keep their terror at bay. Others, like Emre, knew the fastest way to release themselves from the endless lectures and recitations was to learn the material quickly and declare themselves converts.

It could be worse, he supposed. The boys that the physician deemed unfit for training had to serve the recruits their food and clean the tebaq and the meydan each day. And then there were the ones who arrived as newly christened eunuchs, their wounds still barely healed, their souls anguished. These boys often came from southern lands with their members removed ahead of time, for Allah forbade the castration of a man by one of the Faithful, but did not forbid the purchasing of someone already mutilated.

The amir·stopped in front of Izem, his arms crossed. "Is there a problem, tawash Izem?"

"This one is unwilling to accept his name," Izem said, bowing in deference. "His training must not continue until his name becomes his own. I have tried beating him. I have tried making him write it in the dust of the meydan a hundred and one times, but he willfully refuses to respond when called. I will not continue to work with one who is so unwilling to learn."

Badahir scowled darkly at them both. "Leave him with me, please."

Izem bowed and retreated.

"Come with me." Badahir took Emre's hand and led him through the meydan, down several cool, dark corridors, and up the stairs of one of the citadel's towers. When they emerged on the wall, he greeted the guards with a nod and pulled Emre to the crenelations, facing west.

"Zahed, why do you shake with fear?" Badahir asked.

"Because you here to throw me from the walls of this great house, Amir," Emre said in broken Arabic, his voice trembling. "I ready to die. I join with ancestors."

Badahir laughed, then responded in Turkic. "Are you not yet convinced that I intend to keep you? Why would I throw something so valuable from the citadel walls? And here, you have made yourself even more perfect. You are ready to die! Your soul is prepared!"

Seeing Emre's confusion, he pointed to the west. "What do you see there?"

Emre squinted through the haze of cookfire smoke and dust. "Two great mountains and a smaller one," he said, relieved to speak in a tongue he readily understood.

"Those are not mountains, young man. They are tombs, built a thousand years ago by men who feared the oblivion of death and time. They are a legacy to the life of one man each and the kingdom that he ruled. Now look this way." He swept his hand to the north, then east and the south. "What do you see there?"

"A bunch of mosques and stone houses built on streets that stink like shit," Emre sneered.

"What you see and smell all around you is the kingdom of the Mamluks. We are no people, Zahed. Like you, we were all taken from our homes. Me? I am Catay. My birth parents sold me to a band of Mongols, who took me to Baghdad and sold me to my father in Acre."

"Your father?" Emre looked up, confused.

"Amir Mu'izzi al-Sharisa, the man who brought me here and helped me to understand the future that lay before me. When I came to Cairo and started my training, I became a new man. This city is full of people from all the corners of the earth. They come because we have wealth and knowledge, and because we control the most powerful army the land has ever seen. And you, Zahed, have been brought here by me because you belong in this city. Some day, you will become a leader of Cairo."

Emre scowled and turned back to the west. The image of the tombs hovered on the horizon, their foundations obscured in a cloud of haze.

"I would never throw you from the walls, Zahed. I have confidence that if you distinguish yourself in your training, you will become wealthy beyond your imagination. Like me, you will control the fates of other men. 'Badahir' is the name I received when I arrived in Cairo. My birth name is inconsequential because when I came here with al-Sharisa and found Allah, the most glorified, I became a new man."

"I do not wish to be a new man," Emre shot back.

"You wish to remain always as a thirteen-year-old boy? You never wish to father children or see a world outside of your tribe? Shall I take you to the north and put you back into your mountains where you can forage for food until the winter snows come and you freeze to death?"

Emre felt his eyes sting with tears.

"If you wish to go, I will free you where you may find a life of obscurity as someone's household servant. If you wish to be a part of a monumental army that will last a thousand years, you will accept your name. You will call me master and submit to your training with Izem."

The leather of the amir's cuirass creaked as he turned and walked toward the stairs of the citadel wall, disappearing into the darkness. Emre saw the guards looking at him curiously. They were local-born - small and mahogany-skinned, their bodies muscled and compact as they held their spears upright. Emre wondered if they had ever been told that they were valuable and important when they were thirteen years old. He doubted it. Even his own father never spoke such words to him in Cilicia. He hurried down the stairs after Badahir.

7

—.—

CAIRO. SEPTEMBER 1281

Across the city, all faces in Cairo turned toward Mecca for the observance of zuhr, the mid-day prayer. Yusuf al-Hikma ibn-Shihab had managed to urge his camels and servants inside the city gates just in time to find his way to the mosque that Baybars had built eleven years prior. It was not difficult to locate, for Baybars had been determined to leave as much physical evidence of his greatness as possible. Above its spiky walls, the tall, glassy dome of the structure hovered over the rooflines of the palaces and warehouses like a rising sun.

A truly superb place to pray on my return, Yusuf thought, as he hurried toward the mosque's entrance.

After instructing his servants to take his supplies ahead to the house of the Amir Badahir, Yusuf removed his shoes as he entered the gates of the spacious sahn and set out in search of a basin in which to wash. A cacophony of voices rose above the city – the muezzins calling the faithful to prayer. Yusuf paused, drinking in the sound. He had been on the road for too long.

An attendant hurried over to him, pausing to cast a scandalized glance at Yusuf's dusty beard and sweat-stained robes.

"As-salaam 'alaykum. Are you here to er... pray?"

"Wa 'alaykum as-salaam," Yusuf replied, smiling. "I realize I look atrocious, but I have just entered the city after traveling from Antioch. I wish to thank God for keeping my men and me safe on our journey."

The attendant, a small, nervous man in white robes with a too-big white taqiya on his head, wrung his hands anxiously. "Well, I suppose if you complete wudhu quickly before the prayers start, you should be fine. Do you have a rug of your own that you wish to use, Amir?"

Yusuf laughed, his black eyes sparkling. "Not an amir quite yet, but soon, God willing! I would be pleased to use a rug that you can provide."

The attendant gestured to his right. "This way to the wudhu, and make sure you are quick about it." His feet slapped loudly against the stones of the sahn as he pushed his away against the tide of worshippers who searched for space to unfurl their rugs.

Yusuf smiled again. Although the polished limestone pavers were hot under his bare feet, it felt wonderful to be rid of his stinking boots after a long journey through the Sinai, and the water from the fountains at the wudhu was cool and fresh from an underground spring.

After he had washed his feet and legs, hands, arms, and face, he took the rolled rug from the attendant and set it down at the edge of the sprawling courtyard where other men had already gathered. All faced the lavish mihrab, a curved niche in a wall that indicated the direction of Mecca. Sitting at the very back, Yusuf could only see the sweaty backs of the worshippers' robes and head-coverings; dots of taqiyas, long keffiyehs, and expertly wrapped turbans.

Yusuf stood at the foot of his borrowed rug, and the prayers began. He murmured the words as his body automatically performed the motions, his heart rushing with thanks and relief. It had been a difficult journey, and there were several times when he did not think he would make it to Cairo. Bedu had attacked his caravan and captured two of his camels, killing a soldier and making off with a precious goatskin of water. It had been a hot, thirsty trip. Here he was, however, in a mosque built by Baybars, who his new master had served as an amir and advisor. Yusuf reminded himself to focus on his prayers, but his mind wanted to wander to the adventure that awaited him.

At twenty years old, Yusuf was a rising star among the Mamluk elite, having served almost his entire life under al-Shihab, his first master. His battle prowess was admirable, but Yusuf provided the most value to the amirs and their personal armies as a translator and strategist. It became clear to al-Shihab that Yusuf possessed intelligence far beyond the other young men in training. This suited Yusuf more, anyhow. He disliked battle, the fluids of other men spattering in his eyes and mouth, the gurgles and screams of his victims. The smells. It bothered him that they spent more time attacking villages these days than targeting their real enemies, the Mongols in the north and the Franj occupiers in Acre and Tyre, who sometimes allied with them.

Yusuf's lip curled. The word "Franj" had originally just meant "French." After the other Christians from the Italian peninsula, the island of Britain, and the Holy Roman Empire to the north of Francia demonstrated that they were equally as cruel and fanatical, the word took on a derogatory meaning. To Yusuf and the other Muslim occupants of Palestine and Cairo, "Franj" was synonymous with "occupier."

Very few of the Mamluk amirs were careless enough to admit that they – slaves and soldiers purchased and kidnapped from their homes – were also occupiers. There was a difference. The Franj had not only occupied the land when they invaded, but they desecrated sacred places, robbed the people of their wealth, and imposed their strange brand of polytheism on the Believers with their worship of 'Īsā, whom they called 'Jesu Christi,' peace be upon him.

The Mamluk soldiers may have come from all countries and religions, but they were returning the Faith in Allah to this land, and for that, they must remain in power. They were here to protect the Believers and rid the land of the infidels once and for all. After the Christians were eliminated, then the Mamluks could turn their full attention to securing the borders against the Mongol scourge, thus earning themselves riches and bringing glory to Allah, may He be ever merciful.

Yusuf rose to his knees with practiced efficiency and looked to his right, along with a thousand other men in the sahn.

"Peace be upon you, and the mercy and blessings of Allah."

There was a gentle rustle as all heads turned to the left.

"Peace be upon you, and the mercy and blessings of Allah."

The blessings of Allah, Yusuf thought, his heart swelling with joy. *I am blessed to be here.*

8

— · —

DAMASCUS. NOVEMBER 1281

Tamrat strolled around the small square at the Touma Gate as the shops began to open, hands clasped behind his back, face beaming genially underneath the brim of his yellow pointed hat. It was late fall, and the air in Damascus was cool and smoky from the morning fires that warmed houses and heated porridge pots in the city, but the cloudless sky promised sun and pleasant temperatures that day. Pleasant enough, perhaps, to take Sara and Dejen to the river for the afternoon meal, where they could get away from the crowds and the smell of the streets for a few hours.

He glanced up at the giant stone edifice of the Touma Gate, with its pale limestones and arched entryway. The Ayyūbīd royal family had restored the old barbican, and the stones still looked fresh and unchipped. His eyes wandered from the militaristic arrowslits to the stalls of matchstick poles and thatch along the inside walls that sold everything a new traveler to the city could want – pistachios, pointed slippers, money-changing services, tallow candles, fortune-telling, carved bowls and cups, and of course, prostitutes.

Khadir was nowhere to be seen, unsurprisingly. Tamrat's occasional business partner and expert translator was perennially late. He checked the position of the sun, then continued to stroll, greeting the guards and stall-keepers cordially. He squinted into the darkened alley in the direction of the man's house, searching for his friend's large, lumbering frame. Instead, his eyes landed on the tiniest of silhouettes.

The little girl crouched in the shadows behind a neat stack of cedar logs that had recently been delivered from Lebanon, stripped of their branches and bark. Street urchins were not uncommon in Damascus. Indeed, they were just a part of the scenery in any cosmopolitan city throughout the Levant and the West, but Tamrat had never developed the skill that others possessed, which allowed them to ignore the dirty, thin little faces in the crowds and dark corners. This little girl caught his interest because of the grim determination in her wide-set eyes. She avidly watched a wealthy sheikh and his entourage as they entered through the gate, biting her bottom lip in apprehension.

The sheikh sat on a carved cedar palanquin with four slaves carrying him past the stall vendors and toward the main road through the city to the mosque of Salah ad-Din. The little girl stood and walked casually around the square, pretending to take an interest in the stalls, earning narrow-eyed looks from the vendors, who were clearly acquainted with her. When she was close to the sheikh, she suddenly darted underneath his palanquin, tripping one of the slaves. The palanquin tipped sideways as the slave fell and spilled its moneyed occupant into the street.

The girl snatched the sheikh's purse as he lay dazed in the dust and had squeezed herself through a hole in the stone wall before anyone had the presence of mind to call a guard.

Tamrat laughed at the spectacle of the enraged nobleman sprawled on his hands and knees and the frenzied guards as they chased after the tiny thief. But then he became troubled; if this little girl continued to try to rob nobility, she would end up dead or with her hands cut off as soon as she was caught. Only the greatest desperation would cause a child to think of doing something so dangerous. He tugged his beard in thought as he strolled out of the square. Well, he was involved now.

Since Khadir did not show up today, the only remedy was to come back tomorrow and see what happened.

***

The following morning, Tamrat saw the little girl again as he bantered with a sweet seller over a little packet of cardamom biscuits for his wife, Sara. He paid for his purchase and proceeded to walk toward the alley where he lived. Although he could not see or hear her, he felt sure she was nearby, for he had flashed his coins flagrantly at the sweet stall.

The crowd in the alley thickened as his neighborhood woke up and emerged from their houses. He felt a bump and a little tug on his leg and saw a girl in a shabby dress with a matted head of hair weaving her way through the crowd with his money bag clutched in a grubby fist.

"Thief!" a voice roared, and the pedestrians in the alley turned, stopping to watch.

Khadir was holding the girl by a handful of her hair, and she squealed, bit, and scratched at him. He gave her a firm slap across the face as Tamrat rushed toward them.

"Give it back, you filthy child. Give Master Tamrat his purse back!"

"I thank you, Khadir, for watching out for my purse. I can take it from here," Tamrat said, patting the big man on the arm.

Khadir ripped the money bag from the girl's hand and gave it to Tamrat, thrusting her at him.

"You are too kind to these pests, Master Tamrat. They will rob you until you have no roof over your head."

"Ah, but I prefer the great blue ceiling that God provides," Tamrat smiled back at him. "It would be a pleasure to no longer need a house. I hope to see you at my workshop this week, Khadir. I have some interesting new translations to show you from a Roman tablet discovered in an abandoned brewery."

Khadir raised an eyebrow, then smiled. "A recipe for a new ale, perhaps? On the morrow, I shall come. Good day, Master Tamrat!"

The little girl was watching him sullenly. She squirmed, trying to loosen her garment from Tamrat's grip while he spoke with Khadir.

"Now, what shall I do about the little girl who has been following my purse since the Gate of Touma? I must appear much more valuable than I am." He pulled his graying beard pensively. "Hold out your hand, child, and do not run." He emptied the contents of his purse into her hand, and the moment he released her dress, she turned and darted into the crowd, her little legs churning.

"I come this way every morning when the sun rises," he called after her. "You may steal from me again tomorrow if you wish!"

***

Six-year-old Sidika crouched in the shadow of the narrow alley and assessed her prospects. On this day, they did not look promising. Usually, the little square just inside the Touma Gate buzzed with haggling merchants and customers, shepherds urging their animals toward the slaughterhouse, and the occasional loud recitations of a Sufi mystic. But today, the gloom of the overcast sky appeared to have penetrated the mood of the square. The merchants frowned over their piles of dates and goatskin slippers, and the customers – few that there were – skulked past the wares, unwilling to buy, hands grasped resolutely around their purses. That was fine with her. The man called Tamrat had told her that he came this way every day, and she meant to see if he was as good as his word.

Sure enough, he emerged into the square and greeted a vendor selling fresh, warm flaps of ruqāq bread, which he placed in a cloth sack. He continued to walk along the stalls, bantering amiably with a vendor selling olives. Withdrawing a clay jar from his sack, he removed the cork plug and handed it to the man at the stall who filled it with the plump green fruits. Tamrat paid the stall vendor and tucked the jar into his bag. He stopped and looked around, shading his eyes, then walked purposefully in her direction. Sidika backed further into the shadows.

Tamrat whistled as he walked past her and casually pulled his outer robe back to reveal his money bag, dangling loosely at his belt. Sidika jumped from the shadows, snatched it, and dashed down a narrow alley and into the darkness. Behind her, she could hear Tamrat chuckling.

The next day, the scene repeated itself, although this time Sidika did not run away quite as fast as before.

From then on, Tamrat appeared almost every morning, and about a dozen yards after he turned into the alley from the square, Sidika would jump out and grab his purse. Sometimes he made funny faces at her or screamed like a startled woman, and Sidika would put a hand over her mouth and giggle as she ran off. Sometimes the purse held a few coins, and other times it contained a piece of fruit or bread. Once, she found a little carved wooden bird inside, which she hid behind a loose stone in Bekir's warehouse so the other children wouldn't find it. When she was alone, which was rare, she would take the bird out and gaze at it, marveling that someone had taken the time and effort to create it for her.

One frosty December morning, Tamrat appeared in the square at the usual time, but he was not alone. A tall woman was at his side. She wore a loose gown of deep blue wool, fastened at her throat by a silver brooch with a rough garnet in its center. A white scarf with a blue edge modestly covered her jet-black hair, but she looked around boldly at the vendors and other men in the street. This morning they spent time at the shops, purchasing dates, bread, packets of powdered plant dyes, and thick sheets of paper. Sidika bit her lip. He never seemed to mind being robbed, but what would happen with this woman nearby?

As they walked down the alley off the square, Tamrat winked at her, but he kept his purse covered by his robe. Sidika's stomach growled, and she thought apprehensively about what would happen to her if she returned to Bekir empty-handed. Tamrat was an easy source of income, and Sidika had grown lazy. She tailed the couple as they slowly wove through the crowd and turned down the Street of Scribes, stopping at a set of stairs in front of a small house to sit down. The woman reached into her bag, withdrew some fragrant pieces of bread, and Sidika's stomach growled again. Tamrat looked up and smiled directly at her as she crouched in the shadows like an alley cat. Sidika approached slowly, feeling exposed and vulnerable as she walked across the street toward them. They seemed to be expecting her.

"My wife, Sara," Tamrat said proudly. "She is a healer. My darling, this little girl is the reason why you have been compelled to make me a new purse almost every day."

Sara had deep-set black eyes that crinkled around the edges when she smiled. She smeared some tangy olive paste onto a large piece of warm bread and held it out to Sidika, who took it shyly and smelled it. It had been months since she had tasted olives.

"What is your name, child?" Sara asked.

Sidika backed away and ran. Bekir would be angry that she had no coins, but her stomach gnawed at her constantly, and the bread smelled fresh and warm. Today she would suffer his wrath, and hopefully, Tamrat would have coins with him instead of a wife tomorrow.

***

Bekir kept seven young children in his warehouse near the mausoleum of Salah ad-Din, which fronted as a storage house for camel feed, empty crates, jars of wine, or anything else that needed temporary shelter on the trade routes. The children scoured the streets during the day, slipping their dirty hands into the robes and scrips of the men walking the streets, surrendering their earnings back to him in the evening in exchange for a threadbare blanket and a pile of straw to sleep on, and a handful of stale bread to eat. Bekir called them his Little Hands.

Sidika had lived with the Little Hands for a year and had only hazy memories of how she ended up in Damascus. Bekir claimed that the Mongol woman who found her after the death of her parents, whom Sidika only knew as 'Horse Aunty,' sold her to him in exchange for a meal, but Sidika remembered the woman's anguished cries when he ripped her from Horse Aunty's arms. Life with Horse Aunty had been difficult, cold, and always on the move, but Bekir was worse. No matter how little food they had to eat, Sidika knew that Horse Aunty loved her.

One day in the Touma Square, Tamrat brought a boy with him. The boy was slender and graceful, with rich, dark skin and unfathomably deep brown eyes. Sidika and the boy looked at each other shyly for a moment.

"It was Dejen who carved the little bird for you, child. He wanted to meet you because he used to live on the streets just like you." Tamrat told her.

Dejen grinned broadly. He reached into his small bag, withdrawing a smooth, stiff tablet of boiled leather. Taking a handful of dust from the ground, he scattered it across the tablet and dragged his finger in the dust to create a symbol: ﻳ.

"See? This is 'yā,' and this one..." he traced another symbol into the tablet: ﻭ, "is 'wāw.' Do you recognize them?"

Until that point, it had never occurred to Sidika to notice letters. Damascus was a highly educated city, but those privileges did not trickle down to urchins like her. She understood that the squiggles carved into the stone on the mosques and synagogues had meaning but had never known how to puzzle anything from them. Dejen let her try to draw the letters on the tablet herself, and she stayed, engrossed in the magic lines that made sounds until the shadows grew long. That night, she returned to the warehouse after sunset, her mind ablaze with questions, and Bekir beat her until both of her eyes swelled shut.

One early morning, as the children sleepily filed from the warehouse to their work, Bekir grabbed Sidika by a skinny arm and dragged her into a garbage-strewn alley. Tamrat stood there, his face scrunched into an uncharacteristic glare. Bekir shoved her onto the pavers.

"She was almost useless, anyhow. Spent too much time avoiding her work, which I am sure you will find when you compel her to do anything she does not wish to do." He pulled a dagger from his sash, brandishing it at Tamrat's beard. "Now, you remember our agreement; I know not how you found me or why you want her, but you take this child and do not tell the city guard about the others."

Tamrat nodded and held out a small bag of coins. Bekir snatched the coins, spat at the ground, then slammed the door of his warehouse and barred it.

Sidika's mind raced. Locked out. She had never been locked out! Her bed and her carved bird were inside. How would she eat? Rejection and fear gripped her little heart, and she began to wail.

"Now, now," Tamrat knelt and looked into her eyes. "Do not cry, little one. You shall come live with Sara, Dejen, and myself. You will no longer need to rob sheikhs and merchants for your bread."

Sidika backed away. She had already had one master and didn't relish the idea of another one. Bekir was a predictable evil. This Tamrat and his family might be fine enough while in the street, but who knew what horrors they would subject her to behind closed doors? She turned and ran away as fast as she could.

9

— • —

CASTLE BESAN, NORTHERN PALESTINE. FEBRUARY
1283

A t the castle of Besan, juvenile shouts and the clacking of wooden practice swords echoed across the nearby town and Roman amphitheater – the raucous music of a practice joust. In a dusty field outside the walls, boys tilted at the tall, T-shaped quintain with a mannequin sitting atop, its straw-stuffed head wrapped in a turban.

Henri carefully closed the kitchen door behind him, shutting out the noise of the jeering boys. The kitchen was almost always busy, so he had found it so hard to steal food for Minou, but she had not eaten since yesterday and could no longer wait. Today he was in luck; the kitchen was empty because all eyes were on the rehearsal - a precursor to a formal joust, sponsored by King Hugh, to be held next week as a way to introduce the newly minted knights to the community. At ten years old, Henri was still too young to compete, and it was easy for him to slip away unnoticed as Sir Geoffroi, and his knights argued over the rules. For a moment, he stood in the doorway, savoring the stillness and warmth of the dim, smoky kitchen. He rarely had any time alone at Sir Geoffroi's.

He found the warm pans of milk set out to ripen into tangy yogurt and dipped into one with a small clay cup. A leg of a roasted hare from yesterday's mid-day meal found its way into his bag, wrapped in a dirty scrap of muslin, along with a pistachio cookie for himself. Then, he turned to leave.

Otho the cook, a tower of food-stained robes and knife-scarred fingers, stood between him and the door, blocking his escape. He held a wooden ale paddle menacingly in one hand.

"Stealing food? Are you not training to be moved to the Templars, where they will feed you even less than Sir Geoffroi does?!" Otho shouted, his face turning purple with anger.

"No, well, it is only a little bit, and it is not for me—"

"I do not care if you are nicking a crumb of bread for a mouse or a barrel of spoiled wine for a dockside tavern! No one steals from this kitchen! Sir Geoffroi will hear of this and have your brown buttocks warmed with his belt in front of all the household!"

"Wait, please! It is for my cat, Minou. If she grows strong and fat, I will give her to you to keep the rats from your storerooms!"

Otho looked at Henri with narrowed eyes. He was unforgiving against thieves in his kitchen, but the rats had got at a lamb and barley pie only yesterday and spoiled it. And had he not been complaining only last week that he needed a mouser to patrol the pantry and the grain cellar? The boy spoke sense, though Otho hated to admit it.

"How did you come to find this creature?"

"Found her in a sack, Master Otho. Someone tied her up and threw her into the river to drown. I think it was Madame LeVache who did it."

"Very well, but you cannot feed meat to a kit. How big is she, lad?"

Henri snatched a pomegranate from the table and held it up.

"Here, then," Otho grunted. He tore a piece of bread from a plump, leavened loaf on a shelf and dropped it into Henri's cup of soured milk.

"Soak it good and make it into a mash. The little beast should eat that until she can hunt on her own, and then you will deliver her to me to work in my kitchen."

"May I come and see her when she lives here?"

Otho turned on Henri, incredulous. "Why ever would you want to do that? Now, get out before I change my mind!"

Henri hurried away, sloshing the milk as he left, and Otho looked after him. That boy thought he was the same as the other students at Sir Geoffroi's. It was almost as if he did not know he was a Saracen.

"It's not right," Otho muttered as he stoked the coals in the great oven. "Absurd, the way Sir Geoffroi allows that child to mix with the others like he is one of them." He heaved a great iron pot down from a shelf and looked around for help, but the slaves were at the pigsty fence, surreptitiously watching the joust.

Otho stalked outside. "Himmet!" he bellowed. "Get back in this kitchen and fill the pots or I will put you in one of them and make a stew of you!"

Himmet rushed into the kitchen, snatched a pail, and ran back out to the well. Born on the estate to one of the slaves who worked in the laundry, the boy bore a striking resemblance to Sir Geoffroi, as did most of the bastard children in the castle.

"Was that young Henri of Maron I saw coming out here?" Himmet asked when he returned, staggering under the heavy pail.

Otho grunted in reply.

"He may be only ten years old, but he has far more skill than any of the older boys when it comes to the sword. Have you seen the way he moves?"

Otho slammed his knife onto his worktable. "Are you going to blather at me or fill that pot? Besides, it is not proper that a Saracen be given more credit than his betters."

"Well, the only student here who is richer than Henri of Maron is Prince Amalric, 'ent he? Seems the Saracen is living up to become more of an ideal knight than the Franj students, I would say."

Otho narrowed his eyes. "Is that what the other boys think?"

"Sure enough. 'Tis plain to see. He will be wearing the white and red as soon as he turns eighteen. That's my predicament."

"I think you mean 'prediction,'" Otho said, tapping his finger on the table. "That boy is too soft to be a Templar. He is too soft to even be a Saracen, for that matter."

Himmet laughed mirthlessly. "Ah, Sir Geoffroi and the other boys will harden him. If they are not beating the stuffing from him on the practice field, then they will make sure he knows his place. Mark me."

***

Noblemen, especially those with large families, found it convenient to have their sons trained by an experienced fighter and returned to them finished. Sons were rowdy and unrestrained around the serving girls, so noblemen of Acre who wanted to preserve the peace of their households packed their boys off to Castle Besan, far to the north of Acre and Tyre, so Sir Geoffroi and his knights could pound their youth out of them.

The trainees at Sir Geoffroi's had little time for leisure. When not practicing their drills with sword and lance, they learned to squire by polishing helmets, oiling spurs, and rubbing grease into leather saddles. When not engaged in any of these activities, the boys could be found sitting on a hard bench inside the small stone chapel within the castle grounds, listening to the ancient, half-deaf prior Marcheux wheeze through a sermon in Latin. The moments for a ten-year-old boy to play or to sit alone and dream were scarce. Henri found that the best time for daydreaming was in church. In the dimness of the room, he could let his mind wander without serious consequences, as long as he pretended to pay attention.

Today, he had brought Minou with him. The little creature was still so small that she could comfortably sleep in the leather scrip he always carried at his waist, and no one was the wiser. He reached gently into the bag's leather recesses, felt her silky ears, and rubbed her bulging little belly. Drowsy and content from the milk and bread, she purred quietly. Keeping her nearby helped ward off the loneliness, the feeling of otherness that followed him everywhere at the castle. It also helped to know that he had a secret, although now the bald, distended cook was in on it. At least this way, Minou could stay at the castle if Henri donated her to protect the pie cupboards.

As the sermon concluded, Minou began to stir. A little orange paw shot playfully from the scrip and buried a claw in his hand. Henri jumped up from his bench and pushed his way through the other boys toward the door before she tried to wriggle out of her hiding spot. If the other boys knew he had something that he loved, they would surely take it from him.

"The Saracen is eager to leave the church, I see," he heard Joscelin de Loire remark behind him. "Does it make your horns hurt to sit in this holy place, devil?"

Henri ignored the taunts and ran into the courtyard, through the small gate, and into the warren of Scythopolis, the ancient ruins that had stood for a thousand years before the castle's construction. Down a crumbling colonnade, through an arched doorway, and over a wall was his secret place – a small sunken chamber of stone with a floor of soft grass. He placed Minou into her slatted wooden box, which he had made comfortable with some fresh straw and several broken clay cups of water.

"I will return tonight," he whispered before he scrambled away.

It was his first night of serving duty. Squires were required to assist their knights in any way needed, including serving meals and refilling a knight's cup. Henri was only a page, so he would practice pouring wine for Sir Manfred von Bremen, who joined them at the table this evening. After receiving hasty instructions from one of the older boys, Henri was given a copper pitcher filled with sour-smelling wine and told to stand behind the old knight until the level of the man's cup dropped below two-thirds. Carefully, Henri refilled the cup without sloshing and stepped back to his place, his stomach snarling at him as he breathed in the rich scent of meat wafting from the table.

Sir Manfred raised his cup again and again for Henri to fill and was soon quite drunk. After the meal, the man stood, swayed a few steps from the table, then vomited into the straw on the floor of the hall. Henri's mouth dropped open in shock. His father, Lord Rogier, and his guests never displayed such behavior over their wine.

Sir Geoffroi looked on from his throne-like seat at the head table, his narrow-set brown eyes scowling.

"Well, boy, go and clean it up!"

Hours after Sir Manfred repeated his performance and returned for an encore, Henri wearily trudged to the dark, narrow hall where the boys slept on pallets on the floor. Although Sir Geoffroi was a stern master to all the boys, Henri was usually the target of his ire. Rumors swirled that Sir Geoffroi had refused to accept Henri for training until Lord Rogier agreed to pay twice what was required for room and board; ten bezants a season for the privilege of sleeping on a straw-stuffed pallet in a room with twelve other boys and eating scraps from the knights' table. Henri drifted to sleep, dreaming of his feather-stuffed mattress and his bed at home.

***

The weeks passed in monotony until it was finally the day before Kalends – the end of the month – when Rogier would come to visit. Rarely did any of the other boys receive visitors or contact from home, and they watched with veiled resentment as the lord of Maron rode through the gate each month, greeting his Saracen son with a broad smile and saddlebags stuffed with gifts.

On this day, the younger boys were in pairs in the small courtyard, circling each other with shields raised high, wooden practice swords darting out to strike. Henri and another ten-year-old sparred near the stable, and Rogier handed his horse to a groom before hiding behind a wall to watch. Henri only had eyes for his opponent, a weak-chinned Englander named Bliant. At this moment, Bliant's eyes were wide with fear as Henri doggedly edged him back toward the shelter wall, striking with his sword and the edge of his shield.

"Henri, stop. You are backing me into a corner!" Bliant shouted in a panic. "Stop pushing me back!"

Henri smiled. "If I was a Mamluk 'askari, would you whine to him about being backed into a corner too?"

"You are a bloody Saracen. Close enough to a Mamluk!"

From his hiding place against the wall, Rogier frowned, but Henri charged forward with a yell, slammed Bliant against the shelter, thrust the point of his sword under the boy's shield, and jabbed him lightly in the gut. "You are dead."

"Devil!" a voice called out. "Perhaps you should try to back me against a wall and see what happens!"

Joscelin de Loire and his opponent had finished their sparring and watched the two younger boys.

"I am not allowed to fight someone older than me." Henri glanced at Sir Geoffroi, who stood by with his arms crossed.

Joscelin was fourteen years old and already squiring for one of the castle knights. He raised his shield and picked up a rusty iron sword that leaned against a wall.

"Did I not just hear you claiming to be a Mamluk? Fight like one!"

The older boy charged, and Henri pulled his shield up just in time. He and Joscelin collided, and the force threw Henri onto his back in the dust. Joscelin tossed his shield to the ground, placed his foot on Henri's hip, and grasped his sword over his head with both hands, preparing the final blow. Henri, still struggling for breath, managed to raise his small shield in time to block the blow, and the impact slammed the shield into his mouth so that he tasted blood.

"Come on, Saracen! Are you too frightened to fight against one of God's soldiers?" Joscelin grunted and slashed down with his sword. "When I spill your guts with this sword, your soul will travel straight to hell!"

Henri kicked out with a booted foot and pinned Joscelin's sword to the ground with his heel, catching his opponent off guard as the weapon clanged against the stony soil of the courtyard. Henri leapt to his feet, threw his weight against the taller boy, and they both fell heavily against the courtyard wall. Swiftly, he drew his wooden practice sword across Joscelin's throat.

"You are dead too," Henri panted. "And headless."

Sir Geoffroi marched between them and grabbed Henri by the back of his padded leather armor. "That is enough!" he shouted. "Henri of Maron, if I have to keep punishing you, there will be no chamber pots left in this castle for you to clean!"

"But he attacked first!" Henri argued. "With a real sword!"

Sir Geoffroi wrenched Henri off his feet. "Listen, you half-breed b—" He stopped abruptly when Rogier stepped out from behind the stable, his arms crossed.

Sir Geoffroi dropped Henri and shoved him toward his father. "There. Now your father has witnessed your shame. You are not to fight with the older boys."

Rogier regarded Sir Geoffroi coldly but said nothing. He turned and walked toward the castle gate and Henri, hanging his head, trotted to the stable, hung his wooden sword and shield on a peg, and hurried after his father. For a while, they walked side by side in silence.

"I am sorry I shamed you, Father," Henri finally spoke.

Rogier took a deep breath and exhaled slowly. "What I saw back there was not just. It was not right for you to be accused of starting that fight, nor is it acceptable that those boys call the future viscount of Acre and a marquis of Francia a Saracen and a devil. But Henri, you must know that I will not ask Sir Geoffroi to make it stop." He turned and noticed his son's hurt expression. "The truth in life is that no one will play fair – in battle or out of it – and you must protect yourself without expecting that your opponent will follow any set of rules or code. You must become immune to the words that come from their mouths."

"Did anyone call you names when you were of an age with me?" Henri asked bitterly.

"Yes, they called me 'horse face' because I had not grown into my teeth yet, and they also called me an abomination because my brother and I are twins who look exactly alike. For this, they also accused my mother of being a wanton woman. However, those boys all died in battles and arguments or accidents. I still live because I had to learn to be tougher than them. I had to learn to control my anger."

"And when they killed my brother, did you control your anger then?"

Henri knew the words stung his father, but he did not care. Since his brother's death, it seemed like his mother and father did not even notice that Henri lived. He wished his father would punch Sir Geoffroi in the face and throw Joscelin into the water trough, but he also knew that if Rogier had intervened, the boys would only taunt him more cruelly. He just wanted to go home to al-Hadiqa.

"Father, cannot your men train me to be a knight? Surely Durant would make a fine teacher—"

"Durant cannot be spared from his duties to the house and our villages."

"Hire a trainer, then! It would cost you less than what you pay to keep me here."

"It is not safe for you to be at home, Henri," Rogier said quietly, and Henri knew that his father was referring to the kidnapping.

"The kidnappers are dead, and I want to come home!" Henri felt his throat tighten and his eyes sting. He missed his mother, his friends, and even his little sisters. He missed roaming in the citronnier, catching frogs in Yasaf creek, and listening to the insects humming as the sun slowly set over the sea. Every day at Sir Geoffroi's felt like a fight for his life.

Rogier put his hand on Henri's head and rubbed it affectionately. "I know, son. I want you to come home too, but you must stay here. It will get better, and you will become a knight when you are finished with your training, just think of that! Now, tell me about this 'Minou' that you mentioned in your letter. Are you courting a lady of the castle?" His eyes twinkled, and Henri smiled up at him.

"Come, Father. I will show you!"

10

— ● —

CASTLE BESAN, NORTHERN PALESTINE. FEBRUARY
1283

Henri opened his small locked chest of belongings in the
hall and discreetly withdrew a fragrant khushkanānaj
from the parcel that his father had given him. He stuffed the
sweet, crumbly cookie into his mouth before anyone could
notice and dropped a second one into his scrip for later. The
boys at Castle Besan knew that when Rogier came to visit, he
brought cookies or cakes from al-Hadiqa's excellent kitchen,
and Henri often shared his gifts willingly, but today he did not
wish to share, not even with Amalric.

It was late winter, and although the sun still felt far away, a
smell of spring tinted the air. A few clouds dotted the sky over
the mountains in the northeast, and a whiff of impending rain
floated in on a mild breeze.

Henri slunk through the ruins of Scythopolis and found
Minou's box. The locals in Besan township were afraid of the
crumbling city and maintained their distance, as did the boys
in Sir Geoffroi's care. Still, he would not be able to keep her
here much longer, for she was growing, and whenever he left
her, she cried loudly. When she was a full-grown mouser, it
was less likely that someone would try to drown her or that
one of the other boys would torture her, but until she was
larger than a melon, she was vulnerable to the cruel mischief
of his fellow trainees.

The box was empty, and he stared at it dumbly for a moment. He clicked his tongue to call her, but there was no downy orange kit bounding toward him like usual. He scanned the muddy ground around the box, but he did not find so much as a paw print.

A stone fell as someone climbed over the crumbling wall, and Henri looked up in alarm.

"Henri, Sir Geoffroi is looking for you," Amalric said, his expression grim. "He said I would find you here."

Henri's heart dropped. Running back through the courtyard and into the boys' hall, he found Sir Geoffroi and the other students standing near his pallet.

"Henri, come here!" Sir Geoffroi barked, his voice echoing through the vaulted room.

"Sir, is something wrong?"

"My gold pendant, which was a gift from King Louis, is missing. Joscelin says that he saw you sneaking out of my room this morning."

"I was in your room, sir, to change the pots, per my punishment for fighting Joscelin."

"Well, the pendant was in my room last night next to my washbasin. I placed it there, but when I wanted it today, it was gone. Give it to me now, and your punishment will be reasonable."

"Sir, I do not have your pendant," Henri stammered. "I know nothing of it."

Sir Geoffroi snatched Henri's scrip and turned it upside down, dumping out a small dagger, a ball of string, a dog-eared piece of folded paper, several marbles of polished stone, and the crumbling cookie. Then he ran his hands along Henri's arms and legs and made him take off his boots and searched those too. Behind him, the other boys snickered. Finding nothing, Sir Geoffroi snatched Henri's ear and pulled him painfully to his trunk.

"Open your trunk," he commanded.

Henri decided not to argue. Kneeling, he opened the lid. Sitting on top of the linen-wrapped parcel of cookies was a shining gold pendant with the image of Saint Nicholas of Myra stamped on it. Henri gasped and looked up.

"My lord, I did not put that here. I promise that I did not take your pendant!"

Sir Geoffroi's weathered face was rigid with anger. "Bring the little beast here!" he barked.

Joscelin stepped forward. Minou slept peacefully in his hand, curled up like a ginger pillbug with her tail wrapped around her paws.

Sir Geoffroi snatched the kitten and thrust her into Henri's arms. "And this! You are hiding animals now? Are you training to be a knight or a farmer's daughter?!"

Henri said nothing.

"Kill it, and then afterward, you will receive punishment," Sir Geoffroi said coldly. "I train warriors, not thieves and soft-hearted infidels."

"Please, my lord, I will take a stronger beating. Please do not kill her!"

"I will not kill her, boy, *you* will! We keep animals for eating or for working, not as pets. As punishment for your dishonesty and theft, you will kill that cat. Perhaps that will teach you not to steal your master's things!"

Henri stepped back and snatched Minou to his chest. "No," he whimpered. He could feel hot tears running down his cheeks. A few of the boys jeered at him, but Amalric watched the ground and did not join the others. Sir Geoffroi reached for him, but Henri turned and ran. The boys moved together to block his escape, so he dropped Minou to the ground.

"Go!" he shouted, pushing her with his foot toward the door, but she simply looked up at him and swatted playfully at the laces of his boot.

Sir Geoffroi picked Minou up by her scruff, and she cried out sharply as he pulled his arm back to swing her head at the stone wall.

Henri felt himself go blind with fury. Yelling, he charged at his master, butting him in the stomach. Sir Geoffroi lost his footing and sat down hard on the stone floor, dropping Minou, who trotted toward the open door, her tail erect and fluffed with agitation.

Sir Geoffroi laughed, a low, dangerous sound, from where he sat with his legs splayed. "Oh, how glad I am that you struck me, boy. I have been waiting for it!" He sprang to his feet and grabbed a fistful of Henri's dark, curling hair.

"Never steal from me again!" Sir Geoffroi punctuated each word with a strike from the back of his hand. "Go on, defend yourself! Hit me again! Hit me!"

But Henri sank to the floor, dazed, his face and neck swelling with bruises. He did not hear the other boys walk silently from the room or Sir Geoffroi as he plucked his pendant of Saint Nicholas of Myra, the patron saint of children, from Henri's chest, rising to leave and slamming the door on his way out.

11

— • —

"Come, Zahed. Tonight you will dine with me and not with the other boys in the tebaq."

Badahir squinted at Emre in the bright sun and paused to appreciate the sight as the young man slid his sword back into the leather sheath at his belt.

After five years of living and training in Cairo, he had grown tall and robust, his curled hair bleached to the color of honey in the strong Egyptian sun, and his hazel eyes stood out vividly in his deeply tanned face. Although he had not quite surpassed Badahir in height, it was clear that he would tower over his master before he reached his twentieth year.

"Yes, Amir. Is there a reason you honor me thus?"

"There is something I wish to discuss with you."

"Tawash Izem says I must sweep the floor of the tebaq this night."

"Do we not have servants and slaves to sweep the floor? Why is Izem punishing you?"

"Because he says I am stubborn and sullen, Amir."

Badahir chuckled. "Still as troublesome as ever. Well, I will talk to Izem. You would be dismayed to miss what I wish to tell you this night." The amir gave him a one-sided smile and motioned for a servant, who rushed to his side. "I will see you at my house this evening after you have cleaned up."

He strode from the practice grounds, the sun glinting off the jewels embroidered into his blue tunic, his servant hurrying behind him.

Emre looked around to ensure no one was watching, then spat at Badahir as he retreated. Although the other boys considered themselves fortunate to be in the amir's care, Emre remained defiant. The other boys talked of fathers who would beat them and mothers who worked them relentlessly, but Emre only remembered his mother and father's loving smiles that faded along with his memory of the mountains of his homeland. The fine food of the tebaq tasted like sawdust in his mouth, and the rich robes might as well have been made of camel hair – such was his longing for his home.

That is why, hours later, he still did not understand what possessed him to show up outside the amir's house near the palace complex. Curiosity, perhaps.

Like most grand houses in Cairo, Badahir's palace looked plain from the outside, with tall limestone walls and typical wooden mashrabiya windows protruding high above the street, their carved screens concealing the cool, lavish rooms inside.

A servant instructed him to bathe, a somber ritual that the Mamluks of Cairo took seriously. Normally, for a guest, this would mean a rinse of the mouth, water combed through the hair and beard, scrubbed feet and arms, and finally, face. As a Mamluk in Badahir's household, Emre was not a guest, but not entirely family, either. The servant sized him up, then led him into the amir's hammam.

In the mountains, Emre had bathed when they were near a stream or a lake, but the experience was rarely pleasant, even in summer. Here, however, the hammam was steamy, and instead of a basin, he was led to a pool in the floor and instructed to take all the time he needed. The water was warm and scented with herbs, and when he emerged, pink and steaming, an attendant presented him with a clean blue linen tunic and loose sirwal pants that tied at his ankles. His hair was combed, oiled, and his head left bare. A richly dressed servant approached him and bowed low.

"Esteemed fursān, the amir is asking for you."

Emre still had trouble remembering that, although he was a slave to Badahir, he was held in high regard by the local-born of Cairo and was considered lucky indeed to have joined the Mamluk army. The foot soldiers of the city viewed him with reverence, and the citizens of Cairo cowered and bowed to him in the street. None of it made sense to him. He was an outsider. He was *owned*, with no rights or freedom. In his tribe, the slaves were beaten, stripped, and given the worst jobs, such as digging and cleaning latrine pits or killing the snakes inside the tents. But here, he seemed to reside in a strange cleft between servant and prince.

The sun had set by now, and the amir's tree-lined courtyard glowed with the flickering light of oil lamps and long-burning torches. In the center, a tasseled canopy hovered over a low table, surrounded by rugs and large pots of cut roses and irises. Emre's eyes widened. The plates and goblets on the table were of hammered gold and silver. Servants padded quietly to the table on bare feet bearing platters heaped with grilled meats, flatbreads, steaming vegetables, fiery sauces, and delicately decorated sweets. Plump silk-covered cushions glowed in jewel tones in the dim light.

At first, Emre was so overwhelmed by the lavish settings that he did not notice the amir sitting amongst it all in a scarlet robe and turban, watching him. He had never really looked closely at the amir before because they had never been alone in a setting that was not intended for Emre's military training. The man was not tall, but he was wiry and strong, with taut muscles in his neck from swinging a sword and stretching a bowstring. His skin was darker than Emre's, and his hooded black eyes sparkled like stones in a riverbed. A tidy graying mustache drooped down both sides of his mouth, and a triangle of neatly trimmed beard adorned his chin.

"It is not polite to stare, Zahed," the amir beckoned him. "Please, sit and let us talk."

Emre slowly approached and sat on a cushion.

"How was your training today? Izem tells me that you have been showing remarkable ferocity lately that will make you a promising leader in battle."

"Perhaps it is because I imagine my arrow burying itself in Izem's neck," Emre said, surprised by the fierceness in his voice.

The amir looked at him for a moment, a small smile on his lips. He picked up a flagon and poured a deep red liquid into Emre's goblet and then into his own. "Shorbot? It is pomegranate, spiced with clove and rose. Quite refreshing."

Emre picked up his goblet. The flavor rushed across his tongue, sweet and tangy and fragranced. Because he took all of his meals in the tebaq with the other boys, he had never tasted anything like it. The amir watched him closely, his black eyes twinkling with amusement.

"You are my guest tonight. Eat! After a full day of training, you must be sure to keep your strength."

Emre did not know why the amir had summoned him, and he felt the familiar contrarian stubbornness coming over him. He would not eat this man's food – would not give Badahir the satisfaction of providing for him – but the curls of steam rising from the roasted meat tortured his stomach, and his mouth watered. He had not eaten since the morning meal, and after a full day of training, his head spun with hunger. Slowly, he picked up a flatbread and tore off a piece with his teeth. Across the table, Badahir clucked disapprovingly.

"I will ensure to add table manners to your training next week. How old are you, my boy?"

"I am not your boy," Emre replied.

"You look about sixteen, maybe a bit younger." The amir's accent was no longer strange to Emre after years of hearing the Kipchak and Catay lilt to the Turkish language in Cairo.

"Had my father lived, he could have told you the exact day I was born. Perhaps you should not have killed him. Then you would know the answer." Emre felt the old anger rising in him. Usually, he kept it under control, but his hunger made him reckless.

Badahir refilled Emre's cup. "Still angry, I see. Well, good. Stay angry – but I shall help you learn the arts of subtlety and discretion."

"Perhaps tawash Izem is not such a wonderful trainer after all. How would you be any different?"

"Zahed, you alone can decide to make yourself pleasant. Tawash Izem can only beat you until you simply lie about your true feelings. I can teach you to channel them."

"My true feelings are that I would like to leave and return to my home. I would like to find my sister and be allowed to live as I wish."

Badahir frowned. "Did your sister not perish? Zahed, it is time for you to look to your future, to live your life not in your memories but with the full appreciation of what you have now—"

"You killed my parents!" Emre shouted, jumping to his feet. In the shadows of the courtyard, he detected movement. Guards. "My mother... she was *with child*, and you killed her!"

"Step back. It is fine. I am not in danger." Badahir spoke sharply to his guards, who had drawn their swords and approached silently on leather-soled slippers. He rose and circled the table, putting his hands on Emre's shoulders. He looked straight into the boy's eyes.

"I did not know those were your parents when I killed them, Zahed, but such is the way of war. Qalāwūn sent me to your tribe with a command that I was to take it, for your tribe's elder consorted with the Mongols, and we could not allow an alliance to form. Your father resisted. Your mother attacked with sticks and stones."

"You complain about sticks when you put your iron sword into her belly," Emre said bitterly. "Why did you not kill me as well? Why do you not do it now? I would rather die than stay in this place! I will join my parents and my sister."

"Zahed..." Badahir's voice was gentle. "Your tribe was starving when we found them. You all would have starved to death. The Mongols would only have enslaved you, and not as charitably as I have done."

Emre tried to push the memories down, but they forced their way into his mind. The winter had been frigid, and the threat of Mamluks and Mongols was on all sides, preventing them from finding good grazing land for their pathetically small herd in the lower plains of Cilicia. Every few days, another member of the tribe died from hunger or pestilence. The elder insisted on allying with the Mongols so that their herds could graze on Mongol land.

Badahir pulled Emre into an embrace.

"Do not touch me!" Emre said, but as he spoke, the tears left unshed for years clouded his vision, and he began to blubber into the amir's red robe. No one had put their arms around him since his childhood.

"I spared you because you attacked me with such intensity that I knew you would become the kind of warrior that inspires the poets," Badahir spoke softly. "I saw you come running across the hills from the river, snatch up a burning tentpole, and defend your parents with such skill and bravery that I knew I must have you here. Zahed, now that your basic training is complete, I have instructed Izem to train you differently than the other boys. Starting immediately, you will be trained to become my right hand."

Emre pulled back and stared at the amir, swiping the tears from his face with his sleeve. "Your right hand?"

Badahir smiled. "I have no son. Oh, I have four wives who have borne me many daughters, and stillborn sons, and sons who have not lived past their third year, but there is no one to pass on my skills, my legacy," he swept an arm around the courtyard, "and this. You are the most loyal creature I have met, and I want to have that loyalty, Zahed!"

"I am not your son," Emre whispered. "I am the son of Temur and Adja, who you killed a thousand miles from here." But the words no longer filled him with rage. They only revealed the hollowness within him. Temur and Adja were dead. His sister, Ela, was dead.

Badahir leaned forward. "Let me make it up to you. Have I not been good to you? From the moment I saw you, I singled you out as my favored one. I have invested time and money to make you into one of the most fearsome warriors this land will ever see, as bold as Baybars himself! Other boys I have watched fail without sentiment, but you, Zahed, I have pulled up again and again. I ask you to stop living in the past and think about your future. Take what I offer you!"

Again, Emre felt tears spring to his eyes, and he sniffed loudly. Was he disloyal for feeling a tiny spark of hope? For five years, he had lived in the harsh tebaq - undergoing grueling physical conditioning, hours spent praying and learning the Qur'an, Arabic lessons - and he never knew why Badahir pushed him so hard. Now he saw that all of this led to something, to another home and another family. Emre bowed his head, the tears now spattering the carpet and the cushions at the table.

"What must I do?"

"Tell me your name. Say the name that I gave you!"

"My name is Zahed."

12

— ※ —

The Citadel, Cairo. April 1283

"**B**ut my lord Qalāwūn, if we sign this peace treaty with the Franj, we will never be rid of them! It will allow them the opportunity to thrive while our back is turned. We must keep them at bay, or else they will retain their foothold on this land, even as far as regaining Jerusalem!"

Yusuf felt his voice begin to shake with the frustration he felt. He was the most junior advisor in this group of amirs, and they had been in council with the sultan for hours. Yusuf's backside ached from sitting cross-legged on the rug in front of Qalāwūn's throne, and his stomach growled, but more than that, his head ached with the effort of trying to find new ways to move the stubborn ruler from his position.

Sitting next to the sultan on a velvet cushion, Turuntay, his wazir, eyed him coldly.

"You forget yourself, Yusuf. Did Bahadir al-Mu'izzi fail to teach you manners in addition to loyalty to your sultan?"

Yusuf glanced nervously at Zahed, who stood silently near with his arms behind his back. The little brat would probably give Badahir a full report when they returned home, earning Yusuf another lengthy lecture. Badahir had purchased Yusuf four years ago to be a strategist in his army and ra'is – a commander of his spy network of qasids – yet the man rarely took Yusuf's advice. Badahir was too preoccupied with his attempts to become governor of Damascus to disagree with the sultan, even if it was not for the good of Islam. No matter what Yusuf advised, Badahir always listened to Zahed in the end, who was clearly the household favorite, despite his youth and indifference toward Islam.

"Peace, Turuntay," Qalāwūn murmured to his advisor. "Yusuf is as passionate about the Faith as you and I are passionate about preserving wealth and commerce for our people. Both are important. Let us listen to what he wishes to say."

The amirs and their emissaries sat in the magnificent throne room in the citadel, where Qalāwūn now reclined on a wide couch upholstered with thick purple velvet. A delicately carved canopy of acacia wood rose above him, covered in hammered gold and inlaid with semi-precious stones: deep red garnets, lapis lazuli, and marbled green malachite. Near the dais, carpets layered atop each other, where the amirs and courtiers sat in audience. In the steady light of the oil lamps, everything glowed with richness and beauty. Yusuf set his jaw. He wanted to be on that throne someday. Was he willing to ignore what he knew to be moral and right to get there?

He was not.

"Consider, Lord Sultan," Yusuf proceeded cautiously, "that the Franj are on the precipice of annihilation right now. Truly, the Mongol scourge on our northern borders is an existential threat, but they are docile at the moment. Remember also that the Franj have been wily in the past, and if they were to form a strong alliance with the Mongols, which my qasid spies in Acre and Limassol indicate might be possible, then our enemy would be on three sides instead of two. It would be a simple matter to eliminate the Franj from Palestine if we were to remove their stronghold in Acre, which is their spiritual seat after the loss of Jerusalem."

Qalāwūn nodded slowly but said nothing.

"My lord," Qalāwūn's son, al-Ashraf Khalil, stepped forward. "Yusuf ibn-Shihab speaks wisely. We must not ignore one enemy for another when there is a chance they could merge into a single beast. Let us cripple one limb before they become too strong for us. If we can convince the Mongols to convert and defeat the Franj, this will not just be a victory for Islam, but a demonstration of the strength and cunning of our army!"

Qalāwūn glanced at his older son and heir apparent, as-Salih Ali, who sat stoically by his father's couch.

"And what say you, Ali? Do you agree with the younger men? For although youth makes them reckless, it also seizes upon more opportunity, and risk can be beneficial. This I learned from my friend Baybars, whom I loved."

Ali did not hesitate. "No. I agree with you, Father. In this case, diplomacy and peace with the Franj is the best course of action."

"Father!" Khalil complained. "Who is the ruler here? You, or my brother?"

Qalāwūn leveled Khalil with a dangerous glare. "Do not raise your voice at me, 'Lil. Ali will be your sultan someday, and I allow him to counsel me with Turuntay. We seek a truce with the Franj at this time because they are useful to us. We do not do this to let them live in peace. We do this to benefit from the wealth they bring to us - wealth that we will need to raise a large enough army to eliminate both them and the Mongol scourge at once, God willing."

Khalil ground his teeth audibly. He hated it when his father referred to him as "Lil." Ali had no such diminutive. Sitting cross-legged on the dais next to the sultan, Ali seemed to swell in stature slightly as his father embarrassed his younger brother.

Qalāwūn sat in contemplation for a moment, then cleared his throat uncomfortably.

"I might as well tell you all now since the news will be all over the city soon, anyhow. I have decided that you, my sons, will wed the daughters of Amir Sayf in order to secure peace with the Mongol people. In the presence of these amirs, I officially make this announcement."

Ali looked sharply at Qalāwūn. "Father?"

"Why did you not consult us!? Amir Sayf... is a... a..." Khalil broke off. To his right, Amir Sayf crossed his arms and smiled self-indulgently.

"You both will wed Mongol wives and bear Mongol children. This shall engender more good feeling between the lords of the Golden Horde and our family," Qalāwūn said. "There are more ways to win battles than by the sword, my son. Sometimes it is better to win with the marriage bed. And now I am ready to sup, as are all of you, I suspect." He turned to his wazir.

"Turuntay, please have the scribes draft a peace agreement and send a message to Lord Beaujeu and tell him our intentions. He will treat with the Franj king and the Patriarch of Acre on our behalf, for he is also favorable to keeping our relations cordial and profitable." Qalāwūn rose from his seat, and the amirs in the room stood and bowed respectfully.

Zahed strode forward from his place at the back of the room, touching Yusuf on the shoulder.

"Ra'is Yusuf, will you return home with me or stay here? I should like to provide Badahir with an update as soon as possible."

Something about Zahed always unnerved Yusuf. The boy spoke woodenly, and he never smiled. Although he was intelligent, loyal, and a fearsome warrior, he was vacant in the same way that the slave girls were vacant when Yusuf took them to his bed. It galled him that this damaged child should be Badahir's favorite when Yusuf tried so hard not to make a single mistake.

He looked toward the door. Ali remained near the sultan's couch, stunned. Khalil had stormed out, and Yusuf decided not to follow his friend, who would surely be in a dark mood after being insulted and then having his betrothal announced in such a way.

"Yes, Zahed, let us present a report to Amir Badahir together. I am sure he will have many questions."

13

— ◦ —

FAJAR, THE HILLS OF IDMIT. AUGUST 1286

S idika skipped alongside Dejen as they picked their way over the summer-dry hills and back to the tiny village of Fajar. In the heat of mid-day, a few insects chirped listlessly, and the air above the rocks shimmered beneath the unveiled glare of the sun. Dejen looked sideways at her for the briefest moment, then his large brown eyes flicked back to the trail ahead of him. The little girl who frolicked like a sprite on this day could not be more different than the terrified creature that they had taken in when they lived in Damascus.

It had been a mighty effort to welcome Sidika into their family after her life of petty crime. When Tamrat finally coaxed her home for her first night, she stole all of Dejen's clothes and sold them in the market, using the money to buy herself some pistachio sweets and a jug of wine, which she drank until she teetered into a midden behind a smithy and fell asleep. Eventually, a pack of stray dogs chased her away, and she wandered the darkened alleys, wailing and wringing her hands until Tamrat found her again. After that, she fell into a pattern of disappearing for days, causing anguish for her new parents, and reappearing nonchalantly when she ran out of money or food. The independent life suited her, and Tamrat's house was a good place to resupply when she could not support herself.

But all of that changed when winter came and the snow falling in the city became her jailer. When she could not avoid spending time with her new family, she found she also could not avoid loving them. By the spring, when Tamrat declared that they would move south to the hills near Acre, Sidika knew she would follow them anywhere.

Here in Fajar, they were able to build a stable and keep a gentle-eyed donkey, a little piebald goat, and a flock of chickens for fresh milk and eggs. Tamrat and Dejen constructed a small stone enclosure next to the stable, and Sara cultivated herbs and vegetables, which Sidika helped to tend. The years passed, and she melted into her new family like honey into warm porridge. Her life on the streets of Damascus faded, as did the blurry memories of traveling with Horse Aunty and Uncle Güyük with the herds of stout Mongol horses, looking for fresh grazing land – until they were forced to flee to Damascus when she was very young. Bekir's mean-eyed face and yellow teeth were harder and harder to recall, and the memories of mistreatment and hunger rarely caused her to wake crying in the night any longer.

Even the face of the boy who hid her by the river on the day her parents died was fading from her memory.

She stopped skipping and ran back to Dejen, who carried a splendidly marked polecat in a sack. The polecat had been shot so quickly with Dejen's bow that it did not have time to evacuate its scent glands, but that did not stop the creature from emitting a powerful stench.

"Ugh, Brother, why did you shoot that fessyah? It will make the entire house stink!" She grabbed her nose and pretended to gag dramatically.

Dejen looked at her sideways. He was sixteen, still small-boned and serious-eyed, but wiry and strong. Underneath his blue keffiyeh, he preferred to keep his thick curled hair cropped close, and always he wore around his neck the silver and garnet pendant that his mother had given him.

"This little beast's fur will make a fine pair of mitts for you this winter, Sister. Do you remember how cold your hands were when the snows came last January?"

Sidika moved to walk upwind of him. "It has such darling little ears. What a shame that it stinks. I would try to tame one to live at our house."

"Not likely that Mother and Father would let you. Polecats attack chickens."

Sidika was quiet for a moment, thinking. Dejen was always very practical, which was desirable in an older brother, for he gave good advice. Whenever something troubled her mind, she and Dejen would go hunting or fetch water from the well together so they could work out life's problems.

"Dejen, do you remember your mother and father? The ones who bore you?"

"No. I was taken from them when I was a small baby."

"Would you not like to try and find them someday?"

"How could I, when I do not even know how I came to live in Cairo, nor where my people came from?"

"Surely, there must be a way. Perhaps Father could try to find out the next time he is in Cairo. Perhaps you are a Nubian prince!" The thought was so thrilling that she hopped up and down next to him, and Dejen smiled at her.

"I used to imagine I was. Do you wish to find the woman who bore you, little bird?"

"I think I came from very far away," Sidika said slowly. "And I do not think that Horse Aunty was my real aunt, but I do not know why I was with her or why she gave me away. Bekir said she sold me in exchange for a loaf of bread and a few cabbages."

"If that is the case, he got a good bargain because then he sold you to Father for fifteen bezants."

"That swine," Sidika said under her breath.

Someday she would return to Damascus, slay Bekir, and free the children of the Little Hands... if she could gather up the courage to go to the city again. Sidika's fancies were noble, but they remained in her head under a curtain of fear.

The stony road curved through a canyon and shunted them onto a gentle slope covered in yellowing grass. Below them, the little village of Fajar sheltered in the lee of a steep, rocky mountain that protected it from the strong winds that came off the sea, which was a barely visible blue smudge to the west. The wind soughed through the gray-green needles of the coniferous trees, ruffling the children's clothes and the leaves of the low, thorny brush. Sidika breathed deep and smelled hot stone, the homey scent of dried grass, and the pungent resin of a nearby carob tree.

Dejen was quiet for a moment. "If you want to find your parents, Father and Mother will help you. But you might find them less appealing than the parents that we have now."

"No!" Sidika said quickly. "I do not wish to leave. We shall stay together always."

She slipped her hand into Dejen's, and they walked slowly down the hill toward their home.

Sara shrieked as soon as Dejen brought the polecat into the house and chased him into the garden, laughing and holding her nose.

"You and your father must douse that fessyah in vinegar before I will look at it again! Go on, get out!"

Sidika took up a bundle of dried comfrey, chamomile, and a handful of rose hips and ground them under a stone that her mother had cleansed in boiling water. When they had been reduced to a fine powder, she measured them carefully into a clay jar and corked it. Then she took up rue, mugwort, and camphor leaves, grinding them fine and adding them into a copper basin with some new oil.

"Mother!" she shouted. "The midwife's infusion is ready to be cooked!"

Sara dipped a finger in Sidika's potion, tasted it, and then scooped a spoon into it, looking closely at the mixture of herbs and oil.

"Very good! Now, how will you cook it?"

"Over a low flame for as long as it takes the standing stone's shadow to move between two marks, but not boiling it, or else it causes the decoction to burn. Then I shall cover it with a cloth and let it cool completely," Sidika recited, indicating the sundial in the garden.

"And for what will we use this oil?" Sara asked, smiling. On this day at home, she had her head uncovered, and the sun caught the strands of silver in her black hair, making them glow.

"For rubbing on the legs and belly to ease the pains after labor. Also, it may be used to ease the monthly pains of sin."

"Sin?" Sara's forehead wrinkled. "I have never described it thus, my dear. Do you mean the monthly bleed?"

"Yes. Madame Karima says so."

"Ah... I see."

"Do you not agree that a woman is unclean at this time, paying for her sins?"

"My dear, men sin just as much as women, and they do not bleed. I believe that it is a means by which a woman's body purges old blood and nothing else. If men also bled, they would call it a blessing from God."

Scandalized, Sidika picked up her bowl of herbs and oil and walked out to the little clay oven behind the house. Placing her potion on a small pile of coals and marking the sundial with a pebble, she followed Sara to the garden.

"Does not Hashem also say it is the case that a woman is unclean at this time? I have seen you retreat from the family when you bleed to find your solitude, even to the mikvah in Mimas on occasions."

"Cannot a mother have solitude from time to time?" Sara replied, snapping a cucumber from the vine and placing it in a reed basket. "Can I not go to the mikvah to make myself ceremonially clean, even if I do not think that a woman's bleed is evil?"

Sidika was quiet for a moment. "Mother, are we very different?"

Sara looked up sharply. "What do you mean?"

"Well, the women in the village say that you are unchaste and that Father knows unnatural things. And why do we not live with others of our kind, with other Jews? "

Sara sighed. It did not matter where their family fled; the rumors always followed.

"Why do they say that I am unchaste, my daughter? Is it because I will visit the sick that they view as cursed, or because I am not afraid to tell a man when he is improper toward his wife? Do they say your father knows unnatural things because they cannot read as he does? The villagers have much wisdom that they learned from their elders and from the land, but also much superstition. We must balance both so that we do not succumb to fear."

"Cannot we teach them to read?"

"Your father tried, but they do not wish to learn, and why would they? Reading does not help them sow their gardens or tend to their livestock."

"It is folly to stay ignorant." Sidika tossed her hair, pleased with herself.

"Aye, and it is folly to point out the faults in others when you have not walked in their path. I suggest you keep your remarks to yourself, Daughter."

Sara was satisfied when Sidika pulled her scarf further over her head in shame.

"Mother?"

"Yes?"

"Will I also bleed?"

"Yes, Daughter, and you will also have the ability to bear children and nourish them. You will give life."

"I do not want to bear a child," Sidika remembered how Bekir's eyes lit up when a girl in the Little Hands came of age, and how those girls would usually get with child and then he would throw them out when the child was old enough to walk on its own.

Sara did not know what thoughts ran through her daughter's mind, but she saw the look on the girl's face. She pulled Sidika close.

"Do not fear it. Your father and I will not give you away until you are ready and you have found the right man."

Sara kissed Sidika on the tip of her nose and looked into the girl's green-brown eyes. *Where did you come from?* she thought again for the thousandth time. *My little jewel, why would someone let you go?*

14

Castle Besan, Northern Palestine. December 1288

"Well, how many times have you done it?" Bliant sneered. "Roderick says he does it once a week with Ermelda, who works in the kitchens, even though she is old Jacob's wife, and her face is bespoiled by the pox."

Henri's lip curled. "I would not waste my seed on a kitchen maid. Roderick just cannot find a woman of quality."

Bliant let out an incredulous laugh. "A woman of quality? There are no women at all around here, let alone quality of any kind. Maybe you have been having your way in the sheep pen, like Himmet."

Henri turned and snatched Bliant by his tail of greasy blonde hair. "Make such an insinuation about me again, and I will remember you when I inherit my father's title," he hissed.

"Ow, Henri! Lemme go!"

"Your father skived off to Britain and left you here, penniless. Take care that you do not become a kitchen slave yourself," Henri snarled, releasing Bliant's hair.

It was a damp, stormy December day, and the boys were in the bowels of the castle, straightening and tidying the piles of mail shirts and coifs in the armory. In one month, Henri would turn fifteen and receive his investiture as a squire. He was not sure who he would be squiring for yet, but it did not matter to him so long as he could make his way toward knighthood as fast as possible and leave Sir Geoffroi's care.

"What kind of foulness are you boys discussing?" a deep voice behind them rumbled, and they both jumped.

Usually, a knight could be heard coming from afar due to the various bits of metal constantly jangling from his person, but on this day, Sir Moffat had caught them off guard because he did not wear his armor and spurs. Two other knights sauntered behind him and pushed the boys out of the way, reaching for helms and swords.

"Henri 'ent been with a woman before, and he is too embarrassed to admit it!" Bliant blurted out.

Henri seethed as the three knights threw their heads back and laughed.

"Well, unless you take a lover here at the castle among the chamber pot changers, it is unlikely that you would have been with a woman, eh?" Sir Moffat giggled. "Here now, Henri. Were you not bragging only last year that you were bound for the Templar Order? This does not sound like holy talk to me."

"May I be excused, Sir Moffat? I have much to do," Henri muttered sullenly.

He was tired of this place and these people. After nine years of torment from Sir Geoffroi and the other boys, Henri had become aloof, choosing to read or hunt rather than engage with his peers. At first, he read in the great hall, but that only earned him additional taunts, so he would hide a book in his scrip and read with his back against the crumbling wall of an ancient olive press in the ruins of Scythopolis, behind the castle. His father had sent him a poorly bound Arabic copy of Plato's *Republic* that Henri was trying to work his way through, and it demanded his attention. The sooner he finished his work in the castle, the sooner he could return to it.

"I suppose you may leave," Sir Moffat drawled, his face lit with amusement. "Are you sure the Templars would take a Saracen into their midst, Henri? Even though you have eyes like a Franj, you look like you ought to be driving a camel."

Henri was so used to the taunts that he did not even feel his temper rise. He sighed and pushed past the knights, who laughed behind him as he made his way down the damp-walled passage toward the sleeping hall. The echo of his footsteps bounced along the stones, and his mind felt troubled.

The possibility that the Templars would not allow a Saracen into their ranks had occurred to him. Being a Templar came with prestige and honor, and above all, absolution of all sins. He wanted to talk to his father about moving from Sir Geoffroi's to the great Templar citadel that hung off Acre's southern edge and enlisting as a squire, but knowing Rogier's attitude toward Templars, he was afraid to ask.

"Henri, wait!" Sir Moffat trotted up to him, smiling. "My apologies for making light of your... situation." He waved vaguely at Henri's face. "Truth is, I do not care who your mother is. You have the most promising sword skills of any of these boys, and I want you near me. I have asked Sir Geoffroi for you to be assigned to me as a squire next month."

Henri's mouth dropped open. "You have?"

"Yes," Sir Moffat laughed. "Sir Geoffroi said he may not allow it because, between the two of us, we will steal all of the merchants' wives in Acre."

Henri looked at him blankly, and Sir Moffat winked, then squeezed his shoulder. "It is a compliment, Henri. I would not go taking any vows of chastity just yet if I were you."

Sir Moffat turned and strode down the hall, whistling cheerfully, and Henri stared after him, trying to understand the man's meaning.

***

The month passed swiftly. Sir Geoffroi kept Henri busy fulfilling the remainder of his duties as a page until he passed his fifteenth year in early January. Rogier rode to the castle underneath a waxed leather cloak to watch his son take vows as a squire on a cold and wet day. As his father shook the rain from his hair, Henri regarded him, his lip curled sullenly.

"Well met, Father. I am surprised to see you on this day."

Over the years, as Rogier refused Henri's repeated pleas to come home, the warmth between father and son had disappeared.

Rogier forced a smile. "Sir Geoffroi told me that you are to be bound to young Sir Moffat. You know," he lowered his voice, "I could have you come home to squire for Sir Itier instead."

Henri looked at his father with hard eyes. "So, you want me now?"

"I always wanted you to be home with me, my son, but it was not safe for you at al-Hadiqa, and—"

"And I was much safer here, yes, you have told me, Father. My fellow trainees protected me by locking me out of the sleeping hall on rainy nights,l attacking me every time I walked around a corner, or when they skinned my cat and threw her hide into my bed while I slept. I think you are right: If keeping me here was wisdom, then I was much safer at Castle Besan... away from you."

"Right now, you are. I should whip you against the stable wall for that kind of talk!" Rogier snapped.

He left that evening before the feast.

When the revelry and celebration finished, the new squires moved their belongings into the knights' quarters, where they would sleep from that evening on until they were knighted themselves. After Henri had dragged his trunk and straw mattress into the large chamber that Sir Moffat shared with three other knights, he began to undress for bed. Sir Moffat laughed and clapped Henri on the back.

"Come, now! The night is still young. Let us go into Acre, for there is something that we must do."

"What must we do, Sir Moffat?" Henri asked. He felt jittery and excited. Sir Moffat treated him like an equal, not a child, and certainly not like a Saracen. Because the knight had requested him especially, Henri felt tenuous confidence. Perhaps he was worthy.

Sir Moffat winked at him. "Go saddle my horse and prepare my clean livery. We must look our best this evening."

Henri pulled Sir Moffat's red velvet surcoat from a cupboard and smoothed it on the man's bed, setting a pair of black wool hose next to it along with a pair of red-dyed buckskin shoes that had gold thread embroidered on the toes. Then, he hurried outside and saddled Sir Moffat's destrier and his own smaller horse – a silky black Arabian mare named Raven, a gift from his father.

The sun was beginning to set when they thundered out of the castle gates and onto the main road toward the city. The long torches were lit and flickering against the walls of Acre by the time they arrived and made their way through the Saint Nicholas gate. Having spent the bulk of his nine years with Sir Geoffroi cloistered inside the castle, Henri watched the rowdy evening crowds and the night kitchens with wide eyes. Slowly, they wound their way through the narrow streets until they arrived near the harbor, which was still seething with activity, despite the growing darkness.

Sir Moffat reined his horse in front of a loud tavern and swung down while Henri nervously looked around at the dark streets.

"Come, young man. I have a gift for you."

Henri jumped down and tied the horses to a post near the tavern, tossing a few copper coins at the guard outside the door to keep the animals safe. Then he pushed aside the greasy camel hide that hung over the door and walked inside.

The room was dim, but the sound inside was a roar of singing, laughing, and people trying to talk over each other. Men drank wine from rough clay cups and tossed dice at rickety tables, while an old man wiped plates with a cloth and an unsmiling woman loaded stale-looking bread onto a platter behind a low counter. The woman wore her loose kirtle without a chemise underneath, and Henri could see the curve of her thigh and the side of her smooth white buttock as she walked across the room. He stood frozen in the doorway, then slowly began to back away before anyone noticed him.

"Henri!" Someone shouted his name.

Sir Moffat beckoned him through a door at the back of the room, and Henri hurried to his new master, keeping his eyes downcast. Sitting at a table nearby was a woman who wore a pair of men's hose and no covering over her breasts.

"Sir Moffat, what are we doing in this place? Surely you cannot have business here?" Henri tried to keep his voice steady, but it was beginning to change, and sometimes it cracked embarrassingly, which it did now.

"Well, I will not have the likes of Bliant claiming that my squire is unworldly," Sir Moffat said, looking over Henri's shoulder and smiling slyly. "I have secured a companion for you this night. The next time that pimpled dullard insinuates that you are inexperienced with women, you will know what to tell him."

Henri's heart dropped. "What?" he stammered and felt a hand on his shoulder. He turned.

A woman with a hard face and a partially unlaced dress looked at Sir Moffat with narrowed eyes.

"Marta, tonight I would like you to usher my new squire into manhood," Sir Moffat said.

"A bit young, isn't he?" Marta said, lifting Henri's chin and examining him. "And he is a Saracen – that will cost extra."

"I was younger. Come, Marta, have you ever seen a prettier Saracen boy? Surely it will not be a chore to deflower him."

Marta shrugged indifferently and took Henri's hand.

"W... wait, Sir Moffat, I would rather not," Henri stuttered, "I do not think Sir Geoffroi and my father would approve...."

His head spun and his pulse thundered. He wanted to get on his horse and ride home – all the way home to al-Hadiqa. He wanted to crawl into a lemon tree and hide from Sir Moffat and this woman.

Marta was pulling him down the darkened hall toward a series of doors.

"You will be fine, Henri!" Sir Moffat laughed and took a pull at a large cup of wine. "Do not shame me by acting a coward, or I shall rightfully ask Sir Geoffroi for a different squire!"

Marta opened the door to a dark, foul-smelling bedchamber, pushed Henri through, and slammed it behind her.

15

━ ❋ ━

Tripoli, April 1289

"Forward! Come on, men! The day is nearly won! Finish them!"

Somehow, despite the screams of dying men and horses, Emre heard Yusuf's shouts clearly above the din. As *ra'is*, Yusuf had command over Badahir's troops in battle. It was to his face that the blue-clad warriors of Badahir looked, and to his voice that they turned their heads. He was mounted, holding his jeweled sword aloft over his head, face flushed and eyes sparkling with war lust, his turban-wrapped helmet still firmly in place. He looked like the perfect warrior of God: towering and awe-inspiring.

Checking to make sure there were no Franj lances aimed at him, Emre glanced at the hill where his regiment's flagmen stood. The sapphire-blue flags were swirling, thrusting toward the city walls, and the massive kettledrums of the Mamluk drumlords beat a relentless rhythm of attack. *Dum da dum da DUM! Dum da dum da DUM!* The charge was still on.

Emre turned back to face the walls of Tripoli and saw a Franj soldier sighting at him with a crossbow. He jerked his round shield up just in time as the bolt thunked through the copper-plated wood, scratching his hand underneath. Lifting his curved bow, he nocked an arrow and pulled back with his shield still in his hand. The arrow hit the Franj in the forehead, just below the edge of his leather helmet. He watched the man's body tumble from the walls, but the defenses at Tripoli were so thin that no other soldier came to fill the gap. Emre nocked another arrow and sighted a nearby Franj, pulling the string back until his muscles screamed. Just as he loosed the arrow, he heard the thunder of the drums change to a new beat.

Dum ta ta DUM DUM! Dum ta ta DUM DUM! Dum ta ta DUM DUM!

He had only heard this rhythm in the meydan during practice, but every Mamluk fighter recognized it immediately.

The walls had been breached. It was time to enter the city.

Emre saw the Franj knights scrambling like ants near a flooded nest, rushing around a cloud of dust where the wall had collapsed. Some fired their arrows down on the Mamluks forcing their way through the breach. Others scrambled over each other to flee the wall and hide.

"Zahed!" Yusuf yelled. "Up!"

The ra'is and his sturdy Arabian charger were bearing down on him, and Emre grasped the back of the high-walled saddle, swinging himself up behind Yusuf, who guided the horse toward the scrum of men and rubble. The flaming thatched roofs and timbers of the stables and workshops along the inside of the walls were belching puffs of oily black smoke which blew in the hot wind, and it was not possible to see clearly or get through the crush of bodies.

"Another breach has opened at the northern end of the city!" Yusuf bellowed over his shoulder. "We shall enter there. Do you remember what to do? What is about to happen will be gruesome but necessary. We do this to secure the land for Allah and push the Franj back to where they came! We do this to bring wealth and power to our master."

"Yes, I remember," Emre shouted back, his heart pounding as they trotted up a steep hillside and toward a less crowded opening.

"You and I will first make for the largest church in the city. That is where we will find precious metals. My qasids have also told me how to find the house of the ruler, and we shall bring back what we can for Badahir."

Emre swallowed and nodded. Ahead of him, the screams of men grew louder, and he saw a wall of mail-clad Franj turcopoles on foot, pushing back against the turbaned infantry of the sultan's army. The highly trained Mamluk 'askari waited behind them, allowing the unmounted soldiers to take the brunt of the enemy force.

"Cowards!" Yusuf screamed. "Who ordered you to wait behind lesser men?"

The 'askari looked up at Yusuf on his horse, his dark brown eyes ferocious, his blood-stained cuirass glittering. He raised his lance and urged his horse forward, stabbing down at the Franj soldiers from on high. Behind him, the 'askari raised a cry, and some of them pushed their horses forward, crushing the Franj and their own foot soldiers in their eagerness to get into the city.

"In the name of God, the great, the victorious!" Yusuf yelled, raising his lance again.

Still behind him on the horse, Emre looked back toward his regiment's flagmen on the bluff. Badahir stood on the hill next to the blue flags, which waved wildly back and forth, and next to him stood Qalāwūn, the sultan, dressed in an elegant black and silver samite tunic underneath his silver armor. Somewhere in the confusion, the sultan's son, Khalil, also fought to take the city, but Emre could sense no concern on the old sultan's face.

Suddenly Yusuf and Emre lurched and landed painfully in the dusty street. A dying Franj had managed to thrust his lance into the barrel of Yusuf's horse, and the beast screamed, stumbled, and fell. Emre was on his feet instantly, shoving the point of his lance into the injured enemy's neck. Behind him, he heard Yusuf yelling profanities one minute and praises to Allah the next.

Yusuf was nearly thirty years old and had been in many battles before, but this was the largest battle Emre had seen.

Fighting outside the walls had been exhilarating. The Franj against which he played target practice were so small and far away that it was as if he hunted sparrows or hares in the desert. But now, up close, men died all around him loudly, and although he did not understand their language, he knew that they screamed for their mothers and lovers as the life left them. The air fouled as men were disemboweled, and the dusty streets became slippery with blood.

A boy of about thirteen charged at Emre, holding a wooden club above his head.

"Zahed, grab him!" he heard Yusuf shout.

The boy wore a fine linen cotehardie and hose. He looked rich and terrified, but he ran and prepared to swing his club at Emre's face. Emre ducked out of the way and held out a hand.

"Stop it, in the name of God!" he yelled in Turkish. "You will be spared!"

The boy charged again then jerked as the tip of Yusuf's lance emerged, protruding through his stomach.

"Zahed! What are you doing? Get your head back where it belongs!"

"But that was just a boy," Emre sputtered as Yusuf wrenched his lance back.

"Aye, and so are you. You know the job. Capture the women and children, kill the men. Now get going!"

Emre heard a scream to his left as three Mamluk soldiers dragged a woman out of a house and began to tear at her clothes.

"Hey!" Yusuf bellowed, stomping toward them. "What are you doing? The women are not for you lot! Tie her up and move her to the wagons, then get on with your duty!"

Nearby, a house burst into flames, and three women, each clutching a small child, ran out, their dresses on fire. The soldiers caught them easily, wrenching the children from their arms.

"Here!" one of the 'askari barked at Emre, handing him two little girls. "Take them back to the wagons and then return here."

Tears and soot streaked the faces of the girls. One of them had no shoes. Emre tried to lead them by their hands, but both girls kicked and bit, so he tucked one under each arm and carried them like sheaves of wheat to a wagon waiting outside the walls. It looked identical to the wagon that had carried him away from his burning village in Cilicia ten years before.

Emre stumbled back into the city, fending off the remaining Franj soldiers near the wall. A few of them yelled curses at him, but he hardly noticed. He turned down an empty alley, his heart throbbing in his chest.

This was just like what had happened in his village, only larger. There was more death, more orphaned children. He felt the bile lurch up in his throat and vomited loudly against a house. The door to the house flew open, and a Franj rushed out, holding a wooden chair aloft. The man was old and plump, a stall merchant or a laborer of some sort. Emre jumped back as the chair swung and then crashed against his shoulders.

"No, stop! I will not hurt you!" Emre yelled, but the old man swung his chair again, knocking the round shield from Emre's arm.

"Please stop!" Emre begged.

The old man picked the chair up and threw it, hitting Emre in the stomach. Reflexively, Emre wrenched his sword from its sheath and sank it into the man's belly with a sob. Inside the house, he heard screams. Two other 'askari had come running down the alley, and they charged into the house, dragging a woman and small child outside.

"Good work," one of the 'askari said. "You are Badahir's heir, are you not? We shall tell him of your deeds."

Emre nodded and continued down the alley. Two young men ran out of their houses, yelling and swinging swords, but they weren't trained soldiers, and their heavy weapons slashed at empty air. After ten years of daily training, Emre was one of the most elite fighters in the world, excepting the Templars and the Hospitallers. He quickly slew the men and kept walking. A woman in a window fired an arrow at him, which bounced uselessly off his armor. He whipped his bow up and fired back, and she collapsed. He had become what he hated. Now he was the one inflicting death and misery upon children and citizens who had done nothing to deserve it. He wanted to kill the soldiers, the vile white-clad warrior monks, not the innocent.

This was his largest battle, but not his first. Only a month ago, he and some of Badahir's 'askari had raided a Mongol camp near Rutba, slaughtering every man and carrying the women off. Badahir had offered one of the women as a gift to Emre, but the sight of her, hair flying, spitting with rage, revolted him. He demurred and accepted two shaggy, sturdy Mongol ponies instead.

This is to be my life with Badahir; an endless circle of slaughter and kidnapping until I am slaughtered by someone else.

Emre leaned a hand against the side of a house and vomited again. He had never asked for this life. He had never wanted it. Despite his best efforts to escape notice, Badahir continued to heap praise and responsibility on him that he did not deserve or desire. He wiped his mouth wearily and then looked back at the two men he had killed. One he had struck in the head, and there was very little blood on the man's hempen tunic and hose. Emre glanced left and right, then dashed down the street and dragged the body into an alcove. He was done with this. Badahir could choose another heir.

***

Yusuf bowed wearily and swept his arm behind him to a cart piled high with gold and silver crosses, chalices of silver and semi-precious stones, bolts of silk, and swords with jeweled pommels. Nearby sat a group of women and young children, their yellow and brown hair dull from dust and smoke, their faces tear-streaked.

"My lord, your men have secured these spoils for you. They fought admirably today."

Badahir's face beamed. "As did you, Yusuf! From what I saw on the hill, you may soon become an amir of forty. Your daring and cool head in that battle was something I did not know you capable of. Surely, I was blessed on the day when I purchased you from al-Shihab."

Yusuf glowed with pleasure. Badahir was a demanding master to please. If he continued to distinguish himself, Badahir might free him, thus allowing Yusuf to expand his household, even take a second wife or a third. And most importantly, he could focus on his work as an administrator and eventually be released from fighting other men's battles. He would purchase a house that faced the great tombs so he could gaze upon them each morning. He would donate a waqf and start a madrasa of his own near the banks of the Nile.

"Where is Zahed?" Badahir was looking expectantly over the heads of his other men.

"Last time I saw him, Zahed was in the city, facing off against an old man defending himself with a broken chair," Yusuf said lightly. It was best not to insult Zahed in front of Badahir, but he could not help a slight jab at the boy. In battle, Zahed had looked as frightened as a treed kitten.

Now Badahir's brow knit with concern. "Did no one see him after the battle? He would have returned to me as soon as the fighting had finished."

Without meaning to, Yusuf glanced at the rows of broken Mamluk bodies lined up in the sun awaiting burial. Badahir gripped Yusuf's shoulders hard and looked straight into his eyes.

"Ra'is Yusuf, you must find Zahed for me. You must bring him back, whether he is injured or—"

Yusuf could see the fear in the older man's eyes. "I will do this, Amir. I will bring him back to you."

Hours later, Yusuf trudged wearily into his master's tent. Badahir and several other amirs sat around a brazier, warming themselves and talking of their next moves. Yusuf bowed low to the ground, buying himself a few more minutes to organize his scattered thoughts and decide what to tell the distraught old man.

"Excuse me, Amir. My men and I have searched the city. We were unable to find Zahed, dead or alive. However, they did find this." He held up a shining metal cap and a long indigo cloth.

Badahir snatched the cap and fingered the engraved words along the inside of the band.

Zahed, the beloved son of Badahir.

— · —

Part 2

March – November 1290

"Yesterday I was clever, so I wanted to change the world. Today I am wise, so I am changing myself."
~ *Jalāl ad-Dīn Mohammad Rūmī*

16

ACRE. MARCH 1290

The excited cries of the sailors startled Philip out of his reverie, and he glanced up from where he sat in the ship's stern.

"God be praised, we made it," he heard Brother Alaran mutter, hoisting himself to his feet and staggering slightly as his long white robes snagged under his boots. They had stopped at Cyprus after the journey from Marseilles, but the two-day crossing from the island to the Bay of Acre had been stormy and rough, and many of the Brethren prepared their souls for death within sight of Acre's white beaches.

Philip scowled at the outline of the city rising from the bay and forced his memories down. No one in the Order knew that he had ever been to Acre, and dwelling on the past always made it difficult to remember who he was now – a Templar and a respected knight. No residents of the city would remember his past as a mercenary, living hand to mouth. No residents save one.

Passing the Tower of Flies, a stinking fortress that jutted stubbornly out of the harbor's entrance, they sailed smoothly over the barnacle-crusted iron chain that protected the port from invading ships. During these days of peace, the chain always remained lowered.

On the shore, a crowd of men agitated. The Templar ship was a handsome vessel, with a blood-red cross emblazoned on her mainsail, which meant more knights to protect the city and news from all the ports between Marseilles and Acre. As soon as the ship's lines were secured, the excited citizens at the dock were shouting for news of Francia or hawking sweet cakes and fruit at the weary travelers.

Philip picked up his small sack of belongings, which contained a spare robe and undergarments, a wooden case containing his tooth-washing salts, beard comb, silver shears, and an ornately wrought jeweled dagger which was bound in wool and string. Tucking these under his arm, he disembarked and made his way through the gates at the busy harbor, continuing to the nearby citadel of the Templars.

Having distinguished himself to his superiors in his local preceptory, Philip had traveled from his post at Avalleur to Mas Deu in Francia, where he lived for a year before obtaining a post in Acre, the seat of the Templar Order. Although this post was his ultimate goal, he took little pleasure in his achievement as he regarded the steep, sloped walls of the fortress where the golden lions sat, each with a paw raised in greeting. The walls, nearly thirty feet thick in some places, oppressed him, even though he now belonged inside as a brother of the Order.

The last time he had looked upon these walls, he had been an outsider—a bastard. According to the Order's exclusive rules, he had no more right to enter the gates than the street urchins who begged for alms outside, and that thought gave him strength. To hell with their exclusionary rules and self-serving piety. Without hesitation, he strode through the arched gates. After he completed his work at al-Hadiqa, he would come back and get his revenge on these elitist narcissists—every last one of them.

After a light meal, a brief tour of his new quarters, and a lengthy session in the chapel with the rest of the Order at the hour of nones, Philip's first task upon arriving was to find a hiding place for his dagger. A floorboard underneath his cot appeared to have been used for a similar purpose by a previous brother, and Philip twisted it up easily, hiding the dagger and a bulging sack of coins. Then he donned his clean robe, combed his graying beard, and set out to meet his new commander. The air sweltered, and his wool robes prickled uncomfortably.

In the meeting hall, his commander, Brother Rother, greeted him.

"The head of your preceptory recommended you highly to me, although I could never bring you to Acre while he lived. I must admit, I thought that Lord Fons Bleaudi's son was a bit younger than you." Brother Rother looked at Philip solemnly. "You must resemble your mother, for I certainly see very little of your father in you."

Philip smiled through his irritation. "As you know, my mother died when I was young, and I lived away from the estate with the Brethren in Baudelu since thirteen. After my older brother Georges died, it was God's greatest blessing that I reunited with my father. It was such a blow to me to have him die only a fortnight after I returned home to Fons Bleaudi."

He maintained a sorrowful countenance with little trouble. Philip had been repeating the lie for so many years that it flowed easily off his lips until, most of the time, he believed it himself.

"Well, I am glad to have you, Brother Philip. Your skills and leadership are highly regarded by those who have fought with you. It is indeed an honor to live here at our headquarters, where the most important of the Order's work happens, although you may find that some things are not as lax here as they are in the smaller preceptories."

Philip raised an eyebrow, and Brother Rother smiled. "First, we shall take you to the barber and have that tail removed from your head. While you are here, you are to keep your hair short and tonsured. Second, let us seek out the draper for a new robe or two before you expire of heat in those woolens."

They were walking toward the stables, and commander Rother reached into a stall, grasping the bridle of a sturdy white destrier.

"This and these two other horses are yours, and a squire shall be found for you, although we are running a bit short of them at the moment. If you have a squire in mind already, please name him, and I can see if we can arrange to have him assigned to you."

"Does the son of Lord Rogier of Maron reside in the castle? I hear he is a promising fighter and would like to test his skill as a squire for me."

The commander's forehead wrinkled. "Young Henri? He does not reside here, although we would like to have him join the Order, for there is no surplus of noble-born sons in Out-remer to induct into the Brethren. No, he trains elsewhere, despite how hard we begged Lord Rogier to have the boy given into our care."

"I see," Philip mused. "Well, then... no matter. If the boy does not wish to bring honor to his family by joining the Order, I am sure I can find a more worthy squire elsewhere."

"Henri is Lord Rogier's only surviving son," the commander said. "I believe Lord Rogier is more interested in heirs to inherit his fortune than having a distinguished son. But I wonder how you came to hear of the boy?"

"Lord Rogier's father and mine were close friends. It was through Lord Rogier's letters that I know of Henri."

"Well, Lord Rogier's firstborn would be of age to take vows very soon had he lived, but the child was killed many years ago by brigands. The devils took Henri too, but Lord Rogier caught them and killed the scoundrels before they could do damage to both his sons."

Philip affected a look of concerned interest.

"And did Lord Rogier's wife bear any more sons?"

"Indeed, no. They have only Henri and his two younger sisters. It is God's punishment to Rogier for marrying a Sara-cen. I hear that Henri is a bold fighter but so rash that he is not expected to survive his first battle, which is why Lord Rogier should send him here. A little of the grand master's discipline would temper his arrogance. Ah, well, enough of this gossip. Your first assignment is to go out into the city and familiarize yourself with it. We often do battle in these very streets when the merchants' guilds are squalling amongst themselves, and that could very well be your first fight. Walk about and report to me what you see. I will assign you to something more worthy of your talents in a few days. Be back in time for vespers."

Philip bowed as his commander retreated, then called for a groom to saddle his horse. Soon, he was riding into the warren of reeking, twisting streets in Acre. It had been nearly ten years since he last prowled the ancient city, smelled the spices in the souks, and heard the chatter of a dozen different languages from people of a hundred more skin tones and costumes.

Most of the memories were bitter.

Deep in one of the souks, he found an old woman at a tailor's stall and commissioned a new set of clothes: brown hose, a dark blue tunic, and a floor-length, roughspun cloak with a hood. Then he traveled to each of the city's towers, eventually climbing to the pinnacle of the Round Tower on the northwestern tip of Montmusard. There he stood, gazing to the west.

The brilliant reflection of the sea troubled his pale green eyes, but still, he stared at the empty, deep blue horizon. Some day, he would leave this parched wasteland and return to Francia, not as Brother Philip of Fons Bleaudi but as Lord Philip of Maron, Viscount of Acre and Marquis of Maron-en-Rouergue.

17

— • —

THE CITADEL, CAIRO. APRIL 1290

Yusuf watched as the spy bowed low in front of the sultan. Despite the late hour of the evening, the amirs had assembled in Qalāwūn's throne room in the citadel, this time at Yusuf's request. He took a moment to reflect on how his position in life had changed, and he quietly thanked Allah for His gracious generosity. In the year since Badahir named Yusuf his heir in Zahed's place, he had created an extensive network of surreptitiously placed *qasids* who reported on Franj movements in the remaining enemy-held cities throughout Palestine and Syria. Some of them even hid among the merchant guilds and nobility. Christians could easily be convinced to report on the movements of their comrades... for a price.

He looked down again at the prone man on the thick rug at his feet. Shams, one of his best qasids, was embedded in Acre. Shams was sleeping with the wife of a prominent Venetian merchant, which was how he gathered vital trade information, as well as gossip about the interminable tensions between the Venetian and the Genoese quarters in the city. The man's blue keffiyeh puddled on the carpeted floor as he crouched, and the sultan stood from his couch in surprise.

"What? What was that you said?" Qalāwūn demanded.

Shams remained in his prone position. "It is as I said, honored sultan. Two thousand Sicilian soldiers have landed in the city of Acre with intent to launch another assault against Islam and against your graciousness."

Qalāwūn stepped from underneath his covered dais and paced across the top of the marble steps. Although it had only been two years since his son Ali had died, the old sultan looked as if he had aged ten. The servants whispered that Qalāwūn cried himself to sleep at night and visited the grave of his child every week on Jumea. They also hinted that Qalāwūn suspected Khalil of poisoning his older brother to secure the throne for himself. Yusuf had known Khalil since he was a young man of eighteen. Khalil was a fearsome warrior, hardened and unrelenting. He was a man of unshakable faith and principle, and he had done terrible things in the name of conquest for his father, but a murderer of his own brother? Yusuf had his doubts.

"Where is Turuntay? I would have him here with me."

Next to Yusuf, Khalil snorted and crossed his arms.

"Is there a problem, Khalil?" Qalāwūn asked, the annoyance clear in his voice.

"No, my lord," Khalil bowed.

"Good. Although it appears probable that the Franj broke their peace treaty with me, I would first like Turuntay to consult the original contract."

"My lord," Yusuf ventured carefully, glancing at Khalil, "I remember the terms of that contract well. It clearly stated that peace would exist between Cairo and the Franj in Acre, Tyre, and the surrounding settlements so long as the Franj did not send for significant reinforcements to their troops, which would indicate an intent to instigate battle—"

"Did I ask for your opinion, Yusuf ibn-Shihab?" Qalāwūn snapped. This sultan was more even-tempered and mild-mannered than Baybars, but the man was in his sixties and spared little patience for younger amirs.

Khalil, taking his cue, stepped forward. "My lord and esteemed father," he began. Heads turned. It was unusual for Khalil to evoke his patronage in the presence of the other amirs.

"I believe that the Franj prepare for war against us. I not only have the word of this qasid here but of other spies that Yusuf placed in Acre and Tyre. My lord Father, this is what we have waited for! Peace with the Franj has been profitable, but they war against themselves so often that they are disorganized and divided in their goals. The one thing that could unite them is if the Mongols present another opportunity for an alliance, which would surely cut us off from all the north, Damascus, and our other great cities. Yusuf ibn-Shihab speaks wisdom. He is honored for his cunning and knowledge. Do not dismiss him. Do not dismiss me, your son!"

Qalāwūn's thin face quivered with emotion. He stood still on the marble step, his shaking hand hovering close to his scabbard as if he wanted to pull his sword and run it through his rebellious son in front of his entire council. Instead, he willed his hand away and sighed deeply. Turning, he trudged back up the steps and sat heavily on his royal couch, muttering something. Khalil shot an anxious look at Yusuf, then approached him, unasked.

"My lord, what is wrong?"

Qalāwūn looked into the amber eyes of his son. "I wish your brother Ali were here at my side," he sighed.

Khalil's face grew hard, and he retreated down the steps and out of the gilded double doors of the throne room while the other amirs waited in uncomfortable silence.

"Yusuf ibn-Shihab," Qalāwūn commanded in a deep voice.

"Yes, my lord," Yusuf bowed low.

Qalāwūn waved an impatient hand, and the other amirs slowly filed from the room. He waited until the door slammed behind the last of them.

"Badahir named you his heir. He was my friend, and I trusted his wisdom. I never felt at ease about Zahed al-Habib ibn-Badahir. That boy had the look of a traitor about him, although Badahir loved him as his own son. Badahir saw wisdom in you, and so do I. Tell me, does my son Khalil wish for war so that I will die in battle and he may take my place?"

Yusuf's mouth dropped open in surprise. "No, my Lord Sultan! Your son Khalil is a warrior for Allah, *subhanahu wa ta'ala*. He intends only to rid your lands of the infidel scourge. His faith and loyalty to Islam are strong, as are his love and regard for you!"

Qalāwūn saw the passion in Yusuf's eyes and nodded slowly. He didn't feel as passionate as Yusuf and Khalil, but he was born on the steppes of the Cuman, where his had been a religion of the earth. Professing love to Allah was a means to an end, but here was his son and this young amir who believed with their whole hearts. Qalāwūn envied their conviction.

The only god Baybars had worshipped was conquest, and the only one Qalāwūn bowed to was amity, for he had seen too much violence in his sixty-eight years. Perhaps Khalil was the perfect man to take up the throne after all. Perhaps he could take the empire that Baybars had united and usher it into a new era of righteousness and prosperity. Maybe peaceful relations with the Franj were not ideal, but Qalāwūn was tired of fighting, of the sounds and smells of war, and of arguing with amirs. Let the next generation take it.

"Very well," he said wearily. "Tell me everything. I want to understand completely how they have broken this treaty and what we must do to ensure they are taught a lesson they will not forget."

18

___ · ___

ACRE HARBOR. AUGUST 1290

D ogan hauled up his net, hand over hand, from the side of his small boat one last time and gave Ahmed the command to row them back to Acre harbor as the sun drifted closer toward the liquid orange horizon in the west.

It had been a poor day's catch, and Dogan had lingered on the waves for too long, hoping that more time would equal more fish. He frowned at the half-full baskets in the stern of the boat. It was a disappointing yield, and the shoppers in the souks would be mostly finished for the day. There was still a chance he could sell his catch to the inns and night kitchens, but they always expected a discount. Dogan cursed his luck, then prayed to Allah for forgiveness. At the oars, Ahmed rowed pensively. The boy always had his head in the clouds.

Because of the peace treaty with Qalāwūn, the harbor at Acre was crowded these days. A maze of large-hulled galleys and shallow-draught cogs all vied for space at the narrow quays to unload their hulls full of riches. Ahmed expertly navigated their little skiff through the puzzle of creaking, sloshing ships until they bumped up against the stones of the harbor a short distance from the docks, and Dogan leapt from the boat to tie her up, whistling tunelessly. The sun had almost set, and crowds of pilgrims and soldiers, newly arrived from the West, milled about in an agitated throng on the shore, unloading their cargo and shouting to each other in their local dialects.

Dogan had been born near this harbor, as had his father and his grandfather, who remembered when the great Salah ad-Din ruled Acre. Dogan preferred to spend his time bobbing on the waves near the long, straight coast rather than keep his feet grounded in the city, for the occupiers from the West could be unpredictable. He paid his taxes so he could freely work and worship as an Arab and a Muslim in his homeland, and he kept his head down. Someday, when he died, his son Ahmed would bury his bones in the hills outside of town, take his boat, marry a virtuous woman, and carry on his legacy, *inshallah*.

On shore, Dogan stretched his legs, pulled a long robe over his head, belted it, and adjusted the sun-faded keffiyeh on his temples. Nearby, Ahmed sorted the fish, tossing what they didn't want back into the sea and keeping everything else in a reed basket.

Dogan looked at his son. Ahmed wasn't built for physical labor. He was fine-boned, starry-eyed, and moved with slow grace. *He should be studying the Qur'an to become a khatib or a healer*, Dogan thought. *Would that I had the money and prestige to educate him.* He smiled at the boy, then turned to check that the boat's lines were secure.

"Father?"

He heard the alarm in Ahmed's voice and looked up. Five Franj had left the crowd near the docks and approached. In the dim glow of the sun's final moments, Dogan could see that they were tall and armed with swords.

"All will be well, my son. Perhaps they need directions to their church."

But something in the manner of their approach made him nervous. They walked with purpose, and one of the men carried a clublike torch. In the wavering light, their eyes and swords glittered.

"Well met," Dogan said in halting French. "Do you require anything, sirs?"

The men continued to advance.

"Ahmed," he said sharply, "perhaps they only speak Latin. Can you ask them what they want?" Ahmed's Latin was rudimentary, but Dogan spoke and understood none of it.

His son asked them a question, and the men stopped, their faces semi-obscured by darkness. Then the man closest to Ahmed drew his sword and, before Dogan could react, plunged it into his son's belly. The boy let out a high-pitched scream and crumpled into the basket of fish.

"Stop!" Dogan cried. "In God's name, what are you doing?! You have killed my son!"

Two more men raised their swords and slashed at Dogan, and he jumped back, glancing wildly down at Ahmed. His son lay facedown on the ground, motionless. In the darkness, Dogan couldn't see if he was breathing or not, but when one of the attackers thrust his sword into the boy's exposed back, he knew his son was gone.

Dogan turned and ran, and five pairs of feet slapped the stones behind him.

19

—·—

ACRE. AUGUST 1290

P hilip leaned back in his flimsy wooden chair, toying idly with his small clay cup of wine on the table. The Inn of the Three Palms was not too humble, not too proud, and the wine they served was most adequate; bright and refreshing, free of flies, and barely any taste of vinegar at all. On this day, he wore his dull-colored disguise as a day-laborer: woolen hose, a tunic, and a worn leather arming cap that clung to his skull, its strings dangling carelessly near his shoulders. Thus disguised, he could relax and take his ease without fear of discovery from any of his Brethren, who would never take the time to look twice at someone who was not a noble or a knight.

A figure darkened the doorway of the inn, and Philip looked up. The man strolled casually to the table and sat down, hailing the innkeeper for a mug of ale.

"Were you followed?" Philip asked.

"Why would someone follow me?"

"You are a naturally untrustworthy-looking man, Marcouf. If I saw you slinking around the city, I would follow you out of principle."

Marcouf smiled, his broken teeth glinting in the thin light coming through the door. "I was not followed, and I have what you need."

Philip leaned over the table, and Marcouf drew a small clay bottle from his tunic, sliding it across the table with dramatic self-importance. "They will host the feast in three days' time. The house will be full of guests. Therefore, it will be easy to allow the confusion to incriminate someone else. I have been retained to transport bags of grain to the house from my village. I am known to Lord Rogier, so my presence will not be a great surprise. He requires grain from the stores of my village to supplement his party for the feast of the Transfiguration."

"And the family?"

"Only Lady Nasira and the girls. I do not expect young Henri to be present, as he spends most of his time hunting or warming the beds of the merchants' wives. What am I to do about the girls?"

"Leave them for now," Philip said absently, tucking the bottle into the shabby leather scrip at his hip.

"Right. Lord Rogier's study is inside the courtyard but near the back gate which leads to the stables and citronnier."

"I know where his study is. What about Ibrahim? Is there a plan to distract him?"

Marcouf scratched his chin thoughtfully.

"Spill your grain," Philip said, "that will bring Ibrahim running, especially if it spills in a place where the guests are assembled."

"Here now! The harvest was small this year due to the cold. I will not go wasting good grain!"

"Then you can help them pick up each damned kernel and continue the distraction. Ibrahim must be out of the way. That old Saracen rarely lets Rogier out of his sight."

Marcouf grumbled and snapped his fingers for another drink.

"I want to be paid ahead of time. Half now and the rest when you are finished. My family, we did not thrive during this year's harvest, and now the lord takes more of my grain for this feast, which his citizens are not even invited to attend."

Philip pulled a leather drawstring bag from his scrip, counted out five coins, and placed them on the table. As Marcouf reached for them, Philip pinned the man's hand to the table and leaned close.

"If anything goes wrong," he whispered, "it shall be your fault. I will see you thrown in prison with the criminals of Acre and hung. I can make your stay in prison uncomfortable."

Marcouf snatched his hand back. "I know the risks! I just want enough money to get my family back to Toulouse, where we no longer have to fear the Saracens and look at this cursed, dry land. The 'Holy Land,' they call it. Bah! If it were so holy, you would think Jesu Christi would lend a hand once in a while. My village has been raided twice already by infidels, and we cannot resist a third time. This land is death."

Philip smiled. "Aye, it is death for some and opportunity for others."

20

⸺ ∘ ⸺

AL-HADIQA, ACRE. AUGUST 1290

Al-Hadiqa, the estate of Rogier Maron, nestled in a shallow valley near the Yasaf creek, which wound through the green, rocky plains of Acre like a piece of carelessly dropped string. The house was built in a lavish local style, rectangular and flat-roofed, with arched windows and ceilings and intricately carved screens that concealed cool, dark rooms. Niches and alcoves in the walls contained glass and copper lamps that flicked dancing shapes of light and shadow on the walls tiled with blue and white mosaic. Long, flowing drapes, thick rugs, lovingly crafted furniture, and tapestries with delicate motifs of birds and flowers ornamented the rooms.

The main house was built around an inner courtyard surrounded by an arcade with lush gardens and trickling fountains fed by an underground spring to keep the family cool in the hot months of summer. Behind the house, lemon and cinnamon trees reached their branches toward the sky, contained within the limestone walls of the citronnier to protect them from the torches of raiders and thieves.

In the hot afternoon sun, servants moved languidly through the groves, picking lemons to supply the wealthy citizens of Marseille and Toulouse with the coveted sour fruits. Some would be sliced thin and spread in the sun to dry or packed in clay jars of salt to preserve them. Others would be shipped slightly green and nestled in straw to arrive fresh after their long cross-Mediterranean journey to Francia.

Lady Nasira of Maron sat on a rug in the citronnier, sewing in the shade of the trees and soaking in the sound of the leaves as they shifted restlessly on a hot breeze. Now that her children were older, Nasira spent more time sewing and reading than in her younger years, when she was often chasing a toddler or closely monitoring the household. At present, she didn't even know where any of her children were, and she stitched without hurry. At the whisper of a skirt in the long grass, she looked up to find Blanche, her middle child, standing with a halo of Palestinian sun shining around her head, like the gold-leaf paintings of the heavenly angels in St Andrew's Church.

"What is it, my beautiful one?" she asked.

Blanche was slender and tall, like Nasira, and like her mother, she had large, dark-fringed eyes and shapely brows. At fourteen, her womanhood grew on her each day with a grace that attracted notice among the fathers of young knights and widowed merchants. Acre was an outpost with few marriageable French women. Although Blanche was half Arab, Nasira knew that many men would be more than willing to overlook her heritage to wed the pretty young daughter of a noble of Francia and the wealthiest private citizen of Acre.

"I wanted to be sure you had not fainted in this heat," said Blanche, "and to ask if you would take a meal with me."

She smiled, holding up an earthenware jug of cold ale, freshly drawn from the cellar and sweating with condensation. Behind her, a servant brought hammered copper cups, a round loaf of thick-crusted bread, and a bowl of plump green olives swimming in oil and spices.

"Dear girl," Nasira smiled and made room for Blanche on her rug. Overhead, the lemon trees shivered in the afternoon breeze, and shadows danced across Nasira's face. "Where is your sister? Shall she join us at our picnic?"

Blanche wrinkled her nose. "She is with Master Mehmed, challenging his theory of dividing numbers by zero."

"Ah."

Nasira knew that Saruca, her youngest daughter, was likely to drive away this new tutor as she had with so many others. She bit her lip, wondering where they would find a replacement. Both of her daughters were headstrong in their unique ways, but Saruca's way happened to be highly alarming to learned men.

Blanche tore off pieces of the bread and poured the ale. For a few moments, they munched in companionable silence.

"Mother, why have you never told me how you met my father?"

"Does it matter how I met your father?"

"It does." Blanche tossed her hair. "If I do not know how you met Father, how will I know what to expect when meeting my husband?"

"You can expect your father to negotiate the best possible marriage for you, which should give you comfort."

"But what if he chooses a man who is old? What if I do not feel any affection for him?"

"Feelings do not really matter in a marriage, my dear," said Nasira sardonically.

"It mattered for you two. Father broke with his family to marry you. It is a romantic story."

"Romance? You have been hearing too many bard's tales in the city."

Nasira had never told her children this story truthfully; that Rogier had walked in on his father, Lord Jean-Rogier, trying to force her onto the table in his study when she was a chambermaid in his household. Rogier struck his father over the head with a chair, and the old man died immediately. A week later, Rogier, the young new master of the estate, dismissed all the servants, including her. When he appeared months later at her uncle's house asking to speak with her, she had no idea how drastically her life would change.

Nasira returned from her memory and swallowed nervously. Blanche continued to look at her with innocent anticipation. "I was a guest at the house, and your father and I met in... in your grand-père's banquet hall," she finished lamely.

"An Arab guest? But you were not high-born, Mother. What cause had you to be at the house? Indeed, it is less of a scandal that you are Arab and more abhorrent to our peers that you were not of noble birth."

"I was there to help consult on the best local servants to hire." She couldn't tell her daughter that she herself had been a servant. Her children already received considerable scorn because of their low-born mother, but they had no idea how truly low she had been.

"What did you do when you first saw my father? Was he handsome?"

"He was very handsome. At the time, he had fair hair, not gray, and of course, his eyes were very green, like Henri and Saruca's eyes."

"What did it feel like?"

"Almost like... fear." She got too close that time. "I mean, love is frightening. Fear and love are not so very different sometimes, I think."

Blanche sat quietly for a moment. "Mother, when did you know you loved my father?"

This one Nasira could answer truthfully. "A month after we were married. He took me riding on his horse up in the mountains, and we could see all of Acre and the sea. I still felt as if I hardly knew him, but we talked for hours on that day. He told me that he would go up there to contemplate the beauty of the world and the largeness of God. I had never been to those mountains, though I had spent my life looking at them. Your father opened my world."

Blanche seemed satisfied and poured another cup of the rapidly warming ale. Nasira took a deep breath, relieved that Blanche did not question her further.

It was unacceptable to Rogier to have an uneducated wife, so her first year as Lady Maron had been filled with lessons; learning to read, learning to talk, learning to walk, and learning that his family forbade him to bring her to Francia and that his twin brother had used Rogier's scandalous marriage as grounds to illegally claim the ancestral estate.

None of the other nobles in Acre were likely to know her parents, so Rogier simply told them that Nasira was from Cairo. Since she was a woman, no one questioned her about it, for they were not interested in noble lineages that they could not easily trace. She shook away her memories and glanced sideways at her daughter. Blanche's creamy-brown cheeks were flushed, and her eyes sparkled. A slight smile danced around the edges of her mouth.

"I noticed that the son of Georges Foutrier seems to be paying quite a lot of attention to you in church."

Blanche blushed redder, hesitated, and then spoke shyly. "He is very handsome, is he not? He does not resemble his father at all."

Not yet, thought Nasira wryly.

"My child, you know that your father married me for love, and I do wish you will also have that same joy...." She thought of what it would mean if Blanche aligned herself with the Foutrier family. She found the senior Foutrier to be odious, but an alliance between two successful merchant families in Acre could be a benefit. "However, you also have a responsibility to your family to make a wise choice. We marry to secure the stability of the family."

Blanche looked down at her hands. "You and Father did not do so. Why must we never discuss your family if that was not the case?"

"It was... that is to say, we were not...."

What was she supposed to say to this child? There was no explanation about her marriage to Rogier that was acceptable. They had gone against both of their religions and all of society to be together.

Blanche's hands clutched into fists in her lap.

"You and your brother and sister have suffered because your father married me. Your father and I are examples of what should not be done," Nasira said sternly. "By marrying me, your father was being selfish."

Blanche whipped around, brown eyes blazing. "Selfish indeed. You are both examples of extreme hypocrisy!"

She stood, leaving in a whirl of skirts and flying grass seeds. The pitcher overturned and ale soaked into the wool rug. Nasira raised her eyes toward heaven in exasperation. True, she no longer chased toddlers, but teenagers were a different challenge.

All of her children were strong-willed, and none worried her as much as her son Henri, but Blanche was prone to romantic fantasies that would surely set her up for disappointment. Nasira stabbed her needle through the gown that she was trying to complete. This is what she got for marrying a stubborn Franj.

She breathed a prayer under her breath to God – she did not specify which one – that her children would all reach adulthood. *Blanche is rash and romantic, Saruca too intelligent to escape the notice of the Church for much longer, and Henri, well, Henri is...* her eyes pricked with tears.

I no longer know who Henri is.

21

AL-HADIQA, ACRE. AUGUST 1290

Lord Rogier of Maron thundered into the courtyard of his estate in a cloud of dust. Hopping down from his horse, he handed the reins to a groom who had come rushing to his aid, hastily wiping the crumbs of a late lunch from his chin.

"Where is my son?" Rogier asked, unbuckling his sword belt and pushing his woven mail coif from his sweaty forehead.

Salih, the groom, bowed. "Young master Henri is out hunting. He has been gone since the morning, my lord."

Rogier growled and spun on his heel. "Inform me as soon as he returns, Salih, and please send Ibrahim to my study."

Salih bowed again at the retreating back of his employer. "Yes, my lord," he said, and led the magnificent horse through the courtyard and towards the stable.

Rogier strode on long legs through the empty courtyard, his pale eyes scanning for signs of his family. "Emine!" he hollered. A petite serving girl in a white dress appeared from the kitchen, her brown apron stained with pomegranate juice.

"Yes, my lord?"

"Prepare a hot bath and a knife for shaving. Find me when you have everything ready," he said, opening the heavy wooden door that led to his study.

The room was cool and dark, the walls covered with delicately embroidered tapestries. Chests of books and parchments were stacked neatly in a corner away from the glass-paned window, and more books were piled on a table in the center of the room.

Despite the coolness of the house, Rogier removed his black surcoat, his mail hauberk, gloves, and wiped a greasy slick of sweat from his graying temples. His head ached from too much time riding in the dust and unrelenting August sun. Tomorrow he would host a celebration of the Feast of the Transfiguration for the notables of Acre. The young new king, Henry de Lusignan, along with the royal household, the grand master of the Templars, and the wealthiest merchants and nobility in the city would all attend. Rogier pressed his fingers against his aching head and wished he could call the whole thing off. He sighed, nudged the thick glass-paned shutter open, and looked out toward the rooftops of Acre. This cluster of humanity and churches was almost all remained of the West's glorious "Kingdom of Jerusalem" in Outremer.

Two hundred years earlier, bands of bedraggled knights and pilgrims from the squabbling villages of Francia and the Italian peninsula had staggered into Jerusalem, claiming the inhabited city as their own, much to the astonishment of its Arab and Jewish citizens. Slowly, the locals fought back to push the Western invaders further north and toward the sea until all of Christian Outremer clung tenuously to a few small coastal settlements and the wealthy trading city of Acre. Despite the whittling away of the Western conquests and the loss of the city of Jerusalem, the ideological "Kingdom of Jerusalem" was still alive in Outremer and still preached from the pulpits to the town squares in the West. This hot, contested Holy Land was where the residents of the West aspired to die in order to be closer to God.

A gentle knock at the door brought Rogier back into the room, and Ibrahim entered. Slightly built, with expressive hands and kind eyes, Ibrahim was a stable, calming presence who had managed the family's estate for nearly twenty years as a steward. He wore a white turban wrapped neatly about his balding temples and a crisp indigo robe of buttery soft linen, belted at the waist with a thick sash of brown and white striped cloth. He bowed slightly and waited for Rogier to speak as he paced near the window.

"I just returned from a meeting with Brother Georges de Languedoc. When will Henri return? I must speak with him," Rogier asked.

"He is hunting, my lord. For how long, I do not know."

"Can he be found? Will he come back to the house, or is he going straight into the city?"

"I know not, my lord. I suppose it depends on his success," Ibrahim spread his hands apologetically.

Rogier continued to pace. "That boy spends far too much time taking his ease and visiting married women," he muttered. "It is time to send him away from Palestine."

"Is everything well, my lord?" Ibrahim asked. Moving to a cloth-covered pitcher of wine on the table, he poured a small cup and handed it to his master.

"No, all is not well. Can you take down a letter for me? I must write to my brother."

Ibrahim raised an eyebrow. Rogier was a viscount of Acre and master of many villages outside of the city, but he was also marquis of a modest fief in Francia, whose ownership had been contested by his twin brother for twenty years. Ibrahim, priding himself on his professionalism and discretion, withheld comment and began collecting paper, quills, and ink, seating himself at the heavy wooden table in the center of the room.

"What will you say to your brother, my lord?"

Rogier exhaled heavily and turned from the window.

"Gaspard, let us cease this foolishness and return to our normal relations as when I was still with you in Maron-en-Ruergue. There is nothing to be gained in arguing, for it only divides the strength of our claim. In a year's time, I will send my son to you for his protection so that he may begin to familiarize himself with the fief in the event that he shall collect his inheritance, an event that may be near...."

His words drifted, and Ibrahim set his quill down.

"Pardon me, Lord Rogier. Surely you are not suggesting that you will perish soon?" he asked, concern clouding his placid face.

"I am not aging in reverse," Rogier said, just as the door to the study slammed open and his son entered, dirty with sweat and dust from a morning of riding.

Henri stood as tall as Rogier, green-eyed and brown-skinned at seventeen years old. The other young nobles of Acre chafed that Henri had riches, status, and the favor of every woman who crossed his path. The city leadership rolled their eyes at his aloof attitude towards his civic duties as a member of the noble class. Aware of his good looks, he frequently wore a mocking smile that enraged every older man in his presence with its implied insolence. He was the kind of youth who filled men with the desire to hit him in the face, even if he committed no crime.

"Do you require something?" Henri demanded, tugging his leather gauntlets off and dropping into a chair.

"Were you in the city last night?" Rogier asked. "I did not see you come home."

"I came home after you were in your bed," Henri said, yawning. "I need to bathe. There has been little rain, and the roads are dusty."

"You will not travel to the city tonight or any other night until I tell you that you may," Rogier said tersely. "Now go upstairs. Emine has already drawn you a bath."

"What is this? You cannot forbid me from going into the city without reason," Henri protested.

Lately, everything that his son did or said irritated Rogier. "Get up," he commanded, pushing Henri out of the study toward the mosaiced hammam where the family bathed. Emine was there with a manservant, a steaming copper tub, a sharp knife, and a stack of woven towels.

"Please shave him," Rogier said to the servant. "Emine, you may leave us."

As Emine exited the room, Rogier noticed his son's eyes follow her. Henri put a hand to his face, covering his fledgling beard protectively. "Will you explain to me why you are acting strangely? You cannot shave a man's beard without his permission!"

"Hamza," Rogier said, switching to his son's familiar nickname. "I would treat you like a man if you acted like one. You will shave your beard because it is not safe for you to wear it or go into Acre at night."

Henri looked at Rogier, confused.

"Did you see anything when you were out last night? Any violence in the streets?" Rogier demanded.

Henri shook his head. In truth, he had been gambling at an inn, and after losing a considerable sum of silver bezants, he sought solace in a pitcher of wine with Amalric and one of the lesser Lusignan cousins. He didn't return to the house until the monks began their matins in the monasteries and the street sweepers made their way through the dim alleys.

Rogier dragged his fingers through his silver hair. "The new Sicilian troops that the king ordered have become unruly. They are roaming the streets of Acre at night and killing men with beards. Arab men with beards," he said significantly, noting how his son's smooth brown skin contrasted with his own perennially sunburned, freckled complexion. "I met with Brother Languedoc and Grand Master Beaujeu this afternoon to learn what is to be done. It seems the Templars are unable to stop the murders, for there are more Sicilians than knights in the city right now."

"Well," Henri said, standing, "I am only a half-Arab man with a beard, so no harm should come to me, and if you would knight me, then there would be one more in the city to combat the Sicilians."

"Sit down and shave your beard or I will have Salih lock your horse in her stable, and I will send you to Francia to live with your uncle," Rogier said through clenched teeth. "Men are dying in Acre. Innocent men!"

"Poor men," Henri said bluntly. "Saracens and Jews. Why do you care about them?"

Rogier eyed his son dangerously, and Henri sat, scowling at the servant as he approached with the shaving knife. He pouted, and for a while, the only sound in the room was of the knife rasping over his chin.

"I saw you looking at Emine, Hamza. Have you touched her?" Rogier broke the silence.

"No," Henri shot back, and Rogier could hear the lie in his voice. Rogier dismissed the manservant, and Henri rubbed his bare jaw in annoyance.

"Well, since you say you have not bedded the servants and you are clearly lying, I think it is time for me to tell you how I really met your mother."

"You already have. Seems your mind is fading in your old age, Father."

Rogier could have punched him at that moment. Instead, he turned on his son. "What is wrong with you? I brought you back here to live as you demanded. You have everything you could ever want or need, yet you continue to insist on being an insufferable ass!"

"Why do you not knight me?" Henri shouted, and Rogier leapt to his feet.

"I will not give you a title and let you loose on the population of this city until you have demonstrated that you have some redeemable qualities, Hamza. Learn to be a man of honor first!"

Henri clenched both his fists, but before he could strike his father, there came the sounds of shouting through the open window and a great crash. A cart of grain had overturned, and its golden contents spilled across the courtyard where guests would be arriving soon. Ibrahim walked out and spoke to the driver of the cart, then began to give commands for the mess to be cleaned up.

"Well, we shall have sand in our bread tomorrow, it appears," Rogier grumbled. "Hamza, I allowed you to move home on the condition that you would obey my orders when I told you to stay at the house. I am ordering you now. You will remain inside these walls, or I shall have you returned to Sir Geoffroi in chains."

"I am nearly eighteen, Father! You cannot continue to treat me like a ten-year-old child!"

Rogier's eyes misted for a moment. "I miss the ten-year-old Henri that I knew."

"If you wanted that boy to stay the same, you should have protected him."

Rogier fled the room. Impossible. The situation was impossible. He had done what he thought was best to keep his son safe, but he had destroyed all of Henri's humanity in the process. He was so focused on keeping his son alive that he failed to notice that his son had turned hard and arrogant.

Back in his study, a servant was sweeping the floor. Rogier dismissed her.

"My lord," she curtseyed quickly, "there is new wine for you in the pitcher and some bread and potted fish for your refreshment."

"Thank you. I wish not to be disturbed, please."

He dropped heavily into his chair and dragged the silver platter of bread toward him. The door creaked open again behind him.

"Please knock when you enter...." Rogier's words died in the air.

A ghost stood in the room with him, white with deep red blood dripping from a wound in his heart, just like the last time Rogier had seen him twelve years ago. He blinked.

"How did you get here?" Rogier breathed. "You are dead."

"Aye, stabbed through the heart," Philip walked to the table, pulled out a second chair, and sat across from Rogier.

"You live..." Rogier's voice trembled. "But I saw you die, I—"

"Killed me yourself? Well, you certainly tried, but God is good. Not only did he return me to health, but he returned me to you." Philip's smile was full of malice. "You managed to put your dagger in the one place that could not kill me."

"You have been here the whole time? How did you live?"

Philip smirked. "Not exactly. Praise be to Jesu Christi that Palestine has some of the most excellent healers. That is about the only good thing I can say about this place."

"Where did you get those robes? No Templar preceptory would take you such as you are, Philip!"

Philip's jaw twitched, but he remained composed. Reaching across the table, he poured two cups of wine and pushed one of them toward Rogier.

"Such as I am, I would not be this way were it not for you."

"Your fate is unfortunate, but it is not my fault."

"And yet you still thrust your dagger into me. Father's dagger. It seems you felt that you had some control over my fate after all."

"Can you blame me? You killed my firstborn! You kidnapped my son!"

Philip nodded in acknowledgment. "It is unfortunate that your heir died, Rogier, but you forced my hand. I merely planned to hold onto your sons until you granted me a share in the inheritance. It is you who are responsible for that accident."

"Tell me why you are here before I have you dragged to the dungeons in the citadel." Rogier's voice was low and dangerous.

"Ah," Philip chuckled. "That will not be easy, I am afraid. You have wealth, but I have authority. They will not jail me on your word alone." Philip took a long sip from his cup and looked at it appreciatively. "This is quite fine wine. It hardly tastes of vinegar at all. I commend you for your vineyards."

Rogier stared at him coldly.

"All I wish to do is talk to you, Brother."

"You are not my brother," said Rogier.

"I am a brother in the army of the Lord. I am someone's brother."

"Yes, and we will discuss how that happened in a minute, but first, I wish to know how you managed to get in here and how much I can pay you to leave Acre forever."

"You have grown mellow and diplomatic in your old age, Rogier. I expected you to hide behind your guards as soon as you saw me."

"Obviously, it is impossible to kill you, and I know what truly motivates you. Does Beaujeu know of your tarnished past, or are those robes a disguise that you purchased in the souks?" Rogier's mind raced. If he called for the guards, Philip would kill him immediately. He had no weapon, and his arm, injured many years ago, hung nearly useless at his side.

Philip smiled and plucked at the white linen on his shoulder.

"Do you like these? I am afraid they are genuine, Rogier. My past and future are both forgiven. I am as untarnished as that gold necklace around your daughter's lovely throat." He pushed his chair back, and Rogier tensed. "How much will you offer me to leave? I miss Francia and would not be opposed to leaving this stinking place forever."

"I will pay you a hundred florins in gold if you leave this place and never contact my family. This is enough for you to live comfortably wherever you wish."

"Two hundred."

"Fine, two hundred."

Philip smiled again and raised his cup. "Now, that was very easy. I am a simple man, really. It must have been my humble upbringing." His eyes glittered. Rogier slowly raised his cup to his lips and took a small sip. Philip tipped his cup back, draining it.

"Now leave."

"What about my money?"

"I do not keep two hundred florins in my house, Philip. I am sure this does not surprise you."

"You are just as paranoid as our father. I want that gold now, Rogier. Are you keeping it with the Templars? Then you shall ride to the citadel today and get it."

The room swam gently around Rogier, and Philip seemed to float in his seat. Rogier looked dumbly down at his cup.

"You... poisoned me," he slurred.

"Not poison, Rogier, just a little potion to help you feel relaxed."

Rogier stood clumsily and clutched the edge of the table as Philip walked toward him. He tried to step back but stumbled, falling against an iron-bound chest, and Philip was on him instantly, pulling him up by the collar of his black velvet tunic. Slowly, Philip withdrew a jeweled dagger from his robe, and Rogier's eyes widened with fear.

"Recognize this? Yours and mine are twins, and I would like to have the other one, Rogier. Then I will possess two daggers that have tasted the flesh of the men of Maron."

"I no longer have it, and you are not a Maron," Rogier breathed and clutched weakly at Philip's throat. Philip brushed his hands away, then pulled Rogier up and slammed him against the top of the table, spilling the cups of wine.

"Do you really think that I could be paid to leave you here unharmed? Two hundred gold florins is just a little sweetness on top of the joy I will take in killing you."

Rogier grasped at the bread knife on the tray near him, spilling the oily dish of fish across the table.

"I see you are still not relaxed enough, Brother. Take some more wine!" Philip snatched the pitcher and forced the spout between Rogier's lips, pouring the wine into his mouth. Rogier gurgled and choked, and Philip clapped his hands over the man's mouth and nose.

"Drink, and I shall give you a painless death. Painless and powerless. You used to be a lion on the battlefield, but you are weak as a kitten right now."

Rogier gasped, spitting the wine at Philip's face, spattering his pure white robe.

"Very well, perhaps it will not be so painless after all," Philip snarled. He ripped Rogier's tunic open, exposing the freckled chest, placed the tip of his dagger, and then leaned all of his weight on it. Rogier exhaled loudly, and deep red blood bubbled up from the wound in his heart, puddling on the floor. Philip backed away and looked down at his stained robe. He pulled it over his head, revealing his laborer's clothes underneath, then balled the robe up and stuffed it in a sack. He checked to ensure Rogier no longer breathed, then opened the door quietly, peeking down the hall. Seeing no one, he slipped into the hall and toward the stables. It was done. His heart rejoiced.

Rogier of Maron was finally dead, and now only one more obstacle remained in his path.

22

— · —

AL-HADIQA, ACRE. AUGUST 1290

Lord Rogier of Maron had only been dead for a few hours before the clergy and local nobility besieged his house. Nasira dried her eyes, brushed out her long hair, and pulled it underneath a black wimple. With a few terse words, she sent the servants scurrying to procure refreshment and spread sweet-smelling grass in the great hall, for undoubtedly the unwelcome guests would be spending the night and would need a place to sleep.

It would have been a relief to welcome visitors into her house who meant to offer comfort, but Nasira had lived among the Acre nobility long enough to understand that no one felt sympathy for her or her children. A few of the lords and knights present looked truly aggrieved at Rogier's death, but the rest sipped on cups of wine and chatted together amicably as if they were at an afternoon feast.

Because it was August, Rogier's body was swiftly relocated into the cool of the cellar until arrangements could be made for a proper burial. Nasira wanted to take care of her husband's remains in the way of her own people; burial before sunset, time spent in prayer and devotion, and most of all, the fellowship of friends and family who cared about her. *None of these men care about me or my family*, she thought. The desire to run downstairs and throw herself on Rogier's stiffening corpse overwhelmed her senses as the men moved about, oblivious to her grief. Rogier's death had happened so swiftly that she and her daughters still sat with a searching look of incomprehension, unable to participate in the conversation around them. Even ten-year-old Saruca, who was not inclined to be sentimental, seemed subdued. She sat quietly in a dark corner, looking at her feet.

"Excuse me, my lady." A voice startled her. It was Madame Habiba, her lady's maid of twenty years. Many years older than Nasira, Madame Habiba had seen her mistress through tumultuous times of joy and grief, raising and losing children, sharing and keeping secrets. When she looked upon Nasira, her eyes softened with affection. "Several men have asked to speak with you. Will you take some wine first? It will calm your mind."

"Where is Henri?" Nasira's voice sounded like a whisper.

"He is downstairs, my lady...with Lord Rogier." Madame Habiba twisted the sleeve of her gown, a nervous habit that she had developed over the years.

"Please send for him. He must be here to assert his claim on his father's property."

The time for mourning was over now. Each man in this room had some sort of scheme to influence her son to obtain a portion of her husband's enormous wealth. Although he was unprepared to take on such skilled criminals, there was no more time to train him.

As Madame Habiba curtseyed and hurried off, a figure all in white strolled over to Nasira and bowed.

"My deepest condolences on the loss of your husband, Lady Nasira. Rogier and I were comrades in the fight against the Saracens with King Louis, and he saved my life."

Nasira forced a smile. "Yes, he took an arrow for you. I must thank you, Brother Languedoc, for had the enemy not chosen to try to take your life, my husband might have died in battle before now."

Brother Languedoc did not smile back. Nasira had never seen anything but stern disapproval on the man's face.

He glanced around the room and leaned closer. "And how is young Henri? I have heard much talk of him around the city these days."

"I hope he has not done something too terrible of late, Brother Languedoc," Nasira said with a raised eyebrow. "He is nearly eighteen years of age, and it is not possible for me to have him supervised, although I am well-informed of his antics."

Brother Languedoc glanced around again, quickly. "Well, he will need a firm hand to correct his behavior. Since it would be adultery for you to remarry after the death of your husband, you can give Henri to the Templars for training and discipline. He would be welcomed into our ranks." He bowed again, and as he walked away, she could hear his spurs tinkling on the stone floor.

Wretched Templars! Nasira thought hotly. *And he, the most churlish of them all. Adultery, indeed!* She had no interest in remarrying. Rogier had been the love of her life, but she did not see it as a sin against God if a woman whose husband had lived an upright and moral life were to take another husband for her own protection and that of her children.

The chatter in the room grew quiet, and Nasira looked up as her son entered the hall, his face twisted into a glare of contempt. The merchants, priests, and lords gathered around him, but he brushed past them, walking straight toward her.

"You sent for me?"

"Hamza," she whispered harshly in Arabic, "do your duty and speak with these men. The impression you make upon them now will set the tone for your entire rule as viscount of this city."

"I have nothing to say to them," he responded, turning to leave.

Nasira grabbed his wrist. "Then you shall lose everything, my son. Speak with them. Assure the merchants that you will meet with each of them in time and invite the nobles to hunt with you."

"Very well," Henri snapped, his face hardening. He turned to the crowd of expectant guests and favored them with a dazzling false smile. "My lords!" he called out in a loud voice. "Esteemed members of God's church and fellow merchants. I thank you for coming here to my house in my family's darkest hour of grief. Right now, when we need peace and reassurance, your generosity in blessing us with your presence and ensuring that our new wine does not grow old and unconsumed is most appreciated."

The smiles on several of the faces of his guests faltered.

Henri continued. "I know that there is much business to be done. After all, it is not often that a mighty lord of Francia and Acre leaves an enormous fortune to a son that you all deem so singularly unworthy to receive it, but so he has. I am afraid the entail of my father's property remains firmly in place."

There were no more smiling faces in the room.

"My family and I are not your carrion to be picked over, so you may leave at your earliest convenience. I will send a servant for each of you when I am ready to speak with you."

For a moment, the room echoed with stunned silence, then one of the older merchants threw his cup of wine to the ground and spat.

"And so goes the house of Maron," the man declared. "This is what becomes of letting your line become fouled by Saracen blood!" He stalked from the room.

The others followed, some also throwing their cups to the ground, others simply favoring Henri and Nasira with a glare of distaste. Against the tide of retreating men, a wispy-haired, white-robed figure approached, his back slightly bent.

"Patriarch," Henri said, bowing and kissing the old man's hand. "Of course, my words did not include you, for I know your fortune is even larger than mine."

"Oh, Henri," Bishop Hanapes, the Patriarch of Acre, sighed. "Your father worried this would happen."

"My father..." Henri's lip curled slightly. "I doubt my father worried about me much, but he certainly disapproved of me. I see that you have taken his place."

"I have watched you grow, young man, as has every citizen of Acre, in anticipation of the great man you may someday become. I thought there was nothing you could do any longer to surprise me, yet here you have done it. Well, they are furious with you. Best to get some sleep and put it straight tomorrow." The Patriarch reached up a skeletal hand and patted Henri on his shoulder.

"Lady Nasira, I bless you in the name of Jesu Christi. May you find solace during your time of grief. Remember the Lord God tried his servant Job and tested his faith. You are also undergoing your test."

Nasira bristled. The Patriarch's insinuation was clear. He and everyone else would be watching her to see if she renounced her conversion to the Church now that Rogier was dead.

"I trust that God will give me peace," Nasira said, lowering her eyes modestly.

The Patriarch nodded and retreated.

Red wine puddled in the cracks between stones in the floor, and servants rushed around, sweeping up dropped food and straightening the overturned furniture. Nasira sighed. She felt overwhelmed and numb.

"Hamza—" she said, taking both of his hands in her own.

His eyes resembled Rogier's so uncannily that it hurt her to look at them. Henri had Rogier's straight forehead and sensitive brow. He had her skin and wavy black hair, but that was where the similarities ended. He towered over his peers in height, and his temper, which only seemed to grow in size as he aged, seemed to come from the Devil himself.

"I am off to Sir Hugh's," Henri said, kissing her cheek. "There is no need to ask the servants to wait up for me. I will sleep there."

Nasira's mouth hung open in shock. "Your father's body lies cooling in the cellar, and you are leaving this house to go to a feast? His murderer could still be here! Have you taken leave of your senses?"

He was walking toward the large double doors that led to the courtyard from the hall, sweeping his summer cloak of black embroidered silk across his shoulders. "The militia has surrounded the house and will patrol the halls this night. And there is nothing wrong with my senses. I desire to see my friends."

"Those men are not your friends!" Nasira shouted at him, but Henri was gone.

23

———.———

TEMPLAR CITADEL, ACRE. AUGUST 1290

Philip's exhilaration was unquenchable. He lay back in his cot, hands behind his head, and relived each moment of his encounter with Rogier, remembered the feeling of that dagger sliding through flesh, scraping bone, and the wet coughs that Rogier took as he breathed his last few breaths.

News of the viscount's death was all over the city almost immediately, and Philip glowed as he heard the astonished discussions in the halls of the citadel from his Brethren. He had done this. For the first time in his life, he was notable, and he would soon be rich.

The door to the solar creaked open, and a white-robed knight approached, sitting on the side of Philip's cot.

"So," Brother Alaran said slowly. "This was your work, was it not?"

Philip closed his eyes, smiling with satisfaction. "Indeed. The world is freed of a great wickedness now that I have taken revenge on Rogier of Maron."

"Did you get the money?"

"Not yet. Do not worry, Alaran. You will receive a share. Rogier probably keeps it here at the citadel. What is the name of the sergeant in charge of the treasuries and lending?"

"Thomas Cartwright."

"We shall have to pay this man a visit in the coming weeks. And how goes your investigation?"

"The easiest time for us to leave would be in the month of September... a year hence."

Philip sat up on his cot. "Why?"

"It is said that King Philippe will send a delegation of officials to Acre who will stay from the month of June until the feast of the Birth of the Blessed Virgin. There will be much distraction when they leave, and it will be our best chance to slip away without notice. We will travel by camel to Damascus in disguise and then proceed to the Holy Roman Empire, where we may settle and live our lives as we wish."

Philip nodded slowly. "I am impatient, I admit, but this should give me the time I need to settle everything."

The muffled sound of bells ringing filtered through the stone walls of the solar.

"What is that?" Philip asked. "The hour of terce just struck only recently."

Brother Alaran stood and adjusted his robe. "The bells are ringing for Rogier. Apparently, he was a more influential citizen than you realized, Brother."

Philip's face hardened. Rogier was dead, but the man's shadow still followed him.

"Alaran, there is something you must do for me."

"Name it," Brother Alaran replied. "I am still in your debt."

"There is a certain man in the village of Ma'an Barid named Marcouf Charettier. I think that the grand master and the Maron family would be most relieved to find him so that justice can be served for the death of Lord Maron. The pain of not knowing who is responsible for this atrocity must be overwhelming for Lady Nasira of Maron."

Brother Alaran cracked a rare smile. "It shall be done."

24

AL-HADIQA, ACRE. AUGUST 1290

H enri leaned over the short stone wall atop the colonnade of his house and looked down into the courtyard. Emine, the chambermaid, crossed the space below him
with a swaying gait, her hair wrapped up in a turban that
artfully displayed the back of her slender brown neck. Henri
normally would have watched appreciatively, possibly even
gone downstairs and followed her to the kitchen, but today
he could only focus on the vast responsibility that came with
his father's empire. He was inheriting riches and all of the
troubles that came with them.

Because he had shown little interest in the business of
growing and exporting lemons, spices, and sugar back to
Francia, Henri largely ignored the daily operations of the
house. It had been Rogier's wish that eventually his son could
be shipped to the West to marry a king's daughter and produce
royal heirs, leaving Nasira and the girls in the Holy Land.

"Your duty is to return to Maron-en-Rouergue and wed a
noblewoman, and for God's sake, do not allow my brother
Gaspard and his vile son to wrest control of the fief from you,
else your mother and your sisters will be selling themselves on
the street, and you will find an arrow in your back," his father
would tell him.

I cannot find it in myself to be interested in lemons, Henri
thought dully, chipping bits of limestone from the wall and
dropping them down into the fountain below. His destiny did

not lie in lemon shipments but in glory on the battlefield and as a future statesman of the Kingdom of Jerusalem. Perhaps he and Amalric would even recapture the Holy Sepulchre, earning themselves the Pope's favor and lifelong pardon for future sins.

"My lord?" A voice interrupted Henri's thoughts. Emine stood before him, her hands clasping and unclasping. She had quietly slipped up the stairs without him noticing. "Do you require anything?"

"Not at this time," he replied, turning back to the court-yard. She was impertinent for approaching him without being asked, but he hadn't the energy to correct her, so he excused it. Emine took a step closer and put her hand on his.

"May I speak with you, my lord? Somewhere more private?" She looked at him from under dark lashes.

Henri wrenched his hand back and then grabbed her roughly by the arm. "You presume too much," he snarled. "If you seek to secure yourself an estate and a title of your own now that I am to inherit, you will be tossed to the street and whoring in the Venetian Quarter before the day is over."

Emine's eyes widened. "But..."

He released his grip, and she staggered backward before running down the stairs and disappearing into the kitchen below.

Despite his father's severe threats that Henri was never to bed the servants, Emine had visited him in his chamber sev-eral times this year. He thought of the secrets Rogier revealed to him – the real story of how his father and mother met and the truth of why their family could not return to Maron.

It would have been helpful information to have had years earlier, Henri thought angrily, *to know that my mother was a serving wench and his family in Maron-en-Rouergue has disowned us. If my father had kept his prick inside his trousers, I would be married and knighted by now.*

He had told his father as much and earned a stern reproach.

"My son," his father had said, "I loved you when you were young, and somewhere between your first steps and your first woman, you became intolerably arrogant. If I could bequeath all of my holdings to Blanche instead of you, I would."

The loving last words of my sire, Henri thought bitterly. *If I am a disappointment, it is due to his poor example. Or maybe because he sent me to live with Sir Geoffroi and his trained devils.* Still, Rogier's words stung, and Henri knew they would not hurt so badly if they did not contain some truth.

He looked up at the sound of suede slippers on the stair. Blanche approached and leaned against the wall next to him, eyes fixed on the courtyard below.

"How was the full moon feast with Sir Hugh, Brother?"

"It provided the distraction I needed."

"Such an honor you did our father by insulting his friends and then leaving to attend a party while our mother still grieves."

Henri ground his teeth. Blanche, opinionated and sarcastic, could always find her way straight into his bad temper.

He set his jaw. "I am the lord of this estate now, Blanche. Take care of what you say, or I will marry you off to a Jew."

"Do you suddenly take issue with Jews? It was my understanding that a half-Saracen lord of the Holy Land could not afford to insult anyone," Blanche responded lightly.

"You are right, of course, dear sister. Instead, I shall send you to a convent," Henri responded, his temper rising.

Blanche laughed coldly. "A punishment indeed, although Saruca would enjoy a convent well enough." Her long brown hair dripped over the railing, and she swatted it back over her shoulder. "You would send me to live with the Sisters if I did not pose such an opportunity for you to expand your wealth and influence by marrying me to the goutiest old noble you could find. Go on and tell me, who have you chosen?"

"No one will have you," Henri retorted irritably. "Where is Saruca?"

"Here and there. She avoids you when you are in a foul mood, Henri. It would take God's own luck to find her unless you stop behaving like an indulged tomcat."

Henri pushed himself from the wall and swept to the end of the colonnade and down the stairs. In the dooryard, his father's militia milled about, dressed in the black and yellow colors of the Marons of Acre. Waving away their shouted questions, Henri walked through an arched doorway, emerging into the white-walled citronnier.

He found his youngest sister where he expected to find her – barefoot and slowly stalking through the grass under the lemon trees. The tender, glossy leaves of the young trees released a resinous scent in the late summer sun, and the air smelled warm and sweet. In the shivering shade, Saruca moved with tentative steps, physically in the grove, but her eyes darted after unseen prey, and she whispered softly to the air. Henri stood partially hidden in the arched entryway and watched as she moved in a slow circle, fingertips brushing the trunk of the nearest tree.

When she was a young child, Saruca never spoke, and the Patriarch of Acre diagnosed her as a mute. "She is one of God's children," the old man said, "and you should accept God's will that she will remain silent."

Distraught, their mother secretly took her to a Sufi mystic, and when the Sufi said the same, she took little Saruca to a wise woman, a local seer and midwife named Madame Ardukin. The old woman consulted the stars and declared that the girl had been born under a rare sky. Henri had to agree. There were none rarer than his baby sister.

"Saruca," Henri called softly from the doorway.

A smile spread slowly across her narrow face. "Hamza, have you come to greet them too?"

"Greet who? I see no one."

Saruca's pale green eyes fixed him with a serious and unblinking stare. "The shadows in the citronnier... they have arms and legs, and they dance."

Henri did not know how to respond. Ever since Saruca's nurse had beaten her for not making eye contact when she spoke, Saruca had an unnerving way of staring straight through people. Looking at them, but not seeing.

"You must not speak of things like this."

"Father let me speak about whatever I wished," Saruca said, pressing her ear against the trunk of a tree and listening.

Henri sighed. Both of his sisters were out of control. Blanche spoke her mind too freely, and Saruca was practically a witch. Although he wished to blame his mother, he knew that the real responsibility lay with his father. His sisters would have to be reformed and quickly. He would start by getting Blanche married and out of the house.

"Saruca, would you like to have a lady's maid of your own, like Madame Habiba is for Mother?"

"No, I thank you," she gave him a small curtsey. "Although I do wish to have another tutor. Master Mehmed told me this very morning that when I reach the age of twelve, I should cease to study mathematics."

"Seems reasonable to me. At twelve, you will be old enough to marry."

Saruca laughed. "Oh, Hamza. I do not wish to marry a man! How silly you are!"

"Saruca, you should—"

"Should, should, should...." Saruca muttered, wandering off. Henri sighed.

"Saruca, can you hear me?"

She looked at him without focus, then placed her hands on the trunk of a tree, spun in a circle around it, and continued to whisper to herself. "Should, should, should...."

25

AL-HADIQA, ACRE. AUGUST 1290

H enri spent his first few days as master of the estate only speaking to people he trusted – a small circle limited to his mother, Prince Amalric, and Ibrahim. That Rogier had taken a local Arab as a steward was just another of the Maron family's many scandals over the years. Local Arabs, although tolerated by the Franj, were considered a plentiful and inexpensive labor force. Although they often found employment in the great houses as servants, or slaves if they declined to convert, they rarely served as advisors to prominent Franj knights and nobility. Roles of responsibility and council were reserved for pilgrims who opted to stay in Outremer, sometimes even a down-on-his-luck knight looking to earn some coin to fund his return to his homeland. Rogier had little trust in his countrymen, so employing a local man suited his pleasure. Ibrahim, for reasons entirely his own, was trustworthy, discreet, and unswervingly loyal.

Now, Ibrahim watched thoughtfully as his youthful new master paced in the same room where Lord Rogier had been vibrantly alive less than a sennight ago. Henri had slept little in the previous five days. A dark blush of fatigue shadowed his eyes, and the length of his temper shortened with every new complication, real or imagined. After a full day of trying to accustom Henri to the running of the estate, Ibrahim began to ponder his age, his personal wealth, and the option of leaving under cover of darkness for his cousin's house near Nablus. If the ill-humor of his young employer did not kill him first, the impending attack on the city certainly would.

For weeks, rumors had circulated in the dim, smoky tea shops in the Muslim neighborhoods of the city about a force of Mamluks mobilizing in Cairo and recruiting volunteers from as far north as Aleppo. Although it was unclear where exactly they were heading, they were said to be massive in number and rabid in their desire to wrench the entirety of Palestine from Christian hands. And now there was news that a group of Arabs had been slaughtered in Acre by a mob of crazed Franj soldiers, and the sultan threatened retributive war.

Ibrahim wasn't sure what to think about the Mamluks – the army of loyal slaves. They were a brutal, zealous band of warriors who routinely terrorized the villages surrounding Acre, but so were his master's people. The French, Venetians, Sicilians, Genoese, English, and Teutons, collectively known to the Arabs as the "Franj," had instituted the suppression and slaughter of Muslims, Jews, even local Christians, and profited from it. He often felt that there were no good men left in Acre, and now he had the charge of young Henri, who was arrogant, spoiled, and ill-prepared to deal with any threats, Mamluk, merchant, or otherwise.

Ibrahim sighed and raised his eyes to heaven. *Allah, why did you place me with this family? Why Nasira? Surely my master was fair and kind to me and my job here is done. Must I really stay for Lord Rogier's degenerate son?*

Allah was silent. Ibrahim waited a few more minutes to be sure God wasn't pondering an appropriate answer, then cleared his throat like a barrister before a closing argument.

"Lord Henri, perhaps we should now go over the manifests from the last citrus shipment to Marseille."

Henri strode towards him eagerly. "Yes! My thoughts exactly." He paused, unsure.

"The parchment on the table, my lord."

"Ah, yes, of course." Henri plucked a thick, creamy sheet of paper from the table and studied it. "I knew that."

"The one beneath that, my lord," Ibrahim said with practiced calm.

Henri froze, and his ears turned scarlet. Ibrahim stifled another sigh, walked across the room, and put a hand on Henri's shoulder. Henri flinched.

"Master Hamza," he said, using the childhood nickname reserved for family and close friends, "since your father rarely discussed his business ventures with you, I shall be pleased to teach you everything he taught me. Your father and I were close partners in this matter."

Henri remained silent, tense. Ibrahim knew the young man's fear was battling with his pride. Less predictable than his father, Henri could allow his insecurity to rule instead of common sense, and he frequently did.

"Lord Henri," Ibrahim continued, "your enemies gather at your door. Your father's fellow countrymen are looking for a sign of weakness in you, so we must show strength. Let us review these manifests, and then tomorrow we will take a tour of the groves. There is much I wish to show you."

"Very well," Henri said, eyes looking past Ibrahim at the floor. Ibrahim silently thanked Allah that Henri seemed teachable today.

"Right, then. The first thing to know is that the last shipment of sugar left Acre five weeks past, and I just received word from your father's business partners of its receipt in Marseille. You are to receive compensation in the form of ten wheels of fine cheese, five sides of bacon, fifty sacks of wheat, and three dozen casks of new wine from Cyprus, which should fetch a fine price in this year of strong commerce." He leaned over a letter on the table, reading for a moment. "Oh, and three gold florins."

The door to the study slammed open and a breathless servant appeared, escorting a tall Templar knight whose white robes were dusty from a hard ride.

"Lord Henri," the knight said without smiling. "I am Brother Alaran. Grand Master Beaujeu sent me to fetch you. We believe we have apprehended the scoundrel who murdered your father."

Henri and Ibrahim quickly exchanged a look, then Ibrahim rushed out of the room to call for Salih to saddle horses. A short time later, the three of them were galloping in the heat of the mid-day sun toward Acre.

At the citadel, Brother Alaran led them into the central garrison and down several sets of stairs until they were deep underground. Here, the waves relentlessly battered the western side of the citadel, and their thunder rumbled rhythmically through the prison. The jailer met them and unbarred a thick, banded door, which screamed on its rusted hinges.

"Come on. Out with you!" the jailer growled.

A filthy man emerged with his hands chained together and his shoulders hunched in exhaustion. Before Ibrahim could get a look at him, the prisoner was shoved into a dark stone chamber with a table and chairs, at which Henri, Ibrahim, and the knight were seated. The jailer attached the man's chained hands to a ring high up on the wall, so his arms stretched over his head.

Ibrahim stood suddenly. "My lord, may I approach the accused?"

Henri nodded, his eyes narrowed with venom. Ibrahim slowly walked to the prisoner and looked at his face. His eyes were blackened, and a deep gash on his temple still oozed dark blood. His head lolled forward as if the effort to hold it up were too great.

"Marcouf?" Ibrahim whispered. "Is that you?"

"Ibrahim..." Marcouf groaned. Ibrahim turned to the table where Henri and the Templar sat.

"How did you come by this man? He is a resident of Ma'an Barid, one of the late Lord Rogier's villages to the north."

Brother Alaran turned to Henri. "Is this true, Lord Henri?"

Henri's wide-eyed look of blank ignorance darted from Ibrahim to the knight. "It... it must be true, although I have not met this man before."

"He toppled a cart of grain on the day that Lord Rogier died," Ibrahim said, forehead wrinkled in thought. "But I do not remember him being around the house without other people close by, and never did he go inside."

Again, Brother Alaran turned to Henri. "Lord Henri, what is your assessment?"

"I... whatever Ibrahim says is the truth."

Brother Alaran pressed his mouth in a disapproving line. "My lord, I would prefer to continue questioning this man without your steward present. This is a Christian matter."

Ibrahim looked at Henri with a spark of defiance, but when his master asked him to leave the room, he walked out without comment. After he left, he heard a howl of pain as the questioning began.

Marcouf Charrettier was a recent settler in Outremer, having moved to the village of Ma'an Barid two years prior. Ibrahim had assigned the city dragoman to help the man's family integrate into the village and find work for him. Although Marcouf seemed shifty and prone to complain, he hardly struck Ibrahim as a murderer, especially of a nobleman, which brought with it the penalty of death in the severest and most painful manner.

The door opened after a while, and Henri walked out, pale-faced and twitchy. Brother Alaran followed him as the jailer took Marcouf's limp body down from the ring in the wall and brushed past Ibrahim without comment.

"My lord?" Ibrahim asked.

"The prisoner says that another man did the deed, but he could not identify him by name or description. Brother Alaran says that all the guilty ones try to blame their crime on another. Marcouf will go before the citizens' council to present his case and be executed if he found guilty, although, in my mind, the guilt is written all over his countenance."

"Marcouf Charretier was with me when your father was murdered," said Ibrahim. "He is one of your own citizens, my lord!"

"We do not know exactly when my father was murdered," Henri said. "But you may testify for him at the citizens' council."

"The word of an Arab will not be effective against a Templar knight. He has a wife and five children in Ma'an Barid who will become destitute if he dies. They will starve."

"And that is his punishment," Henri said firmly, finding his resolve. "Not only will he give his eye for my father's eye, but he will die with the knowledge that he has failed his wife and children. If I could have executed him myself in that room, I would have done it."

Ibrahim looked at Henri for a moment. The boy's expression was hard.

"My lord, please do not do this. Not until there is further evidence. Do not throw this man's family out—"

"I am the authority, not you, Ibrahim," Henri cut him off. "It shall be as I say. Do not argue against my decisions again."

Ibrahim could see that Henri's hands were shaking slightly, and he bowed his head respectfully. "Yes, my lord."

26

— • —

I t was the persistent noise that woke Sidika from her sleep, or perhaps she could feel the intensity of the grief in the next room, even in her dreams. Bright moonlight falling through the open window illuminated the indent in her father's straw-stuffed pallet where he had lain, the coverlet now thrown back. The peg on the wall where his robe hung was empty.

In the next room, she heard the noise again. Moaning. This was the third night that he crept from their room to cry alone. Hugging a wool blanket about her shoulders, she padded on bare feet into the main room of the house and sat down next to him.

Tamrat wiped his nose with the sleeve of his robe. "I am sorry I woke you, my dear," he sniffed. He wore his blue and white *tallit* – his prayer shawl - draped over the crown of his head.

"I was not sleeping," she lied.

"I miss them. I just... miss them!" He buried his face in his hands, and the sobs shook him so hard that Sidika feared he would fall over. "I miss your brother's smile," he went on. "Your mother's brave spirit...."

Sidika put her arm around his shoulders, laying her curly head on his shoulder, and felt his sobs subside. Slowly, Tamrat put a hand on her hair.

"You are a blessing, Sidika," he whispered. "I could not face this alone, and here you are. You have lost two mothers now."

"And two brothers," she whispered, "for I am convinced the boy at the river on the day we were attacked was a brother or a cousin. No one but my own kin would have risked so much to keep me alive."

The harsh, cold light of the moon drove through the cracks around their wooden door and the skylight cover on the ceiling. Sidika stood and pulled at the hemp rope, which slowly lifted the skylight open. The silvery light flooded the room, painting stark shadows on the floor.

"Look, Father." she pointed to the perfect round disc. "Mother is there, watching us now. She will come back every night to check on us, and when she is too tired, she will rest in the darkness knowing that we are taking care of each other."

Tamrat wiped his eyes. "That is a beautiful heresy, daughter."

Sidika looked up thoughtfully. "Horse Aunty believed in the Great Sky. Perhaps it is not true, but the idea that every natural thing can represent a loved one gives me comfort."

"Where is your brother, then?" Tamrat asked, and Sidika's face lit with a smile.

"Every time I watch the swallows in the evening, I think of Dejen, flying over our heads with such lightness and joy."

Fresh tears sprang into Tamrat's eyes and dribbled into his beard. "I am blessed, blessed to have you with me, Daughter. Will you take up your brother's work and continue in his footsteps? Will you carry on the healing knowledge that your mother gave you?"

"Yes, Father," Sidika said.

The prospect seemed too weighty to discuss now, while her mother and brother's deaths still pounded at the doors of her heart every day. She was not as good a student as Dejen. Instead of collecting herbs with Sara, she often disappeared into the hills to climb trees or explore the limestone caves in the crags. She knew she had squandered her time with them.

"I shall be your son and your daughter for you, and perhaps you will find a new wife—"

"No! Sara and I were together since I was fifteen years old. The moment I saw her collecting almonds at her uncle's farm, I knew my fate was sealed. I do not wish to discuss such things, although I know you do it to try to be helpful."

Helpful. Now that her mother and her best friend were taken by fever, she must care for Tamrat, the animals, and their house. Her grief was held at bay by the shadow of responsibility that solidified every day and the knowledge that her childhood was over. Sara had managed to quietly care for her family and the health of the village. Dejen had assisted Tamrat in his work and hunted meat for them to eat. What value did she bring to this family? As she often did, she wondered what had possessed Tamrat and Sara to take her in. A street urchin, twice orphaned. A thief and a Turk. A girl.

"Come, Father," She pulled Tamrat to his feet. "A night of sleep is what you need. It is the medicine that God provides. I still have some of Mother's valerian root tonic, which will help to calm your mind. And tomorrow, let us set about finding a way that I can learn to mix dyes as Dejen did."

She pushed him gently back to his bed. For her, grief would have to wait.

27

— · —

HOUSE OF MAFEO DI ORSINI, ACRE. SEPTEMBER 1290

E mre heard the loud complaint of iron on iron as the door to his prison swung open slowly. Mafeo stood in the entrance, his trim figure silhouetted by the flickering oil lamps behind him. Even though the light was not bright, Emre shielded his eyes. It had been a week since he had seen anything brighter than the smoky flicker of a tallow candle.

"Well?" Mafeo demanded. "Are you ready to come out, or would you prefer another few days in the hole?"

A few days earlier, Emre would have haughtily told Mafeo to leave him in his cell, which was wide enough for him to sit, but not to lie down. The extra days had changed his mind, however. Acre sat on a coastal plain, and the cell underneath Mafeo's house was soggy and brackish. The damp penetrated his bones and he was cold, stiff, and starting to sniffle. He bowed his head penitently.

"I am sorry, Master Mafeo, for my disrespect toward your concubine. Truly she is both genteel and comely to look upon. The words that I spoke were neither called for nor true."

Mafeo shifted his weight from foot to foot. "Well, they were not called for; that much is correct. You are my property, and if I tell you to keep your mouth shut, you will comply. I should leave you in here until your teeth fall out and you lose your sight, but you are the best manservant I have had in a dozen years. If you promise to behave, I shall restore your position and have your wounds treated."

I am not a manservant, Emre thought bitterly, *I am your slave, and there is a difference.* Still, he held his comment and bowed again. His years of hiding his grief and anger in the Mamluk meydan had trained him for this.

"Get him cleaned up," Mafeo grunted to the jailer. "I am to meet my betrothed in three days, and I cannot have him looking like this."

Rough hands pulled him up the stairs and into the brilliant sunlight of Mafeo's small courtyard, and he was tossed unceremoniously into the stable next to a pen of rooting pigs. He picked himself up painfully and limped toward the kitchen. Stealing a honey cake from an unattended tray, he then slouched toward the bathhouse to try to scrub away the week of vermin and human filth from the hole.

The bathhouse was warm and welcoming. The flickering oil lamps soothed his eyes, and although the domed ceiling did not contain the lavish mosaics of wealthier houses, this one had two pools of differently scented water. He was stripped of his filthy clothes and scrubbed vigorously with sand and rough woven cloths until his skin glowed pink and raw. Two slaves picked the nits from his scalp until the tortuous itching no longer bothered him and then washed his hair in rose-scented soap. After that, the barber arrived to shave him and attempted to trim his hair, which curled wildly around his ears.

The barber then examined the red, swelling cuts on his feet, prescribing a poultice of dung, fenugreek, and macerated sage leaves to be applied while the moon remained full. Emre refused.

"I demand an Arab physician!" Emre yelled until Mafeo stomped into the room, hollering for silence.

The barber puffed his chest with indignation. "Is this young man your slave or your heir? There is nothing wrong with this poultice. It will draw the bad humors from the flesh."

"Zahed, you will do as the barber tells you or return to the hole," Mafeo threatened.

"Master, he wishes me to put animal dung on my wounds!" Emre insisted. To his ears, it sounded strange when Mafeo used his Mamluk name, but he had decided not to correct it. His real name had become his special secret. "This medicine of the Franj only causes more pestilence, not less!"

Mafeo took two steps across the room and slapped Emre hard across the face. "I will break your pretty face open, and then the barber will put dung on it too," he hissed, then rounded on the barber.

"You would have my servant smell of a stable when I am off to meet my new wife? Find another treatment, or a Saracen physician will be brought. I wish no harm to come to him."

The barber murmured an acknowledgment and bowed fearfully as Mafeo turned to leave. Everyone knew that those who disagreed with Mafeo di Orsini could find their house burned and their children in a debtor's prison. Emre smirked, for it was enjoyable to see someone else on the receiving end of Mafeo's notorious temper. He spared a moment of pity for Mafeo's new betrothed, but he was joyful about the upcoming union. With Mafeo distracted by a wife, he would have less time to beat his slaves.

***

Two days later, Emre stood silently behind Mafeo as they waited in the anteroom of a finely furnished house near the Venetian Quarter. It wasn't the finest house that Emre had visited in his year as a slave within Acre's walls, but he also knew that the family of Maron-en-Rouergue had another, larger home in the hills, plus many villages to the north and east of Acre. Emre sighed. Once Mafeo's household merged with his new wife's, he would probably move to the country, where the air might be easier to breathe, but there was far less amusement. His eyes glazed over as he thought back to his attempted escape from the attack on Tripoli and the life as Badahir's heir that he had left behind.

Two days after Tripoli burned, a band of Bedouins had found Emre wearing the clothes of a dead Franj and fainting with thirst near a dried streambed. They gave him a waterskin, assessed his physical state, and promptly whisked him to the slave market in Acre, where the Mamluk slave buyers prowled the pens looking for young men who would make good recruits. Well known as Badahir's heir, he crouched in a corner and hugged his knees to his chest, shaking and coughing and generally trying his best to look ill and unappealing until the Mamluk buyers left.

Mafeo, however, had seen the whole thing and bought Emre immediately. The moment they crossed into his new master's courtyard, Emre, with his hands still bound, was thrown to the ground and Mafeo's guards kicked and struck him with sticks until both his eyes swelled shut and he spat blood. Mafeo watched, his arms crossed.

"You are a liar," Mafeo said. "You will receive this same beating every day until you understand who I am. I have men castrated if they cheat me in business. I have whores strangled if they defy me. I will take your life from you as fast as I take the life of a beetle beneath my shoe. I require a man who is discreet and vicious, and you, my lying Mamluk, will suit perfectly. If you can be broken."

Emre closed his eyes, thinking of the days that followed. He had suffered beating after beating as Mafeo attempted to tame him, and finally, he had succumbed to reluctant acceptance. Emre burned. He always accepted eventually.

Next to him, Mafeo shifted and fidgeted, snapping his fingers irritably. "Zahed, bring me some wine. This young brat has kept me waiting until my mouth feels like dust."

Before Emre could move, he heard a door close and a young man came bounding down a staircase, adjusting his sash. He was strikingly handsome, with light brown skin, black hair that curled at the nape of his neck, and green eyes that were so pale they looked distant and indifferent. He wore dark blue hose, a close-fitting white tunic belted with a wide black sash of silk, and a ring of silver with a large golden-colored stone on his right hand. A long dove-gray robe edged with black and silver stitching flapped around his sides as he walked. He glanced briefly at Emre and appraised Mafeo with a cool stare. Emre held his breath. No one looked at Mafeo in this way unless they were very secure in their own power.

Behind him, an older Arab man in a fine black thawb and taqiyya walked sedately down the staircase and stood at a respectful distance, his hands folded at his waist. Mafeo smiled ingratiatingly.

"Well, my boy, shall we begin? Let us send our slaves to the cellar to fetch us wine—"

"Ibrahim is my steward, Signore Mafeo, not my slave," the young man interrupted. "He will be present and proactive throughout these negotiations."

Mafeo's eyes widened. "A Saracen steward! Well, considering the circumstances, I should not be surprised. Come, Lord Henri, let us begin anew as if I said nothing before."

This woman must be very worthy, for Emre had never seen Mafeo show deference to anyone, not from the negotiating table to the throne room. Lord Henri inclined his head and strode toward a delicately carved door leading off the main room.

"I want you to watch him and that steward of his," Mafeo whispered to Emre as they followed slowly.

"But Master," Emre replied, "my understanding of Latin is not strong, and he will surely negotiate in that language."

"Never mind that. Just watch their faces, and if one of them tries to reach for a weapon, you will defend me."

Emre nodded, and they entered a room tiled entirely in delicately cut mosaic stones of veined black and white marble, with a large stone fireplace against one wall. The windows were paned with pieces of thick amber glass, which let in golden shafts of sunlight. Lord Henri gestured to several chairs around a polished olivewood table, and wine was brought.

"First," Lord Henri leaned over the table, "betrothal to my mother implies that you will be gaining her portion of the estate, not any part of the estate that my father left to me and my sisters. Although I have not yet come of age, I am the heir of Rogier of Maron, and therefore you have no paternal rights over me."

Mafeo seemed taken back by this but smiled. "Perhaps there is a misunderstanding, young man—"

"You may call me 'Lord Henri or Viscount Henri.'"

"Ah, of course. Lord Henri, it was my understanding that it would be your sister's hand we negotiated for on this day."

"My mother felt that my sister is too young, and I agree. I will promise Blanche to you, but she will not marry until she is fifteen, which is nearly a year from now if you are willing to wait."

From where he stood, Emre watched Lord Henri. If the young man felt ill at ease negotiating his own mother's marriage contract, he did not show it. As he leaned across the table, the lean muscles of his back moved beneath his robe, and Emre felt his heart race as he took in the sharp cut of his jaw. Mafeo had told Emre to watch, but he hadn't told him not to appreciate. He felt eyes on him and glanced up. The old steward was looking at him, his deep-set brown eyes troubled.

Lord Henri and Mafeo haggled back and forth, and Emre grew faint with the heat until the door opened with a blast of cool air, and two somberly dressed Arab men entered the room.

"These are my masters of the law, signore. They are here to witness and record all we agree upon," Lord Henri explained.

"Do you not also bring a priest to witness?" Mafeo asked. He glanced nervously at the two men, who leaned over the marriage contract, their quills scratching.

"We will bring the final documents to the Patriarch and have him approve."

"The Patriarch? Surely he is not involved?"

Emre noticed sweat beginning to bead on his master's temples.

"Why, yes, signore," Lord Henri said sweetly. "Nothing but the best for my mother. She is a kind woman, and her beauty is legendary. And there is her money, of course."

"Of course. Well, as you know, my family has fathered popes, and that blood runs through my loins. She cannot object to such an alliance. Of this, I am sure." Mafeo pulled himself up and, for a moment, seemed to gain lost confidence.

Ibrahim rose as if signaled and spoke to a servant, who turned and ran from the room.

"What is this?" Mafeo asked, glancing at one of the two sheathed daggers that Emre always kept in his sash. "What are you doing?"

Lord Henri smiled. "I only wish to ensure that my mother feels comfortable with these proceedings, signore. Forgive me – it is a Saracen custom. We do not marry our women away to men that they do not desire."

The door opened, and the servant escorted a woman inside. She was tall and willowy, with long fingers and creamy brown skin. She wore a floor-length dress of black and silver brocade, and a purple wimple covered her hair. Her dark eyes surveyed every man in the room, and she adjusted her head cover modestly. Lord Henri took her hand and turned to Mafeo.

"Mother, this is Mafeo di Orsini, who asks for your hand in marriage. What do you think of him?"

Now, the beads of sweat were dripping from Mafeo's temples into the collar of his red velvet cotehardie. The woman gave him an unreadable look, and Mafeo struggled to hold her gaze. Emre watched, his mouth hanging open in fascination. Then Lord Henri's mother lowered her eyes, curtseyed gracefully, and held out her hand, which Mafeo took in his sweaty palm.

"Would this alliance be advantageous to the Maron family, my son?" she asked, her voice rich and mellow.

"I believe so, and my men of the law have not started yelling yet, which bodes well."

"Signore Mafeo," she said, her French lightly accented. "Will you promise to be the father my girls need right now and protect them and secure marriages that benefit all of the family?"

Mafeo stared at her, entranced. Although she had a tall seventeen-year-old son standing next to her, in the amber glow of the glass windows, she looked ageless.

"I do promise, my lady. It is my greatest wish to secure the interests of this noble and unique family."

Lady Nasira nodded slowly, then gave her son a long look. She bowed again and retreated from the room with the men staring after her.

"Does she approve?" Mafeo breathed. "Tell me that she does, for I think I have just seen an angel that walks upon the earth. Truly, the holy virgin herself was not half as pleasing to look upon!"

Lord Henri rolled his eyes, and Emre saw Ibrahim's fists clutch the edge of the table until his knuckles whitened.

Lord Henri turned to his lawyers. "Draft up the marriage proposal according to the terms you have heard from Signore Mafeo and me. When my mother has signed it in her hand, we shall take it to the Patriarch."

"Her hand?" Mafeo said weakly. "She can write her name?"

Lord Henri stood. "My mother can read and write, as can my sisters and myself. And now, if you please, I must ride out to my estate to see to some urgent matters."

Ibrahim, the steward, quickly saw them out, casting a critical, lingering look at Mafeo before closing the door.

"Come, Zahed," Mafeo said, frowning. "We have much to do."

"Yes, my lord," Emre muttered. The young lord of al-Hadiqa had just managed to force his master into an arrangement that he had no control over. Perhaps a life in the country outside of Acre's walls would not be so bad after all.

28

— · —

FAJAR, THE HILLS OF IDMIT. SEPTEMBER 1290

"Very good," Tamrat exclaimed. "Very good indeed, Daughter! No one would know the difference between my hand and yours! Truly you were born with a gift that took me a lifetime to achieve!"

Sidika blushed and set her quill down. She adjusted the blue and white scarf tied around her unruly hair and looked around their tiny house. Day faded to dusk, and the sky above her father's skylight slowly turned pale gray, deepening the shadows inside. Parchments, seashells filled with powdered dyes, pots of inky water, horsehair brushes, knives, blotters, and quills covered their simple wooden table. In a corner, shelves bowed under the weight of unbound manuscripts. She yawned and stretched to relieve the cramp between her shoulders.

"Father, the light is fading, and it is time for me to prepare supper. Shall we put this away for the evening?"

Tamrat looked up at the skylight and then patted Sidika on the shoulder. "Let me make the meal this evening, my dear. You have earned a rest. Clear the table, and I shall cook something grand for you!"

Sidika crossed her arms with an amused smile. "Porridge and onions? Because that is all we have. Father, I must go hunting. I know you do not like it, but we have no meat."

Tamrat's smile faltered only for a moment. "Ah, but it shall be the best porridge you have ever tasted. I shall sing to it while I cook. It deepens the flavor!"

Sidika did not reply, her brow furrowed in thought.

Tamrat sighed. "Daughter, you know that I have nothing against you hunting, but I worry about what would happen if another hunter discovers you. You could be taken advantage of far away in the hills, with no one to help you."

"If you trust me to kill a beast, do you not trust me to fell a man if I must?" she asked. "He is merely a different kind of beast."

"I hope you never have to," Tamrat said over his shoulder. He walked to where they kept their tabun, a little clay oven they kept outside to cook without overheating the house. The coals in the tabun still glowed dimly from the morning meal, and he stoked them, tossing a few pats of dried dung on the fire before replacing the lid. Sidika had gathered the fuel herself, and Tamrat felt a pang of guilt. She did too much while he stayed lost in his work – too much for one young girl.

If only Dejen were here to help.

He shook the thought away. He must remain cheerful for Sidika. He must not let his mind go to that dark place that overtook him when he thought of his son.

When the porridge had finished cooking, well-seasoned with plenty of coarse salt and fragrant herbs, Tamrat brought the steaming pot back into the house. Sidika had cleared the table of their tools and set out two bowls, a rushlight, and two clay cups of heavily watered wine. The two settings looked forlorn on their large table, and Tamrat hesitated, disappeared into their small room, then returned with something in his hand.

"This is for you, my daughter. For your hair," he said awkwardly.

Sidika took the delicate bundle from him – a slender hair ribbon of lavender silk with a complicated mosaic of silver threads stitched into each end – and held it up to the light.

"Father, we cannot afford such things," she whispered, looking at the ribbon.

Tamrat gently removed the rough scarf tied around her head. "Lavender will look the best against your hair," he said. "Now, put it on so I can admire my good taste in women's paraphernalia."

Reverently, Sidika braided the long ribbon through her fawn-colored curls and tied it.

Tamrat smiled. "My beautiful girl. You could grace the court of a king!"

"Father, why?"

Tamrat patted her on the hand. "You have been such a good daughter, and you have lost much. You deserve something frivolous, like the grand ladies of Acre have."

Sidika smiled and kissed him on the cheek. "But I would rather have Mother and Dejen back again, Father. I would rather have them than all of the gold and hair ribbons in Palestine."

Tamrat smiled sadly. She was fifteen and more beautiful than she realized, with slender limbs and large hazel eyes set wide on her face. Her rich olive skin glowed in the lamplight, and Tamrat wondered, as he had every day since she came to live with him, who her birth parents had been and why they would abandon a child so fair and intelligent. Already two village men had come to him to speak about her. Sara would have known what to do, but he felt helplessly unable to meet the task of finding her a husband.

It was his own fault. He had chosen to live in this village, separate from the community of other Jews who could support him... whose sons he could observe for potential matches. But who could he possibly match with such a girl? He sighed and set his spoon down.

"I miss them too, my daughter. I miss your mother so much that it hurts me, like a sickness in my body. When I think of Dejen, I want to die with him. But I have you, my dear," he patted her hand again, "and you make my life worth living."

He looked around their modest house. The son of a prominent moneylender, Tamrat could have gone into the family trade and made himself rich, but he had been a studious and quiet child. A beautifully written phrase interested him more than a palace in the city. To him, a blank paper and a full dish of ink contained more value than fine clothes. In the cities, Jews had to work in the unpopular trades, and Tamrat knew that the only way he might be able to fulfill his dream of learning to scribe was if he studied at the great scriptoriums in Cairo, where it didn't matter that he was not Christian. When his skill increased, he returned to Acre and eventually became one of the most well-respected scribes north of Jerusalem.

He had a few Franj clients, but they preferred the flat and heavy-lined look of their Western artists. Tamrat gladly traded the lost revenue from the wealthy Franj residents of Acre so that he could take commissions from patrons in Damascus or Cairo, even as far as Baghdad, who appreciated his style of art and prose, which he had taught his children.

His children.

He pushed away the ache in his heart that rose whenever he thought of his adopted son. Dejen's spirit shone on his face as if his heart was a thing on fire, catching everyone around it. Had he lived, Dejen would have taken over Tamrat's work as a scribe and done good for the world. Sidika, trapped up here in the hills, was also trapped in her past, a refugee from everyone who had left their mark on her. She trusted rarely and let her true self show even less. Where her brother gave himself freely to everyone around him, Sidika pulled within herself, like an anemone on the rocks of the sea. How could he give her away to a village man, where no one knew how to read or write, and women were worked until their backs hunched and their skin dried from the relentless sun and wind?

Tamrat sighed again. "You may hunt, Sidika, but you must promise to disguise yourself as a boy so that you will not be followed by any of the village men when you go out."

Sidika grinned.

"And you must not do anything to endanger your hands because they are your livelihood if anything should happen to me."

Sidika's smile vanished, and she looked at him seriously. He was all she had left. He must take care as well, or else she would be left alone, and who would marry an orphaned Turkish girl who knew how to scribe? Tamrat and Sara had educated her, creating a girl who was almost an impossibility. He feared they had burdened her with a future of loneliness.

He put his arm around her, and she rested her head on his shoulder.

"I love you always, my daughter," he said.

"And I you," she whispered back.

29

— · —

AL-HADIQA, ACRE. SEPTEMBER 1290

"What do you mean, the servants are unhappy?" Henri asked, incredulous. He sat at his table in the great hall, eating a late meal after a full day of arguing with Genoese warehouse owners. After a frustrating day in the city, Henri had retreated to al-Hadiqa to nurse his injured pride and plan a new route of attack. The seeds of a plan were growing as he picked at a platter of venison roasted with pomegranate seeds when Ibrahim interrupted him.

"It is as I say, my lord," Ibrahim repeated calmly. "There is considerable malcontent among the servants of late."

"Well, why?"

Ibrahim paused, choosing his words carefully. "Your father had a different manner of interacting with them, my lord. He knew their names and their families. He protected them and often spent time with them."

Henri glanced at the young serving girl standing in the corner, still and frightened as a rabbit.

"I never noted my father doing anything particularly special. They are servants. They should be happy that they have paid work and are not kept as slaves."

Ibrahim kept his face impassive. Turning to the girl, he smiled lightly. "Harra, would you please give Lord Henri and me some time to speak alone?" She hurried from the room, and Ibrahim turned back to his new master.

"Your father always took the servants' complaints seriously, my lord, for without them, we would surely be unable to continue to live in Acre. Your family is unique. You do not have a large household of cousins and uncles and half-siblings here like they do in the other great houses, and your father sired no living bastards that we know of to take on as helpers. These servants keep the estate running."

Henri snorted and returned to his meal. "I keep this estate running," he declared, waving a jewel-handled silver spoon at Ibrahim. "And if they wish to leave, they are welcome to find another master who pays them as well as I. We can always hire new servants."

"It is easy enough to hire servants, yes," said Ibrahim, with as much control as he could muster, "but it is not easy to train new servants. It is not easy to find people who will remain loyal to you." He took a deep breath. "There is another problem. Your militia are saying that they will leave the estate this night."

Henri was dumbstruck, still holding his spoon aloft. "Leave? All of them?! Where will they go?"

"Sir Parsiprestre says he will return to the Occitan, and three men are going with him, including the cellarer. Sir Itier and his brother have decided to join the household of Lord Vauquelin, and the others have not decided where they will travel."

"Well, tell them they cannot leave!" Henri yelled. "Have they not sworn fealty to my father?"

"Yes, but not to *you*, my lord. You may yet be able to convince them to stay, but you will have to act fast."

"What is it that they want? Do I not give them clothes and food and shelter? Are they bored? Tell them to go raid a Saracen village!"

Ibrahim tactfully did not answer. Turning to leave, he paused at the door.

"My lord, militias come and go, but many of your servants and their families have remained with the estate since you were a child, even though other landowners attempted to lure them away. Have you never wondered why they did not leave?"

Henri felt his anger rising. His father's shadow saturated every stone in the house and stalked his every move. "I am the master here, not my father!" he yelled after Ibrahim. "He was not a perfect man!"

But Ibrahim was gone.

"By all accounts, my father was more interested in the welfare of his servants than his own son," Henri grumbled. He tossed his spoon on the table. "Harra!" he bellowed, and the little serving girl trotted into the room, bowing low. "Clean this up and lock the silver away."

He found Sir Parsiprestre and his men in the dooryard, saddling their horses, which they had laden with supplies and their personal belongings.

"Sir Parsiprestre, where are you going?" Henri demanded.

"We are leaving," Sir Parsiprestre said without looking up as he strung the bridle on his horse.

"I have not given you and these men my blessing to go."

Sir Parsiprestre snorted. "I do not require your blessing to piss, little Hamza."

"I am the master of this estate now, and you will address me as 'lord,' and if you and these men leave these grounds, I will ensure that no knight or noble of Acre hires you after me!" Henri seethed.

"We will return to our homeland, thus saving you the trouble of trying to sabotage our prospects, *Lord* Hamza."

"But... but why are you leaving? What do you want?" Henri hated the note of desperation in his voice.

"I have no wish to remain employed by an indulged tyrant and watch everything your father built be tossed away like the contents of a chamber pot. I pray for the health and safety of your villagers and hope that your honored mother and sisters will find husbands soon, although not the one of your choosing. Mafeo di Orsini is a snake if I ever saw one."

Henri reeled with rage. While his father lived, these men had obeyed without question, treating him and the family with respect. As the men mounted their horses, he dashed into the stable and snatched a spare sword from the wall.

Sir Parsiprestre had his back turned when Henri lunged at him. At a shout from one of his men, the knight turned in time to block Henri's blow with his own weapon, then pushed the young man to the ground.

"You may be a fair fighter on the practice course, Hamza, but you are no match for a real warrior," Sir Parsiprestre hissed, leaning on Henri's chest. "You are a vain, spoiled princeling, and you do your family dishonor by continuing to live. The only thing that stayed my hand from slitting your throat as soon as Lord Rogier died is my respect for him, Ibrahim, and Lady Nasira, who is too good for all of you."

Quick as a scorpion, Henri's sword slashed out, not at Sir Parsiprestre, but at the man's horse. The animal screamed and staggered, its left fetlock bleeding where Henri had severed the tendon. Henri struck again, thrusting his sword into the animal's belly. Sir Parsiprestre cried out and would have run his sword through Henri's heart at that moment had his men not grasped him by the arms and pulled him back.

"Parsiprestre, stop!" Sir Itier yelled. "Kill this young fool, and Brother Georges Languedoc will have you hunted and hung from the walls of the city!" Then he turned and smacked Henri across the head with the pommel of his sword.

***

Henri awoke alone in the dooryard, blinking at the darkening sky. Sir Parsiprestre's lamed horse lay near him in the dust, its throat slit. Nearby, the hulking bodies of three other horses rested in a growing pool of black blood, their bellies opened, and their bowels spilled into the dirt in glistening cascades. Inside the stable, Salih, the groom, was screaming.

Henri tried to sit up, but his head exploded in sparks and thunder, and he fell back again. His clothes were damp, and he smelled urine. Sir Parsiprestre and the other men must have anointed him while he was unconscious.

Ibrahim ran from the house and shook him by the shoulders. "My lord, do you live?"

"No..." Henri groaned.

Ibrahim scrambled over to inspect the dead horses, then into the stable. Salih was moaning and crying as Ibrahim led him out, holding him up with an arm around his back.

"I was returning the master's horses from grazing," Salih yelled, his voice high and terrified, "and I came back just as those devils left! Why did they do this, Ibrahim ustadh? Why would they do such a thing?!"

"Peace, Salih, they are only horses," Ibrahim clucked at him. "No lives of men were lost."

"Men?" Salih shrieked. "I care not for men! My children! These beasts are my children! Why do these people take everything from me!" He dropped to his knees and grabbed two fistfuls of dust, which he poured over his bald head in anguish. "Again, they take everything from me!"

Henri raised his head. "Does Raven live?" he asked thickly.

Ibrahim shot him a silencing look. "Come, my lord, let us get you to your bed. Sir Parsiprestre stole your father's horse and took his displeasure out on these animals but spared your life, God be praised." They walked into the house, Henri leaning on Ibrahim while Salih draped himself over the belly of a slaughtered horse and cried loudly behind them.

30

AL-HADIQA, ACRE. SEPTEMBER 1290

All the rest of that week, Henri avoided riding whenever possible and kept to himself. Without Sir Parsiprestre and the militia, the estate and villages were at risk from raids. Without trade allies, the merchants were already starting to move against him, quietly "forgetting" to invite him and Ibrahim to their meetings at the Court of the Chain, where most of the city's high commerce occurred. Although his mother and Ibrahim were patient, Henri could sense their frustration, and it chafed at him.

Only a month after becoming the master of my estate, and I am losing control of everything, he thought dully one day, staring into another empty wine cup. *Perhaps everyone is right. I am only suitable for bedding noblewomen and spending money.*

Nasira tolerated Henri's sulking with dignity. She had expected this kind of response. The Marons of the Rouergue in Francia ruled a fief on the rough edges of King Philippe's control, where for millennia, the princes and dukes had fought battles of pride and honor to protect their lands. Nasira knew that the Marons never forgot an insult because it was essential to their survival. But her son was half of her blood. He would come around. For all his attempts to be as hard and strong as his father, Henri could never hurt someone without being agonized by guilt.

Ibrahim gave Salih several days off to rest and insisted that Henri accompany him to the market to purchase more horses to replace those that Sir Parsiprestre killed or stole.

"Buying horses and camels for the fields is a servant's work," Henri grumbled as Ibrahim led the way through the crowded animal market.

The old steward resolutely marched Henri past the picket lines of foreign-bred destriers, past the graceful coursers and the palfreys, to the large corrals of less handsome beasts destined to pull sledges of hay and power the oil presses.

Ibrahim discussed the qualities that he was looking for; a gentle disposition, strong back, bright eyes, nothing older than five summers. After he had chosen several mature animals and one soft-eyed foal that pleased him, he asked Henri to negotiate a price for the beasts, which the young man did sullenly. The horse merchant grinned when Henri agreed to pay three times the animals' worth.

"I hope to do business with you again, my friend!" he said, slapping the scowling youth on the back.

"My lord, we will be out of money in a year if you negotiate like that," Ibrahim said, shaking his head.

Henri snorted and rubbed his temple, which was still tender and bruised from Sir Itier's blow. "If you are such an expert, why did you not intervene?"

"Because your father and Sir Geoffroi always intervened, and you never learned anything," Ibrahim said firmly, tying the animals to his saddle. "You are the master of the estate, and in this early stage, you should always know who is spending your money for you. You trust me implicitly, but should you?"

"My father trusted you. Should I throw you out of the house and find someone I trust on my own experience instead?" he challenged, and Ibrahim smiled.

"You may do that if you wish, but I have worked for your family since before your birth. It will be hard to find someone who knows the estate as I do. However, I will tell you if I think you are making a poor decision. If I did not, I would be doing you a disservice. You may wish instead to have a steward who only tells you what you wish to hear."

A sharp cry interrupted them, and Ibrahim's expression darkened. He cast a sideways glance at Henri, put a hand on his back, and guided him through the crowd toward the noise.

"Where are we going? Saint Anthony's gate is in the other direction," Henri said, his voice filled with impatience.

"There is something you must see," Ibrahim said. "It is another thing that your father shielded you from."

They pushed through the dense crowd, and the screaming grew louder. Ibrahim nudged men out of the way until they arrived in front of several circular hedges of sharp sticks, their pointed tips jabbing in the air. One pen held men, another, young boys, and the third contained women and girls.

A woman was on her knees, her hands bound, and her tear-bloated face pressed against the hedge. She looked toward the pen of young boys and wailed in a language that Henri could not understand.

"What is going on?" Henri demanded. "Will someone not quiet that woman?"

Ibrahim pointed. A boy of about eight was having the ropes on his hands cut away. A man in long black robes and a black keffiyeh took the child's hand and led him away while two other boys were also similarly removed. The little boy looked back at the crying woman and dissolved into tears, but Henri could not understand his words.

"What does the child say?" he asked.

Ibrahim shook his head. "That is probably his mother, and they are probably from Armenia or the Cuman steppes. The boy has been sold into the Mamluk army. He will train every day until he is ready to fight, then he will die for the sultan, having forgotten who his parents are. The sultan will make him fight the Franj or the Mongols, and if he distinguishes himself, he will receive riches and land as his reward. Someday, you may meet this boy on the field of battle."

"Slavery is a reality, Ibrahim," Henri said, crossing his arms. "These people are spoils of war. If they did not wish to become slaves, they should have left their village before it was ravaged."

"You speak as if they had a choice," Ibrahim said, looking at Henri with liquid brown eyes. "You have the choice and the means to leave, Lord Henri. You have other homes to go to, but most do not."

Henri crossed his arms petulantly. "Well," he began, but before he could say any more, a well-dressed Franj merchant stepped up to the crowd and cleared his throat.

"Of course, it is not unusual to see such displays in the slave market, is it not, my friends?" A few of the men nearby nodded their heads. The merchant continued. "As you can see, this woman," he gestured to the mother, coughing and blubbering into her bound hands, "has strong maternal instincts. She will make an excellent wet nurse, or perhaps a sow for your own bastards, eh?"

A laugh rose from the crowd of onlookers. Eventually, a wealthy Venetian merchant purchased the woman, and led away.

"What will happen to her?" Henri asked Ibrahim, and the old man sighed.

"She will never see her child or her home again. She will work for that Venetian signore as a slave in his house, and he may take her to his bed against her will if he so wishes, for she is his property now."

Henri felt a flush of discomfort rise to his face as he thought about his mother. His father had refused to buy slaves for al-Hadiqa, and Nasira was honored in their home, despite her low-born status. Was giving his mother away to an unsuitable marriage just another type of slavery?

"Ibrahim," he said, anxious to change the subject, "why was Salih so upset about the horses? Horses die often, and I have seen him slaughter a horse when it was lamed. I do not understand his reaction."

Ibrahim was quiet for a moment as he led Henri back to their waiting mounts.

"Salih had a wife and seven children some years ago. When the knights of Acre came to his village one day, they found his wife working in a field, and they raped her. All of them did. Salih tried to stop them, but one of the men ran him through with his blade, and then they killed his wife and children, even the two babes. They killed his goat and his mare, but the mare had a foal, and somehow they did not see it, so the foal was spared. It was the only thing left living in his home.

"Salih was fevered for days, and no one would come near to help him, for surely he was cursed by God to have such a thing happen to him. The foal lay down next to him for warmth, and slowly he healed. Since that time, Salih has always preferred to be with horses instead of people. His horses are like children to him. He talks to them, and they understand him. Seeing the horses slaughtered and you with your sword lying beside you must have reminded him of that day when his family was murdered."

"Why would he live in Acre with a Franj family if he was so terrorized?" Henri asked.

"Your father heard the knights bragging about what they had done to Salih's family, and so he went out to the village and took Salih and the foal to live at al-Hadiqa. One of the animals that Sir Parsiprestre slew was Salih's horse. His foal. The only Franj that Salih trusted was your father, and your father was rich enough to have great stables with many animals."

"My father was not as wonderful as everyone thought," Henri said glumly. "He spent more time caring for his townsfolk and servants than his children."

"Your father did a great deal to help you, my lord, but he ensured that you never saw him doing it," Ibrahim said firmly, and then he refused to speak for the rest of the ride home.

Ibrahim untied the horses when they arrived at the house, then handed Henri the lead rope for the young foal. "This foal is for Salih. You should give it to him yourself, my lord."

Henri stepped back, affronted. "I did not intend to purchase a horse for a servant. You deceived me, Ibrahim!"

Ibrahim gave Henri a long look. "Very well, my lord, if you wish to keep the animal for yourself, you may do that, of course. I will leave it up to you to decide what is right."

***

The towering stone stables at al-Hadiqa had ten arched stalls that housed the family's finer animals and a tall wooden structure for the workhorses. It was here that he found Salih running his hands along flanks of a dappled Percheron that Sir Parsiprestre had spared, talking to it in consoling tones.

The old groom turned and saw Henri with the foal, and his eyes watered.

"Yes, my lord, do you wish to ride?" He wiped his nose with his sleeve.

Henri held out the rope. "Salih, for the anguish you suffered, I wish you to have this foal. She is a strong little beast, and sweet-tempered."

Salih covered his eyes with a weathered hand for a moment and then slowly took the rope. The foal pushed her face into Salih's chest, and he reached out a tentative hand to stroke her velvety nose.

"Thank you, my lord," he whispered, but his eyes remained mournful as he slowly led the little animal into his small house attached to the stable and shut the door.

Ungrateful man, Henri thought, stalking back into the main stables. *Giving him a horse ought to have at least put a smile on his face.*

He walked past his mother's bay palfrey and his sisters' ponies until he saw an elegant, glossy black nose poking out from the last stall. Raven neighed quietly in recognition and brought her delicate muzzle up to his hand. He scratched her between the eyes, and she whinnied with pleasure, leaning into his hand and bumping him affectionately with her head. *How did I manage to lose three horses and an entire militia in one day*, Henri thought miserably. *Why did I never ask Father how to gain a soldier's fealty? Why did Sir Geoffroi never teach me?*

His father had bought Raven when Henri was fifteen years old and helped to break and train her. It was one of Henri's only good memories of Rogier past the age of ten. In the quiet stables, he felt his eyes sting and his throat tighten. Everything was out of control. Rogier ran his villages and managed his household with ease, but Henri had ruined everything.

He heard a determined step on the stone floor and saw Nasira walking toward him, anger radiating from her posture.

"Mother?"

Nasira held up a piece of parchment, and Henri recognized it with dread. As the inheritor of the estate and title, he was expected to help protect the ever-dwindling trickle of Franj pilgrims on their way through the Holy Land by chasing off Bedu and Mamluk raiders. His father had managed to retire from his knightly duties due to an old injury to the shoulder, and he kept his small militia of fighting men barracked at the house for protection and to stand in for him when he was called to patrol. But Henri had lost the militia and so must go in their stead.

"This says that you will be taking Sir Parsiprestre's place!" Nasira waved the parchment. "We have a militia so that you do not have to fight."

"We *had* a militia. Until I hire new men, I will go on patrol. After all, I may not be knighted yet, but I am capably trained."

"But you would be killing your own people! Arab people! And who will be here to protect us since we are unguarded?"

"Ibrahim is here to take care of everything while I am gone, and Durant is the most lethal man I know," Henri said, willing himself to keep his temper under control.

"When you are on patrol, you will be asked to kill men just like Ibrahim. How can you look him in the face, Hamza?"

"The Saracens that we encounter are nothing like Ibrahim. He is the most civilized and well-educated savage in this city and has nothing in common with the filth that prey on Jesu Christi's holy pilgr—"

His mother's slap was so quick and strong that the air cracked with its sound and his sentence hung, unfinished, between them. Henri's pride stung more than his cheek, which colored dark red, and he stared at her coldly. Head tilted up, hands on her hips, she glared back.

"Yes, you have no choice, I know," Nasira said, "but do not blithely write off Ibrahim and your kin as savages and thieves, for you are both one of them and one of the usurpers who took their home."

"I am not responsible for the sins of my father and his father," said Henri through gritted teeth, "nor do I wish to be associated with your low-born people."

Nasira fixed her son with a fierce look of disapproval. "You cannot hide who you are, my son. You are responsible for the choices that you make. You can choose to repeat the sins of your ancestors or to stand against them. You can choose to right the wrongs of your father's generation and that of his father's."

"Protecting the Kingdom of Jerusalem is not a sin. God commands us to keep and protect his Holy Sepulchre," Henri snapped.

"The Holy Sepulchre has been lost for a hundred years, and if you think that protecting the Kingdom of Jerusalem is why your father and your grand-père came to Palestine, you are greatly mistaken!" Nasira's eyes flashed, and she stormed from the stable.

"This is an impossible situation!" Henri shouted after her, invoking a chorus of snorts and alarmed whinnies from the stable's equine residents.

"Did you say something, my lord?" Ibrahim entered the stable.

"Saddle Raven and pack some provisions. I am going for a ride."

"To where will you ride, my lord? It is late."

"I care not. As far from here as I can go in a night."

31

— · —

FAJAR, THE HILLS OF IDMIT. SEPTEMBER 1290

Sidika crouched in the lee of a boulder, her hazel eyes fixed, unblinking, on her prey. Before her, a young doe arched her tawny neck cropping flowers from their stems, unconcerned and off her guard. Sidika's arms burned and shook with the strain of holding her bowstring taut, her arrow nocked. The doe's body was within an inch of being perfectly positioned for a quick kill, and Sidika debated whether to make a sound, causing the creature to look up, to wait, or just to take her chances. It had been a week at least since she had tasted meat, and a kill this size would feed her and her father for a month after they dried and smoked the venison.

Suddenly, the doe stopped chewing, raised her head in alarm, and looked away from Sidika. The animal sprang into the air, then dropped, an arrow sprouting from her throat and blood blooming along her flank. She tried to leap again, but the arrow had embedded itself to the fletches, and she stumbled on slender legs, collapsing into a bed of parched grass.

Sidika stood from her hiding place, the arrow still nocked. She looked around for the other hunter but saw only trees and brambles. Raising her bow above her head, she called out.

"I also hunted this doe. Please show yourself, and perhaps we can come to an arrangement."

A rustle in the dense shrubbery drew her attention, and Fakri al-Ghalib emerged with twigs and leaves snagged in his brown keffiyeh. He smiled broadly, and Sidika suppressed her instinct to leap away as the doe had done.

"Why, Sidika, you hesitated," he said, grinning, "a pity, for I should have liked to see if you could make such a clean kill as mine!"

"Fakri, you followed me," she said, crossing her arms.

"Nonsense. We are both accomplished hunters. I knew that this animal and her kin frequented the area, and so did you."

Sidika shrugged her shoulders in reluctant acknowledgment. "Fakri, I was a breath away from making that kill myself. Would you not be willing to share some of the meat?"

Fakri bowed elaborately. "Of course, my lady," he said, eyes wandering along her lean frame, scandalously clad in comfortable hose and a too-large gray cotehardie that had belonged to her brother.

"An 'arrangement,' you say?"

"I am willing to pay you, only I have no coin with me now. I will pay you a dinar for one-quarter of the meat after it has been cut from the bones," she said in as businesslike a tone as she could muster.

Of late, when she walked past him or met him in his pottery workshop, Fakri's eyes always seemed to be on her. Widowed, and at least fifteen years her senior, he was likely to approach her father soon. He knelt next to the doe and lifted the animal's head, muttering a quick prayer over it.

"Oh, I will give you this meat for free, Sidika. No payment necessary."

Sidika moved back several paces. "As I told you, one dinar and no more than that. If this is unacceptable to you, then I shall move off and find a doe of my own."

He smiled and took out his dagger. Expertly slitting the large vein in the throat, he drained the animal's blood to the ground as he spoke.

"I have discussed it with my son, and I plan to speak with your father this very week, Sidika. We were fated to meet here. The hand of God is upon this encounter. I had doubted whether you would be suitable, but now I believe. It was not an accident that we both hunted the same prey." He stopped and stood up, blood dripping from the dagger.

Sidika took another step back. "Fakri, as you said, this is the best hunting ground in these hills. It is a coincidence that brought us here and nothing more."

She continued to back away and he moved slowly forward, so smoothly that he seemed to float towards her.

"I have not had the comfort of a woman since my wife died two winters ago," he said, "and I will be most pleased to welcome you into my home if you convert. I do not think that I can keep myself from you, Sidika. I have watched you these many months, and I burn with desire for you! I shall speak with your father, but you may give me your answer now. I have seen the way you look at me."

"I what? I do not look at you, Fakri, except to look with pity." Sidika raised her bow and nocked her arrow, pointing it at his crotch. "Move any closer to me, and I shall free you of your manhood, which seems to have overtaken your wits."

Fakri stopped, confused, and then his expression darkened. "Come now, it is unbecoming enough that you wear those abominable clothes, but to threaten a man's life is a mortal sin."

"It is not a mortal sin when a man takes another man's life in battle," Sidika argued, pulling her bowstring toward her cheek until again her arm shook with strain.

"A man may take a life in the name of God, but a woman must be full of grace and without violence. Come now, Sidika, put the bow down."

"Move away from me, Fakri!" she yelled. "Keep the meat for yourself and stay away from my father's house. If you step closer, I shall not be responsible for what happens with this arrow!"

Fakri smiled patronizingly and held out his hand to take the bow from her.

"You are frightened, that is certain, but so was my first wife when her father gave her to me. Now hand me the bow!" He sprang towards her. Sidika aimed slightly to the right, released her arrow, and Fakri screamed as it grazed the skin of his thigh. He dropped to the ground, stunned, and Sidika lowered her arm.

"Stop your crying," she grumbled. "I only took the skin from your leg and not your entire manhood as I had promised. Here, bind it with this." She tossed him a clean rag and a wine flask from a leather scrip slung low at her waist.

"You bitch and whore's daughter!" Fakri raged. "Filthy Turkish vermin! I do not need to ask your father's permission to take you if I want you!"

Sidika looked down at him with amusement. "If it makes you feel more like a man to think that, I will not stop you. Also, I decline your proposal of marriage."

"It is not yours to decline, you dog of an orphan!" Fakri spat, dumping the wine on his leg and binding it with the cloth.

"Of course, you are correct," Sidika said, squatting down to dress the doe herself. "I decline your proposal on behalf of my father, who is not here to decline for me." She expertly pulled back the doe's skin and sawed off two large hunks of flesh from the flank.

"You will never get a better offer, Sidika, although now I begin to reconsider it!" Fakri raged as he struggled to tie the bandage off.

Sidika wrapped the meat in a piece of waxed cloth and put it in her scrip, then cleaned her knife and walked over to the man, still prone on the ground. She patted him on the arm, squatted next to him, and began to retie the bandage.

"I am glad you are reconsidering your offer, Fakri," she said, wrapping the bloody cloth around his thigh. "Have you considered the widow Nimet? She fancies you." She gave the bandage an unnecessarily strong tug.

"The widow Nimet is nearly thirty years old!" Fakri yelped as the bandage squeezed his thigh.

"You are right, and God forbid that you marry someone your own age. Well, Fakri, it seems God does not shine his face on you with favor as you thought. I am sorry that you and your miserable son will be lonely, but perhaps since every woman in the village declines your offers, *you* are the problem, not them." She stood, slung her bow across her shoulder, and left him seething on the forest floor.

"The whole village shall hear of this!" she heard him screeching after her.

"I hope that they do," she called back cheerfully.

The sun was only halfway in the sky, and two large pieces of venison were good, but not good enough. She turned east and walked further into the hills, where they became craggy and snake-infested. Prowling amongst the pale rocks and limestone caves, she shot two large hares, which she bound by the ears and hung from her belt, and one small quail, which she placed in her scrip with the venison. As the sun began to transit toward the western horizon, she reluctantly turned back to the road.

Hunting was an occupation that required her complete focus, driving all other thoughts and distractions from her mind. Killing and skinning the animal was not her prize; it was the serenity that came from a focused mind and a single purpose that she craved. Lately, since the deaths of her mother and brother, she wandered into the hills to hunt more frequently, seeking that focus.

The road to her small village was little more than a narrow, dusty mule-track in the summer-dry highland scrub. She ambled home, enjoying the sounds of insects humming in the heat and the smell of the warm rocks and pines as the late afternoon sun wrapped around her in a gentle embrace. So absorbed was she in her thoughts that she did not see the man and his horse until she was nearly upon them, and in the narrow canyon where they stood, there was no place to hide. She stopped abruptly, the hares swinging by their ears at her waist.

The man had been watching her, leaning against a large stone with his arms crossed across his chest. A tall black horse stood in the shade, greedily cropping the tender grass that grew near a small stream. Sidika considered turning back, but she knew she could not outrun a man on a horse. Options and eventualities raced through her mind. Perhaps she could scramble up the rocks and hide in a cave until he left? She was sure she could climb faster than he, for he wore heavy chain mail. She knew herself to be close to the village but not close enough to be heard if she called for help.

While she stood in the road, pondering whether to flee or fire an arrow into his face, the man straightened lazily and called out, "You there, boy! I require assistance."

Sidika's racing thoughts stopped. She had obeyed her father's request and wrapped her hair in a turban before setting out in the hot sun. From a distance, with her hose and cote-hardie, the man had mistaken her for a village boy. Fortunately, the man looked wealthy and preoccupied, which meant he wouldn't look at her closely. Crossing her arms casually over her small breasts, she swaggered toward him.

"My horse has thrown a shoe," he said, and as she had hoped, he did not look her in the face. "Is there a smith or a farrier nearby?"

He seemed impatient. Sweat sparkled on his temples and soaked into the fabric of his black surcoat, which had a stripe and three yellow spots on it. The saddle on his magnificent horse was of fine leather, with polished gold fixings, and the saddlecloth was as black as the horse's coat, with the same crest of a yellow stripe and three yellow spots as the crest. Sidika bowed, lowering her voice.

"There is a village nearby, my lord, and for a florin, I will fetch the farrier for you."

He had been rummaging through his saddlebag but stopped abruptly and turned.

"A florin? Are you a peasant or a Genoese merchant? Do you think I keep florins on my person while I travel, like some naïve pilgrim from Rome?"

Sidika cursed herself. She had gone too far. A florin was enough money to support her and her father for two years. As rich as this peacock looked, he wasn't stupid enough to carry such money with him.

"Five dinars, then," she responded quickly.

Maybe she could keep him off his guard.

"Just take me to your village, and we will negotiate later," he said, grasping the bridle of his horse.

She bowed again, turned, and walked ahead of him, covertly trying to loosen her belt so that her tiny waist was not clearly defined. It did not matter, since the man and his horse walked slowly behind her at a distance and took no further notice of her.

Sidika's mind spun. What would she do when she reached the village? The sun would set soon, and it was still a long walk to her house. He would have to stay the night somewhere, and there were no inns or boarding houses. She could charge him at least three dinars to stay the night in their house if she and her father slept in the stable, and if she fetched the farrier, she could charge another six. Nine dinars would be enough to have their copper pot mended, buy more green malachite, and perhaps even purchase new shoes for her father.

With these thoughts to occupy her, they reached the village sooner than she hoped, and the sight of the tall man with his beautiful horse and Franj armor spurred the grubby children playing outside to alert their parents to the presence of a noble stranger. Hearing the commotion, her father emerged from the house, his hands and cloak spattered with spots and smudges of black ink from his work. Seeing Sidika, he snatched up his robe and ran towards her.

"Daughter, is everything alright? Who is this man?"

The stranger started, turned to Sidika, and looked at her in surprise. "Daughter?"

"Yes, Father," she said quickly, looking past the stranger. "I am unharmed. This man's horse has thrown a shoe, and he requires a farrier."

"Ah," her father said, and his face broke into a luminous smile. "Young man, we have no farrier in our village. There is one several miles from here at the foot of the hill, but the sun is setting. Come, you will stay with us tonight, and tomorrow we shall fix up the hoof of that beautiful creature of yours."

He put his hand on the man's back and pushed him towards the house. Turning to a boy standing shyly nearby, he spoke kindly.

"Ali, take this horse and tie her up in the stable. The freshest hay is on the western wall. Give her that, for surely she is a grand lady!"

Ali took the horse's reins and looked at the beast reverently as he led her to the stable. Sidika's father was leading the stranger towards the house.

"I am Tamrat, young man, and you are most welcome to stay in our house, for there are bandits and beasts out in the night, and it is not safe to find a farrier until tomorrow. I see you have met Sidika already?"

The stranger shot Sidika a confused glance but was pulled into the house before he could comment. Sullenly, Sidika walked to the small yard at the back of their little house, dressed the hares to sell in the market, and cut the venison into strips to be salted. As she worked, Rahat, who was of age with her, hurried into the yard. Taking up some of the strips of meat, she quickly helped Sidika pack them into the salt.

"Who is this that you have brought to our village, Sidika?" Rahat asked.

"Merely a stranded Franj looking for a place to sleep, as you and the whole village saw, Rahat," Sidika replied without looking up.

Rahat, a year older at sixteen, was the best friend that Sidika had in this village, but that did not mean much. The other women avoided Sidika, most likely because wearing boys' clothes and engaging in arts such as hunting and reading were frowned upon, and her mother had been regarded as something between a miracle healer and a witch. Sidika's heart felt a familiar stab of pain, and she glanced in the direction of the still-fresh graves on the hill near the house.

"That is no mere Franj. That is a lord of Acre or Tyre," Rahat spoke under her breath. "Sidika, he is the most handsome man I have seen, although I suppose that says very little of us living here in the hills."

Sidika realized that she hadn't looked at the man directly. She tried to recall what he looked like; a full head of dark hair, taller than average. She shrugged her shoulders. "You say that because your husband is twenty winters older than you."

"Eighteen winters older than me," Rahat replied tartly, "and if I were you, I would change out of those men's garments, brush out my hair and get myself inside before that prize decides to return to whatever castle he came from!"

Sidika slammed the lid on the cask of salted meat.

"What 'prize,' Rahat? I say a rich Franj is not a prize. He is a curse upon this village. He shall come back with his marauding friends and burn our houses. Besides, he is not to my taste."

Rahat laughed incredulously. "Oh, really, you have taste? I was not aware that you could afford to be choosy." She dusted the salt from her hands and flounced from the yard.

Sidika pulled the feathers from the little quail and dressed it for roasting. After lighting a fire in the oven, she released her relentlessly misbehaved hair from its turban, and it floated in a corkscrewed cloud around her shoulders. Splashing the dust from her face in the water trough, she paused to look at her reflection on the shivering surface.

Sidika had never seen her full likeness. Her father told her of lords and ladies in Acre and Cairo who had polished glass and metal surfaces like water that stood upright in which they could see themselves, but village girls had to content themselves with the animal troughs and stagnant pools near the creek to see their reflections. On the water's surface, she saw her hair, light brown and backlit by the sun, olive skin and hazel, almond-shaped eyes. People told her she was comely to look at, but she did not see that this brought her any benefit.

"Comeliness means nothing if you starve to death," Sidika said aloud. Pretty girls stayed inside and waited to be married. Sidika didn't have the luxury of sitting around like an ornament. Her father needed her.

"What was that, my daughter?" Tamrat walked around the corner. She noticed that he had combed the snarls from his gray beard and now wore his fine black robe. "Come into the house, Sidika. I could use some help making our guest comfortable."

"I am coming, Father. I need to change out of these clothes."

Her father glanced back at the house and then took her hands, his face glowing with excitement.

"Sidika, he reads Latin, and he knows the works of Aristotle and al-Farabi. The first and second teachers! Such a conversation we have already had! Come, come, my dear, never mind your appearance. It is such a great blessing to speak with a fellow scholar again." Tamrat practically danced into the house through the low door.

Sidika looked back and saw the rangy silhouette of Fakri in the dusky distance, limping towards the village, carrying the remains of the doe across his shoulders. She dashed into the house and slipped into the small room where she and her father slept. Ripping the cotehardie and hose off and tossing them in a corner, she pulled a chemise and a roomy olive-green frock over her head and dragged her fingers through her hair, braiding the untamed mess loosely so that it hung down her neck in a thick rope. She tied a narrow fillet of cloth across her forehead and then pinned her blue and white circular scarf to the fillet so that it draped artfully around her face. Taking a deep breath, she emerged from the room.

The stranger sat under her father's skylight in their work-shop. He no longer wore his mail armor, having changed into a clean shirt and hose from his saddlebag, and he held a clay cup of tea in his hand as he leaned over one of her father's manuscripts. Tamrat stood behind him, looking over his shoulder like a headmaster, beaming with pride.

"This took me three years to finish. It was not commissioned. I made this for myself and for my family. Sidika, she reads and writes as well."

"I am most impressed, Master Tamrat. How did you come to possess this skill, and why do you not work for one of the scriptoriums in the city?" the young man asked, taking a sip from his cup.

"Bah!" Tamrat waved the suggestion away with a graceful hand. "In the city, there is always someone to distract you from your work. Up here in the hills, I have no lords pestering me, no priest or rabbi looking over my ear. I can open the door in my roof, let the sunlight come in, and I can work uninterrupted. It brings me peace, like the peace of death. When I am illuminating or translating, there is nothing else in the world that exists."

Sidika cleared her throat.

"Except my Sidika, of course!" Tamrat exclaimed, crossing the room and planting a kiss on the top of her head.

The stranger stood. He was so tall that his hair brushed the ceiling, and he stooped slightly to keep from bumping his head. Now that Sidika looked him in the face, she suddenly forgot her words. He had shockingly pale green eyes. His build was lanky but not scrawny, and she now saw that he was only slightly older than her. She gave a quick curtsey. He did not bow in response.

"Are you the same who led me to the village?"

Sidika nodded.

"Well, you look somewhat less homely in a dress, at least," he commented.

"Sidika, my daughter, I think that I saw you put a bird on the fire for our supper, yes? Come, Lord Henri, we shall prepare the table while Sidika finishes cooking." Tamrat bustled the young lord towards the large table, which was strewn with pots of ink, parchments, paintbrushes, and other ephemera of Tamrat's work.

Lord Henri stared without comprehension as the old man handed him a stack of finished pages and instructed him to place them on a shelf. Clearly unused to taking orders, Lord Henri set the papers back down on the table and waited for his meal. Tamrat patiently handed the papers back to him and repeated the instruction to put them on the shelf, then patted the man affectionately on the shoulder. Slowly, Lord Maron moved to the shelf, his brow knitted.

Sidika's temper was boiling at this ill-mannered guest. She stormed outside and rotated the bird on its spit, placing a dish underneath to catch the drippings. Then she loaded a basket with a small melon, some sprigs of fresh mint hastily snatched from the garden, a handful of barley, some leeks, and three round millet cakes. She chopped and mixed the leeks with the barley, the drippings, and some water in her thin copper pot. She added salt and a pinch of her dried cumin seeds and sat down near the fire, stirring pensively while the porridge bubbled. Inside she could hear her father's animated talking, and she smiled, despite her irritation.

He has not had a companion to talk to this way since Mother and Dejen died.

The memory tore off a scab of forgetting that made her grief so fresh she had to put her spoon down and catch her breath. Again, she looked longingly at the graves on the hill.

Inside the house, the table was cleared and set with three bowls. Lord Henri pouted at his seat as Sidika filled each bowl with the barley porridge and pieces of steaming roast quail. She set a plate of melon sprinkled with mint in the center of the table and sat down to eat while her father rummaged in a cupboard, muttering to himself.

"Sidika, where is our good wine?"

"But Father, you have been saving that wine!" she protested. "It is sealed!"

"Saving it for just such an occasion. It is not every day we have such a guest in our house! Come, Lord Henri, tell me again of your library! Sidika would love to hear of it." He continued to paw inside the cupboard.

Sidika turned a sour gaze on Lord Henri, and he looked back at her with a sort of disgusted curiosity.

"It is true, Lord Henri, I do know how to read. You look at me as if I were something you found under the straw in your horse's stable," she said, returning to her bowl of porridge.

"I have never met a woman who wears men's garments," he said.

"I have never met a man who does not know how to set a table," she replied.

"Obviously, you do not spend much time away from your village." He shrugged and tentatively took a bite of his food.

"And what exactly were you doing near my village, my lord?"

"Sidika is hesitant with strangers, and for a good reason," Tamrat said, returning to the table with the wax-sealed jar of wine and three small clay cups. "But she is the best of daughters. I wish, Lord Maron," he said wistfully, "you had come months earlier. I would have liked for you to meet my son, Dejen. His was a rare mind."

Sidika put her spoon down and took a deep breath. Dejen's death was still new and raw, like the wound she left on Fakri's leg. It burned.

"Has your son left for the city?" Lord Maron asked.

"He has left us mortals behind," Tamrat said, setting the wine jar down. "My wife Sara and I were blessed to have Dejen with us for a short time before he was taken by a fever, along with his mother. It struck the whole village. I also nearly succumbed, but Sidika, my brilliant girl, brought my fever down and pulled me back from death."

Lord Henri looked at Sidika again, his expression unreadable, and she squirmed under his gaze.

"Does anyone wish for more?" she asked, not caring what her guest wanted. She did not want anyone who didn't know Dejen to talk about him or even hear about him. Dejen was theirs, not to be shared with strangers.

"If your son were half as talented as you are, he would have had a place of honor working for the Patriarch," Lord Henri said haltingly.

Sidika could tell that giving compliments did not come naturally to the man. Her father smiled and put his hand over the young man's. "You are kind, my lord."

This comment seemed to take Lord Henri back. He looked at Tamrat's hand on his and said nothing.

When the evening meal ended, Tamrat insisted that Lord Henri sleep in their room, and he and Sidika would sleep in the stable. Their guest didn't protest, so Sidika spread their blankets over the sweet-smelling hay as far from their donkey and their goat as possible. There was very little hay, since it was the time before the late summer harvest, and she could feel the hard ground beneath her. While her father snored on the other side of the stable, she rolled restlessly on her makeshift mattress and imagined that Lord Henri was Fakri and she was shooting him in the leg.

32

— • —

Fajar, the hills of Idmit. September 1290

The next morning, Tamrat left at first light with his tallit and phylacteries for his morning prayers, and Sidika rose to feed the animals and milk the goat. As she poured the milk from the bucket into her copper pot to boil for cheese, a shadow fell across her in the bright early-morning sun.

"Sidika, I would speak with your father, please," Fakri said.

She stood and placed the pot of milk over her small fire. "He is out for a walk, Fakri, and I already told you, my father will not consent to marry me to someone whom I do not wish to marry. This he promised me."

"And you do not wish for me, my beautiful one?"

"Do not try to give compliments, Fakri. It only makes you sound ridiculous and unnatural."

"Fine, then I will be straightforward. I need a wife, and you need a husband. You are nearly sixteen, and your childbearing years will come to an end before you know it."

Sidika snorted and stirred the pot with a wooden paddle.

"I have only one son, but together we could make more. Would you like that, Sidika? Sons of your own?" Fakri continued, moving closer.

Sidika ignored him. Fakri moved another step closer and snatched the paddle from her hands, grabbing her skinny wrist and pulling her toward him. "There is no one else in this dogshit village who will marry a woman as strange as you,

Sidika. I am your last chance." His breath smelled of stale garlic and unwashed teeth.

Sidika picked up the pot of hot goat's milk and sloshed it across his chest. Fakri yelped in surprise, then brought the wooden paddle up and slashed at her with it. Pain flashed across her eye as the wood cracked on her cheekbone. She stumbled back, reaching blindly for anything that might serve as a weapon, but Fakri suddenly paled and stepped away from her.

Sidika turned. Lord Henri stood in the doorway of the house, arms crossed over his chest. He had clearly just woken up. His hair was snarled and his clothes were rumpled, but despite his appearance, Fakri cowered and backed away from her. Fakri slunk out of the yard like an injured cat under Lord Henri's icy gaze, and then that green stare turned on her, looking similarly disgusted.

"Where is your father?" he asked.

"Out for a walk. He says his prayers in the hills at sunrise."

There was an awkward silence while Lord Henri took in the spilled milk and the red welt rising on Sidika's face.

"I can handle Fakri myself, Lord Henri. Yesterday I shot him in the leg, and if you had not interrupted me, I would have finished him off today," she said, pulling a long stick of wood from the woodpile and brandishing it like a club.

Lord Henri raised an eyebrow. Before Sidika could say more, Tamrat ambled slowly around the corner and into the stable yard, his hands clasped behind his back, face beaming pleasantly.

"Ah, Viscount! I hope that you slept well! Such a beautiful morning. Had you awoken earlier, I would have invited you to join me to watch the world wake up in the mountains. It clears the mind and strengthens the soul."

Sidika threw her stick down and walked into the house.

Eventually, one of the village boys was dispatched to the next town to fetch the farrier, who arrived carrying a sling stuffed with horseshoes, nails, his hammer, and a small bellows. He gently ran his hands over the flanks of the beautiful horse while the young lord watched on, scowling like a suspicious father. The farrier talked to her quietly as a man speaks to his lover in their chamber, and the horse nuzzled him. This seemed to set Lord Henri at ease.

Tamrat had lifted his hinged skylight inside the house to let the sun pour into the room as he prepared his quills and knives. Standing at his slanted table, he carefully consulted the manuscript in front of him – an ornately illustrated physician's book for the sultan that he was translating from Latin. All of the text had already been painted in flowing muhaqqaq script. Now, all that remained was the illumination of the page with scrolls, fanciful creatures, and dismembered body parts.

On a nearby bench, Sidika ground plant dyes into a fine powder with her mortar and pestle. A chicken wandered into the house and wandered out again. The sun moved slowly through the sky, and the hot summer air soaked into the mudbrick walls. Lord Henri sat down next to Sidika as she mixed blue indigo and yellow weld together, attempting to color match a green that her father needed for an illustration of the bile duct. He watched her in silence for a moment, then cleared his throat.

"I enjoyed the meal you made last night," he said awkwardly, "even though it was simple food."

Sidika shrugged her shoulders and kept grinding, head bent over her work.

"I need another servant at the estate. One of the kitchen maids died in childbirth, and we have space for another. Would you consider coming to live at my house near Acre? All my servants are paid well and have good accommodations. You could come back and visit your father once a month, or we could even find a place for him to stay, for I enjoy his company."

Sidika stopped grinding and stood, picking up her pestle and leveling it at his face. "I am tired," she said through gritted teeth, "of men trying to convince me to do them a service. I will stay here, with my father, because I choose to. He never asks anything of me, and so I serve him and no other man. A kitchen maid, you say? Do any of your other kitchen maids know how to read and write Latin or shoot a target from sixty meters? Can any of them set a broken bone and cure a fever?" She waited for his reply. He stared at her with wide eyes and an open mouth.

"As I suspected. If you so devalue me again, Lord Henri, I will put an arrow in your leg as I did to Fakri back there!" She realized that she was shouting and her father had set his brushes down.

"Sidika!" Tamrat's voice was scandalized. "This is not how we treat a guest in our house!"

"A guest? Father, if you had not invited this self-important lordling into the house, he would have ordered you out of it on his own! He is no more worthy of special treatment than any other man in this village. This peacock is clearly very pleased with himself, and can you wonder why? I am sure that no one has ever told him he is as coddled as an infant at the breast!"

Tamrat wrung his hands. "Lord Henri, I apologize for my daughter. She has been distraught since her mother and brother died."

But Sidika was not finished. Once she started, her temper rolled like a stone down a steep hill, and nothing could stop it. "Lord Maron, have you ever made a meal for yourself? Have you ever saddled your own horse or cleaned your own clothes?"

"I was a squire as a boy, which meant that I had to serve a knight. I had to saddle his horse, clean his armor, and serve him his food," Lord Henri snapped at her, jumping to his feet.

"And I am sure that must have been extremely hard for you." Sidika's voice dripped with sarcasm. "Nobles and knights like you are a burden to the world. This is why my father and I live in this village. We do not wish to be deal with the Teutons, the Templars, the Sicilians, the... Franj! Please, take your horse and leave us so that we can rebuild the illusion that we are the masters of our lives."

"Mademoiselle, that is enough!" Lord Henri's expression was fierce. His pale eyes stared through her like green ice. Her father's mouth moved wordlessly, and he clasped and unclasped his hands nervously.

"Sidika," Tamrat whispered, "my child...."

Sidika threw down the pestle, leaving a smear of dark green on the bench. She ran outside and climbed the hill behind the house, curling up on her mother's grave. Far away to the west, she could see the misty blue expanse of the sea and the double walls of Acre. Eventually, she saw Lord Henri and her father emerge from the house, Tamrat still wringing his hands in apology. Lord Henri mounted his freshly shod horse, tossed the farrier a coin, and rode slowly to the south.

33

— · —

E verything was ready. Mafeo's black hair had been washed and picked free of nits, doused with perfume, and curled around his face with hot irons. Emre ensured that his master's wedding clothes – a red and white embroidered cotehardie and black silk hose – had been cleaned, perfumed, and pressed, and he set out his jeweled red velvet shoes with the pointed toes. His master's nails were clipped and buffed and a gold earring placed in his right ear. Mafeo declared himself handsome, but Emre thought he looked more primped than the Countess of Blois.

The master's horse, a black courser, had a bridle with gold fastenings, and a collar of red carnations adorned its shoulder. Mafeo had hired acrobats and musicians to tumble and play ahead of him, and three small slave girls scattered rose petals as he processed from his house to the church, where the Patriarch would witness as Henri gave his mother to Mafeo.

The prospect of being married in the presence of the Patriarch excited Mafeo, for he was wealthy but not wealthy enough to garner the attention of the most powerful man of the Church in all of Outremer. True, he was a member of the noble family of Orsini, but he resided on a small twig of that grand family tree, and nowhere near enough his hallowed distant cousins – Pope Clement and Pope Nicholas – to garner any serious favors in Acre. In fact, he generally avoided the Patriarch, whose treatises on how pious Christians were supposed to behave always sounded vaguely accusatory, as if the man had written it with Mafeo's vices in mind.

After the ceremony finished, Emre rode in the red and white livery of his master, and because Mafeo felt that his slave's exuberant mop of curls looked unchaste and the turban looked "too Muslim," he had been compelled to wear a brown leather arming cap over his head with his hair tied back in a queue. At least it covered the purple bruise that Mafeo's fist had left on him that morning.

He yawned in his saddle and waved dust out of his eyes from the dry road. Ahead, Mafeo and Nasira rode side by side with a canopy over their heads to keep the sun off them, their horses draped in cloth-of-gold caparisons. Mafeo glanced from time to time at his bride, who rode tall and stately in her blood-red dress, neither looking to the left or the right. On her other side was Lord Henri, and at the front, the Patriarch rode in a white-curtained wagon.

Emre stole a glance at Lady Blanche, who sat as tall and aloof on her dappled mare as her mother. *Franj noblewomen are just as enslaved as I. They have no choice who they may marry, and Mafeo will surely treat these women cruelly.*

Again, as he had done every day since his capture eleven years ago, he thought of his sister, Ela. She would be fifteen now, and his father and mother would be seeking a husband for her too, had any of them lived. He looked ahead and drew in his breath.

They had turned off the main road and were descending into a shallow valley. The air smelled cool and damp after the fetid stink of the city, and the waving grasses here were still green, unlike the late-September brown elsewhere. He noticed a dark smudge of trees growing near a creek, and in front of it a large stone wall with wide wooden gates. Flowers bloomed around the outside of the walls, and he could see the tops of more trees swaying from behind them. Mafeo dismounted after the gates, helped Nasira from her horse, and a fleet of white-clad grooms and servants floated toward them, bearing cups of chilled wine and cool basins of rose water to refresh the travelers.

They were in a small dooryard with another lower wall in front of them that had a lattice of carved white limestone along the top. Another set of doors, these wrought of shining bronze in a pattern of intertwining vines, opened and beyond, Emre glimpsed the reason why this house was called "the garden." Lush greenery lined the courtyard and moss-covered fountains bubbled quietly in each of the corners, bordered by small bushes of rosemary and lavender. Around the edge of the courtyard, a columned arcade supported a portico, and in the shadows, lanterns of copper and colored glass swung on long chains. The honored guests followed their hosts into this Eden, and the gates slammed shut.

Ibrahim approached Jacomo, Mafeo's steward, with a smile.

"I am Lord Maron's steward and the seneschal of this estate. I will be pleased to show Signore Mafeo's servants to their quarters. Will any of you remain at his auberge in the city, or is the whole household moving to al-Hadiqa?"

Jacomo gestured to himself and to Mafeo's cook. "We are the master's servants. The slaves may join yours in the slaves' quarters, and after you and I have met to discuss where to place them, we may move one or two of them back to the house."

Ibrahim blinked at Jacomo, uncomprehending. "Slaves' quarters? We have none. The Maron family does not keep slaves."

Jacomo was incredulous as he looked around. Next to the stables were a smithy and a small sugar refinery. Near that lay the citronnier and beyond, irrigated fields of glistening green sugar cane in various stages of growth. "How in heaven does he manage all of this without slaves? I was informed already that I am not to treat you as a slave, despite you being a Saracen, but I see few fair people working here. Do you mean to tell me that the viscount pays all of these people a wage?"

Ibrahim smiled again. "And allows them to farm their own crops and animals on his property, which they keep for themselves or sell in the city. The citizens of his villages pay only their tithe to the church and a yearly tax to the lord for maintenance of the mill, wells, and irrigation canals and to pay the village militias."

"He does not collect revenues from his mills?" Jacomo asked, eyes wide with surprise. "How did he become so rich if he is so unwise with his money?"

"Lord Rogier was a shrewd businessman who was wise in his trade agreements. And he has family money."

"And his son? What about the young Lord Henri?" Jacomo raised an eyebrow, and Emre leaned in, listening closely.

"His son will be just as wise, but he is young, as you say. This is why Lord Rogier felt it would be best that, should something happen to him, my lady would continue to live at al-Hadiqa until Henri comes of age."

"A most unusual arrangement," Jacomo muttered and clapped his hands three times loudly. The slaves all gathered to him. "Since there are no slaves' quarters here, you all will sleep under the stars tonight," he said. Several of the slaves lowered their eyes but did not complain.

Ibrahim touched Jacomo on the sleeve. "We have plenty of room for all of these people in the servants' hall."

"No. They are not servants; they are slaves. To house them with the servants would give them ideas. I will consult with my master and Lord Maron about building a shelter for them."

Ibrahim's face was troubled, and Emre watched him closely. *They keep no slaves here!* For the first time that he could remember, he felt excitement. Perhaps there were benefits to living outside of Acre after all.

"Zahed!" Jacomo barked. "See that Master Mafeo's belongings are unpacked properly in his chamber and that he has wine and a basin for washing."

"Your master will reside in the late Lord Rogier's room, which adjoins my lady's room," Ibrahim said, his face still troubled. "I will show Zahed where to find each."

They set out through a thick wooden door that led into a dark passage. At the end of the hallway, Emre could see the bright sun on the green courtyard and hear the sound of voices floating toward him, but they turned into another tunnel and took a set of stairs that led to the portico atop the arcade surrounding the courtyard instead. Emre glanced down. The guests sat under canopies of white and gold silk, and servants hurried about with fragrant platters of food and pitchers of wine and ale while a musician strummed a lute and sang gently. Ibrahim opened a carved wooden door and waited so Emre could enter first. The chamber was large, with polished stone floors and a massive bedstand against a wall with a deep blue canopy and drapes. Ibrahim walked across the room and drew the heavy silk curtains, revealing the terrace that looked out toward the west and the sea.

"Lord Rogier kept these closed in the afternoon to keep out the heat, but he allowed the chambermaid to come in and open them in the early morning. Your master may wish to do the same, as the sea breezes in the morning are enlivening."

Emre strolled around the room and looked at the bed. "I do not think that my master will want anyone in his room to open the drapes in the morning. He wishes to get to know Lady Nasira very well indeed."

Ibrahim stood stiffly by the terrace entrance and said nothing for a moment, then walked from the room with Emre trailing him. Emre felt confused. Usually, servants and slaves in a household had a healthy sense of gallows humor about their masters—camaraderie against a mutual foe. Ibrahim seemed interested in none of this.

"Place the chests against the western wall. I will be up later to unpack them," Emre commanded a slave who labored under Mafeo's belongings, and he hurried to follow Ibrahim back down the stairs again.

Ibrahim strode into the sun and toward a separate building with chimneys that belched black smoke and a dozen different delicious scents.

"Here is the kitchen, and the cellar with the wine barrels is through that door."

Ibrahim still seemed annoyed, so Emre nodded meekly and retreated to his master's room. From the top of the arcade, he could hear Mafeo loudly holding forth, his guests listening politely.

"Is she not the most beautiful of women you have seen? Surely our children will be as beautiful as those that she bore her dead husband." He glanced at Blanche, who blushed furiously and stared into her cup.

Next to his mother, Henri watched Mafeo sourly.

Emre filled the basin with scented water, inspected the candles to ensure they were fresh, checked that the chamber pot was clean, then grabbed the wine pitcher and went to the kitchen to refill it. After that, he began to unpack the trunks.

Mafeo was fond of fine clothes, and soon the carved wardrobe was filled with brocade tunics and velvet cloaks, gold-embossed leather shoes with pointed toes, jeweled belts, and hats bedecked with samite and gems. He turned down the embroidered silk coverlet on the bed and ran his hands across the smooth sheet below, feeling the plumpness of the cotton and down-stuffed mattress. He sat down upon it and then laid back, letting the feathers quietly envelop him as he admired the dark velvet canopy overhead with its small stars stitched in gold.

"Comfortable?"

Emre sprang to his feet. Lord Henri stood in the doorway with his arms crossed.

"Pardon me, my lord." Emre bowed low. "I wanted to check the quality of the bed for my master. It was his request."

Henri smirked, and Emre felt his pulse leap in his chest. He could see that Henri was a few years younger than him, although taller. Despite his good looks, he radiated arrogance.

"Is this room prepared?" Henri asked. "My mother has re-quested no escort to the marriage chamber, so there will be no time to fetch anything else that she or your master requires."

"Oh... my master thought that they would be ushered to the marriage chamber by the guests."

"And my mother says no," Henri said firmly. "This is her second marriage, and she has no desire to place herself on display in such a manner at her age."

"I will inform my master, although he may resist, my lord. He is stubborn."

"So is my mother."

Emre smiled slightly. Henri was moving about the room, examining Mafeo's things; an inlaid box of fine lead powder for his complexion, a bottle of rose oil, and a small mirror of hammered and polished metal.

"My lord, is it true what Ibrahim said, that you keep no slaves at al-Hadiqa?"

Henri turned and looked at him for a moment. "There are no slaves at al-Hadiqa, per my father's preference. Why would you ask such a question?"

"Mafeo owns many slaves, and well... some of the slaves have been wondering if they will receive manumission now that they live here."

"Are you a slave?"

"Yes, my lord."

"Well, I am not the same man as my father," Henri said, then turned on his heel and left the room.

34

—·—

AL-HADIQA, ACRE. OCTOBER 1290

Nasira woke early and crept from the bed, making as little noise and movement as possible. She had shared this bed with Rogier only two months ago and the sight of Mafeo with arms and legs thrown out wide like a starfish, sweat beaded on his face and neck, felt like more of a defilement than the things he had done to her only hours before on their wedding night. Rogier always woke with the sun, then closed the drapes so she could sleep longer. She could not remember a morning when he had not greeted her with a smile when she first opened her eyes after spending the night with him.

Quietly, she slipped through the adjoining room into her own chamber. Madame Habiba, her faithful servant, was awake and sitting on Nasira's curtained bedstead, hands folded placidly in her lap.

"Good morning, my lady. How was your first night with your new husband?"

Nasira took in a deep breath and tried to smile, but tears sprang to her eyes.

Madame Habiba was on her feet immediately, pulling Nasira into her arms. "My dear mistress," she said, stroking Nasira's tangled hair. "Was he not a good husband to you?"

"I do not wish to be married to that man, Habiba," she hiccoughed. "I want Rogier. I miss my husband."

"There now, we cannot change the past, my lady. This was only one night, and it is Mafeo's first marriage. It may take him time to understand how to treat a wife. In time, you may come to love him as you loved Lord Rogier."

"Oh, Mafeo clearly has had plenty of experience with women, Habiba!" Nasira pushed away. "But only those that he can treat roughly. He says that he expects me to bear him an heir within the year, but I cannot stomach the thought of spending another night in that room." She clutched a cushion to her face to stifle her sobs.

"Did he hurt you?" Madame Habiba asked gently.

"No. He only frightened me. Please draw a hot bath, Habiba. I want to scour him off my skin."

Madame Habiba kissed Nasira on the top of her head, then hurried from the room, yelling for the servants to fill the large copper tub in Nasira's room. An hour later, Nasira sank into the fragrant water, watching the steam curl toward the ceiling of her chamber as Madame Habiba washed her hair with frankincense-scented soap. The door to the room slammed open, shattering the quiet, and Mafeo stood in it, completely naked. Madame Habiba drew in her breath sharply and averted her eyes.

"I expected to find my wife next to me when I roused this morning, but instead, I woke alone. Come back to bed," he ordered her.

Nasira glared at him from the water. "I must bathe. After the long day yesterday, it is necessary."

"Bathe afterward, Wife. I have need of you now."

Nasira stubbornly sank deeper into the water. Mafeo looked balefully at Madame Habiba, who crouched near her mistress's head.

"Leave us!" he bellowed at her.

Madame Habiba looked fearfully at Nasira, then slowly stood to go. Nasira sat up in her tub.

"Madame Habiba is my servant, and she comes and leaves at my command only. You will not speak to her with such a tone."

"As your husband, I have jurisdiction over the slaves and servants of this household, including your lady's maid, and including you. You will come to my bed. Now!"

"I am neither your slave nor your servant. I am the lady of this house, and if you speak thus to me again, I shall have the guards drag you from it!" she shot back.

With a yell, Mafeo grasped the edge of Nasira's tub and threw his weight against it. Nasira screamed as the tub overturned, sending a wave of water across the room, saturating the woven mats on the floor, knocking chairs sideways, and toppling a table. Madame Habiba was on her knees immediately, dragging Nasira away, pulling a robe over her mistress to cover her nakedness. Mafeo stormed across the room and grabbed Nasira by the top of a wet, glistening arm, wrenching her to her feet. He threw her into his bedchamber and slammed the door behind them, leaving Madame Habiba trembling in her lady's empty chamber, clutching the wet robe to her chest. She could hear the sound of the water as it dribbled through the cracks in the floor into the room below.

"What in the name of heaven and hell is going on!" a voice roared from downstairs.

Henri had seen the water from Nasira's tub as it flowed underneath the door and down the mosaiced stairs. Madame Habiba took a few deep breaths to steady herself, then opened the door and walked down the sopping staircase, back erect, face blank.

"There was an accident, and your mother's tub overturned, my lord," she said calmly.

She wanted to pull Henri into Mafeo's bedroom and demand that he save his mother, but she knew Nasira would not allow it. She must save face for the sake of her mistress.

Henri was quiet for a moment. "Well, I suppose these stairs needed to cleaning anyhow. Ibrahim will send a carpenter to assess if there is permanent damage to the room."

Madame Habiba curtseyed but said nothing. Her fear and rage were too strong. She hated Mafeo, and she hated Henri for bringing the beast into her lady's house. Lady Nasira was noble and brave to save her daughter from that man, but Madame Habiba still wished she had not married him. She looked past Henri and saw Zahed, Mafeo's curly-haired manservant, standing in the hall holding a stack of clean linens. His face was pale and his eyes wide as he took in the overturned tub in the room behind her. It was evident by the expression on his face that he had seen this before.

***

The stairs were given a good scrub with the spilled bathwater and the sodden mats removed and replaced with fresh ones of sweet-smelling seagrass and lavender, woven together in a chevron pattern. Unable to find his mother, Henri met Ibrahim at the newly expanded sugar refinery to watch as the new furnaces were lit. Three of the refinery's servants yawned in the morning light, waiting to be trained on the latest techniques that Ibrahim had brought back from his visit to a sugar plantation in the north.

"Instead of the usual number of canes, these pots can hold three times as much. Therefore, you must press three bushels of cane juice at a time instead of one. Also, it is of vital importance that you use more vigilance when in the stoking room, for I noticed several fires burning too hot last week, and we must not allow the syrup to burn," Ibrahim instructed them in his quiet voice.

The men nodded, then moved towards the tall stacks of cane that they had harvested the day prior as Henri and Ibrahim continued on to the citronnier to discuss a concerning development with some of the younger lemon saplings.

"Thrips. I have seen this before, but it has been many years, and not at your estate. We must have acquired plants that brought the pestilence here with them," said Ibrahim, as he rubbed a ruined leaf between his fingers pensively.

Henri felt glum. "Perhaps it is a punishment from God."

Ibrahim shot him a look, then continued to the next tree. "It is not from God. It is thrips."

"Ibrahim, do you know why my father failed to prepare me for this?" Henri said with a sweeping gesture that encompassed the citronnier, the house, the fields of sugarcane, and groves of cinnamon.

"Thrips are something that no one is prepared for," replied Ibrahim, still examining the diseased leaf in his hand.

"No, that is not what I meant. Why did my father not teach me how to run the estate and the villages when I was young?"

"Did you ever ask him to prepare you? It was his understanding that you did not care for lemon trees and shipping manifests," Ibrahim said, straightening and moving to another sapling.

"I suppose I did not. However, a father should prepare his son. I am less prepared than most, and should it be my responsibility to remind him to do his duty as my sire? Passing on his legacy should have been the only thing occupying his mind, and yet he seemed to have given it no thought whatsoever." Henri kicked petulantly at a stone.

"Lord Henri, when he was not working, your father talked about almost nothing but his concerns for you and his legacy."

"Then why did he leave me so unprepared? Why allow me to spend my days training to be a knight and learning courtly manners? Those skills have been useless to me since he died."

Ibrahim chose his words carefully. "Your father sent you to live with Sir Geoffroi to give you the skills and protection you would need for what was to come. There are threats."

"Threats?" Henri repeated incredulously. "Look around us, Ibrahim! We live in the last great city in the Kingdom of Jerusalem. Threats to me are the same as they are to any other man living here."

"Not exactly," Ibrahim muttered under his breath, then looked Henri in the eye. "It was never your father's intent for you to remain here in Palestine. He wished for you to return to Francia, marry, and protect the family estate. To live the life of a noble, not a nobleman merchant."

Henri felt his irritation close to the surface. "I am protecting the family estate."

"No, my lord. Your uncle may live in Maron-en-Rouergue in Francia, but it is *your* estate. Your father was declared the firstborn of his father, and you are the heir. Therefore, it belongs to you. Your uncle rules that land with a cruel hand, and the people suffer. Your father was unable to return, but you have a chance to right the wrongs done."

Henri turned and continued to walk among the young trees. He was born in Acre. He had never traveled further from this place than the island of Cyprus. Francia was as foreign to him as the land of the Mongols. Although he often heard other locally born men talking wistfully of returning to the land of their fathers, he had no such desire.

He bent to pick up a handful of pale, stony soil at the base of a lemon tree. The other local Franj knights and their families kept a strict social separation between themselves and the city's Jews and Arabs. Henri fell somewhere in between this dichotomy. It wasn't just the tone of his skin or the blood in his veins that separated him from his peers. Who your parents were defined you, and his parents were the most unusual that could be found in the nobility of Outremer. A shield of self-importance and a mask of contempt might be a good ruse, but they didn't help the two halves of him join together.

"My lord," Ibrahim hesitated. "Are you aware of the Mamluk proximity to Acre right now?"

"Yes, although it is not as if they have not blustered at us before."

"They will wipe Acre from the earth like the sweepings of a threshing floor," Ibrahim said glumly. "You saw for yourself that even now, in our own slave markets, we sell young boys to the Mamluk army to use as fighters against our city."

Henri's brow knotted. "We are the most fortified city in the Holy Land. It would take a massive force with bigger horses, stronger men, and better weapons to defeat us. All of which I doubt they have. A force of Turkish orphans is no match for the knights of Acre."

"Your father met them in battle for the last time before you were born," Ibrahim continued. "He traveled far to the south, to the edge of the great desert with King Louis, where he met with a small force of Mamluk fighters while scouting. The king's knights outnumbered the opposing force two to one, yet when the battle was finished, only your father, Brother Languedoc, and a few others escaped with their lives, and your father was gravely wounded by an arrow. He barely survived the trip back to Palestine. This is why he never fought again."

"That mission... I have heard of it. The knights of King Louis were humiliated," Henri said.

"Yes, it was an embarrassment to the Crown that they had failed so spectacularly, but it was not a complete loss. They succeeded in confirming that the Mamluks are well-matched to our own soldiers. When the king died of a bloody flux, no one seemed to care anymore, but your father remembered."

"He actually thought that the Mamluks could take the city? And what do you think, Ibrahim? Do you share his concern?" Henri asked.

Ibrahim smiled. Rare it was that Henri ever asked for his opinion. "Your father was not a man to exaggerate or minimize the truth. If he felt that the Mamluks were a threat to Acre, then I believe him. Also, consider that this estate sits outside the city walls, has no significant fortification, and now no militia. Even if Acre does not fall, the estates and villages will easily be razed to the ground, and we are more vulnerable than most."

A warm breeze lifted Henri's hair, and he looked around the citronnier. Rows of dark-leaved trees shimmered in the heat, and the white limestone walls trapped the scent of fruit and dry soil. Losing al-Hadiqa would be like losing a part of his own body.

"We must protect it. This house must not fall. We will make the women relocate into our home in the city and hire another militia of our own to garrison here."

"That was not your father's plan, my lord," Ibrahim shook his head sadly. "This place was never meant to be your permanent home."

"Well, I run this house now!" Henri snapped. He was tired of people questioning his decisions, assuming that he didn't know how to run his own house, that he was too young and too arrogant to have an inner life. Since the day his father died, he had found himself surrounded by the opinions of others on everything from how to grow his crops to who and when to wed.

A servant hurried through the citronnier and handed Henri a letter with the seal of Sir Jean de Grailly, the Seneschal of Acre on it. When he saw the seal, his heart leaped, and he cracked it hastily. Seneschal Grailly and his father had been discussing Henri's investiture into the knighthood before Rogier died. But as he scanned the letter, his face grew pale.

> *Lord Maron, may God's grace be with you. Per the terms of your agreement with King Henry of Jerusalem, you are required to provide one knight or worthy knave to serve on a patrol of the northern roads at the first new moon. Please have your man report to the Templar citadel for service immediately. If no such man can be produced from your estate, you must go in his stead. In Christ's mercy, Jean de Grailly, Seneschal of Acre*

35

— · —

S idika stepped back from her half-finished manuscript and scowled. "I wish," she said with an agitated stomp, "that we could make finer brushes, Father. It is so difficult to achieve the correct level of detail with these tools."

"Never mind, my dear. You have a very steady hand, which more than makes up for the clumsy tools we must use," Tamrat smiled.

"Perhaps I shall cease learning to scribe and invent a better brush instead," Sidika growled crossly. "As well I should, for you and I both know that these skills will be useless to me once I marry."

"Useless? There are no competent shaykhas for a hundred miles of here!"

"A woman must be trained in a madrasa or by a scholar of renown to be a shaykha, Father."

"So? And have I not made you read the Qur'an and understand its concepts? Such beautiful prose and expressions of devotion in that book!"

"I am not a religious scholar, Father, and neither are you. We should both leave these musings to those who devote their lives to such questions." She glowered at the illustration on the paper before her. It still looked too heavy-handed, and she continued to glare at her brush until Tamrat took it from her hand and set it down on the table.

"I shall buy you some new brushes the next time I am in Damascus, my dear." He hesitated, looking at her sideways. "Truly, my daughter, what do you want in your life? Do you really think you cannot continue to scribe once you are married?"

Sidika stared at him for a moment. "I am a woman. I have no right to want anything."

"I know not where you got that idea. Your mother and I never encouraged it."

Sidika wiped her ink-stained hands on a cloth and removed her ragged wool apron. "You and Mother are not normal, Father. What else can a woman aspire to but marrying a man who rarely beats her, or to bear children and hope that she or they will not die?"

"When I met your mother, she did not wish for any of those things. She made herself a valuable member of the community with her knowledge of herbs."

"As I said. Not normal." Sidika kissed him on the cheek and walked outside to the little oven, whose coals glowed dimly, nestled in a bed of ash. Tamrat followed her out and watched her for a moment as she poked a reticent flame to life with a stick.

"You are also not normal, Sidika. I know of no other young woman your age who is as well educated as you, and I have known princesses and matrons of great houses. I wonder if I did you a disservice, for most men find an educated woman intimidating. Here, now! Perhaps we could find a way for you to join the nuns! They are also educated and spend their days reading and writing."

"Father!" Sidika laughed. "We are Jews. I do not think the nuns would take me. Why do you have a sudden interest in converting me to another religion?"

Tamrat shrugged. "You do not have to convert, and they do not have to know. Since you are a Turk, you could always tell them that, and maybe they will not ask about your religion."

Sidika shot him a flat look. "I feel certain that the nuns would ask about my faith. No, Father, I want nothing. I am happy here with you. I shall take care of you until you die, and then I will either marry or take a job in the city."

"No man would hire you, Sidika. I worry about you. I have promised that you may choose your husband, but how will a village man deal with a wife such as you? You must have some protection and income after I am gone."

Sidika held up her bow in one hand and a quill in the other.

"What were you saying?"

Tamrat laughed. "Yes, I see you can take care of yourself. But my daughter, perhaps we should send you to the land of the Franj. There are learned women there, and some of them write. The von Bingen woman – she even counseled kings!"

"She was a rarity."

"And so are you!" Tamrat pounded the side of the house, sending a shower of dried mud-plaster to the ground.

The world in which he had raised his children was not the world he wanted. He knew that to take Sidika to Francia or the Italian peninsula would mean exposing them to danger and discrimination. He knew that if she did not marry, she would be accused of witchcraft because of her knowledge. He also could not imagine any man who would not be threatened by her intellect. He had cursed her with this learning.

"Father, I am happy," she said, putting her hand on his arm. "I know no other women or girls in this village who are happy. I do not aspire to be a counselor to kings. I just want to stay here with you. I want to keep learning."

"Daughter, I wish for you to go out into the world and move the stars in the sky. Change the thoughts of men and fill their hearts with fear and awe when they see you coming, because they know you have knowledge and courage. I wish all of these things for you, and I know that you cannot have them because you were born a woman. But I can still wish them for you."

Sidika smiled. "But I love you for wanting it, Father, and perhaps I will be so lucky as to meet a man who also feels the same way." She scanned the ground of their small dooryard until she spied two little brown eggs that the hens had left hidden in their dust wallows, then took them inside.

"You should marry a king. You should have the run of your own scriptorium. A hundred novice scribes under your care...." Tamrat trailed off as he followed her in.

"It is not wise to wish for things you cannot have. And besides, if I become truly desperate for the arms of a man, there is always Fakri," she laughed.

Tamrat chuckled and helped her prepare supper. Evening birds swooped over their heads, and a hot breeze swept across the dry hills. When the meal had finished cooking, they sat outside on the bench beside the door, balancing their clay bowls on their laps and waving at neighbors as they walked by.

When they had finished, Tamrat remained outside alone, his face lifted to the heavens as the stars appeared one by one in the mellow autumn sky. *Hashem*, he pleaded, *I am getting old, and I have not been the most faithful of Your people, but I beg you, please let no harm come to my daughter after I am gone. She is too talented and unusual to let her waste away.*

Hashem was silent, and the stars looked on him impassively. Despite the heat of the night, Tamrat shivered.

36

— • —

AL-HADIQA, ACRE. OCTOBER 1290

I t took little time for Henri to secure replacements to garrison the house. Knights were becoming increasingly rare
in Outremer due to the wars happening abroad in Francia and
the Holy Roman Empire, so turcopoles – locally born soldiers
with admirable skill but no title – replaced Sir Parsiprestre
and Sir Itier. Durant, Henri's master-at-arms, oversaw the
men's training, and Henri drilled with them to keep his skills
sharp.

A young man of noble birth who had the proper training
would typically be knighted as he came of age. Some sooner,
and some later. Henri woke every morning wondering if this
would be the day that he would receive his investiture as a
knight, but none of the nobles in the city ever brought the
topic up. The words of his father the day he died echoed in
Henri's mind as he sulked one day, watching Durant and two
of the turcopoles discussing the fortification of the estate's
walls.

*"I will not give you a title and let you loose on the population
of this city until you have demonstrated that you have some
redeemable qualities, my son. Learn to be a man of honor
first!"*

Lately, his thoughts seemed to be turning against him.
His mind wandered on its own toward introspection, and
since the other young men of Outremer studiously avoided
self-reflection, he tried to do the same. It was dangerous to

ponder one's shortcomings when embroiled in a two hundred-year-long holy war.

A shadow fell across him and lingered. Zahed, Mafeo's wild-haired lackey, stood before him, grinning. Henri often saw Zahed slipping from Mafeo's room, quietly peering through windows at Nasira as she walked the grounds, or trailing her when she took her horse out to ride in the early morning. Mafeo himself had become thoroughly intolerable, ordering the workers around in the fields and then offering simpering excuses for his interference to Henri later. His mother rarely left her chamber anymore, did not take her meals in the hall with the other guests, and did not meet his eye when they passed each other in the courtyard. The scale of his mistake tugged at a corner of his consciousness. He had married his mother to a devil. He pushed that one down with the rest of his suspicions about his own character.

"My lord," Zahed bowed, his golden-brown curls flopping across his face. "I wish to offer my help to train your new soldiers."

Henri took a moment to comprehend the slave's words, then stood. "Why would I want your help?"

"Because I have seen battle, and your men are unprepared to take on a Mamluk attack."

Henri eyed him with distaste. His youth spent with Sir Geoffroi had honed his paranoia to a sharp point, and nothing alerted his defenses more swiftly than being challenged by an older boy.

"You come here as a slave, swagger up to me in front of my men, and then tell me that they are unprepared? Why should I take any counsel from you?"

Zahed's face clouded with confusion. "Pardon my lord, I meant no offense."

Henri stood. "Oh, I am sure you did intend to offend me." He raised his voice, and the other servants stopped their work in the courtyard to watch. "Your master is a scoundrel, and I assume you are the same. I have no wish for help from anyone in his household. Would that he had left you at his house in the city."

He turned to go, but Zahed grabbed his arm and wrenched him back.

"You speak as if I have a choice!" Zahed snapped. "You speak like one who has always been the owner and never the owned."

Instinctively, Henri snatched Zahed's tunic and sank his fist into the man's stomach. Zahed gasped for air, and Henri pushed him back against a wall.

"Never touch me again," he said through gritted teeth. "I have seen you do that man's bidding like a cur whose master feeds it scraps from the lowest table."

"You are the one who married your mother to him," Zahed wheezed, "not me. If you want to be angry at someone, make it yourself." He snatched Henri's wrist, twisted it painfully, spun him around, and put his hand to Henri's throat. "And if you ever touch *me* like that, Lord Henri, you will find yourself with my dagger in your side."

"If Mafeo allows you to keep a dagger, then he is an even greater fool than I suspected," Henri grunted, just before he slammed the point of his elbow into Zahed's stomach.

Zahed saw the blow coming, clenched against it, then dropped to the ground, rolling away from Henri, and sprang to his feet again. Before Henri could react, Zahed had pulled one of the bows from a nearby armor rack and had an arrow aimed at Henri's eye. By this time, Durant and the turcopoles had noticed the commotion and come running. One of the men tackled Zahed to the ground, and another put his sword tip to his throat before turning to Henri.

"Your kill to take, my lord. You may use my sword if yours is not close to hand."

Henri looked at the sword and then at Zahed on the ground, staring up at him fearlessly. "No. Let him go."

***

The turcopoles reluctantly released Emre and Henri offered him a hand, heaving him to his feet. Then he grabbed two blunted lances from the armor rack and tossed one to the slave.

"Are you a Mamluk?"

Emre caught the lance and balanced it in his hands. It felt natural. Real. Like the most familiar and solid thing he had felt in years. His arms and legs burned to rehearse the dancelike drills he had learned in the meydan.

"No," he said, letting the weapon clatter to the ground.

Henri charged, and Emre had just seconds to dive for the lance again and bring it up to block the blow. The first contact made his teeth clack together and his arms vibrate. Jumping back, he balanced on the balls of his feet and crouched into a defensive position. Neither man had a shield. With a yell, Henri attacked again, and for a second time, the force of the attack shocked Emre. Lord Henri might be pretty and arrogant, but he was powerful and well-trained. Emre, on the other hand, had been laying out Mafeo's clothes and serving his wine for over a year, and he realized with dread that he would not have the strength to resist for long.

"When your body is spent in battle, your wits must go to work for you."

The words of tawash Izem, his old trainer, sprang into his mind. Henri had him back against a wall, steadily pushing until Emre had almost no room to maneuver. Planting the butt of his lance into the dust, Emre ran two steps up the wall behind him and vaulted away. Henri spun around, stunned.

"Mamluks wear lighter armor than Franj, so they are quicker and more agile in hand combat," Emre panted. Henri feinted to the right, then jabbed his lance toward Emre's stomach, but Emre blocked across his body, easily deflecting the attack. Then, he used the momentum from the maneuver to bring his lance around and crack Henri on the side of the head. Henri grunted, putting a hand to his ear, and Emre realized that Durant and the other turcopoles were standing in a wide circle with their swords drawn, ready to charge if their lord was injured. In that second of inattention, Henri's lance shot out and slammed against Emre's instep. He staggered with a cry. Henri threw his lance to the ground, then tossed Emre a bow and several arrows.

"Salih!" he yelled. "Bring Raven and saddle Persephone. Slave, can you shoot a pomegranate from that tree while your horse circles it?"

Emre stood, his bruised foot throbbing. "I can, and I do not need a saddle. I will ride bareback."

Henri shrugged and launched himself into Raven's saddle. Emre sprang onto the back of Persephone with some difficulty – she was a courser, and taller than the quick, compact Arabian horses that he was accustomed to. Henri circled the pomegranate tree, whipping up a cloud of dust around it. He fired three arrows at the tree, and one of them grazed a pomegranate. Durant and the turcopoles cheered.

Emre urged his mount forward with his knees, pulled three arrows from his quiver, held them all in his draw hand, then fired them in quick succession. The first two passed cleanly through the fruit in a shower of ruby pulp. The third buried itself in the tree's twisted trunk.

"Well, I am out of practice," Emre admitted, sliding from the horse. Durant, he noticed, still had his sword drawn. "These are only two of the skills that Mamluks must learn to perfect. The rest I can show you and your men."

Henri smiled. "Does your master know he has given food and shelter to a Mamluk and brought him into the house of a lord of Acre?"

"I told you. I am not a Mamluk."

But it did not sound right. Emre realized with horror that he *was* a Mamluk. It was the only identity he knew, and he had owned it the longest. Longer than being a nomad of the Cilician mountains. Longer than being a slave and manservant. Longer than being a sullen and angry youth.

"How many other lies have you told to Mafeo?"

Emre tried to think of a response, but Henri turned on his heel and walked toward the house.

"Clean this mess up!" he shouted over his shoulder.

Durant and the turcopoles followed, leaving Emre alone in the dooryard.

37

― • ―

Fajar, the hills of Idmit. October 1290

"Now, Daughter, keep the door barred when you are inside and seek out Rahat's house if you become scared. Are you sure you will not sleep there instead?"

"Rahat and her husband are trying to make a child. I prefer to sleep here."

"Well, er... yes, I suppose that is best," Tamrat blushed, placing some cloth-wrapped loaves of bread in the donkey's saddlebag. "I will return in a fortnight at the most, although I hope it to be a faster journey than that. Would you not prefer to come with me? We could ask Fakri to care for the animals while we are away."

"Do not forget new brushes, Father." Sidika pressed three bezants into Tamrat's hand.

She had thought many times about going back to Damascus. The prospect of staying alone in Fajar was far less terrifying than the chance that she might see Bekir, her old master, again... that he might snatch her quietly away from her father and lock her up in his warehouse or forgotten children.

"No, Father, I shall stay here, and you must not worry about me. It is good that you have received this commission. It will bring us some much-needed money. Please travel safely and do not worry about me." She kissed him on the cheek, and he mounted the little donkey, turning and giving her one last look as she disappeared into the house and shut the door behind her.

***

"What did you just say?" Philip was not sure his ears were working properly.

Grand Master Beaujeu glanced up from the paper he read and looked at Philip, an eyebrow raised.

"Apologies, my lord," Philip dropped to one knee and bowed his head respectfully. "I thought I misheard you. Did you say that Henri of Maron will be accompanying us on this patrol?"

"I did," Beaujeu replied, picking up his quill. "It seems the young man no longer has any knights to contribute to his debt of service to the city. Therefore, he must go himself."

"But my lord, is not the young man still a squire?"

"Not a squire, no, but not a knight either. However, he is an admirable hand with a sword, and you will find that an asset, although his attitude may leave much to be desired. The Patriarch has been asking of late why the boy has not been knighted, and I want to take this opportunity to observe him. You will give me a report."

"I, uh..."

"Is there a problem, Brother Philip? There are rumors of Mamluk scouts in the hills between here and Damascus and we must increase the men in our patrols. If that means taking on able fighters who are not yet knighted, then it is what we must do. Oh, and Brother Philip..." Beaujeu leaned forward, his gray eyes serious. "No harm must befall young Lord Henri on this patrol, or else I will have the wrath of King Henry of Cyprus, King Philippe of Francia, and the Patriarch following me. See that he comes back alive."

"Yes, my lord." Philip bowed his head again, his mind racing. "May I be excused, Grand Master? I must prepare before we leave this evening."

Beaujeu waved him away absently and continued to scratch at the paper in front of him. Philip hurried from the grand master's quarters and strode toward the towering, sparsely windowed stone structure where he slept. Taking the stairs two at a time, he rushed to the second-floor solar he shared with Brother Alaran, Brother Languedoc, and their three squires. Brother Languedoc stood in the hall, adjusting his robes and looking through one of the narrow arrowslit windows down to the courtyard.

"Peace and blessings upon you, Brother," Philip murmured as he brushed past, but Brother Languedoc stopped him.

"Brother Philip, a moment, please."

"What is it? I must hurry to prepare for our patrol, which leaves this very eve."

"Your squire, Paolo, is ill. I have interceded on his behalf and the commander has permitted him to convalesce in the healing hall."

Philip blinked without comprehension. "Ill? I saw him this morning when he served me my meal. What has taken him so quickly?"

"A complaint of the stomach, I am afraid. He is in the garderobe, shitting so violently I fear there will be naught left inside him but his bones."

"Well, I will pray for the healing touch of Jesu Christi at vespers this eve," Philip said, but he scowled. He had never ridden out on patrol without Paolo. Without his squire, he would have to set up his own tent and mind his own pack animal. "Can a replacement be found?"

"No time, I am afraid. I am truly sorry that this happened to you, Brother. May God keep you safe on your patrol." Brother Languedoc crossed himself, then retreated down the stairs.

Philip's supplies were already packed and waiting in the stable, but the news that Henri of Maron would be joining the party rattled and excited him. Dropping to his knees at his cot, he twisted back the loose board in the floor. His pauper's disguise was there, along with his bag of gold, but his dagger, the curved, jewel-handled dagger that he had carefully concealed for so many years and plunged into Rogier of Maron's heart at al-Hadiqa, was gone.

38

THE HILLS OF MOUNT HERMON. OCTOBER 1290

O n the first night of the new moon, a small company of city knights and robed Templars rode in a cloud of dust to relieve a cohort of men who guarded the roads to Acre against attack. The secular knights, both titled and common-born, rode under their house banners, a blessing for Henri since his livery was all dark. His Maron of Acre family crest was a field of black with a gold line running from the top left to the lower right. In the lower-left quadrant, three plump golden lemons glowed against their black background. Raven's glossy onyx coat was not draped with the cloak-like caparison that some of the other men used to show their house colors, so the three lemons stood out in the dark of her saddle cloth like strange eyes.

The other knights rode large, heavy-headed destriers, but Henri favored his graceful, proud mare and damn the snide comments from the men about his insistence on keeping a woman between his legs. Raven was quick and intelligent, with bright eyes and ears that quirked with curiosity. She obeyed without fault and could outrun the overloaded de-striers across a hot Palestinian hillside on any day. She was also fiercely protective, although if pressed, Henri would have difficulty articulating why. He felt he knew her as well as he knew himself. On this night, he and Raven moved through the darkness together like a single shadowy being.

The Templars rode close together at the head of their retinue, their pale robes glowing in the moonlight. Henri had worshipped them when he was a boy for their holiness and their unmatched prowess on the battlefield. As he grew older, the prospect of celibacy and a lifetime of service seemed a high price to pay, and his father did not argue with this change of mind. Rogier didn't seem to hold the Templars with the same respect and awe as the other Franj of Acre.

"None of these men are blameless," his father would say, "but at least the Order of the Hospitallers can heal the men that they break in half. All a Templar will do for you is say a prayer and stab you a second time."

As brother-knights, these five men were the elite fighters of the Order, but the Templars in Acre served many purposes. The Templar sergeants possessed a breadth of skills, from blacksmithing to banking, and were ever-present in the lives of the local merchants, monitoring the movement of goods and finance, and even brokering discreet loans to bankrupt nobles. They ensured that the many castles, farms, mills, and other holdings owned by the wealthy Order ran with meticulous efficiency. Templar Chaplains oversaw the preservation of the spiritual health of the Brethren and the surrounding community. And Guillaume de Beaujeu, the grand master of the Templar Order, was the de facto ruler of Acre in the absence of King Henry's presence.

Brother Gregoire, one of the younger Templars, reined back and fell in step with Henri. "How are you getting on, Lord Henri? This is your first patrol in the mountains, oui?"

"I am glad to be out with this company, Brother Gregoire. It feels good to be among men instead of my house of sisters and servants."

Brother Gregoire's loud, barking laugh earned him a glare and a shush from his taciturn comrades. He lowered his voice and leaned closer, conspiratorially.

"Ah yes, well, women are poisonous. They serve no purpose but to breed, feed, and make men miserable, is that not so?"

Henri squirmed uncomfortably in his saddle. Despite their occasionally annoying habits, he liked his sisters and his mother, but he was desperate to impress his heroes. Emboldened by Brother Gregoire's favor, he continued, regretting each word as it left his mouth.

"Some of them are even tolerable to look at, but I agree, they are otherwise useless. A pity a man cannot visit his wife when he has needs and then keep her locked in the cellar when she is not in use."

Brother Gregoire laughed heartily. "Right you are! You might have made a good Templar. Of course, with your reputation, it sounds like the lifestyle would not suit you, although it is not as if those rules are never broken."

And in the dark, Henri thought he saw Brother Gregoire wink at him. Henri thought of Master Tamrat's daughter, hunting for pheasants in her brother's clothing and healing her father's fever. The girl might be wild, homely, and ill-tempered, but she was certainly not useless.

After several miles of walking on level terrain, their horses labored up the sloping, scrub-covered hills surrounding the towering Mount Hermon. Normally, the mountains were merely dark green ramps on the horizon – hazy and obscured when the sea winds were unfavorable and occasionally crowned with white, making their ravines and peaks look unearthly. As the ground inclined upwards, the mountains seemed imposingly steep and incredibly real. The company continued up the trail, the horses kicking up puffs of dust, until they saw the flickering light of a fire on the rocks.

"Ho!" shouted Brother Gregoire.

"Who goes?" came a wary reply.

"Those who would deliver you home to your comfortable beds and a cold dish of ale," Brother Gregoire responded with a laugh, and cheers erupted from the camp.

Soon they arrived at the fire, which bustled with activity as the slaves and squires unpacked provisions for Henri's incoming group and saddled horses and stowed bedrolls for the outgoing group. As the sun began to rise, their leader clapped loudly for attention.

"Sir Beauvais and young Lord Henri, you will stay here and watch the camp. Brother Gregoire, Sir Hanlet, and Brother Alaran will all come with me to patrol the road to the south. The rest of you spread out along the road to the north. We are west of Qal-at fortress – do not stray too close to it unless you wish to have your heads delivered back to camp without your bodies. Remain out until terce and then send a man back to be relieved."

Henri nudged Brother Gregoire. "Who is your commander? I have never seen him in Acre before."

"Brother Philip de Fons Bleaudi," Brother Gregoire whispered, "and do not allow yourself to end up on the bad side of his temper. He is as mean-spirited as a cornered weasel."

Henri sighed, recalling some of the more unpleasant moments of his training with Sir Geoffroi and the unchecked cruelty that older knights could inflict on younger men. Although Brother Philip had not spoken more than two words to him, Henri had noticed the man watching him predatorily. This could be a very long fortnight. He jumped as Sir Beauvais clapped him on the back.

"Looks like we have the place to ourselves, young man," he boomed. "Fancy a game of chess?"

They sat with the board perched on a pile of blankets between them for several hours, Henri winning one match, Sir Beauvais winning two. Eventually, a knight reappeared from each direction, requesting to be relieved. Henri enjoyed the company of Sir Beauvais, who was good-natured and talkative, but he readily mounted Raven and set out toward the north to join the group of waiting knights along the road.

And waiting was precisely what they did. Three pilgrims passed them that day on their way to Acre, wearing brown robes and sandals made of wood and hempen rope. A two-wheeled merchant wagon loaded with jars of olive oil rattled past them, and a few local farmers and merchant families, all traveling away from Acre, their eyes averted fearfully from the knights. Henri watched them retreat until their forms blurred in the waves of heat rising from the dusty road.

The next day, Brother Philip ordered Henri to stay in the camp again, this time with Brother Alaran, the knight who had apprehended Rogier's murderer. He was neither jovial nor interested in chess. A stoic Englishman with flinty gray eyes and a craggy face, he preferred to sit at the fire, picking at his nails with his dagger or polishing his equipment.

Henri paced the camp until it was time to relieve the first shift. He and Raven turned to the south this time because Brother Philip had taken watch in the north. The same routine continued day after day until the first week concluded with an extra ration of meat for the men.

On the Sabbath, the Templars led a holy service at sunrise, making everyone kneel on the ground for such a long time that when they stood, small pebbles stuck in their armor, requiring the squires to dig them out of the interlinking mail with sharpened sticks. Listening to Brother Philip intone his lengthy prayer while he tried to ignore the flies that swarmed around the men, Henri again felt grateful that he had not joined the Brethren. *Tonsured hair would not look comely on me*, he thought smugly as he focused his gaze on Brother Alaran's shorn and sunburned head.

The following day, Brother Philip arranged everyone into their groups, and they set off again, with Henri left behind. This time, Brother Philip was one of the two knights returning to be relieved first. He trotted to the camp where Henri and an older Templar named Brother Jean de Lenglée played at tossing stones into a circle.

"Brother Jean, please ride to the north to relieve me. Young Henri, this fire needs more fuel, and what is that?" Brother Philip asked, gesturing to the circle of stones.

Henri felt his temper rise. "It is the squires' job to feed the fire."

"Well, then, manage the squires better, *Lord* Henri," Brother Philip said, brushing past Henri's shoulder. He walked to the circle and kicked at it until the stones scattered.

Brother Jean mounted his horse and favored Henri with a pitying look as he rode off. Brother Philip pointedly ignored Henri as he sharpened his weapons and patched a hole in his saddlecloth, only standing when a cloud of dust on the horizon indicated riders on the road. It was Brother Gregoire who rode back this time to be relieved, and Henri eagerly jumped up and made for his horse, but the voice of Brother Philip stopped him.

"Stay, young Henri. I think I will relieve Brother Gregoire today."

"But Brother Philip, you have only rested for a short time, and I have been here all morning," Henri protested.

"And yet I feel still quite energetic. Please stay here and do a better job of minding the camp this time. Brother Gregoire, Henri is not to play games while at the camp. It is unbecoming of our mission."

"Brother Jean was also—" Henri started, but Brother Philip was already trotting away in the shimmering heat.

"He's a right nasty piece of work when you get down to it," said Brother Gregoire, watching the retreating back ends of horse and knight. "What were you and Lenglée playing?"

They set up the circles of stones again, wagering their ration of ale to the winner.

"Why do we still watch these roads with so many men?" Henri asked, tossing a stone. It landed in the circle and then bounced out again. He frowned. "We have a peace treaty with the sultan. The city is fortified and well-guarded. Surely the Mamluks are not a serious threat to us these days. After all, Acre is a valuable trading port for Qalāwūn as it is for us."

Brother Gregoire tossed his stone. "There is a threat. Henri, do you know what the Mamluks have been saying? They have sworn to wash the streets of Acre in our blood, not leaving a woman, child, or man alive until they retake the entirety of the Holy Land."

"They are always saying that," Henri pointed out, "and are not the Mamluks too busy chasing after the Mongols to also try to kill us?"

"Yes, but they are different now. Fiercer. They are amassing men and armor, and we suspect they have been crafting siege weaponry in the north. This army is more well-matched to our forces than anything we have seen in the past, and it is probably large enough to kill both the Mongols and us. Their tactics are sophisticated, they are well organized, and their horsemen can match ours for skill. Last year we did not worry, but Qalāwūn voided the peace treaty when that wretched group of Sicilians massacred some Arabs in the city a few months ago."

Henri pondered that for a moment. "I am sure we must be secure. We have double walls, a fosse, and twelve fortified towers. And Acre is the Templar headquarters, for God's sake! The most dangerous fighters in Christ's army are in the Holy Land and headquartered right here. Send the Sicilians back to where they came from."

Brother Gregoire shot him an annoyed look. "And punish Christians for killing Arabs and Jews? You had best reconsider your confidence, young man. Even Grand Master Beaujeu is concerned. He has been writing to the Pope and King Philippe in Francia for help, but he cannot raise additional troops because the Sicilians *were* the troops, and now they have probably started a war for us. The city leaders refuse to acknowledge the threat, and the rest of the world has truly lost faith."

"Or just forgotten that we exist," Henri muttered, tossing another stone at the dusty circle.

***

The next afternoon, Henri and Raven set off to the south to relieve Brother Alaran at the second watch. He found the Templar and other knights just below the crest of a rocky crag, unmounted and crouching in the dirt.

"Hush, Henri!" Brother Alaran whispered. "Enemies ahead."

Henri's heart pounded. He secured Raven at the base of the hill and crawled up to the men. Removing his helmet, he peered around a large boulder at the valley below. A cloud of pale dust rolled across the road in the far distance as six mounted men galloped toward Damascus.

"What say you, Alaran?" Sir Hanlet asked nervously. "Shall we harry them?"

Brother Alaran shook his head. "They are too far, and they run away from Acre. Spread out along the road and conceal yourselves. We must search for their spies. Henri, you are with me."

The other knights dispersed quickly. Brother Alaran decided to scout east of the road in the forest.

"Forgive me, Brother Alaran, but might I not go in your stead?" Henri asked, continuing quickly when the older man shot him an annoyed look. "I grew up in Palestine, and I am comfortable with the terrain and the heat."

Brother Alaran was tall, broad, and wore heavy curtains of mail armor. His face shone with perspiration, and sweat dripped down his palms from underneath his white robes. "Very well, but do not do anything stupid because no one will come for you if you get caught."

Henri gratefully slipped out of his black surcoat, which covered his iron-ringed hauberk and kept the metal from becoming too hot in the sun. He stripped off his sweat-soaked gambeson, a lightly quilted jacket that protected his skin from the interlocking metal of his mail, and pulled at leather straps and iron toggles, dropping more bits of armor to the ground until he was standing in his sand-colored linen tunic and a pair of knee-length linen braies. Digging in his saddlebag, he found a roughspun cloth and began to wrap it around his dark hair.

"Maron, what in the name of the Virgin are you doing?"

"Concealing myself," Henri said, wrapping the cloth into a turban on his head and tying it in place.

"Well, if you want to go scampering around the countryside in your underclothes, that is your choice," Brother Alaran said with obvious scorn, "but you look like a dalcop."

"At least I will be a living dalcop when this day is over," Henri said, tucking his flask inside his shirt.

Promising to return before sundown, Henri slipped around the boulders at the top of the cliff and disappeared, dropping down into a shallow crevice. Feeling light and free, he quickly scampered down the opposite side of the hill and crept into a nearby copse of cedars and scrubby juniper shrubs. He kept to the woods, slinking silently on a spongy carpet of fragrant forest duff until the trees began to thin and he could see a flicker of light through the gray trunks, reflecting from a shimmering green lake. Intending to fill his flask, he made for the lake but froze and dropped on his belly when he heard voices speaking quietly.

From Henri's hiding place in the trees, he saw a group of men and horses resting near the water's edge. They wore billowing colorful breeches tucked into their boots and split robes of yellow, covered by hauberks of interlocked scales of leather and metal, making them look like strange fish. On their heads, they wore conical helmets secured in place by tightly wrapped turbans. At their sides, they carried slender curved bows of wood and horn, round shields, and a sheaf of lances lay on the ground near them. They spoke softly to each other in a mix of Turkish and a dialect of Arabic that Henri could hardly understand.

Henri tried to slow his labored breathing. So, this was the notorious Mamluk army, composed almost entirely of slaves trained to be brutally violent and unswervingly loyal to their masters. Occasionally, small groups of raiders would attack his house and were easily chased off, but these men were not of that ilk. They looked purposeful.

Henri watched, fascinated, as they moved amongst themselves. A man sat to the side of the camp with two of the younger soldiers who haltingly recited the Qur'an while he listened, occasionally nodding when they mastered a new verse. The others drilled gracefully with their lances near the shore of the lake, moving in perfect coordination. The leaders talked in a tight huddle near the trees.

Henri slithered closer to the edge of the forest. There appeared to be two groups. One consisted of the six men he had seen riding on the road towards Damascus, and the other group looked as if it had been camped in this location for days. Tents and latrine pits were arranged in an orderly fashion, and bare-chested men hacked at the nearby trees, stripping the branches and piling the denuded logs on sledges. Near the sledges, a pen of camels chewed their cud, their faces placid.

Eventually, the group of six remounted their horses and moved toward the road. Henri followed them at a distance, his dun-colored underclothes blending in with the pale rocks and dust. They walked their horses carefully over the dry terrain, avoiding the road and cutting overland toward the northwest. After following for a while, Henri turned back to the road and Brother Alaran.

By the time he arrived, the sun had sunk rapidly behind the rocky hills, and evening birds tentatively chirped in the branches of a nearby oak, calling question and answer to each other. When Henri returned, the English knight sat on a rock, drawing patterns in the dirt with a pointed stick.

"Mamluks. About twenty of them. Six retreated to the north. The rest appear to be creating a supply dump. They are felling and stripping timber," Henri reported.

"Put your clothes back on," Brother Alaran said, standing up. "We must tell Brother Philip."

The sun had already set when Henri and Brother Alaran arrived at the camp. The other knights from Henri's patrol milled about the fire, cleaning and stowing weapons or hand-ing out wooden bowls of fragrant stew. Brother Alaran dis-mounted his horse, handed the reins to Henri, and sought out Brother Philip immediately. The two men talked, heads close together for several minutes, then Brother Philip clapped Brother Alaran on the back and shouted for attention.

"Brother Alaran has discovered a squad of Mamluks on the north road," he said. "Tomorrow, we will seek these infidels and bring them back to Acre for questioning."

Henri looked hard at Brother Alaran, but the English knight pointedly avoided his gaze.

39

T he following day, Henri and Brother Gregoire were assigned to stay at the camp. Blond, sunburned, and perennially smiling, Brother Gregoire was the youngest of the Templars. He and Henri spent the morning throwing rocks into their circle and speaking of their homes in Acre.

"So, tell me, what is it like to make love to a woman?" Brother Gregoire asked after a long pause in their conversation. "I have heard, well... you have a reputation, it seems."

"What is it like? Wonderful. What is it like to never make love to a woman?" Henri challenged.

"Not always wonderful," Brother Gregoire confessed. "Many of the Brethren are older because they joined the Order after their wives died. Some of us joined before we had wives. Of course, we are supposed to be quite holy, so naturally, we never think about women." Brother Gregoire drifted off for a moment, took a breath, and continued. "Did you know that as a Templar, I am not even allowed to speak with a woman on the street?"

"You are not missing much," Henri said, "they rarely have much to say."

But as he spoke, he thought of his mother and his two sisters back at his home. None of the Maron women ever found themselves without something to say. Indeed, Blanche seemed to have an opinion about everything. He frowned.

Why are my sisters so immodestly outspoken compared to the other young women of Acre?

***

Brother Philip and Brother Alaran returned together that afternoon, their horses walking slowly in the mid-day October heat. A dusty man staggered behind them, his hands tied to Brother Philip's saddle by a long rope.

"What have you, Brother Philip?" Brother Gregoire asked, standing from his seat near the fire.

"I have apprehended a spy!" Brother Philip's face flushed, and his pale eyes sparkled. Henri stared, wide-eyed. The man's feet were bare, swollen, and crusted with black from where the dust had mixed with his blood and dried. His lips cracked and bled, and his head lolled, but there was no doubt in Henri's mind: it was Master Tamrat.

"Help me bind him, Brothers. He must be questioned," Brother Philip barked.

Henri observed Master Tamrat covertly while they bound his hands and feet. "Brother Philip," he heard himself saying, "I do not think this man is a Mamluk spy." A voice whined in his head. *What are you doing, Hamza? Keep your head down!*

Brother Philip eyed him without expression for a moment. Rising, he grabbed Henri's bicep with an iron grip and dragged him away from the prisoner.

"Watch your tongue, fool," he hissed, his eyes bloodshot from dust and sun.

Henri glanced at Master Tamrat, who whimpered in Arabic for water.

"But Brother..."

"Out with it, little lord! If he is not a Mamluk spy, then what is he?" Brother Philip snarled as Brother Gregoire joined them, his white-blond brows tangled with concern.

Henri hesitated. If he told the Templars that he knew Master Tamrat, they might assume that Henri was also a spy, which could endanger Henri's life and his entire family. Surely old men such as Master Tamrat died every day, and very few people noticed.

"Brother Gregoire," Henri turned to his friend. "You said the Mamluks are from Turkey and the Caucasus. Does this man look like a Turk, or does he look like a son of this land?"

"Mamluks are slaves, purchased from Nubia all the way to the Cuman and beyond. They all look different because they are of no particular race. He was trying to avoid being seen by my patrol on the north road, and he was carrying this." Brother Philip held up a scroll of parchment bound with string. Henri reached for the scroll, but Brother Philip snatched it away.

"He is too old to be a spy or a Mamluk—" Henri tried again, but Brother Philip cut him off.

"Listen, there are many older men and even women who would spy for the Mamluks if it meant the death of Christendom in the Holy Land. Assume that every Turk, Arab, Bedouin, and Jew is your enemy, and you will live long."

"May I speak with him?" Henri asked, lowering his head in an attempt to look humble.

"Ha! You? No. You know not the proper way to interrogate a prisoner." But Brother Philip hesitated, looked sideways at him. "However, I suppose you could learn." He opened his saddlebag, retrieving a short wooden club and a small, plain dagger.

"If you wish to question a prisoner, first you must observe someone with more experience." He walked back to the bound man, who squirmed and tried to back away upon seeing the white-robed knight approaching with his club. Brother Philip sank to one knee, his face inches from the prisoner's.

"Who is your master?" he demanded.

Master Tamrat blinked at him blankly, then looked around at the other knights. Brother Philip repeated the question louder, and Master Tamrat stammered, "I... I have no master, sir knight. I am a scribe, and I work on commissions. I am my own master."

Immediately, Brother Philip's hand was on Master Tamrat's shin, and the club came down on his already bloodied foot with a loud crack. Master Tamrat fell backward from his seated position with a scream.

"Give me satisfaction, Saracen, or I will break the other foot!" Brother Philip said. "Tell me where your men are hiding."

"I am not a Saracen!" Master Tamrat sobbed. "I am a Jew, and I traveled to Damascus to meet with a man who wishes to commission a book of the history of Syria!"

"Impossible. You do not look intelligent enough to be a scribe. Your skin is as brown as dung," Brother Philip snarled. He raised his club again, and Master Tamrat shrieked in fear.

Henri's heart raced. To speak out could mean his death, but the old man in front of him cried with the same eyes that had smiled at him only weeks earlier. His rational mind screamed at him to stay quiet, but....

"Stop, wait!" Henri shouted. "Let me talk to him. I know him!"

Brother Philip and Brother Gregoire stared, and Henri continued quickly. "He is indeed a scribe from the hills and a Jew, Brother Philip. It is not possible that this man could be a Mamluk or a spy. He lives a solitary life as an illuminator and translator."

"And how in the name of God do you know this, little lord? Surely you do not socialize with Jews and hill people? Is he a citizen of one of your villages, and if so, why do you not require him to wear garments demarcating him as a Jew? Where is his hat?" Brother Philip's pale eyes stared through him, and Brother Gregoire's expression grew more worried.

"He took me in when my horse was lamed," Henri said, consciously avoiding mention of Sidika, for if the knights thought Tamrat a spy, they would surely come to question her as well. "He was kind to me."

Brother Philip grabbed Henri by the front of his surcoat. "Kindness? Are you a man of Acre or a wet nurse? You spent time in this man's house? What did you tell him? Did he ask you about Acre's fortifications?"

"No, Brother Philip. We spoke of Aristotle and al-Farabi." Henri saw the uncomprehending look on Brother Philip's face. "They are two philosophers of antiquity. This man is peaceful, and he lives in a peaceful village. I doubt he has ever encountered a Mamluk or one of their amirs. Please, let me tend to his foot as he helped me tend to my horse's foot."

"A cunning story, but if this man is guiltless, then why did he attempt to avoid us on the road? If he is a scribe, where is his ink?"

Henri drew himself up and put on his best mask of haughty disdain, which he reserved for anyone who did not properly respect his rank.

"You do not believe me? Although you may be knighted, and I am not yet so, I will remind you that I am also a Christian and of noble lineage. I am a viscount and a marquis of Francia, and my word is honorable."

Far from cowing Brother Philip, this speech only seemed to enrage him. "You," he stepped closer to Henri, "are a half-breed, your father an imposter, and your grand-père was the worst devil that ever walked this earth."

Henri's mouth dropped open, and he stepped back.

Brother Philip continued. "I told the Brethren that it was unwise to bring you along. Your loyalties will always be divided between our holy cause and your thieving Saracen blood." He squatted in front of Master Tamrat and stared at him. "Alaran!" he hollered. "You are sure this man was among the Mamluks that you found at the lake?"

Brother Alaran didn't even have the decency to look guilty. "I am sure," he said smoothly. "Arabs all look the same to me, but I would know this one anywhere. And as you saw, he carries a packet of documents with him."

Brother Philip considered the prisoner silently. Then he drew his small iron dagger from a sheath on his belt. "Henri, come here," he commanded.

Henri put his hand on Brother Philip's arm and whispered fiercely. "Brother Philip, you must listen. Brother Alaran did not find the Mamluk raiders. He stayed with the horses while I scouted. This man was not among them! Sir, look at him! Does he have the look of a fighter to you? Does he look like anything other than a terrified old man?"

"These people are animals," Brother Philip said, gesturing with the dagger at the prisoner. "Saracen or Jew, they know nothing but hate for Jesu Christi and for our way of life! A Jew, you say? A killer of Christ, then."

Henri was at a loss for what to say. "Brother Philip, I am telling you that Brother Alaran lied. He would not know if this man was a spy or not because he never scouted!"

"Brother Alaran is a Templar knight, and he has sworn an oath of holiness and chastity. He would not lie about such things. And you," Brother Philip's face twisted into a sneer, "are just a rich coxcomb, playing at being a knight."

Brother Philip turned to the old man and grasped his hand. Master Tamrat started in surprise and tried to pull his hand back, but Brother Philip slammed it to the ground and thrust the point of his dagger underneath the nail of the man's middle finger. Master Tamrat let out a high-pitched scream, and all conversation around the camp ceased.

"Tell me the truth!" Brother Philip shouted, and Master Tamrat looked to Henri in agony. Henri started to speak, but Brother Philip cut him short.

"Gregoire! Have the little lord's hands and feet bound. I call his loyalty into question."

Brother Gregoire hesitated and then approached. Henri heard the prisoner scream again as Brother Philip dug the tip of his dagger underneath another fingernail.

"Sorry, Henri," Brother Gregoire mumbled as he wrapped a scratchy hempen rope around Henri's wrists and then tied him securely to a nearby pine tree. Henri listened, unable to cover his ears, to Master Tamrat's screams. *Blessed Virgin*, he thought, *do you not protect the innocent? Surely this is wrong?* But there was no answer from Mary. There was no sound at all, except the cries of an old man having his body broken.

Eventually, Henri was untied, his wrists bloody and his nerves frayed. He stood stiffly and fixed Brother Philip with a stony stare.

"Get on your horse and go relieve me with my cohort. They need the reinforcement," Brother Philip commanded flippantly.

Henri didn't move.

"Now, little lord! Get on your horse and go!" Brother Philip jabbed a gauntleted finger towards the north road.

Seething, Henri turned to Master Tamrat, uncorked his flask, and began to dribble water into the old man's mouth, noticing his dry tongue and eyes sunken from dehydration.

"Stop that at once!" Brother Philip screeched.

Henri calmly disobeyed. "If he dies of thirst now, who will you torment later for your entertainment?"

"You, for a start!" Brother Philip grabbed Henri's arm and pulled him violently to his feet, shoving him towards Raven, who neighed and sidled away with alarm.

Henri mounted and looked back at the prisoner. "It will be well, Master Tamrat," Henri said in Arabic. "Tell them the truth, and Jesu Christi will protect you."

"Maron! Speak in French, or else more severe consequences will come to you!" Brother Philip barked.

"Lord Henri, please, young man, where are you going?" Master Tamrat whimpered. "Please do not leave me with these men!"

"I will be back as soon as I can." He urged Raven to a trot toward the road.

***

Hours later, the weary knights returned after a long day of patrolling an empty road in the unrelenting heat. The sun had recently set, and the men gathered around the fire to share some warm ale and a meal of venison stew, the result of a kill that Sir Beauvais had made the day prior. The Templars, abstaining from meat on this day, satisfied themselves with bowls of cracked wheat porridge seasoned with almond milk and cinnamon. Henri noticed Brother Gregoire eyeing the bowls of stew furtively from his place next to Brother Philip.

"Brother Gregoire, are you not content with the food that God has provided us?" Brother Philip asked calmly. "I am sure it is only my imagination that you lust after meat on this day."

Brother Gregoire murmured a reply and kept his eyes on his bowl. Hunched over his food, Henri searched the circle of firelight for the prisoner but did not see him amongst the men. Taking a torch from the fire, he slipped into the darkness as if to relieve himself and searched the edges of the camp until he found Master Tamrat sitting quietly against a rock, still bound. In the wavering light of the torch, Henri could clearly see that the old man had been beaten again.

"What happened to you?" Henri whispered.

Master Tamrat let out a small sob. "They asked me questions, but no matter what I told them, they still cut me. Henri, they took the fingernails from my hands! I am a skilled scribe... I work for the sultan and his amirs. I have a commission right now from Grand Master Beaujeu himself." The old man's shoulders shook as he tried to contain his tears. "My hands... they are my life! What will I do now?"

Henri quickly unsheathed his flask again and brought it to Master Tamrat's lips. The prisoner chuckled. "Ah, young man, you bring water to wet my mouth so that I can spit in your face? After all, I think I have a right after what your people have done to me."

"I bring it so that you can spit in Brother Philip's face," Henri whispered.

"You watch out for that one, young cub. He is a wounded lion who will hurt anything that gets close to him."

Henri glanced fearfully back at the men drawn together around the fire. "Master Tamrat, why did you try to hide from them on the road? That made them suspicious. A dog does not chase a rabbit unless it runs away."

"You are right. These men are like dogs whose master has mistreated them. They are vicious and afraid. I have harmed no man. I have spent my life giving knowledge and healing to others, and this is how God repays me!"

Master Tamrat stopped to slurp more water, and then he sighed. "I avoided them because I was afraid they would detain me. You see, I left Sidika alone, and there are men in that village who would try to take advantage of her. They circle like vultures. I must hasten back to my home before they realize I am gone."

"Believe me, Master Tamrat, from what I saw of your daughter, she is capable of taking care of herself," Henri said caustically, recalling Sidika's biting words before he left her house.

Master Tamrat smiled. "She speaks brashly so that people will not get close to her, even when she wishes that they would."

"Master... you are not a spy, are you? I cannot say with certainty that you are not, and Brother Philip does not believe me."

"I could present you with all manner of evidence, young cub, but would you believe me? I say to you as a man who gave you hospitality that I am not a spy. You are a learned man. Read the documents that they took from me. Whether they accuse me or a kitchen maid, those occupiers are looking for spies, and so they will find spies."

He closed his eyes and sighed heavily, his stomach emitting a loud growl. Henri noticed the savory smell of stew permeating the air.

"I will return," Henri whispered and then sauntered back to the fire. Casually, he took one of the carved olivewood bowls and helped himself to some of the thick stew. Sitting at the very edge of the flickering firelight, he took a few tentative bites from his bowl before slipping away into the darkness and back to where Master Tamrat sat. Under the clear, starry sky, a cold mountain wind whistled across the hills, and the old man shivered against his rock. Henri spooned the stew into Master Tamrat's mouth, then quietly slipped a horse blanket over his shoulders.

"Ah, why are you doing this, young cub?" Master Tamrat murmured. "It will only get you into trouble. They will be displeased if you do not become brutal as they are."

"I will be brutal when the situation calls for it," Henri whispered. "Besides, I have many other vices that these men are not allowed to have." He crept back to the campfire and sat brooding for the rest of the evening.

At first light the next morning, Henri was awakened by Brother Philip ripping away his blanket and dragging him from his tent.

"Get up!" the Templar shouted. "Get up, you half-breed bastard!"

The other knights stirred from their sleep, some of them leaping to their feet and reaching for nearby weapons. Henri sprang to the balls of his feet and into a fighter's crouch on instinct.

"This young fool has been nursing the prisoner. I found the spy this morning with a blanket and some spilled stew on the ground," Brother Philip declared to the other men.

"Perhaps it was a squire who did it," Brother Gregoire said, casting a nervous glance in Henri's direction.

"The squires would not dare," spat Brother Philip. "Maron, come here."

Henri straightened and approached. He and the older knight were of the same height, although Henri was of a significantly more slender build. Brother Philip eyed him for a moment and then spoke.

"Ten lashes for disobeying the order of a Templar and five lashes for being a conceited wretch."

No one spoke. No one moved.

"And..." Brother Philip paused in thought for a moment. "You want to finally learn how to be a man, little Lord Henri? Here is your first lesson." He held out a short scourge with a thick leather handle and seven knotted leather tails. "First, you will give the spy fifteen lashes. Then you will have fifteen of your own."

"No." Henri moved closer to Brother Philip and met him, green stare to green stare. He heard Brother Gregoire intake his breath.

"Be still, Brother Gregoire," said Brother Philip, eyes still locked on Henri. "Our little lord here has not benefited from rigorous training like us, and he must learn how to respect his betters. You and I understand this. In the Order, this kind of disobedience could mean being compelled to eat your meals on the floor with the dogs for a year. Little Lord Henri, you just earned yourself another lash. You now have sixteen, and so does your prisoner. I tell you again, pick up this whip and do as you are told."

"I will not!" Henri shouted, but his voice and his knees were trembling. "This goes against your code. Are you not sworn to chivalry? You are Templars. Holy warriors! This is unholy!"

"Our code orders us to protect women, children, and God's pilgrims," Brother Alaran spoke up. "It does not extend to Saracen spies."

"And the innocent!" Henri's fists clenched and unclenched. His voice sounded thin and shrill to him. "This man is guilty of nothing more than being a traveler who dislikes knights, and can you wonder why? You betray yourselves to be crueler than the Mamluks!"

On the ground, Master Tamrat shook with a gravelly cough, opened his swollen eyes, and addressed him in Arabic. "Ah, my lion cub. You had better do as they ask."

Henri looked at him, his eyes wild, his heart thundering.

Master Tamrat's face was calm. "These feral dogs were always going to get me one day, young cub. Perhaps if you just give me a few tickles with that whip of yours, they will grow bored and let me go, eh?" He smiled broadly through broken teeth.

"I... but..." Henri stammered.

His thoughts swirled. Why was he risking himself for this man? Henri of Maron, Viscount of Acre and Marquis of Maron-en-Rouergue protected himself and no one else. He suddenly did not know who he was.

"What is he saying, Henri?" Brother Gregoire asked.

"He is telling me to do it. To beat him."

Brother Gregoire nodded solemnly. "Then you had better do as he says. Best not disobey two of your elders in one day."

Henri took the scourge with a trembling hand. The other knights turned Master Tamrat over and slashed his robe from collar to waist, exposing his bare back and the tassels on his tallit undergarment.

"*Ana 'asaf*," Henri whispered. "I am sorry." Taking a deep breath, he brought his arm down and the leather tails of the scourge slapped the old man's back.

"Harder, you woman! You have not even broken his skin!" Brother Philip yelled.

Henri pulled his arm back and slashed the tails across the man's back again. This time the old man flinched with a grunt. Fourteen more times he raised the scourge, and Master Tamrat writhed and groaned but did not cry out. Henri's eyes burned with tears, but none ran down his cheeks. Rage prevented him from showing Brother Philip how much he wanted to cry.

"Give me that!" Brother Philip snatched the scourge away.

With a sword-strengthened arm and many years of practice, he swept the whip down with such force that the skin
of Master Tamrat's back split, oozing blood, and his mouth
opened in a scream. Again and again, Brother Philip slashed
until Master Tamrat fell, senseless, to the ground, then he
turned and pointed the weapon at Henri.

"You next!"

***

Later that day, Henri sat on a rock near the fire, the pain still
throbbing through his back in waves and prickles. He had
been left to guard the camp while the others were on patrol,
and Brother Alaran had been left to guard him. Again, Brother
Alaran ignored Henri in favor of polishing his saddle, which
he insisted on doing himself. "A squire would just mess it all
up," he grunted.

Eventually, the older knight stood up.

"I'm off for a piss. Put some more fuel on the fire, would
you?"

Henri slowly got to his feet. Shirtless due to the seeping
wounds across his shoulders, he picked up a few pats of dried
dung and tossed them into the fire, sending up a cloud of ash
and sparks. Hearing a groan behind him, Henri looked around
and then crept to the prisoner's side.

After his beating, Master Tamrat had fainted onto his stomach, and the men left him there in the sun. Blood puddled into
sticky brown pools in the dirt at his flanks, and flies gathered
on the exposed flesh of his back, which was a mass of angry
red and crusty black. He whispered something into the dirt.

Henri glanced up in the direction of Brother Alaran. Apparently, the man had more business to do than pissing. He
scrambled to his flask and poured a thin stream of water on
the old man's face, washing away some dried blood and dirt,
then dribbled the rest into his hand and let Master Tamrat

drink from it like a cat at a dish of milk. He couldn't move the man onto his back or sit him up straight for fear of causing him great pain.

Master Tamrat slurped the last of the water from Henri's hand and then lay his cheek back into the dirt. "You did well, my lion cub," he rasped, a cloud of dust rising at his breath. "You are still an honorable man."

"Do not try to talk," Henri said, refilling his hand with water. "And it is not true that I am an honorable man," he mumbled. "There is nothing good to be said of me."

Master Tamrat drank again and sighed. "Oh, I knew there was goodness in you from the first day you showed up in my village, so angry and scared. You have buried it, deep within yourself, for some reason – perhaps because men treat each other like animals, and there is no safe place in this world for good any longer."

Henri sat, speechless and still.

The old man continued. "Three favors I ask of you, young cub. They will not be easy." His voice cracked.

"Hush, Master Tamrat, there are no favors needed. I will find a way to free you." Henri felt a wave of panic rising in his chest. The old scribe reached up and gently placed a wrecked hand on the young man's cheek. Henri froze, thinking of all the times his father could have touched him and didn't. This wounded hand, deprived of fingernails, swollen and hot, conveyed more than his father's entire lifetime of words had.

"First, I ask that you spend your life learning to reveal the goodness within you. Do not become like those men. Second," he paused and sighed again, "second, I challenge you to become a man on this day. If that devil Templar starts to torment me again, I wish for you to end my suffering."

Silence hung between them. Henri noticed movement and saw Brother Alaran picking his way back over the next hillside, clumsily hitching up his hose and tying it to the garter underneath his mail hauberk.

"You must do this for me. It will not be a mortal sin on your soul, Henri. Please do this, my son. I will not recover from these wounds. This I know," Master Tamrat said, squeezing his eyes shut.

"I promise," Henri whispered.

"Third, and most importantly, you must tell Sidika what has happened. Tell her not to be afraid and that her face is the last one that I saw before I died. Tell her I am happy with her mother and brother now."

Henri balled his fists and started to speak, but the old man interrupted him.

"Young man, you will do as I say, and you will not attempt violence against these men. They care not if I am a Muslim, a Christian, a worshipper of Tengri, or a Jew – they hate me because they want to hate me. These men know I am not a spy because the evidence is there. They will kill me because they want to kill me. Because they are bored, and their hearts are full of anger. Because they do not wish to see a man who looks like me living a free, rich life. Their pain overwhelms their senses, and so they must inflict pain on others in order to feel something stirring within them. You must show them a different way." Master Tamrat let his head drop back into the dust.

"You there! Henri, what are you doing?" Henri heard Brother Alaran shout as he trotted toward the camp.

"Do not be like these men, young cub. Now, do as I ask," Master Tamrat wheezed.

Brother Alaran grabbed Henri's shoulder, shoving him away from the prisoner. "You are certainly slow to learn, little lord!" He cuffed Henri hard across the face.

"The prisoner was asking to relieve himself!" Henri stammered.

"Then let him piss right here and sit in it like the animal that he is."

***

That night, when the knights had assembled around the stew-pot, Brother Philip spoke without looking up from his bowl. "I hear, little Lord Henri, that you have been disobeying orders again."

The hum of conversation and wooden spoons scraping bowls fell silent as each man froze and looked up. Brother Philip continued. "So, it seems that we need to teach you again." Turning to Brother Jean de Lenglée, he casually asked, "Brother Jean, I gave you my scourge, did I not?"

"Yes, Brother Philip."

"Please hand it to *Lord* Henri."

Brother Lenglée wordlessly tossed the weapon to Henri. It landed in the dust at his feet.

"Not going to pick it up, little lord? Well, I guess my arm could use a bit more exercise today." Brother Philip stretched and started to rise from his seat.

"I will take care of it." Henri stopped him, picked up the scourge, and walked out of the glowing circle of the fire's light. The knights grabbed flaming brands from the fire and followed. Master Tamrat lay on his back now, mouth open, breathing shallowly. With every few breaths, a violent shudder rolled through his body. The parts of his face that weren't bruised were flushed pink with infection.

"Is it time, lion cub?" he whispered, looking up at Henri with fever-glazed eyes.

Henri dropped the scourge and pulled his jeweled dagger from his sash, a gift from his father when he passed his six-teenth year. He had spent the afternoon sharpening it under the suspicious gaze of Brother Alaran. Gently, he put his hand on the old man's face, and Master Tamrat began to whisper kaddish under his breath, preparing himself for death.

Henri couldn't breathe. He had a flash of recollection. A circle of jeering boys, a tiny orange kitten, Sir Geoffroi's fists pummeling him.

"I will not continue to prolong this man's suffering," Henri said. "The Christian thing to do would be to end his misery. He is near death already."

Brother Philip laughed. "You do not possess the courage to take a life."

"There is nothing courageous about taking a life unnecessarily. My father taught me this." Henri knelt, his pulse throbbing in his head and drowning out all other sounds as the ground seemed to rise and fall around him. Master Tamrat looked at him with quiet acceptance, and then his ravaged face broke into a smile.

"Do it, please," he rasped.

Swiftly, Henri drew the freshly sharpened blade hard across Master Tamrat's neck. The tendons and artery severed, and hot blood gushed out onto Henri's hand. The old man's eyes never left Henri's. There was a moment of fear, a moment of confusion, and then, a relaxing. Blood poured onto Henri's lap as he watched the light fade in the old man's face.

Then he silently walked back to the fire and sat alone.

40

— · —

AL-HADIQA, ACRE. OCTOBER 1290

P hilip handed the reins of his horse to a groom and hurried across the courtyard to his solar, high up in one of
the citadel's towers. The panic pushed against his chest so
dreadfully that he thought he felt his heart collapsing within
him. He opened the door and peeked inside. It was empty and
dim from the waning light coming through the small window.
Hastily, he peeled off his filthy robes and sloshed some water
into his basin from a large pitcher in the cupboard. He washed
his face, beard, and hands, then looked at his reflection in the
thick wavy glass of the window. Standing in his hose, he could
see how tanned his face looked against the pale whiteness of
his skin, which was always beneath his robes. Templars were
not allowed to be disrobed, even in sleep. He had started to
lose track of the freckles on his chest, their constellations
once so familiar to him.

Dropping to his knees, he twisted up the loose floorboard
and pulled everything out, searching in vain once again for his
dagger.

"Son of a whore!" he swore under his breath. It must
have been Paolo, his errant squire, who stole his dagger,
but he knew he could easily extract a confession from that
weak-willed boy. It surprised Philip that Paolo would have
had the courage to steal anything from him at all.

Philip shook his head and opened his wardrobe, pulling out
a fresh robe. His body, now approaching fifty years old, was

stronger and healthier than it had ever been, and yet when he looked at Henri's young frame, he feared he would not have the strength to kill him when the time came.

The door creaked open, and Paolo shuffled into the room with his head bowed like a pup who fears his master's boot. Philip pulled his robe over his head and tightened his belt around his waist.

"Nice of you to join me." His voice was poisonous with sarcasm. "Change the water in my basin and take my robes to the launderer. Then you will return and tell me how it is that you came down with a sudden illness before a patrol."

"Yes, Brother Philip," Paolo wearily picked up the basin and left the room.

Philip made sure the door was closed and twisted up the loose floorboard again to stare at the place where he had last seen his dagger.

No... I last saw it in Henri's hand as he slit the old man's throat.

After he hadq scrubbed two weeks of camping on the road from his body, Philip waited outside the door of Grand Master Beaujeu's private apartments. Brother Alaran strolled laconically to the doorway and stood next to Philip, hands behind his back.

"Well," Brother Alaran asked in a low voice. "What do you plan to say?"

"I plan to tell the truth as it is, and so must you, Alaran. Lord Henri of Maron was trying to aid a spy for the Mamluks. I did not punish the boy severely, though I would have been within my rights to, and because of that, he killed a man who could have been a valuable source of information had he lived."

Brother Alaran leaned in close. "Yes, Brother, that is what happened. The question that I have is, why did you not kill Lord Henri as well? Sir Jean de Grailly says that he will grant Henri his investiture soon, and it will be that much harder once Lord Henri is a rich brat *and* a knight."

"With Gregoire constantly flirting with him, how could I have done any more harm to the boy than what you all saw?" Philip snapped, just as the door opened and the black-robed sergeant bowed toward them.

"The grand master will see you now."

Brother Alaran and Philip exchanged a look, then followed the sergeant inside.

41

AL-HADIQA, ACE. OCTOBER 1290

Henri threw off his silk coverlet and launched himself out of bed, pulling on a robe and wandering into the citronnier from the house. For the third night in a row, despite the cups of wine and vile-smelling draughts from his physician, sleep was out of reach. The windows of the house were all dark, saving Ibrahim's, and who in hell knew why the man was awake at this hour before prime? Henri had always suspected Ibrahim never slept.

He was so tired that it was difficult to tell if he walked or floated, if his eyes were open, or if he were in a dream. Tamrat's last words drifted around him, and he felt warm blood flowing over his hands and saw the old man's eyes stare sightlessly toward heaven. The lemon trees shivered above his head in a cool pre-dawn breeze, and Henri stood motionless, hands clenched in front of him... clenched around Brother Philip's throat.

"Lord Henri?" Brother Philip wheezed, and Henri squeezed tighter. He no longer felt blood spilling. He felt it pounding in Brother Philip's veins as he strangled the life from him.

"Lord Henri!"

His eyes focused. He was standing in an open robe, belt dangling loose, barefoot in the dark. In front of him, a shadow reached out and Henri jumped back. In the east, the sky began to lighten from velvet black to silky gray, and Henri could see that the shadow wore a turban wrapped around his temples.

"Zahed?"

"Is that you, my lord? I thought you an intruder."

"What are you doing in the citronnier before dawn?"

"I might ask you the same, my lord."

Henri crossed his robe around him and belted it petulantly. Zahed did not speak to him with the respect he deserved.

I deserve no respect, for I have taken the life of an innocent man.

Warm blood spilled into his hands. He could feel it dripping from his fingers. Henri gasped aloud and brushed his hands to wipe the blood off.

"My lord, are you well?" Zahed stepped forward, and in the new light, Henri could see a shadow of concern on the slave's face.

"I am fine. I just thought... for a moment, I thought there was... on my hands... why are you here?"

"Merely passing through on my way to observe ṣalāt al-Fajr at the eastern hill, my lord."

"You mean to pray?" Henri felt his mind clearing slowly.

"Do you not also pray at prime?"

"No. I am usually asleep at prime."

"Ah, yes, I forgot. You have men who pray on your behalf. Well, good morning to you." Zahed stomped past him, disappearing through the citronnier gate, then through the main gate of the house with Henri following. He climbed a low hill then stopped, unfurling a rolled rug on the dirt. Henri stood at a distance, watching curiously.

"You might as well make yourself useful, my lord, if you insist on spying." Zahed ignored the indignant look on Henri's face and thrust a pitcher of water into his hands. "Please pour it slowly so that I may wash."

Henri sullenly drizzled the water, and Zahed cupped his hands under it, running them through his hair and scrubbing his face. After he had finished and rewound his turban, he settled himself on his rug, facing to the southeast, and began to pray aloud. Feeling like a voyeur, Henri seated himself on a rock some distance away and watched the sunrise to Zahed's monotonous intonations. A few high, wispy clouds glowed golden-pink with the coming onslaught of the sun. Blood dripped from his hands and ran in rivulets down the sides of the rock where he sat.

"So, you killed the spy."

Henri jumped. He had not noticed Zahed make his final bow toward Mecca, roll up his carpet, and approach from behind.

"What?"

"I am friends with Faisal, the servant of Sir Beauvais. He tells me that you had some trouble on your patrol."

"Must I remind you that you are a slave, and as a member of my household you are not to divulge—"

"I am not a member of your household. You do not keep slaves, remember? I belong to Mafeo."

"Do not speak of my family or me to your friends."

Zahed looked at him solemnly, holding his prayer rug under his arm. Henri could feel the blood dripping from his fingertips.

"Was he really a spy? The man that you killed?"

"No. He was a scribe and a good man. A very kind man."

When Zahed continued looking at him, Henri mumbled, self-consciously, "You were not there, and I doubt your servant friend understood what was happening."

"The porters and slaves know and understand more than your lordly class seem to think," Zahed said, setting his rug down. He unrolled it again and sat upon it, staring toward the rising sun, which had crested the mountains to the east and shone across the coastal plain, casting long shadows. "I do not envy you, however. The first man I killed with my own hand was a Mongol warrior with a drawn bow aimed at my chest. I thought no more of him until days later, when I rejoiced that I had struck before he could. It would distress me if the first life I took were so close."

"How did you—"

"For three days, you have walked about your house with the look on your face that I remember well from the tebaq on the northern frontiers of our territory. Men who had never killed before - some of them were triumphant. Exhilarated. But the others, they could not sleep for fear of seeing their hand taking a life in their dreams."

Henri fumbled for a response, but Zahed just smiled. "They all became used to it eventually. Or they did not, and those men were removed from war. Sent back to Cairo to try to make new lives as blacksmiths or cobblers."

"I am no cobbler!" Henri sputtered.

"I did not say you were. But what will you do now? Does the man leave a wife and children?"

Henri turned his face away. To reveal Sidika's existence to this man could bring her harm.

Zahed drew in a deep, long breath and sighed.

"When the Mamluks took me, they killed my mother and father in front of my eyes. I saw the life leave them, and although my soul still hurts to think of it, I know their fate. They wait for me... somewhere. In the Great Sky, or in Paradise. I do not know."

He picked up two pieces of chalky limestone from the soil next to his rug and rolled them between his fingers absently. "But I had a sister. I hid her by the river, and then I was captured. I never discovered her fate. She was four years of age." He looked up at Henri. "I think of her every time I say this prayer at sunrise. I wonder if my sister is also watching the same sunrise each morning or if her bones are dried out in the ground somewhere."

"I am sorry to hear of your family," Henri said awkwardly. "It seems to me that your life has been one of sorrow, which has not ended since you were purchased by Mafeo."

Zahed smiled bitterly. "You were right to call Mafeo vile, my lord. I hope you do not think me ill of me for telling you, but you would be wise to question the servants about his treatment of your mother."

Henri felt his stomach churn with dread. If Mafeo were harming his mother, then Henri's destruction of all that his father had built was complete. Zahed cleared his throat and stood, re-rolling his rug.

"If that man you killed was as good and kind as you say and he has a woman waiting for him, she will watch her door every single day until she dies and always wonder what happened to him. It seems to me that you could help both of your lives to move on if you were to go to her. It would put your soul at ease, as well as hers. As well as the scribe's. Peace be with you, my lord," Zahed said with a slight bow before retreating to the house.

42

— · —

The road to the hills followed the coast north of Acre before turning east, and despite the black keffiyeh he secured around his temples, the stretching white sand and blinding reflection of the sun on the restless sea dazzled Henri's pale eyes.

Along the way, he met Templars in towers or on their mounts, watching the road for bandits and pilgrims. He passed fortified houses and castles belonging to the titled knights – land that was awarded by Church and Crown for services rendered for the business of the Cross – and the sprawling abbeys and estates belonging to the wealthy Templar and Hospitaller orders. Living in such a castle brought with it the responsibility of guarding the roads from Saracen raiders; however, nearly two hundred years after the first Franj had arrived in the Holy Land, most of the fortresses had been abandoned, or their inhabitants no longer took their oath seriously.

When the sun set, he stopped at the fresh spring of Le Quiebre, once a great structure in antiquity, now a ruin of ghosts and unusable stones guarding the grand aqueducts that fed Acre and the nearby towns. He could have demanded a bed in the nearby castle – the Franj controlled the land now – but instead, he refilled his leather flasks, built a fire in the lee of an abandoned olive press, and waited for night to come. The flames flickered on the broken stones around him, and the wind whistled strangely through the olive trees.

All of this we took from the Arabs and the Jews. All of this land we destroyed.

Where the thought had come from, he did not know, but he found it heretical and intrusive. Shaking his head, he focused instead on reciting the drills his tutor had taught him years ago to remember the words of al-Farabi and his treatise on society's influence on man in a virtuous city.

"A just city should favor justice and the just, hate tyranny and injustice, and give them both their just desserts," Henri muttered to himself.

He pondered his unexpected visit weeks back with Tamrat and their surprisingly rich discussion about al-Farabi, the "second teacher." At the time, he had felt challenged and uncomfortable by the man's sharp intellect and lack of respect for Henri's rank, but now he wished to revisit the mudbrick house strewn with parchments and pots of ink and Tamrat's twinkling smile. Tamrat had looked at Henri and he had seen someone good. Even kind, gentle Ibrahim looked at Henri with doubt in his eyes.

Morning came too soon, and he folded his bedroll before the sun was up, riding into the tiny village of Fajar just as dawn broke over the stony peaks to the east. Sidika would be awake soon, so he sat on the bench outside her low front door and waited. Raven, he kept untethered, and she nuzzled the side of his face, her grassy breath whooshing in his ear.

The sun painted the side of the little house, reaching the window where Sidika and her father slept, and he heard her stirring within. A short time later, she emerged. The door faced south, and the pink light of the rising sun ambered her eyes, making the wild curls of her hair glow like swirling flames and the silhouette of her slender frame ghostly underneath her thin green dress. He sat still and quiet, watching her, until she turned and jumped back in alarm when she saw him, dropping her milking pail.

Henri stood and picked up the pail, handing it to her. "Do you remember who I am?" he asked without greeting.

She shielded her eyes from the sun, and in the early light, they gleamed like gems.

"It would be difficult to forget you, Lord Henri. You are the highest-born man that I have thrown out of my house, although not the first one." The corner of her mouth tugged up in a reluctant smile.

Henri smiled back sadly.

"My father will not be back for several days, so I am afraid you have journeyed for nothing. He traveled to Damascus to take a commission," Sidika turned back to the house.

"I know," Henri said quietly, and he held up the old man's robe, bloodied and torn from his ordeal with the Templars.

Sidika stared at it for a moment, uncomprehending, then snatched the robe from his hands. "Where did you get this? Where is he?!"

Henri took a deep breath, but no words came to him. Why was she so difficult to look at? Why, on this of all mornings, was she so beautiful in her wild anger?

"Where is he?!" she screamed, shattering the morning sounds of roosters crowing and birds chirping. The door to a nearby house opened, and a sleepy neighbor peeked out before slamming it shut again.

"Dead. Killed on the road to Damascus," Henri said, and Sidika sank to her knees, taking gulps of air as if she were trying not to drown.

Henri awkwardly dropped to his knees next to her. "He said..." His voice cracked, and he tried again. "He said to tell you not to be afraid. He said that he is happy with your mother and your brother."

Sidika let out a low moan and pulled her knees to her chest in the dusty yard. Henri would rather be naked in the public square than sitting with her at this moment.

"He also said that yours was the last face he saw before he died," Henri's brow furrowed. "But I suppose mine was the last face he saw as he died," he mumbled, instantly regretting his words.

With a cry, Sidika lunged at him. "You killed him! I told him that taking you in would bring ruin upon us!" More doors opened, and the street began to fill with curious villagers.

"Let us go inside. You need some wine to calm yourself." Henri looked around nervously.

"Leave me, you demon!" Sidika's face was flushed and bloated with tears. "What did you do to him?"

"I... I gave him mercy," Henri stammered, "he told me to do it—"

Sidika leapt at him again, this time pounding his chest and his shoulders with her fists.

"Franj," a deep voice spoke, and Henri looked up at Fakri, the same man who had accosted Sidika outside her house so many weeks ago. "You will leave this village at once."

"Begone," Henri snarled, and he dragged Sidika through the low doorway into the house. She crumpled on the floor, shaking violently. Henri rummaged around in the cupboard until he found a jar of wine and poured her a cup, which she refused.

"Do you wish to know what happened?" he asked.

She shook her head.

"Very well. Please come with me back to al-Hadiqa, not as a servant but as a member of my household under my protection. You can live with my mother and my sisters, and we will care for you as a ward until a husband can be found," he said in the most businesslike tone he could muster.

Sidika continued to cry on the floor.

"Girl, do you hear me?"

"Leave my house," she sobbed. "I pray that the day I see you again is the day of your death. You deserve to die in fear, among strangers and heathens, as my father did."

"I see." Henri stood. "I thought you might refuse. This is for you, to see that you have a living until you are wed. Do not shame your father and become a prostitute."

He dropped a heavy bag of gold bezants on the floor next to her and strode out of the house, ignoring the fearful stares of the villagers.

43

Damascus. November 1290

Sarangerel stuffed the piece of stale flatbread into her mouth and gummed it quickly, filling the toothless cavern with saliva in order to soften the food. She could feel the sand in the bread, but it mattered little, since she had no more teeth for it to grit and grind against. *And anyway*, she thought, *hens eat stones to help them chew their grain, so perhaps a little sand will help me grind my food as well.* This thought made her laugh, and she opened her mouth wide, guffawing and spitting crumbs into the dust.

Sitting cross-legged on the ground on her dirty camelhair blanket, she could see the swish of long robes and thawbs around men's ankles and hear the scrape of soft leather shoes and sandals as she looked through the crowd.

"No girls, no girls, no women at all. My girl is gone," she muttered to herself as she struggled to her feet. "Where are all the pussies?!" she screamed, causing several of the men walking near her in the square to jump in alarm.

"That is enough. You are done here!" A city guard snatched her arm and tried to drag her away, but she dropped back into her sitting position and cackled as he struggled.

She spat the slimy ball of bread from her mouth into her free hand and proffered it to him. "If you leave me be, I will let you share my meal."

"Filthy old hag!"

"I have already seen your jail, Najib, and my girl is not in it. Take me to her, and I will leave your streets alone."

Najib pushed her back roughly, his arm throbbing with the effort of trying to move her. "Old woman, how long have you been sitting in this square?"

"The years, they are like birds which fly past my eyes and into the Great Sky...." Sarangerel said in a sing-song voice, swaying on her blanket and waving her arms toward the heavens.

"Crazy old witch," Najib muttered, turning to leave.

"Wait!" Sarangerel clutched at the edge of his tunic. "You say I am mad, but it is love that makes me thus. I loved my girl, and she was taken. Twice she was taken. Bring her to me, and I shall become young and beautiful again. Young and lithe, and you would like me, as my husband once did."

Tears glittered in her eyes. "May I have something to drink, please?"

Najib looked left and right, then offered her his leather flask. He watched as the old woman closed her eyes with relief, a dribble of sour wine crawling down her wrinkled chin until the wineskin deflated. Then she lay down on her rug and wiped the tears from her face.

"I lost her. I let them take her twice. Oh..." She drifted off.

Najib looked at his empty wine flask and back at the old woman snoring at his feet. "Well, whoever your girl was, she must have been a rare child to have been kidnapped twice and drive a woman mad."

He decided not to take her to the jailer this day and let her sleep instead on her blanket, where she could always be found in the Touma Square. Doubtless, she would cause another scene tomorrow.

***

Emre waited patiently as Lord Henri attempted again to articulate his apology.

"I mean to say that I thank you for your counsel, Zahed. It was sound advice to ensure that the old man's family was informed of his demise. I wish someone could have done so for you with your sister and eased your mind."

Emre smiled. "I shall see her again someday after I die."

Henri smiled back. "Perhaps. Also, I would like to know more about your offer to train my men in Mamluk tactics. Did you mean it?"

"Yes, my lord."

"But... why?"

Emre thought for a moment.

"Because I have nothing else to do that interests me. Because Mafeo would dislike it. And because you are a Franj who does not keep slaves, even though you could. This inspires me to help you."

Henri looked at the ground. "I do not need help. My men do."

Emre smiled. "Whatever you say. Now, shall we start your men with the lance, or would you prefer the bow? I personally think the bow, since you have a nice wall to defend here."

Henri grinned. "The bow sounds like a good place to start. Let us—" He stopped. A thin cloud of dust rose from the road below the rise of a hill, and he saw two riders clad all in white appear on the horizon. Brother Gregoire and Brother Alaran.

Henri trotted out of the gate, and Brother Alaran held back while Brother Gregoire dismounted. With his close-cropped sandy blond hair, long beard, and white robes flapping in the late morning breeze, Brother Gregoire truly did look like the ideal Templar, and Emre felt uneasy at the sight of him. Tawash Izem always told his students that if they saw the white-robed infidels charging at them, they should prepare their souls for death.

"A word, Lord Henri?" Brother Gregoire beckoned. "It is fortunate that you were home."

Withdrawing a folded parchment from his saddle, he handed it to Henri. "There is to be an inquiry into the death of the old man. Your presence at the castle is required ten days hence."

Henri took the letter and opened it. The summons was written in Latin and French. Although he was not an expert at Templar customs, he knew that parchment was rarely wasted on a message that could be delivered by word of mouth. His stomach turned with sudden apprehension. Henri had assumed that because of his rank and fortune, the Templars had just decided to let the incident be quietly forgotten.

"Why did you do it, Henri?" Brother Gregoire said under his breath. "Now you are in Brother Philip's power. You embarrassed him, and he has talked of nothing but punishing you since the whole bloody mess happened. It is almost as if he has been waiting for this his entire life. I like you, Henri, but you certainly made a foolish mistake by angering the most vindictive member of our Order."

Henri looked up from the parchment in his hand. "He was torturing an innocent man. A good man."

"It happens all the time!" Brother Gregoire hissed. "And keep your mouth shut, or else the next innocent man to have his hands cut off or his feet held to a hot iron will be you!"

"Gregoire!" Brother Alaran called. "Are you going to stay there nattering like an old woman or come back to the city? I want my bed."

Henri walked stiffly back to the house and did not meet Emre's eyes.

***

Philip eased the iron door open, flinching with each scream of metal on the rusted hinges. He had left a pitcher of strong ruby wine on the guards' table, and from the sounds of the raucous laughter above, they had found it, which eased his mind as he slipped into the Templar cellars. Philip was allowed to visit a prisoner whenever he wanted, but he couldn't risk someone overhearing his questions. He slipped through the narrow opening in the door, then slammed it back quickly, just as the guards above let loose a roar of merriment and pounded their table with their fists. Below, in the absolute darkness, it was quiet. Some of the prisoners muttered to themselves, and a few sang breathy songs, but most were subdued, their eyes staring blankly like newts in a cave, their minds wandering across imaginary fields and galaxies.

Philip waited a moment in the blackness before sliding the metal shield back on his lantern. The sudden candlelight elicited a started cry of fear and hope from the prisoners as Philip found the hole in the ground that he was looking for and wrenched the heavy wooden door up.

"Good morning, Paolo," he said pleasantly. All he could see was the top of his squire's dark hair, matted with mud and blood.

"Good morning, Brother Philip," Paolo whispered back.

"Do you have anything to tell me today?"

Paolo's shoulders shook, and he heard the boy's quiet sobs echoing in the dark. "No, Brother Philip. I have no more knowledge today than I did yesterday."

"That is unfortunate. How is that hole? Dark?"

"Yes, sir."

"Terrifying things live in the dark," Philip said slowly. "Devils, demons, and snakes." He held up a squirming leather sack, and Paolo looked up for the first time, his eyes widening. "You do not like snakes, do you, boy?"

"No, Brother Philip." Paolo swallowed. "It was a serpent who tempted Eve in the garden..."

"And?"

By now, the boy's hands were shaking. "And it was a snake that bit and killed my older brother in our tent!" His voice rose to a shriek as Philip began to tip the bag slowly toward the hole.

"Please, Brother Philip, *please*! I know nothing! I fell ill shortly after Brother Languedoc brought me my food. There was never an object that I stole from you because you have no possessions other than your robes and your toilet kit!"

Philip hesitated. "Brother Languedoc brought your food? Why?"

"It was his act of service. I helped him saddle his horse one day, and he insisted on serving me a meal as a way to humble himself before God."

Philip lowered the bag. "And then you fell ill after you ate?"

"Aye, and he called for his squire to bear me to the physician's chamber. It was gracious of him to tend to me."

"Indeed." Philip's mind raced.

"It is unfortunate that the food had spoiled, but it was not Brother Languedoc's fault!" Paolo babbled from the hole. "Several others also felt ill that day, although not as strongly as me. So you see, Brother Philip, it is as I have told you – I did not intend to leave your quarters that day, but I was ill and never alone! I did not steal anything belonging to you because I could not have done so!"

Philip thought for a moment, then looked down at his frightened squire.

"You are correct, Paolo. It was not you who did this deed."

He pulled the ties off the leather sack and tipped three vipers into the hole. Paolo screeched and tried to jump and claw his way up the walls, but Philip slammed the grate and barred it, then retreated up the steps of the jail and into daylight.

44

— · —

T he mornings were the hardest. Every morning of Sidika's life since she was six years old, the cheerful, tuneless whistling of her father woke her up with the singing of the birds as he returned from his dawn walk. He always set out before the sun rose with his three tefillin dangling from their strings, and returned after his prayers, just as the world turned to gold with the newly birthed light of another day. To her, that was a magical time, when he would wake his wife and children with a broad grin and exclamations of greeting. Her father's smile could outshine the sun on a cloudless afternoon.

It had been a week since Lord Henri came and delivered the news that her father was dead. Sidika had lain in her dark room for the first two days, not sleeping, but hardly awake. On the third day, she stumbled outside to milk the goat and gather the eggs. On the fourth day, she remembered to eat something, but only because Rahat came over and prepared a custard for her. Sidika sent her friend home with armloads of eggs.

Now it was the seventh day, and Sidika walked stiffly to the stone basin of water that they kept for washing and splashed some of the tepid liquid on her face. Her hair hung in limp, greasy mats, and her clothes stank from days of sleeping and sweating in them. She stripped slowly, pulled on the second dress that she had outgrown, washed her dirty frock, and wrung it out to hang in the afternoon sun. She brushed the sand from their table, swept the floor, and opened the skylight to let in the sunlight. Then she sat and watched the shadows move slowly across her silent little house.

The absence of her father's constant chatter screamed at her.

On the shelf, the pots of ink and dye powders were arranged neatly next to the stacks of crisp, creamy parchment, the rougher sheaves of paper, and the two manuscripts waiting to be taken to the bookbinders in Acre. Tamrat had been working on the physician's manual for the sultan's healer and a book on the history of Acre for Guillaume de Beaujeu, grand master of the Templars. Now that her father was no longer there to continue his work or protect her, Sidika needed to find a husband, and she needed to do it quickly before she ran out of money or one of the village men tried to force his way into her house. She was well aware that an unmarried woman living alone would be quickly branded a witch or a prostitute, no matter the circumstances of her solitary lifestyle.

Tears dribbled from her chin as she thought of her father's work. He had put his entire soul into each manuscript. Every one of them was an individual work of art and love. She had been learning the way of that art until....

Sidika stood up.

"They do not know he is dead," she spoke into the silent room. Then she began to pace.

Why couldn't she finish Tamrat's work? His clients need not know who the scribe was. She could just tell them that he was sick, and she doubted that self-important Lord Henri would divulge that he knew the identity of her father. She could carry on working in Tamrat's name, and no one would be the wiser. Her father would continue to receive renown and honor, and she would not have to marry yet.

She heard a familiar voice outside the house call out her name.

"Sidika? Sidika, my dove, are you in there?"

Sidika wrenched the door open. Fakri stood outside, and his face broke into a broad, gap-toothed smile.

"Ah, you are more beautiful than the morn—"

"Fakri!" she said sharply. "I need you to create a new seal, please."

"Er... come again?" Fakri asked.

"Wait a moment." She dashed inside, snatching her father's artisan seal from its honored place on the top shelf. Dipping the seal in some ink, she stamped it carefully on a scrap of parchment. Then she took up her quill and scratched a very tiny "S" in one corner, so artfully done that it merely looked like a part of the seal's elaborate pattern.

"You are the village potter. Please make me a new seal that looks exactly like this. If it matches this drawing exactly, I will pay you five dinars. If it does not match, I will pay you nothing," she said, thrusting the paper in Fakri's face.

Fakri stepped back and took the paper from her, squinting at it nearsightedly.

"Five dinars? Your father dies, and already you begin to spend all his money?"

"It is Lord Henri's money," Sidika replied flippantly, and Fakri's shoulders fell.

"Very well. But instead of five dinars, would you take the seal without charge?"

Sidika turned on him, her eyes narrowed. "No," she said. "Please have it done in two days. I shall have need of it."

Fakri turned and left, his head hanging. Sidika slammed the door to the house and bolted it. Standing on a bench, she pulled down parchment and supplies, then placed a sheet on her father's slanted work table under the skylight. Dipping her quill in a pot of indigo ink, she carefully began to sketch the image of Acre's skyline for the grand master's book.

45

— ◆ —

TEMPLAR CITADEL, ACRE. NOVEMBER 1290

I t was the day of the inquiry. Henri carefully kept his morning routine normal, and his countenance relaxed around his mother so that he would not worry her, although he knew he need not bother. Nasira quietly haunted the house when Mafeo was out and stayed cloistered in her chambers when he was home. To look at her drawn and dull-eyed countenance was to experience a wave of guilt, and so Henri secretly felt relief when she no longer joined the family for meals in the hall.

But someone from his household needed to know what was about to happen. He confided in Ibrahim the day before he was due at the Templar castle, and the old steward looked at him sternly, long enough that Henri couldn't hold his gaze.

"I thought you would want to know," Henri said, looking at the floor. "Although he was not noble-born or even Christian, Master Tamrat was a good man. I could not let him continue to suffer. They might as well have been torturing you. And now, nothing feels the same. I no longer know who I am after what I saw, and I certainly do not know who the Templars are. To me, they now seem like devils."

Ibrahim clasped Henri on the shoulder. "What you did for this man was merciful, but I am very afraid for you. Was Brother Languedoc not on this patrol with you?"

Henri shook his head. "No. I need your help, Ibrahim. I wish to ask you if you would accompany me into the citadel during my trial. They have no quarrel with you, and so you should have nothing to fear. But if they decide to imprison me, I need to ensure that word is sent to my mother and arrangements are made for a bribe or a burial."

Ibrahim nodded solemnly, but inside his long, bell-shaped sleeves, his fists clenched.

The next morning at dawn, as he and Ibrahim rode through the gates of the estate, Henri turned in his saddle and looked back at the house. The sun had not fully risen, and as they trotted down the gentle slope towards the main road, the house stood cold and silent behind its walls, a monolith against the star-speckled sky.

It has been attacked three times in the last ten years by raiders, and the groves burned twice, and yet it stands. Whatever happens to me in the city today, I will also stand, he thought, but unease sat on his chest, and Raven's normally smooth gait rattled his innards.

He and Ibrahim said little on the ride toward the city. Eventually, the eastern edge of the world began to glow. A morning bird warbled tentatively in a low copse of gnarled oak trees, and soon two others accompanied it. Usually, Henri enjoyed the singing of the birds at dawn, but today they sounded like a chorus to sing him to his grave. As the sky lightened, his mood became more introspective. Would that he could stop the sun from moving like Joshua had when he was fighting the five kings at Gibeon.

Well, I am not so far from Gibeon right now, he thought. *Perhaps this is still the land of miracles*.

They were in Acre before he felt ready. By now, the sun coaxed mellow waves of heat from the stone walls, and Saint Anthony's gate rang with a babble of voices speaking languages from all over the Levant and the West; people negotiating entry, farmers cajoling reluctant mules, beggars pleading for alms, and sellers wheedling travelers out of their coin.

In the last ten years, trade and commerce in the city had increased threefold with the reasonably stable relations between the remaining trade guilds and a formal truce with the sultan. Although often crowded, Acre now throbbed with humanity in the streets, the inns, and the houses, which sent money flowing into the city treasury and the purses of the local merchants. But with the increase of people came an increase in problems.

Pilgrims arriving by boat came into Palestine with a holy fire burning within them, stoked in the West by bishops and priests who preached death to all infidels. Newcomers often arrived with the expectation that their work for God included abusing or killing the first Jew or Muslim that they saw. The permanent Franj settlers of Acre regarded the recently arrived zealots from the West with disgust. However, tolerating the bad behavior was easier than dealing with the moral ambiguity of punishing men who were instructed by the Pope and his bishops to kill their Muslim and Jewish neighbors in the name of the Church.

Recalling the ruthless slaughter of Arab men in Acre only months prior, Henri shivered under his cloak. Safety was never a given in Palestine, but he had always felt reasonably secure in the city, so long as he kept his wits about him. The locals and the Franj tolerated each other well enough, even if they rarely socialized. But now, his world and his beliefs were changing around him against his will. Although the city looked the same, it no longer felt familiar. Although he looked the same, he no longer knew who he was.

As the sun rose further, the main streets became so crowded that Raven had to nudge pedestrians out of her way with her shapely head. Slowly, Henri and Ibrahim moved with the throng, past the boxy, thick-walled Hospitaller citadel, skirting the Venetian Quarter, and inching past the Church of Saint Lawrence. Finally, they spied the severe walls of the Templar citadel.

Splendid and glowing in the morning sun, the Templar citadel abutted the ocean by means of a thick limestone seawall that grew slimy and green where it met the water's edge.

The citadel's many towers afforded unobstructed views of any incoming marine traffic due to the fortress's strategic position at the very tip of the peninsula that Acre was built upon. Although he couldn't see them from his vantage, Henri knew that the rocks directly beneath the steep-sided seawall were often shallowly covered by water at high tide and exposed and glistening with dark mats of seaweed at low tide. He could hear the roar of the warm sea against the rocks even from where he stood waiting outside the gate.

He and Ibrahim passed through the gate in the curtain wall and into the bailey of the citadel. Unlike his calm, lavender-scented oasis at al-Hadiqa, this space was purely functional. In one quadrant, rows of knights drilled in white linen robes, and even in the relative cool of the morning, they sweated from the exertion of their exercises. A smaller group of black-robed sergeants practiced sparring with wooden swords and shields in another quadrant. A blacksmith's hammer rang out near the stables where shoes were fitted on the hooves of the towering destriers belonging to the Brethren.

Templar knights dedicated their entire lives to fighting for the cause of Jesu Christi, and a young nobleman wishing to become a brother knight was required to give up his fortune and his title and commit to a monastic life of celibacy. A married man must leave his wife and family and do the same, which is why the Order was mostly populated with widowers or second and third sons with smaller inheritances. They were the strongest and most pious of the knights in the city, both feared and admired. Whereas the Hospitallers had developed their Order out of necessity to protect the pilgrim hostels along the road to Jerusalem, the Templars deemed themselves warrior monks – the keepers of the Holy Sepulchre and the protectors of the true cross.

The true cross had been lost to Salah ad-Din a hundred years earlier at the Battle of Hattin, along with the entire city of Jerusalem, but it no longer seemed to matter. The Templars had an unshakable belief in the righteousness of their deeds and the certainty that they would reclaim the sacred city once again in the name of God. Every fighting man within that courtyard, young and old, believed himself to be superior to the other knights in the city in both physical skill and holy purity, and most of the Western world agreed with them.

A groom in black robes met Henri and Ibrahim near the gate and took their horses, while a baby-faced monk asked their names and bade them wait in the arcade. Henri expected to see curious, and even hostile looks from the other occupants due to his presence, and especially Ibrahim's, but no one took any notice of them. Ibrahim placidly adjusted his simple blue taqiya on his balding head, and if he felt nervous surrounded by so many Brethren, he did not show it.

The monk led them along a colonnade and into a long, narrow hall, furnished with two almost equally long, narrow tables. A few knights sat at the tables, hunched over hard bread trenchers of wheat mush and boiled vegetables. Templars were allowed to eat meat only on certain days, and they were expected to take their meals in silence, carefully watching each other for signs of gluttony or greed. A few of the men looked up as Henri and Ibrahim entered, but many more kept their eyes carefully focused on their food or their fellow Brethren.

The monk led them up a long stone staircase and through a heavy wooden door on the opposite side of the bailey. The first person Henri saw in the room was Brother Philip, standing at a wall and peering out of an arched window. Henri had a wild moment of panic as he took in the rest of the room. Brother Alaran, half-obscured by darkness, Brother Lenglée and Brother Gregoire, both standing stiffly with hands behind their backs next to a lavishly carved wooden table. And sitting behind the table was Grand Master Guillaume de Beaujeu himself.

Beaujeu, son of a French noble and cousin to King Louis and Charles d'Anjou, had arrived in Acre when Henri was a baby, quickly establishing himself as a leader of the city, despite the official presence of Bishop Hanapes, the Patriarch of Acre. Henri's father had always maintained friendly relations with Beaujeu because it made political sense. Even with his personal militia, Rogier knew that al-Hadiqa was vulnerable unless they had powerfully armed allies. Thus, Beaujeu had always been a presence in Henri's life, but rarely did they have any direct interaction with each other, except on formal occasions. It was well known that those who trod arrogantly around the grand master could find their household on the losing end of an attack by the Templars, or at the very least, excluded from any say in the matters of the city.

Seeing him now, Henri felt his mouth go dry. Why had he helped Master Tamrat? The old scribe was doomed to die, and now he had condemned himself, and possibly even Ibrahim and his mother and sisters. His heart pounded and his palms dampened with sweat. The grand master spoke.

"Brother Honorus, why does Viscount Henri of Maron carry his sword into my solar?"

The monk who had escorted them into the building paled. Eyes downcast, he hurried over to Henri and Ibrahim, muttering, "Your weapons, please."

Henri handed over his long sword and his jeweled dagger. Ibrahim had a slender, curved shamshir that hung from his belt. Henri knew that he mainly used it for chopping at meddlesome weeds when he was walking the groves, but the monk looked at it with horror, as if it had tasted the blood of a thousand Christian pilgrims.

Beaujeu steepled his fingers, nodding sagely, and Henri knew what to do next. He knelt, like the knights of all the orders usually did in front of their grand masters, and bowed his head. Ibrahim followed his example, dropping to both knees and touching his forehead to the floor between his hands, like a Muslim praying toward Mecca. This subservient pose seemed to please Beaujeu, and Henri was surprised to find himself annoyed. Ibrahim held a valued position in his household, and it offended him that his steward was made to grovel.

"Please, my lord, I beg that you allow my steward to observe discreetly and come to no harm," Henri said. "I asked him to accompany me here to report my welfare to my mother and sisters. He had no involvement in the proceedings that we are discussing today. Indeed, he was at my home when the incident happened."

"Very well," Beaujeu said, with a spare gesture towards a bench in the corner of the room. Ibrahim stood and moved toward it silently, head still bowed, but he raised his eyes for a moment and looked curiously at Brother Philip.

Henri stayed on one knee, waiting quietly, eyes cast downward. The grand master leveled him with a stern frown.

"Brother Philip tells me that you tried to help a Mamluk spy escape from his capture."

At his words, Henri looked up sharply.

Beaujeu held up a hand for silence and shot a flat look at Brother Philip, who watched Henri from his place near the window.

"But Brother Philip has also told me that you killed the prisoner," Beaujeu continued. "You understand that it would have been valuable to keep him alive so that we could question him?"

"With respect, my lord, I did question the prisoner. The prisoner and I were acquainted," Henri said, keeping his eyes firmly glued to the floor, not daring to look up again.

"And what did the prisoner tell you?" Beaujeu had an aquiline nose and sharp gray eyes, which roamed the room continuously, like a bird of prey.

"He told me that he was a scribe traveling to Damascus to take a commission."

"Why then did he avoid our patrols?"

"He told me that he did not wish to meet with...." Henri hesitated, trying to choose his words carefully.

"Yes, Lord Henri?"

"With dogs and occupiers, my lord."

Beaujeu chuckled. "Well, our young man here tells the truth, at least. No one else would dare repeat such language inside these walls unless it were the absolute truth."

Brothers Gregoire and Lenglée laughed nervously while Brother Alaran regarded Henri with unveiled loathing.

Brother Philip wrenched his gaze from the window. "Grand Master," he sank to one knee alongside Henri. "Lord Henri gave the prisoner succor when we attempted to question him. When I gave him the order to question the prisoner further, he instead slit the man's throat, so we are now no longer able to determine his mission. It is also my concern that young Lord Henri will spread vicious rumors and libel about me because he is an Arab sympathizer."

Beaujeu scrutinized Brother Philip silently for a moment, fingers still pressed together. "Brother Philip, would the prisoner have had the strength to continue answering questions if Lord Henri had not given him water and nourishment?"

Brother Philip said nothing.

"Would he have been able to continue answering questions in his fevered state? I understand from the other men that he was, ah... unlikely to recover from your vigorous questioning," Beaujeu continued.

Brother Philip opened his mouth to speak and closed it again. Brother Gregoire spoke in his stead. "Grand Master, it is true that the prisoner was gone with fever when Lord Henri slit his throat. He would have expired of his wounds in painful torment."

Brother Philip shot a contemptuous glare at his colleague.

"And Lord Henri already received punishment for his fraternizations with the prisoner?" Beaujeu asked.

"I received sixteen lashes, my lord," Henri replied.

"Come here." Beaujeu beckoned to Henri. "All of you, leave us. I wish to speak to the viscount alone."

Reluctantly, the knights moved towards the door. Philip and Ibrahim left last, both watching Henri as they walked out. When the door snapped shut, the grand master leaned forward in his seat.

"Come here, young Henri. They are all listening outside the door, so we must speak closely."

Knees trembling, Henri rose from his place in front of the table and then knelt again next to the grand master.

"You are sure this man was not a Mamluk? Tell me why, for the enemy is crafty and often employs locals as spies," Beaujeu said, his voice barely above a whisper.

"He gave me shelter when my horse threw a shoe. Not only did he harbor no ill will against anyone, but he also seemed completely without guile. He was almost as old as...." Henri tactfully stopped himself, but the grand master laughed.

"I am blessed by God. Were I still living in France, I would have died of some pestilence by now. To a man your age, I must look as old as Methuselah."

"He was a scribe, and a talented one. Brother Philip..." Henri stopped.

Beaujeu raised his eyebrows expectantly.

Henri continued carefully. "Brother Philip beat him, tore off his fingernails, cut him, and compelled me to administer the scourge."

Beaujeu contemplated silently for a moment. "Brother Philip has been trained to use whatever means necessary to protect the city and the citizens of Acre. You know, he would have me believe that your Arab blood has made you disloyal to the cause of Jesu Christi and the Kingdom of Jerusalem. Why should I trust what you have to say when I need not do so? After all, I can see the color of your skin and that of your mother as plain as the sun rises each morning."

Shaken, Henri searched his panicked thoughts for something to say and came up empty-headed.

"Do not worry. I believe you when you say that the man is innocent. Despite your reputation for being a vapid scoundrel after you returned from Sir Geoffroi's training, I do believe you have improved with your newfound responsibilities now that your father is dead." The grand master cleared his throat. "I also happened to know of Master Tamrat, as he occasionally took commissions from my secretary. It is as you say. He was a Jew, not an Arab."

"Does that matter, Grand Master? Jew, Arab, or Mongol, the man was innocent!"

Beaujeu shook his head. "To you and me, it matters not, but many of our Brethren here who were not born in Palestine have little incentive to show God's mercy to their neighbors. Brother Philip wants blood, and he will have it one way or another. I could let you go free, or I could punish you now and save you from a worse fate later."

Henri dared not speak. The grand master appeared to be wrestling with a decision. Finally, he stood, pacing the room.

"You have heard about the dissolution of the peace treaty with Qalāwūn? Ah, yes, well, who has not heard of it by this time?" Beaujeu sighed, removed his white cap, and rubbed his eyes. "In truth, the sultan has been looking for a reason to break the peace treaty. I only wish we had not given him such a strong moral platform to stand on."

"Sir, were not the killed men Muslims who had committed crimes?" Henri asked, and Beaujeu scowled at him.

"They were Arabs, with beards. Muslim, Christian, Jew, and all innocent, like your scribe. I will not allow men to be murdered in Acre; I care not about their eye color or style of facial hair. Now listen, here is what will happen to you for your disobedience. First, I require something to be delivered to an emissary well outside the walls of the city. You shall deliver this for me when I ask it of you."

Henri's brow furrowed. "Yes, my lord..." he said uncertainly.

"Second, I need you to sit on a committee of city leaders to determine the fate of those dratted Sicilians who caused this peace treaty to dissolve with their ill-timed and hot-headed actions. Qalāwūn has written to me and demanded that I turn them over to him, and I wish to have a man on the council who has some compassion and local knowledge. You would have been the last man I chose if this were a year ago, but your recent actions have me reconsidering my opinion of you. I knew your father well, and I have watched you grow from a distance. Believe me when I say that I have been unimpressed with what I have seen of you up until I heard of your exploits on patrol."

"Me, my lord?" Henri asked. He was not sure what he had expected from this inquisition, but more civic responsibility was not it.

The grand master's mustache quirked up in a one-sided smile. "You are inexperienced, young man, but it is your duty to become a leader. We might as well begin to train you now."

"Thank you, my lord. Tell me when and where this council is to meet and I shall be there." Henri's heart thundered and he wanted to collapse with relief.

"Also, you will also receive additional public lashes for dis-obedience to a knight commander during a patrol," Beaujeu said, and he waved his hand dismissively, indicating that the meeting was over.

Henri straightened with surprise, and the grand master sighed.

"I cannot let you leave here without punishment, or suspi-cions will run mad around this city. Already Brother Philip has spread rumors of what you did, and if I do not punish you, he will find a way to take the law into his own hands. You could find yourself lying in an alley with an arrow in your back."

"Cannot you control your men?" Henri asked incredulously. "I could have my family in Maron-en-Rouergue block this action."

"We could do this another way," Beaujeu said, leaning for-ward, the blue-green veins on his hands standing out starkly. "I could have all of your land and villages outside the city con-fiscated by the Holy Father in Rome and your house awarded to Brother Philip when he retires from his duties as a knight, should he live so long. Then I could have my cousin, King Philippe, seize your family's land in Maron-en-Rouergue and bequeath it as Templar property, and we could build a new abbey in its place. How does that sound to you?" Beaujeu's gray eyes were suddenly flinty and cold.

Henri swallowed. "I will take the lashes," he heard himself say.

"In public," the grand master added.

46

— ◆ —

AL-HADIQA, ACRE. NOVEMBER 1290

Mafeo contemplated his options. Nasira stubbornly refused to allow herself to become pregnant with his child, and each day that passed without an heir of Mafeo di Orsini was another day that brought Henri closer to inheriting his family's wealth upon his eighteenth birthday, which was only three months away. He ground his teeth. It was clear to him that his wife was consulting the local witches for potions to poison her womb in order to rob him of his legacy. Or perhaps she was just too old. Either way, he felt deceived.

Henri had left for Acre that day, and Nasira was in her chambers with a headache, so Mafeo loitered near the stables until Blanche emerged from the house for her evening ride. He bowed and watched greedily as she curtseyed in response, giving him a view down the front of her dress. She had not covered her hair, and it hung in glossy chestnut waves around her face. A girdle of silver chain circled a waist that was slender and temptingly close. Mafeo felt a tingling between his thighs. This girl was surely fertile, and youth made her even more beautiful than her mother.

"Good evening, Mademoiselle Blanche. Shall I saddle your horse for you?"

"Where is Salih?" she asked, looking around for the head groom.

Mafeo had sent Salih to the far end of the fields to check on one of the farm horses. "I do not know, but I will be pleased to assist you," he said, walking to her dappled palfrey in the stable. The horse looked at him with concern and backed away from the stall gate. He caught the reluctant animal by the bridle and pulled her into the sunlight.

Blanche watched, her arms crossed. "I do not think Najima likes you," she said, a smile tugging at the corners of her mouth.

Mafeo swallowed his irritation and smiled, throwing a saddle cloth on Najima's back. "Nonsense. She is used to Salih's face and not mine, that is all."

Blanche looked unconvinced, and Mafeo quickly cinched the saddle under the horse's barrel before she could bite him on the shoulder. The animal's eyes followed him with increasing malice.

"I was in the city this week, securing my tent for the festival of the Feast of Saint Andrew," he said, stringing the reins through the bridle.

"Really?" Blanche responded with excitement. "My father never allowed us to go to the festival of Saint Andrew. He said that the crowd could be dangerous."

"Well, your father perhaps never attended with his guards," Mafeo grunted, occupied with a saddle strap, "but I see no reason to deny a pretty girl the chance to attend such a delightful event. Perhaps you would like to come this year?"

Blanche froze. The horse craned her slender neck and snapped at Mafeo, and he jumped back.

It was nearing the end of November – the time of year when traveling players from Francia, Messina, and Genoa came to Tyre, Acre, and the other Christian-occupied towns along the coast to play after the Feast of Saint Andrew to celebrate the weeks leading up to Jesu Christi's birth. Henri had no interest in attending, and Nasira felt that the noise and crowds would upset Saruca, which meant that Blanche would be unable to attend without a chaperone.

"I... I had not planned to," Blanche stammered. "But I could ask my brother if I may attend, as long as I take a companion with me."

"Your brother is staying in Acre for a few days. Ibrahim just informed your mother and then returned immediately to town." Mafeo frowned. He would have to send Zahed to Acre to find out what Henri was up to.

"Monsieur Mafeo?" Blanche pulled him out of his thoughts.

"Sorry, mademoiselle?"

"May I bring Emine as my companion?"

Mafeo's mouth turned down. "Emine is a kitchen servant, Blanche. You should not consider her your companion. You need a proper lady's maid. Someone more competent."

The horse was slowly pushing him against the stable wall, trying to pin him. He edged away from the beast and handed the reins to Blanche.

"I will be your chaperone. After all, I am your guardian, and your happiness is the only thing that I care about," he smiled, and Blanche smiled back, her eyes dancing with excitement.

"Now," he said, "when we are at the festival, we shall buy a present for your mother, so do not tell her about our conversation. Let us make it a surprise that you will be there."

***

Ibrahim rode like the wind and cursed his luck. He was a meditative man, and rarely did he ever rush himself or his horse. The horse's name, Ocparna, meant "Diligent," and the beast ran diligently now, even though Ibrahim knew he didn't want to move any faster than a relaxed trot. Today Ocparna seemed to sense Ibrahim's urgency and understood it to be an occasion that required haste.

Indeed, Ibrahim felt more than urgency. A blanket of fear settled heavily on his heart. Never before had he lied to Nasira, but Henri had made Ibrahim swear on his ancestor's bones that Nasira would not know of the public lashes about to be inflicted upon him.

If only Henri knew who my ancestors really were, Ibrahim thought, and then quickly pushed it away. It was unwise to dwell on such things. Maintaining emotional distance was of extreme importance, and yet Ibrahim felt his resolve cracking. Henri could die tomorrow.

"No," he said aloud to the wind. "Merciful Allah, help me!"

He urged Ocparna on and the faithful horse grunted, giving even more speed. The sun sank sulkily into a hazy western sky, and Henri sat in a dungeon somewhere beneath the Templar castle. Ibrahim had only a short time to prepare. He leapt out of the saddle at Saint Anthony's gate and led the horse through the heaving masses of people, down the twisting streets toward the harbor. Somewhere in this city was the one knight that Ibrahim trusted.

It wasn't difficult to find the home of Sir Eirik Einarssen, the northman knight, because it was the only house in Acre with a peaked roof of heavy carved wooden beams. Ibrahim tied Ocparna to a hitching post and pounded on the front door with his fist. After several minutes, Sir Eirik himself wrenched the door open. He wore a scandalously short blue cotton tunic over bare legs, and his red hair stood out in a wild explosion of curls and snarls as if he had just woken up. In his right hand, he held a cruel-looking iron dagger.

For a moment, the great northman sized Ibrahim up. The man was a head and a half taller than Ibrahim and as fierce-looking as an orange djinn. Then his face split into an enormous smile, and he boomed in heavily accented French.

"Ibrahim, is it not? You are the servant of my friend Lord Henri, the viscount of Acre."

"Indeed, I am, Sir Eirik," Ibrahim bowed.

"And what is that troublesome devil up to now? Upsetting some lady, I am sure." Sir Eirik's laugh cut short when he noticed Ibrahim's frown. "My God, what happened to him?"

"Lord Henri is to be publicly flogged in the square tomorrow morning as an introduction to the festival. I did not know who else to come to, for Henri will not allow me to tell his mother and refuses to let the Hospitallers tend to him. I fear for his safety and wish to hide him in your house after the flogging."

Sir Eirik put his hand over his eyes and groaned. "This thing, is it because of the patrol with those Templar devils?"

Ibrahim nodded.

"Asta!" Sir Eirik bellowed. A minute later, his plump, pretty wife appeared around the corner.

"This thing I feared will happen, as I told you. Henri is to be whipped tomorrow morning."

Asta gasped.

"My love, go to the Hospitallers' souk to buy herbs and strong wine. We must prepare poultices. I will stay here with the children."

Ibrahim bowed again. "I shall accompany you, Madame Asta. The shadows grow long, and you should not be out alone."

Sir Eirik growled and wrenched the door open. "And Wife, after this, we move to some other place. I no longer want to live in the same city as a Templar. We shall move north with the Teutons, eh?"

Asta rolled her eyes, pulled on her cloak, and gave her husband a kiss. Then she took Ibrahim's arm, and they hurried into the souk.

47

FAJAR, THE HILLS OF IDMIT. NOVEMBER 1290

For two days, Sidika labored under the open skylight, stopping only to sleep when the sun set or to grab a few bites of food. So engrossed was she in her work that she would not take the time to prepare meals for herself, gnawing instead on pieces of salted venison and stale flatbread. The book for Grand Master Beaujeu was nearly done.

She worked in silence, jaw clenched, forehead wrinkled in concentration. Tamrat skirted the edges of her consciousness, along with her mother and her brother. Setting her quill down, she rubbed her eyes, her mind wandering to the first time she had ever seen her adopted father, then wandering further back into the past.

Horse Aunty. Who was that woman, and what was her connection to the boy at the river?

A hammering on her door broke Sidika from her reverie. Wiping her ink-stained hands on her apron, she cracked the door open to reveal Fakri standing sullenly outside, holding up a delicately carved clay seal. Sidika slammed the door and then re-emerged with a handful of gold. She stamped the seal on a piece of paper and squealed with delight.

"It is exactly what I asked for!"

"So... you like it?" Fakri asked tentatively.

"Enough to pay your five dinars," she said, dropping the coins into his hand.

"Sidika, will you walk with me to the top of the hill? There is something I should like to ask you," Fakri said, his voice filled with tenuous hope.

"I must go. The book is finished!" she said, rushing back into the house.

She quickly dribbled some brown wax onto the linen-wrapped book, stamped the seal down firmly, then ran into her room, stuffing her extra dress and underclothes into a large sack. She braided her hair and draped her best shawl over it, tied her lavender hair ribbon to her wrist, then bustled about the house, snatching stale bread and a vessel of flat ale.

"Fakri, will you please feed the chickens and milk the goat while I am away? You may keep the eggs and milk," she said distractedly.

"I... er... yes," Fakri faltered.

Tamrat's little donkey had never returned after her father died, so Sidika wrapped her provisions in a wide piece of muslin and tied it to her back. She would have to walk to Acre.

"If you will care for the animals and guard my house against thieves, I shall pay you five more dinars." She saw with smug satisfaction that Fakri's eyes widened in wonder. Then she walked from the house and began the long, dangerous journey to the southwest – toward Acre and Guillaume de Beaujeu.

48

— • —

H enri couldn't sleep. Deep under the belly of the Templar citadel, he could sense the weight of the many layers of stone and men above his head, and the darkness was so complete that it pushed at his eyes. His bare feet, liberated of their boots by an opportunistic jailer, squelched on the foul-smelling mucky floor. As tired as his legs were, he refused to sit or lie on the ground. Instead, he leaned against the wall until exhaustion eventually won out, and he crouched on his heels and waited. Only the scrabbling of rats and the quiet sobs of the prisoners in the cell next to him broke the silence. He had heard the jailers deliver the news to them, hours earlier, that they were to be executed. Usually, prisoners were not told in advance unless they were Christian and required a priest or unless the jailer intended to instill as much terror as possible.

Henri knew that he was lucky. He was only going to be flogged as a way to excite the crowd for the real show; the execution of Saracens harassing pilgrims and local Acrean miscreants who were caught thieving or who had committed murder... including Marcouf Charettier, the man who had been accused of murdering Rogier. After his experience on patrol, Henri wondered if those doomed men were even guilty or if they had just been in the wrong place at the wrong time. How many men had died with their necks broken on the gallows due to a false accusation? He thought back to Marcouf's "trial," and an uncomfortable thought tugged at him. *What if Marcouf was innocent?*

His little stone room was windowless except for a slot underneath the banded wooden door, and it let in no light. The jailers sat on an upper level, which conveniently made it difficult for them to hear the cries of their charges. Henri had no idea what time of day it was, and there was no one to ask, so with nothing else to do, he focused his thoughts on Psalm 27.

The Lord is my light and my salvation – whom will I fear?
The Lord is the strength of my life; of whom will I be afraid?

Another verse came into his mind.

Whatever happens to you...
Don't fall in despair,
Even if all the doors are closed...
A secret path will be there for you that no one knows,
You can't see it yet...
But so many paradises are at the end of this path,
Be grateful...
It is easy to thank after obtaining what you want...
Thank before having what you want.

Heresy, a small, weak voice whispered to him, but he no longer cared what it had to say. The words of Shams al-Tabrizi brought him just as much comfort as those of the Psalmist.

After what could have been hours or days, Henri saw a flicker of light at the bottom of his door. For a moment, he stared at it dumbly, unable to tell if it was a lamp or his imagination. He heard one guard speaking to another, telling a lewd joke.

"An' then she said, 'Oh, sorry, m'lord, was that your member? I thought that was a faggot for the fire!'" and they both dissolved into snorting fits of laughter. Henri heard the bar slide up heavily from his door.

All men are this ugly inside, Henri thought bitterly, *but Templars have found a way to trick the world into only seeing their white robes. These jailers are the most honest men in this castle.*

"Alrigh', your lordship. Time for your beatin'," the taller jailer said. He was missing all of his front teeth. "Now, don' try to get away from us, or we'll throw you in with yon S'racens."

The other jailer squinted up at Henri. "He sure looks like a S'racen, though. Are you sure we got the right man? Look at him!"

"This here's Lord Henri, the viscount of Acre. Somehow managed to be Arab and still rich as a prince. An' me almost as poor here as I was in Messina. Life ain't fair." The first jailer spat on the floor and grabbed Henri by the front of his tunic, jerking him out of the cell.

"Sorry, your lordship. If I treat you gentle-like, will you give me some gold?"

Henri said nothing, holding his hands out to be bound. The first jailer tied his wrists tightly, and the second jailer pushed him towards the stairs so suddenly that Henri lost his footing and fell against the wall.

"Ah, pardon me, m'lord. I mistook you for one of yon' prisoners over there," he said, gesturing again to the cell with the Arab prisoners. "Did I damage your lovely clothes?"

"You will not succeed at making me angry by comparing me to my kinsmen," Henri snarled through gritted teeth.

They marched him up the stairs into an antechamber, where he was lifted and thrown into a cart normally used for transporting barrels of ale. One of the jailers hopped onto the cart and tied Henri's hands to a ring attached to the sideboard.

"Have fun, m'lord! I hope you get some good gifts from the crowd!" one of the guards yelled cheerfully, and with a shout from the driver, the horses and cart lurched forward. Henri sighed. He knew what was about to happen.

The cart rolled into the white-hot sunlight, and as his eyes adjusted, he saw the Templars standing in rows in the courtyard, watching him silently. The gates opened, and the cart rattled into the street. Behind him, a line of Templars on horseback followed at a safe distance, their surcoats spotless over glinting mail.

The first projectile to hit him was a warm pat of dung thrown by a young boy. It smacked him on the ear, followed by a rotten lemon, green with mold but still painfully hard. As the cart progressed through the narrow street, the crowd increased and followed, some throwing rocks, but mostly just horse dung and spoiled food.

I used to be them. I was that boy, Henri thought, trying not to focus on the indignity of every missile that struck him. *Sir Geoffroi used to take his boys to the festival each year and laugh as he watched us throw refuse at the prisoners.* Henri couldn't remember the faces of the prisoners he had tormented, only that the other boys would cheer if he scored a direct hit to their mouth or eyes. Since the prisoners were often Muslim, Henri always made an extra effort to yell the loudest and throw the hardest to show his loyalty to the Cross more fervently than the other boys.

After an excruciatingly unhurried journey through the crooked streets, the driver turned the cart into the largest of the city squares. The normally bustling place of commerce now had tents set up for wealthy citizens around the perimeter, giving them a prime view of the platform and gallows. Henri had also been them, sitting under an awning on a pile of carpets and cushions with food, drink, and friends. *Not real friends, though. My so-called friends are in that crowd, and I am here. I can see Seymon and Sir Hugh and—*

"Blanche!" he gasped aloud.

He stared, blinked. Indeed, his young sister sat under a tasseled awning of deep purple and red striped cloth, surrounded by servants. She hadn't seen him yet. Even though the crowd roared their approval at the arrival of their entertainment, his sister remained preoccupied with a man.

Mafeo. Blessed Virgin, please tell me that I took a rock to the head and I am seeing a vision. Henri's mind raced. He searched for Nasira, but she did not appear to be with them.

The crowd surged toward the cart and grasped the sideboards, rocking it back and forth, chanting, "Saracen! Saracen! Saracen!" while Henri tried to keep his balance on his knees. City guards with clubs moved in quickly and viciously beat them back, then helped Henri down from the cart, just as he saw Blanche turn.

Maybe she will not see me.

The guards pushed him toward the raised platform in the middle of the square and hauled him above the crowd like a sheep at the auction block. It was impossible not to see him. About nine feet square, the platform sprouted a wicked gallows with three ropes, lopped and prepared for their victims. The posts of the gallows each had an iron ring attached. In the crowd, pressed up against the base of the whipping platform, he recognized a familiar face.

"Ibrahim!" Henri screamed. "Get Blanche out of here!"

Ibrahim staggered and looked around, then raised his hands in a gesture of helplessness.

"She's there! She is with—"

"Quiet, your lordship," said the voice of Brother Philip close to his ear, and the knight cuffed Henri across the cheek.

For a moment, his head swam and the crowd vanished from his sight. Brother Philip had a strong arm and was well-practiced in using it to knock men senseless. Dazed, Henri watched Brother Alaran climb the platform. He slashed Henri's tunic off with a dagger, then tied each of his hands to the rings in the posts, spanning his arms between them and tightening the ropes to ensure the skin on his shoulders stretched taut.

Grand Master Beaujeu stepped up to the platform and motioned for silence. Today he was dressed in his full, glittering mail, pristine robes, and he carried his baculus – a long ceremonial staff with a carved octagonal head that could be used to absolve the penitent or whack the misbehaved. He glared at the crowd until they quieted uneasily.

"This morning, before all of you, we punish this man for insubordination to a senior knight." He raked the crowd with his hawkish stare. "A Templar knight," he added significantly. "Henri of Maron, viscount of Acre and marquis of Maron-en-Rouergue, you are sentenced to twenty lashes with a scourge to be administered by the man you defied."

The crowd murmured and agitated when Beaujeu spoke Henri's name and title. "Brother Philip, please carry out the punishment," He gave Henri a hard look before dismounting the platform.

Above the titillated murmur of the crowd, a young voice cried out. "Henri! That is my brother! Grand Master, this is a mistake!"

Henri saw Ibrahim turn and look about, then push through the crowd toward Blanche's voice. The crowd began to chant again. "Saracen! Saracen! Saracen!" The noise of it shook the timbers of his platform.

Good, Henri thought. *At least Blanche will not have to see this.* He tried to prepare himself for what was to come, but at the edge of the platform, a face came into focus in the press of shoving, yelling people. Hazel eyes, wildly misbehaved hair. Sidika. He looked at her, and she held him with serious eyes. They were the color of a deep lake – green, brown, and amber. For a moment, he could hear himself breathing above the crowd, and by the rise and fall of her chest, he knew that she was breathing with him. Time stopped. The screams of the crowd became the call of birds in the hills. She reached a slender hand toward him and he closed his eyes, imagining it, smooth and strong on his cheek.

Then the first blow landed on his back.

Because Henri had been flogged by Brother Philip once before, he felt confident that he could endure it again. He hadn't considered that this time Brother Philip had a larger audience to impress or that the scars on his back were still tender from his last ordeal. The second blow landed, and Henri's eyes stung with tears. Each tail of the scourge pulled strips of skin away from his body, burning like hot irons. Then the third blow struck his open wounds. He gritted his teeth and breathed heavily. His nose began to dribble. Above the pounding in his head, he vaguely heard the crowd chanting and cheering, and perhaps it was only in his imagination that he could hear Blanche screaming above them all.

Henri tried to find a single point to focus on, and again his gaze found Sidika just below his platform, looking as if she were trying to will him out of his chains. She had a soft purple ribbon wrapped around her wrist that stood out against her faded green dress.

Henri smiled. "You get your wish, mademoiselle," he gasped at her, a dribble of bloody saliva stretching down to the platform from his mouth. "Today, I think, you will see me die among strangers and heathens."

He clamped his mouth shut and breathed through his nose, clinging to Sidika's gaze as if she was the only thing holding him from a descent into hell. She stared back, solemn and quiet as people jostled and yelled around her.

The sixth blow fell, and his head spun. The seventh, and this one hit his neck and the base of his head. His hair tangled in the scourge's tail, and Brother Philip yanked it back with such force that Henri was violently pulled back and his hair ripped out.

The eleventh blow fell, followed by more and more again. *Twelve. Thirteen.* Henri's thoughts clouded, and he hung his head. *It is nearly done*, he thought. *I had sixteen lashes last time. Blessed Virgin, I am going to die.*

At the sixteenth blow, he screamed involuntarily, and he cried out even louder at the seventeenth. Looking down, he saw blood puddling at his feet. *Is that mine?* He closed his eyes.

Eighteen. Who is making all that noise? Is that me? His vision went black. The chants of the mob dissolved into the buzzing of a million angry bees.

Nineteen.

His head dropped, and he remembered no more.

49

—·—

E mre stumbled into an inn near the harbor, ordered a cup of wine, and hastily drank it down with a trembling hand. He had fled Mafeo's tent in the noisy square, with Lady Blanche's screams echoing in his ears. His master had wrapped Blanche in a protective embrace, pushing her face against his chest to block her from the spectacle, but over her head, Mafeo watched with vicious enjoyment as Henri lapsed from consciousness.

During the day, Mafeo had lavished Lady Blanche with attention, pouring her wine for her and even presenting her with a delicately embroidered sheer silk veil to protect her face from the sun. "It is a gift, my dear," he said with a flourish of his hand. "Yours is a face too beautiful to allow the sun to see, for he is jealous of the beauty of others and seeks to destroy it."

Emre swallowed his disgust with unease. He knew what Mafeo was up to. His master acted this way toward every woman he planned to seduce, and fourteen-year-old Blanche was drinking it in. The question was, should he tell Henri, or should he let Mafeo's nature take its course, which would conclude with Blanche underneath him sooner or later? It would serve Henri right for ignoring his sister. If Emre's sister had lived, he would treasure her. Sometimes he imagined her now, Ela at fifteen years old, talking to him.

Emre sat up straight, forgetting about his wine. Where was Henri being taken? If he were given a Christian physician, in all likelihood he would die, either of a pestilence or from being bled, even though he had lost so much blood already. Emre placed a coin on the table, then fought against the crowd and back into the square, where three condemned prisoners dangled from the gallows, necks broken, their purple, swollen tongues protruding from their mouths. Someone knew where Lord Henri was, and he would find out where, if it took him all night.

***

Sidika hurried against the crowd toward the Templar citadel, her linen-wrapped bundle clutched tightly to her pounding chest. She had fled the square after Lord Henri fainted from his wounds. She charged forward, ignoring the protests of the young men who tried to vie for her attention. *He defied the orders of a Templar. Did he defy them and kill my father, or defy them and try to save my father?*

Sidika shook the thoughts from her head and looked up. The steep, slanted walls of the citadel loomed over her. A gilt statue of a lion sat at attention on the ramparts, looking toward the horizon with one paw raised. Suddenly Sidika felt foolish. She was just a girl. Her father belonged here, doing business in a place like this, but not her. How could she walk through these gates? She turned away, ready to flee.

"Young woman?" a voice behind her asked. "Do you require something?"

Sidika whipped around. A man stood behind her, wearing a somber black robe with a red cross stitched over his heart. He held a scroll of rolled parchment in pale, delicate fingers.

"I am here on behalf of my father..." she faltered. "Master Tamrat ben Moshe." That was all she could say. She suddenly forgot why she had come, but the man's face lit up.

"Ah, yes! Tamrat often speaks of his children fondly. I was so sorry to hear of your brother's passing. He was a talented young man."

"You knew Dejen?" Sidika asked, her head swimming.

"Of course. I am the secretary to the grand master! We have our own scriptorium here, and I could have any one of our illuminators do the work..." the man chattered on as Sidika looked around wildly, realizing she had no idea where he was taking her.

"...but Master Tamrat's illustration is so fine, much more in the Byzantine or even Mamluk style, I will admit, but it captures more detail..." the man guided her up a staircase and into a large room occupied by a single table.

And there he sat—the man with the power to have a viscount of the city flogged in the public square. Grand Master Beaujeu had removed most of his finery, and his strange, octagonal scepter lolled across the table.

"What is this?" he demanded, his severe face deepening into a frown at the sight of Sidika.

"Tamrat, the scribe, sent his daughter to deliver the book you ordered, my lord. I am most pleased, for I spent many days with him working over the finer details of the illumination, which you know I have no talent for." The man seemed practically giddy. Did he not know that Tamrat's killer was just scourged in the public square?

The grand master glared at Sidika. "Young woman, where is your father?"

"Ill with a consumption, my lord. He requested I bring this book in his stead," she answered, willing her hands to stop fidgeting.

"Does he expect me to also hand payment over to you?"

"Yes, my lord."

The man's gray eyes were like nails that pounded through her skull. He turned to his secretary.

"I know you are excited to see the book, but please leave us. Send my servant Flavius in here to ensure propriety."

The man bowed and retreated, closing the door behind him. The grand master gestured to a hard wooden stool in front of his table, and Sidika sat primly on its edge. The door opened, and another black-robed man slipped into the room, crossed it silently, and stood in a corner in the shadows.

"I only give payment to the man who has done the work," Beaujeu said. "Your father must come here when he is well again."

Sidika felt panic rising in her chest and scrambled for an answer. "My father is old. It no longer suits him to travel this far. Please, my lord, look inside the book and see for yourself that it is of the quality you would expect from Master Tamrat."

Beaujeu untied the strips of linen that bound the parcel and cracked the seal. Slowly, he flipped the embossed leather cover open and leafed through the pages, a small smile growing at the sides of his mouth. "Magnificent," he muttered, "truly wonderful." He flipped to the last pages. "And these you did yourself, of course," he said.

Sidika sat perfectly still. "Excuse me, my lord? I am only a woman. I do not know how to read or illuminate a text."

The grand master's gray eyes twinkled. "Of course not. How thoughtless of me." He stood and walked to one of the arrowslit windows near his table.

"My servant Flavius is deaf, and so we can speak freely. Your father is buried on a hill at the base of Mount Hermon. I am sure Lord Henri could show you where it is, since it was he who tried to keep your father from being tortured. I still cannot fathom why he would do such a thing, for I have never known the young man to commit a selfless act, and yet you saw him bear the punishment for it, I am sure."

Sidika's hands now shook visibly. "I happened upon the square as I attempted to find you today, Grand Master."

"What is your name, young woman?"

"Sidika, my lord."

"Ah, a Turkish name. It means 'Truth,' does it not?" Beaujeu reached into a purse hidden under a flap on his belt and pulled out a few coins. "Your father often spoke of a daughter of his who could read and write as well as him and his son. Can you write a line of text describing what you saw today in the square for me?"

He pulled a small pot of ink, a scrap of paper, and a quill from a locking cabinet. Sidika willed her hands to stop shaking and took the quill, dipping it in ink.

I saw a man crying to his servant to shield the face of his sister while he took his punishment.

Then she dipped the quill in ink again and quickly sketched the figure of a man, his back bent in agony. Beaujeu nodded sagely and placed a small stack of coins on the table.

"You are indeed talented, Mademoiselle Sidika. Thank you for completing your father's work. I will tell no one of Tamrat ben Moshe's passing if you will continue to carry on this artistry in his name, unless you wish to retire and find a husband instead."

"No!" Sidika jumped to her feet and quickly sat again. "That is to say, I have not found a suitable man to wed, my lord."

Beaujeu smiled, then waved his hand to his deaf servant, speaking slowly. "Flavius, please fetch my secretary. You may leave the door open behind you."

Flavius stood and walked from the room, his eyes downcast, and left the door wide open. Sidika could hear his sandals slapping the stones loudly as he ran.

"Your father once told me that his daughter was a talented healer. Lord Henri is staying in the house of Sir Eirik Einarssen and is sure to perish after the beating he received. It seems he had the forethought to tell the Hospitallers to take their black tar poultices and boar's gall tonics and throw them in the sea. I thought you should know."

Sidika nodded mutely, and Beaujeu escorted her to his secretary, who led her back to the gates of the castle.

"Excuse me, good sir," she whispered, "where can I find a seller of herbs in the market?"

"The souk in the Hospitaller quarter has merchants with many healing and cooking herbs," he replied.

Sidika looked up at him. "And where is the house of Sir Eirik Einarssen?"

50

—•—

S ultan Qalāwūn sat upright on his velvet couch as usual, but Yusuf could see the exhaustion in the man's face and the slope of his shoulders. In front of him, standing with feet planted and arms crossed, Khalil, the sultan's eldest surviving son, stood, defiant. Qalāwūn heaved a deep sigh and handed the dog-eared letter to his wazir, Turuntay, then pulled himself slowly to his feet.

"Let all who are witnesses hear this: My son Khalil and amir Yusuf ibn-Shihab are correct. The Franj who occupy Acre have indeed broken their treaty with us by supplying themselves with new troops, who also slaughtered innocent Muslims in the streets."

The amirs in the room murmured, some gesticulating in agitation.

Qalāwūn held up his hand for silence. "Therefore, I intend to march upon Acre, and we will demand the surrender of the perpetrators from outside of the city gates – our entire force of twenty-five thousand. If Allah grants us success, we shall march north and catch the Mongols off their guard while they are calm, and maybe we can dispatch two enemies at once, God willing."

Several of the amirs cheered heartily, but Khalil and Yusuf did not. Yusuf knew that this did not align with Khalil's vision for the battle, and his outspoken friend would say something.

"My lord, would it not be better to wait and gather a larger army before approaching Acre? It is a well-fortified city, and without a massive force, we will not succeed."

Qalāwūn turned on his son, his face deep red with rage. "All of you, leave us!" He shouted to the assembled amirs. "Khalil and Yusuf, you stay."

After the other amirs had hurried out of the chamber, Qalāwūn stepped swiftly down from the dais and stood in front of his son. Khalil was shorter than Qalāwūn, but the two both shared the same expression of disappointment mixed with disgust on their dark brows.

"Is this not what you have advocated doing for months, my son? And now you contradict me in front of the other amirs?! Trying to make me look the fool will not inspire me to name you my successor!"

"Father," Khalil kept his voice soothing, "I do not contradict. I offer counsel. We cannot take Acre with twenty-five thousand."

"And why not?" Qalāwūn snapped. "They have far fewer numbers than that. Could you not have discussed this with me in private before you blurted it out in front of the whole war council!?"

"I did not have the intelligence in your letter until the war council convened," Khalil said through clenched teeth. "Perhaps if you included me in your work instead of Turuntay, I would have known this ahead of time."

Yusuf could hear Khalil's voice straining with control. He knew that Khalil wanted to scream at his father, and by Qalāwūn's posture, he suspected the old sultan was barely restraining himself from putting his hands around his son's neck.

Yusuf cleared his throat respectfully. "A compromise, then. My lord sultan, I know that you cannot spare your garrisoned armies at the northern borders, but what about the people? Many have suffered under the heavy hand of the Franj and would be willing to take up arms against the enemies of Islam. Let the people fight for you and boost the size of your army."

"What good would they do except become arrow fodder?" Qalāwūn said haughtily.

"Indeed, arrows that would not be hitting your trained Mamluks. The civilian soldiers could provide intimidating numbers and necessary distraction so the 'askari can do their work."

Qalāwūn paused, and in that pause, Khalil spoke. "This strategy makes sense, my lord! Let us send riders to all the towns between Nubia and the Caucasus and gather the faithful to us. It would be an honor for the men of Allah to fight for their faith and their freedom! They would willingly undertake this risk to bless their families and communities!"

But instead of answering, Qalāwūn sank to his knees on the steps to his dais, clutching at his heart.

"Father?" Khalil knelt next to him. "What are you doing?"

"Your father is unwell," Yusuf said, hurrying up the dais and yanking on the thick braided rope next to his couch. Somewhere, deep within the walls of the palace, they heard a gong, and in moments the room was swarming with palace guards.

"Our Lord Qalāwūn is ill," Yusuf said authoritatively. "Take him to his chambers at once and send for his physicians."

Yusuf sighed. Suddenly his future and the fate of the sultanate seemed precarious. War was on the horizon, the sultan was gravely ill, and the Mongol armies massed at their borders. Acre would be the sacrifice needed to protect the Mamluk realm that Khalil was about to inherit.

Khalil stood pale and motionless, watching as the guards gently lifted his father onto a litter and bore him away. Yusuf walked down the steps and put his hand on the young man's shoulder.

"You should get some rest, my friend. You may need to take command of the armies and claim Acre and the throne sooner than anyone thought."

***

To be continued...

51

— ◊ —

GLOSSARY

- **Alham** – A unit of measurement approx. 50 cm or 19.5 inches. Typically described in Mongolian culture as the distance of one stride.
- **Amir** – A lord or general in the Mamluk army. Similar in status to a lord.
- **'Askari** – A freed Mamluk soldier. 'Askari were considered highly skilled and loyal enough to be freed, but still remain within the household of their master. Similar to a knight.
- **Auberge** – Apartment. A personal abode.
- **Braies** – A trouser undergarment of light material worn by men in the middle ages.
- **Caparison** – A drape made of thick material, such as felt, fabric, or chain mail that covered a warhorse from head to hoof. Caparisons gave the horse some amount of protection from projectiles in battle and helped to identify its owner.
- **Caruca** – The approximate amount of land that a team of eight oxen could plow in a single year. A unit of measurement for land in the middle ages.
- **Confrere** – A knight of a non-religious or organized order (non-Templar, non-Hospitaller, etc.)
- **Cotehardie** – An outer garment that was worn over a shirt as a tunic. The cotehardie was worn hip-length for men and floor-length for women and could be laced or

buttoned on the front, back, or sides for added fit. (See Surcoat)

• **Dalcop** – A medieval insult roughly meaning "idiot" or person of low intelligence.

• **Enceinte** – In large fortifications with double walls, the outermost wall is the enceinte, the inner (often taller) walls are the curtain wall, and the space in between is called the outer bailey.

• **Faris** – A Mamluk warrior or trainee warrior. The equivalent in the West would be a knight warrior.

• **Farrier** – A tradesman who was responsible for the care of a horse's hooves, including trimming the hoof and shoeing the feet.

• **Fessyah** – "Stinky" in Palestinian Arabic. Sometimes used to refer to the marbled polecat, a relative of the North American skunk.

• **Fosse** – Sometimes called a "moat." A large channel or canal built outside of a fortified structure, sometimes filled with water.

• **Kaddish** – A Hebrew prayer of thanks, praise and a wish for universal peace. Kaddish can be recited as of regular synagogue liturgy or for a person who has recently died.

• **Lauds** – The morning or dawn prayer in the Catholic liturgy of the hours. Usually around 5 a.m.

• **Livery** – The identifying "uniform" of a knight and his household. The livery had a distinct coat of arms or crest, flag, and colors to identify him and his household to his peers.

• **Madrasa** – A Muslim religious school, usually supported by a waqf or monetary donation by a wealthy patron. The Madrasa often housed and fed the students and scholars who taught and attended.

• **Mamluk** – A soldier in the Turkish military. The Mamluk army evolved throughout the centuries, but when this story takes place in the 13th century, the Mamluks were mostly slaves who were purchased or taken captive from the eastern part of the modern Turkish state, or as far east as the Caucasus and western China.

- **Manumission** – The act of setting a slave free by his/her owner. Manumission could be earned through years of service or granted as a gift.
- **Mashrabiya** – A wooden structure that protruded slightly from the side of a building. The mashrabiya usually had carved, wooden screens that allowed ventilation and privacy at the same time.
- **Meydan** – A large, often circular or square arena where Mamluk soldiers would train. In later years (after the 13th century) the meydan became more and more lavish, sometimes featuring gardens, fountains, and spectator areas, essentially becoming city squares.
- **Mihrab** – A shallow niche carved into the wall of a mosque or holy place, often ornately decorated, which indicates the direction of Mecca.
- **Muhaqqaq** – A type of Arabic script known for its beauty and complexity. Muhaqqaq calligraphy is considered a form of fine art and the most beautiful of the six main types of Arabic scripts.

- **Nones** – Ninth-hour prayers in the Catholic liturgy of the hours. Usually around 3 p.m.
- **Outremer** – The "Western" name for Palestine and Syria. Literally means "across the sea" in Old French.
- **Patriarch** – The Patriarch of a city was its highest holy leader, often in charge of managing city affairs and wrangling local trade guilds in addition to guiding the spiritual health of the community.
- **Phylacteries** – Also known as tefillin. Small leather boxes containing verses from the Torah. The tefillin are affixed to the arms and forehead with leather straps and are worn during morning prayers.

- **Preceptory** – A community of Templar knights who live together apart from the Templar headquarters (located in Acre during the 13th century).
- **Prime** – The first of the liturgical hours, when prayers are recited by monks, nuns, and devout Christians. Usually around 6 a.m.
- **Qasid** – A Mamluk secret intelligence agent or spy.
- **Quintain** – A t-shaped structure of wood used for practice at tilting and jousting. Quintains sometimes had a sandbag attached that could swing around and strike a horseman in the back if he failed to hit the target.
- **Ra'is** – A Mamluk commander.
- **Sahn** – Courtyard or room where prayers are performed in a mosque.
- **Salāt al-Fajr** – The first of the five daily prayers recited by devout Muslims. Usually recited early in the morning at sunrise.
- **Samite** – Silk cloth interwoven with gold or silver threads and heavily embroidered. Samite was extraordinarily expensive in the middle ages and rare even for a monarch to wear.
- **Seneschal** – In the context of Western 13th-century culture, the Seneschal refers to a steward, caretaker, or "senior guard."
- **Sennight** – An archaic term for one week (seven nights).
- **Shams al-Tabrizi** – The best friend of the famed Sufi poet, Rumi. Shams al-Tabrizi was murdered (some suspect because of his potentially sexual relationship the poet) but Rumi claimed that Shams (also a poet) continued to talk to him and dictate poetry and wisdom after his death.
- **Shamshir** – A curved sword in the scimitar family.
- **Sirwals** – Trousers that are wide and billowy and tie closed at the ankle.
- **Souk** – A market street in a middle eastern city. Souks can be general or specialize in a narrow range of goods.

- **Surcoat** – A fabric or leather vest, much like a cote-hardie, that was worn over a knight's armor. Surcoats could be short or long, but if they were long, they were often split under the waist to allow a knight to sit comfortably on his horse. Surcoats performed a dual function of protecting the knights of warm climates from the sun, which heated the metal of their armor, and identifying them to their colleagues in battle.
- **Tallit** – A fringed garment worn by Jews as a prayer shawl. Traditionally, the tallit is white with blue stripes in a specific pattern.
- **Taqiya** – A round, embroidered cap worn by men to cover the top of their head.
- **Tawash** – A eunuch in charge of training young Mamluks in the meydan. (See Meydan, fursān)
- **Tefillin** – See phylacteries.
- **Thawb** – An ankle-length, loose garment with a hood and wide sleeves worn by Bedouins and Arab locals in medieval Syria and Palestine. A version of the 13th-century thawb is still worn in present-day Egypt.
- **Tonsure** – The typical hairstyle for a Catholic monk or brother knight. A circular spot shaved onto the top of the head and a fringe left on the sides.
- **Turcopole** – A hired foot soldier, light cavalry, or archer. Not knighted. Turcopoles were often the local Arab and Armenian Christians.
- **Ustadh** – A Mamluk title for "master."
- **Waqf** – A monetary gift or trust given by the wealthy to support a madrasa or a shaykh. (See madrasa)
- **Wazir** – An advisor or counselor to a high-ranking amir or a sultan.
- **Wudhu** – A fountain located within a mosque complex where the faithful can perform ablutions before the daily prayers.

THE LAND OF GOD

NORTHERN PALESTINE. DECEMBER 1293

Abdul planted his feet in the sandy ground and grunted, straining to shift a large limestone block. It had not looked difficult to move the stone when he was standing above it on the ruins of a pillar, but now that he had attempted it and the palms of his hands were raw, he was about to give up. And yet, he couldn't. He knew that there were riches beneath this stone, and so far, Abdul's senses had never failed him. Some said he could smell gold. He certainly could smell something, but the strong wind blowing in from the jewel-blue Mediterranean sea snatched the scent away before he could identify it.

"Jalal!" he hollered, hands on his hips as he evaluated his challenge. "Come help me."

He heard the scrape of Jalal's sandals as he leapt from stone to boulder and occasionally tiptoed along a shattered timber toward him.

"This stone is too big, Abdul. Come, I found a cache of pots behind the hammam. Still intact, although the oil inside of them is rancid."

"No, Jalal," Abdul rubbed his stinging hands together, "this one. I have the feeling about it."

Jalal argued no further. He knew his little brother better than anyone, and everyone knew that Abdul was blessed with intuition, given by God himself. He nodded, then put his hands on the edge of the stone. Abdul braced his shoulder against the other side and counted down.

"Wahid... itnan... talata!"

Jalal heaved, Abdul pushed, and the stone shifted and toppled onto its side with a great muffled thud.

"Oh, God and His angels!" Jalal clapped a hand over his mouth and nose. Staggering backwards, he fell onto a pile of broken stones, retching loudly. Abdul pulled a corner of his wool keffiyeh over his nose and peered into the shallow hole that the stone had covered. The stench of flesh, sealed and rotting in the cool, damp darkness for two years, rose from the hole, and no amount of fresh sea air could carry it all away. But who cared? In the white-hot sunlight, gold blinked back up at him, alive with a rich yellow glow. Abdul reached into the hole and tugged at a glittering necklace, which was clutched in a bony fist. He tugged again. Sometimes the dead refused to relinquish their riches without a fight.

Drawing his curved shamshir from its sheath on his belt, he hacked at the brittle bones of the wrist until the hand and the necklace came out of the hole together. Tossing this into the sand next to him, he felt around the head. Yes, this was a woman – the skull was small, and he could feel an earring hanging onto what was left of her earlobes – now just a slimy black mass of putrefying flesh. He pulled out her second earring and noted without emotion that there were long blonde hairs snagged in the clasp.

"Jalal! Come, I need your help before the others notice." He cast a concerned glance at the ragged scavengers who picked through the cracked stones and collapsed houses.

After two years, it was unusual to find anything of high value here, despite how large the city had been. Thirty thousand people, all gone – dead or fled – their homes destroyed with such violence that it was hardly possible to tell there was ever a city here at all. Everything that the citizens could not take with them now hid like cockles under the sand and rock, and as each treasure was unearthed, the seekers became more and more desperate.

Abdul did not fancy a fight today. His leg still ached from the place where another scavenger had slashed him in a brawl over a cache of rusting blacksmith's tools a few weeks ago. Jalal crawled back to his feet, looking pale.

"I do not like this, Abdul. There are ghosts here. You remember what happened to Mustafa."

Abdul handed Jalal a rock. "Break the fingers off this necklace and be quick about it. Act casual, or else the others will come." He did not want to think about Mustafa.

"A dead Franj walked into Mustafa's tent, Abdul. A holy warrior no less – tall and yellow-haired and dressed in white. He said we would all go to hell!"

"Shut up!" Abdul hissed, grabbing Jalal by the front of his loose brown thawb, which he had tied up around his knees for easier mobility over the stones. "Mustafa is a liar and a simpleton."

"But he has not left his tent since, and Omar hears a woman screaming every night from under the sea. Khalid hears her too!"

"Shut up, *shut up*!"

From a distance, Abdul heard a shout. Several of the other men were tripping and sliding over the broken houses toward them. Abdul plunged his hand back into the hole, right into the woman's rotting abdomen. After scavenging the ruins of the destroyed city for over a year, there was little that could turn his stomach, but the repugnant feeling of his hand inside the soft, rotting flesh made his head spin. He pushed her corpse aside. Underneath it was a smaller body and skull. Her baby. Many of the women under these stones were found with their bodies curled protectively around smaller skeletons.

He shoved the baby aside as well and smiled. A soggy leather sack was there. He pulled it out and peeked inside. A few tarnished silver cups with pearls embedded in them glowed dully. He stuffed this in his sack along with the necklace and the earrings, quietly thanking the woman for giving up her treasures.

Whatever atrocities happened to you before Acre fell, I am sure it was terrible. And I am sure you deserved it.

***

The Land of God **is available for purchase at your favorite bookseller.**

What readers are saying about *The Land of God*

"A brutal and gripping tale! What a great depiction of the devastation of the attack on Acre! I couldn't stop thinking about it even when I wasn't reading."

"It kept me spellbound from page one to the very last word! The tension and relationships are beautifully written and will keep readers coming back for more. I got chills up my spine more than once."

"What a wonderfully captivating and emotional book. It took an unexpected turn at the end and I am so eager for the next one. So far, the series has been everything I enjoy about historical fiction novels."

— ◆ —

EXCLUSIVE CONTENT FOR MEMBERS OF MY NEWSLETTER

Want to receive free chapters, offers, and become a part of the community? Sign up at www.elizabethrandersen.com

I am an independent author and reviews from readers are **<u>vital</u>** to helping me succeed in the crowded, competitive world of writing. Your review of *The Scribe* not only means a lot to me, but it will also mean a lot to other potential readers.

— • —

ACKNOWLEDGEMENTS

It was on an airplane, taking off from Vaclav Havel airport in Prague, that I finally decided to do something about the idea that had been spinning in my brain for almost a year. I was finally going to write a book about leprosy in the 14th century! Clearly, the path from there to here was full of twists and turns because I ended up with a novel about a group of teenagers on the eve of the siege of Acre, a topic that consumed my life for two years of research and two more years of writing. From the bottom of my heart, I want to give thanks and apologies to the brave and loyal friends and family who read my first attempts at a book that would ultimately look nothing like the finished product.

To Iman Ayyeh, who helped me with my understanding of Islam and Islamic culture, all the thanks in the world. Thank you for only laughing at me a little bit when I butchered the names and pronunciations. Many thanks also to Vahan Dede for helping me with my Turkish and correcting some mistakes in spelling and understanding of Mamluk training.

To Brent, Ed, James, Debbi, Chelsea, Aria, and Rachel, thank you for giving thoughtful feedback, even when it was a challenge to find time to read. And to Mari, the first person to finish the first draft. You are a trooper.

Thank you to Raanan Schnitzer for helping me to see, smell, and experience Acre and Israel when my research trip was canceled due to the global COVID-19 pandemic.

Theodor Jurma created the maps of Acre and the Levant in record time, which are so beautiful that I screamed when I first saw them. Likewise, Olly Bennett at More Visual Ltd. did a fantastic job on the book cover of my dreams. I also thank Cecily Blanchard, who took a published book with editorial problems and made it into something I could be proud of (except for that sentence that I just ended with a preposition!)

There is an online community of incredible, helpful people who I have never met in person who encouraged me out of my self-doubt and lifted me up, even though they did not have to, in the competitive, fierce world of writing. To all of them, my sincerest gratitude. I cannot wait to someday return the favor.

Thanks also to my mom, the book's first super-fan, who got angry on my behalf whenever someone criticized my work, and will probably be angry at every poor review I receive.

Finally, to Jordan, my long-suffering husband, and Soren, my patient son, who listened to me typing until the early hours of the mornings and tolerated mountains of research books that invaded their personal space. Thank you for allowing me to pursue my passion.

ALSO BY ELIZABETH R. ANDERSEN

THE TWO DAGGERS SERIES

A spoiled noble. A kindly scribe. And a world about to change.

The battle for dominance of the Holy Land begins...

The war for Acre is over. The battle for the two daggers is just beginning...

Made in the USA
Monee, IL
15 August 2022

11452900R00194